For Molly Friedrich
with many thanks

more . . .

SHARON McCONE MYSTERIES
BY MARCIA MULLER

A Wild and Lonely Place
Till the Butchers Cut Him Down
Wolf in the Shadows
Pennies on a Dead Woman's Eyes
Where Echoes Live
Trophies and Dead Things
The Shape of Dread
There's Something in a Sunday
Eye of the Storm
There's Nothing to be Afraid Of
Double (with Bill Pronzini)
Leave a Message for Willie
Games to Keep the Dark Away
The Cheshire Cat's Eye
Ask the Cards a Question
Edwin of the Iron Shoes

MARCIA MULLER

A WILD AND LONELY PLACE

WARNER BOOKS

A Time Warner Company

WARNER BOOKS EDITION

Cover design by Diane Luger
Cover illustration by Phill Singer

Warner Books, Inc.
1271 Avenue of the Americas
New York, NY 10020

W A Time Warner Company

Printed in the United States of America

Originally published in hardcover by Warner Books.
First Printed in Paperback: July, 1996

10 9 8 7 6 5 4 3 2 1

Thanks also to:
Toni Alexander, Sharon McCone's travel agent
Suzanne and Rex Stocklin, guides on a scary journey
Collin Wilcox, flight instructor to an
earthbound author

And to Bill, without whom . . .

6,500 Feet Above The Tehachapi Mountains

The vast arid waste of the Mojave was behind us now, but the deathlike loneliness of the tiny airfield and the shroud of white smog drifting from the chemical plants at Trona had left nightmare traces in my mind. Below sprawled the Tehachapis, their wrinkled, jagged peaks thrusting aggressively. They seemed to telegraph a warning: we can claim you.

I pulled my gaze from them before my imagination could cloud my judgment, looked instead at the last ridgeline separating us from the Central Valley and an easy flight home. Piece of cake, as Hy would say. Only Hy wasn't saying anything just now—hadn't for some time.

Anxiously I glanced into the Beechcraft's rear seat, where he'd crawled after I'd awakened him with difficulty at Mirage Wells. He was slumped against the side—unconscious again, and maybe better off, since the chills had passed and the fever raged again. The little girl sat rigid beside him, silent as she'd been the whole grueling journey. Her dark hair was matted, her face begrimed; her eyes had a bottomless quality that said she'd seen too much in too few years. I wished Hy were able to hug and reassure her, but for the moment my smile and the words "Not long now" would have to do.

She didn't respond.

Well, who could blame her? After we were on the ground, I'd hug and reassure her. And get badly needed medical help for Hy.

I checked the instruments, looked back at the ridgeline. The morning sun was turning its striated brown rock to gold. Some of my tension was draining away, but the grit of the desert was still on my skin, overlaying the clamminess of the tropics. I made myself feel it so I wouldn't become careless.

So much could go wrong yet. Could go wrong at any moment, as events of the past days had proved—

The impact felt like slamming into a concrete wall.

My stomach lurched and I felt a surge of panic. I scanned the instruments as the plane shuddered. The VSI showed we were descending fast: fifteen hundred feet per minute, sixteen hundred . . . When I looked up the ridgeline tilted crazily, then leaped to the top of the windscreen. All I could see was a fractured stone cliff face.

Downdraft—bad one.

Extreme clear air turbulence here, and why the hell hadn't Flight Service warned me? Not that I'd've had any choice but to brave it. . . .

I glanced into the rear seat again. Hy was still unconscious; no help from that quarter. The child's eyes were wide, her face drained of color. Afraid I'd betray my panic if I spoke, I tried instead for a reassuring smile, but it didn't come off.

Okay, I thought, *you know what to do. You've watched Hy deal with downdrafts a hundred times or more. Stay calm and change course. Get away from that ridge, turn toward lower ground.*

I turned. Another draft slammed us. For a minute the Beechcraft shuddered so violently that I imagined its wings being torn off.

Two thousand feet per minute now and still falling!

Sweat coated my forehead and palms. I gripped the controls, struggling for focus.

"Mountain flying course," I said. "Mountain flying—what did they teach me?"

My mind refused to function.

Oh God, not this! We've come too far, through too much. Twenty-three hundred.

This can't be happening! I can't die this way.

Twenty-five hundred.

Jagged brown peaks below. Sunny gold cliff ahead. The last things I'll ever see.

Sunlight, you idiot! Mountains facing into the sun create updrafts. Get closer to them, not farther away.

Find an updraft, and you can use this machine as a glider. Find one, and you'll clear that ridge.

I began to test the controls, banking toward the cliff.

For God's sake, McCone, find an updraft!

PART ONE

NORTHERN CALIFORNIA

MAY 18 – 22

One

I had just left Adah Joslyn's office at the Diplo-
bomber Task Force headquarters when I ran into Gage Renshaw.

As I walked toward the elevator of the decrepit Federal
Building annex on Eddy Street, I spotted him turning away
from the drinking fountain and brushing at some water drops
on his rumpled blue tie. There was a dark stain on the lapel
of his equally rumpled gray suit that might also have been
water but could just as well be the remains of some long-past
meal eaten on the run. Gage had the ability to go for days
without noticing such things, but of course he noticed me
instantly. His dark eyebrows quirked up and his mouth widened in a smile that gave him a distinctly satanic look.

"Well, Sharon McCone," he said. "What brings you here—
as if I couldn't guess?"

"Hello, Gage." I nodded pleasantly enough and kept walking. The conversation with Joslyn that I'd just concluded had
disturbed me, and I was in no mood to spar with an old
adversary—even one whom I'd forgiven most of his trans-
gressions.

Renshaw stepped in front of me and placed his hand over
the elevator's call buttons. "Visiting the SFPD's representative
on the task force?"

I looked pointedly at my watch. It was only a little after one, and I had a long gap in my schedule, but I hoped Renshaw would take the hint.

"Hear anything interesting while you were in there?" he asked.

"Only that the TV special last night brought out the usual nut cases." I peeled his hand off the call buttons and punched Down. The single elevator was absurdly slow; I leaned against the wall and crossed my arms, prepared to suffer Renshaw's curiosity until it came.

He regarded me through his dark-rimmed glasses, cool gray eyes amused. The dim light from the fixture above our heads cast shadows on the bony planes of his face and made him look like a middle-aged Abe Lincoln. He said, "Of course, you wouldn't tell me if you had—heard anything interesting, I mean."

"Of course. And if I were to ask you why you're here, you wouldn't tell me, either."

"I think our motives are fairly obvious, and similar. Every investigator in town is whoring after the million-dollar reward the feds've posted for information leading to the bomber."

Now there was a false note if I'd ever heard one. Gage's firm, Renshaw and Kessell International, specialized in corporate security and counter-terrorism services, and a million dollars was nothing to them, compared to the handsome retainers they collected. His very presence in San Francisco was suspect, as he worked out of RKI's world headquarters in La Jolla.

I didn't comment, though, just raised my guard an inch or two and waited to see where this conversation was going.

Renshaw came over and leaned against the wall next to me. His white forelock—startling in contrast to his shaggy dark mane—flopped onto his brow; he tossed it back with a practiced twist of his head. "The figure one million does have a nice ring, Sharon."

"Uh-huh."

"Not much chance of one individual claiming it, though."

"Why not?"

"In my experience, an investigation like this requires teamwork."

"Meaning?"

"Meaning you might be better off joining forces with an organization that has greater resources than yours."

"An organization such as RKI."

"We've got capabilities you've only dreamed of."

"Then why on earth would you want to co-opt me?"

"Well, there is your connection with the task force. You can't convince me that Inspector Joslyn hasn't been feeding you information."

She had, but Renshaw didn't need to know that. I pushed away from the wall and punched the call button again.

"Besides," Renshaw added, "you and I have worked well together in the past."

I stared at him, astonished. "*Worked together*? You tried to use me to get a lead on Ripinsky—so you could kill him!"

"And you used our money to save him. Touché. Anyway"— he waved his hand dismissively—"all that's in the past. Ripinsky's a partner in the firm now. He, Kessell, and I have reached an understanding. You and he are . . . well, whatever you are to each other. That makes us practically family."

"You and I are not family. We will never be family. And McCone Investigations doesn't enter into cooperative arrangements with firms whose practices are . . . incompatible with ours."

Renshaw tried to look wounded at my thinly veiled slur upon RKI's professional ethics, but the effort was lost on me. I'd long before learned that he was incapable of being insulted. If anything, he took pride in his dubious transactions and extralegal shortcuts.

"Okay," he said after a moment, "let me make you a proposition. Come back to the shop with me, take a look at what we're got on these bombings. If it intrigues you, you share what you've got with us, and we work together. If you're still not interested, the subject is closed."

The elevator finally creaked to a stop, its doors wheezing ominously as they opened. I stepped on, and Renshaw followed.

"Why such largess, Gage?"

"Oh, let's say for old times' sake."

"Don't give me that. You must need my connection to the

task force very badly. And it isn't because, as you put it, you're whoring after a million-dollar reward."

He hesitated. "Okay, it's not. But come back to the shop anyway. What've you got to lose?"

"Only my self-respect."

"That's nothing."

"Thanks a lot." But already he'd intrigued me. I said, "I can be there in half an hour. But remember—I don't owe you a thing."

"Not yet, anyway."

As I drove to RKI's building on Green Street between the foot of Telegraph Hill and the Embarcadero, I thought about my earlier conversation with Adah Joslyn.

My friend was slumped behind her littered desk when I entered her office, a pencil skewered through her thick dark curls, a scowl creasing her honey-tan face. Even on what was obviously a bad day, she managed to look elegant. Her beautifully tailored jacket and pants had something to do with that, but I'd seen her look the same in sweats. Adah's elegance stemmed from a combination of inner qualities: composure, confidence, assertiveness, her way of meeting the world with a level, honest gaze.

A fifteen-year veteran of the SFPD, Joslyn had been the answer to the prayers of a former chief beset by complaints that the composition of departmental personnel did not reflect that of the community they served. In order to get the media, the mayor, and various citizen-watchdog groups off his back, he'd cast around for a minority figure to award with a high-visibility promotion, and in Joslyn he found her. She was not only half African-American and half Jewish, but also a decorated, talented cop. When she took her place on the elite Homicide detail, she quickly proved that she wasn't there as mere political window dressing and soon won the admiration and respect of her most serious detractors.

A month ago Joslyn had been tapped as one of the department's two full-time representatives on the newly formed Diplo-bomber Task Force. There she joined agents of the FBI, the ATF, and the Postal Service in the search for the individual who had bombed two Washington, D.C., embassies, two cars belonging to foreign diplomats, two homes of delegates to the United Nations, and two consular offices here in San Francisco. In the past five years the bomber had killed three people and badly injured three others. Pressure for his capture from both our own government and foreign powers was enormous.

The pressure must have really been on today; Adah's scowl didn't soften when she saw me. She waved her hand at her desk and said, "Do you believe all this shit?"

I eyed the stacks of message slips, each a different color. "Phone tips?"

"Damn eight-hundred hot line's jammed. One of the callers told the operator he'd been on hold for fifty minutes."

"Anything useful there?"

"Who knows?" She pointed to the largest stack—blue, weighted down by a stapler. "Those're the real whackoid callers—the ones who claim the bomber's an extraterrestrial or Elvis or the ghost of their dead mother-in-law who hated foreigners. The pink pile's tips from folks who sound like they're out to cause somebody trouble—the ones who accuse their boss or a family member or the next-door neighbor. Still, they've got to be checked out. These white ones"—she poked a third pile—"are from what you might call theorists. They're cool, logical, persuasive; they've got it all figured out. Usually they're wrong, but every now and then you spot a glimmer of truth that can lead to a breakthrough. And this yellow bunch're from people whose memories may have been jogged by the TV special—folks who may have noticed something significant at some time and forgotten about it till now."

"And these green ones?"

"First priority. Suspicious callers. Our interviewers have been trained to pick up on certain things; sometimes it's as subtle as a change in vocal tone, other times the person knows one of the details we haven't made public."

"And how soon are you supposed to finish checking them?"

"By my calculations, about an hour ago."

I was silent, overwhelmed by the size of her task.

Joslyn pushed back from the desk, stretched her long legs out in front of her, and sighed. "You know," she said, "I never used to envy you. The long hours you put in, the way the partners in that law firm ragged you, the shit you'd have to take off sleazes—none of that seemed worth the salary you drew. I'd tell myself, 'Hey, compared to McCone's, my life's not so bad. I've got official status, the respect of the community, a good salary and all kinds of benefits.' Woman on the way up, I was, maybe make captain someday."

I leaned on a corner of her desk. "Well, you're still a woman on the way up. And I'm still doing all those things you don't envy me for."

"No, you're not. You've got your own agency now, you call the shots. And me . . . well, the shield has gotten kind of tarnished."

I frowned questioningly.

"No, nothing like that. I'm still an honest cop. But the shine's definitely off the metal. Official status? Doesn't mean squat. Respect of the community? Forget it. Salary and benefits? I can think of a hundred jobs where I'd do better. And I'm not a woman on the way up anymore."

"Why not?"

"I'm pushing forty and still an inspector; that wasn't in my game plan. And after Bart Wallace moved to Vice, I never got a new partner. Somebody's on sick leave, they send in Joslyn to pinch-hit for a while. Somebody's new on the squad, they're temporarily teamed with me. But then the regular partner comes off leave or the new guy learns the ropes and gets assigned to somebody else, and I'm back to operating solo."

"But what about your appointment to this task force? That was a coup."

"Hah!" Her hand swept across the desk, stirring the message slips. "What I got here is paper-shuffling, and what I am is a goddamn clerk for a bunch of federal agents who think they're too good to share their ideas with me. No, the Department stuck me on the task force because years ago they trotted me out as their poster girl, and now they don't know what to do with me. You see, in their hurry to revamp their image, they forgot to look closely at my background check; if they had, they'd've thought twice about promoting a girl from Red Hill." Red Hill was what Adah called Bernal Heights; according to her, it had once been a hotbed of communists.

"You're not saying that Barbara and Rupert—"

"I'm not saying my crazy parents have hurt my career, but they sure haven't helped. You know them. She still goes to her Marxist study group every Wednesday night, and you'll find her on the front line of every lunatic-fringe protest. And he still turns up at every open meeting at City Hall to tell them who and what he doesn't like in local government—which is everybody and everything. I love them and I wouldn't change them, but they're not exactly assets."

I doubted the situation was as grim as she painted it, but it wasn't good, either. "So that's why you asked me for help on this investigation," I said. "You want to crack the case and show them all up."

"I want to hand them the bomber, say 'fuck you,' turn around, and walk away. You help me do that and, like I promised, I'll recommend you for the reward."

Again I was silent. For two weeks now Joslyn had been acting in direct violation of policy. She'd given me copies of reports and files, briefed me on the progress of the investigation. Together we'd brainstormed till both our heads ached. I wanted to crack the case, too—and not only because of the reward or for Adah's sake—but now I wondered if I hadn't been abetting her in a risky and potentially ruinous course of action. Maybe I should back off.

She must have sensed what I was thinking. "McCone, don't listen to me," she said quickly. "I'm having a bad day, that's all."

"You know that's not all. We need to talk."

"Talk? We've been talking." She hitched her chair up to the desk and glared at me. "I'm out of time for you. Get the hell out of here and let me work. I'll call you when I've got something interesting."

I nodded dubiously and left her alone.

Maybe, I thought, it was only the stress of the assignment that was getting to Joslyn. After all, a message was being sent to the task force from local and state government; from SFPD, ATF, FBI, and Postal Service headquarters; from Congress; from the White House itself: the Diplo-bomber is making international relations very iffy; get your asses in gear and find him.

*   *   *

After circling the surrounding blocks for some fifteen minutes, I finally found a parking space near the looming cliff
face of Tel Hill and walked past decorator showrooms and
antique shops and small cafés to RKI's renovated brick ware-
house. On the sidewalk I paused, however, reluctant to go
inside. Even being on the premises made me uneasy.

My feelings weren't due to the type of business they conducted; counter-terrorism contingency planning and hostage-
recovery services were necessary for corporations operating
in today's high-risk environment, and if RKI's methods were
somewhat unorthodox, they usually worked. Nor were the
feelings due to the fact that most of RKI's principals and
operatives had murky pasts; my lover, Hy Ripinsky, owned
a past that crisscrossed those of Gage Renshaw and Dan
Kessell, and now that he'd told me about it, I understood both
the forces and the mistakes that had driven him. The potential
for violence that I sensed in RKI's people didn't concern me;
I'd long ago been forced to recognize the same potential
within myself. And as for ethical considerations—well, I paid
them a lot of lip service, but as recently as last fall I'd availed
myself of the firm's help on a difficult case.

No, what really bothered me was that I might be becoming
too much like those people.

There was a time when I'd viewed everyone—both victim
and perpetrator—through idealistic, compassionate eyes. No
longer. There was a time when I'd gone strictly by the book,
but then I'd found that the book was something that a lot of
people in my business talked about but few had read. Toward
the beginning of my career, remorse over having killed a man
in order to save a friend's life had dogged me for years. But
last spring I'd cold-bloodedly shot another man and called it
justice. I wasn't sure that I liked the woman I was becoming,
but she was formed of life experiences I couldn't eradicate.
You work with what you are, I often told myself on those
dark, lonely nights when my misdeeds caught up with me.

I told myself that now, crossed the sidewalk, and pushed
through the building's lobby entrance. The armed guard at the
desk looked up from his closed-circuit TV monitors, surprised.
"Mr. Ripinsky's not in the office this week, Ms. McCone."

I set my bag and briefcase on the desk and went over to the security gate. "I'm here to see Mr. Renshaw."

"Sorry, he didn't tell me he was expecting you." He made a cursory check of my things, then buzzed me in. "Let me get your badge."

Since Hy had struck his deal with Renshaw and Kessell last winter, they'd kept my photo I.D. on file with those belonging to frequent visitors to the San Francisco offices. Not that I used it all that much; Hy seldom used any of RKI's facilities, preferring to work out of his ranch in Mono County or the cottage we jointly owned on the Mendocino coast. He was, in fact, at the cottage right now, and I planned to join him on the weekend.

The guard handed me the badge, and I attached it to my lapel. "Mr. Renshaw's in the projection room," he told me. "You know the way?"

I nodded and went through an unmarked door and down a long white corridor.

Renshaw was waiting for me in the last row of padded chairs, his feet propped on the one in front of it like a teenager at a double feature. I half expected him to be clutching a grease-stained bag of buttered popcorn. Wordlessly he indicated I should sit beside him, then fiddled with the buttons on the console between us. The lights dimmed and the projection screen shimmered.

I'd sat here before, in this exact place, the day he told me he intended to kill Hy.

"Do you mind if we go over the chronology of these bombings?" he asked.

"That wouldn't hurt."

A slide flashed onto the screen: a large, austere building, its windows blown out. Glass and rubble littered the foreground, and a military guard stared down at it as if he wondered where it had come from.

Renshaw said, "Brazilian Embassy, Washington, D.C. March, nineteen ninety. The bomb was in a package delivered by mail, postmarked D.C. No fatalities, but the clerk who opened it was disabled."

A second slide replaced the first, showing a plain sheet of paper that bore a single sentence: *VENGEANCE IS MINE.*

The letters were Italic—Palatino Italic, to be exact. Joslyn had told me they were a brand of rub-on lettering commonly sold in art- and office-supply stores from coast to coast.

"His message isn't very original," Renshaw commented, "but he makes his point. This was also postmarked D.C., arrived at the embassy the day after the bombing. No fingerprints, nothing distinctive about the paper or the envelope."

"As was the case with what they recovered of the packaging the bomb came in."

The next slide showed a black Lincoln Continental standing in front of a restaurant called Fino. The car's doors had been blown off, and a body in a dark suit lay twisted on the backseat, legs extending toward the bloody pavement.

I said, "Also D.C. August of ninety. The car belonged to the Saudi Arabian ambassador. He and some of his attachés were inside the restaurant. The package was on the backseat; apparently the driver noticed it and investigated. The same message, in the same typeface, on the same stationery stock, was delivered to the embassy the following day. Again postmarked D.C."

Renshaw clicked slowly through the next few slides. "He hit the office wing of the Pakistani Embassy in November of that year. No fatalities, same message the next day. Now we move to New York City."

Another slide: a torn-up living room. Large mirrors on its walls were shattered; their shards reflected a jumble of ruined furnishings. A primitive wood carving stood in the foreground, decapitated.

I said, "Co-op apartment in the east eighties belonging to an official of Ghana's United Nations delegation. The bomb was inside a florist's box delivered by messenger. The messenger was never identified, and all the florist's personnel were checked out and eliminated as suspects. No fatalities, but the maid who accepted delivery was badly injured."

Renshaw said, "January of ninety-one, right?"

"Right. The usual message arrived at Ghana's U.N. offices the following day, postmarked midtown Manhattan."

Renshaw kept advancing the slides. "The bomber really had it in for the U.N. He blew up the head of the Yemeni delegation's car in June of ninety-one, severely crippling the son of a minor official. In February of ninety-two the Mexican ambassador's apartment was hit. A lot of destruction, but no fatalities or injuries there. In December of ninety-two the entire Panamanian delegation was at a Christmas banquet at a midtown restaurant. A messenger with a package for them seemed overly eager to leave; restaurant management got suspicious and called the bomb squad, but the man got away and was never I.D.'d. Of course, the usual message arrived after each incident."

"And then he took a couple of years off."

"Until last December."

The next slide showed the bombed-out facade of the store-front offices of the Libyan Trade Commission on Howard Street here in the city.

"One fatality," I said, "again, the clerk who opened the package. It was mailed from the main post office, as was the message that followed."

Another slide: an office with furnishings knocked helter-skelter. There was a big hole in the rear wall, and on the floor chalk marks outlined where a body had fallen.

Renshaw said, "Belgian consular offices. Last month. Bomb and message both mailed from the Lombard Street substation. One fatality."

He left the slide on the screen, and we contemplated the destruction silently. I couldn't imagine what he was thinking, but I was entertaining emotions, rather than intellectual concepts.

Somewhere in this city was a person who methodically plotted and carried out monstrous crimes. A person who'd gotten away with them time and again. He could be any nationality, could come from any walk of life. Could look as ordinary and harmless as the wrappings that concealed the bombs. Could kill or maim again at any moment. The thought of such a creature walking the same streets as the people I cared about chilled me through and through.

Renshaw had only guessed at part of my interest in the Diplo-bomber case. I wasn't sure if even Joslyn was aware of it. Yes, a million-dollar reward was attractive; I'd be a fool if I didn't want to claim it. But there was more.

Last August a hired killer had blown up a house that had stood on the Mendocino coast property that now belonged to Hy and me. I had been his target, but someone else had died in my place, and other lives had been ripped apart as a result. Time had passed, people had healed, the rubble had been cleared from the cliff top; the place seemed beautiful and serene once more. But often at night I could sense violent ripples beneath the surface of that serenity, could hear the echoes of grief and loss in the waves and sea breeze. The aftershocks of that bombing would never be stilled.

I couldn't do anything about the tragedy in Mendocino County, but I sure as hell could take steps to prevent any more bombings in San Francisco. I was, as Adah told me when she asked me to help, "a flat-out fine investigator, if sometimes a pain in the butt."

I turned to Renshaw. "Okay, Gage, we've reviewed what's public knowledge. Now show me something new."

He smiled thinly and advanced the slide.

An imposing house: creamy white plastered brick, with a mansard roof and heavy cornices. The arched windows were elaborately ornamented, and carved pillars rose beside the massive front door. Yew trees stood like sentinels at its corners. I'd seen it before but couldn't place it.

Renshaw said, "Azadi Consulate, Jackson Street near Octavia."

"Azad—isn't that one of those oil-rich emirates?"

"Right. Oil rich, progressive, and politically stable. They've maintained the consulate since the late sixties, do a high volume of business with our West Coast oil companies."

"But they haven't been—"

"The target of a bombing? No."

The next slide showed another sheet of plain paper lettered in Palatino Italic: *BE FOREWARNED*. Below a sentence was taped, obviously a headline clipped from a newspaper: BRAZILIAN EMBASSY BOMBED.

I asked, "The Azadis received this after the first D.C. bombing?"

"Yes. And again after each subsequent one." He showed slides of the messages in quick succession.

Odd. According to Joslyn's files, none of the other diplomatic missions who had been bombed had reported receiving such warnings. But then, neither had Azad. "Did these come to the consulate, or to other Azadi delegations as well?"

"Only the consulate here." Renshaw switched the projector off and the screen went blank.

"Okay," I said, "what's RKI's connection to Azad?"

"We handle their security in San Francisco, D.C., and New York."

"How'd that happen?"

"They were impressed with how we dealt with a situation for an American company operating out of their capital in the late eighties. When these messages started arriving, they decided to beef up their protective measures at all three of their U.S. locations and contacted us."

"Did they also contact the authorities?"

"No. Mrs. Hamid has an aversion to negative publicity and, besides, the authorities hadn't done anything for the bomber's other targets."

"And Mrs. Hamid is . . . ?"

"Malika Hamid, consul general here."

"A woman consul general? Interesting, for an Arab country."

"As I said, they're progressive."

I thought for a moment. "Do you buy the idea that they didn't contact the authorities because of Mrs. Hamid's concern about bad press?"

He shrugged.

"There's got to be more to it than that."

"If there is, no one's told us."

"And you haven't asked."

"It's not our policy to question our clients' motivations. Not that I wouldn't mind finding out, and that's where you—"

A pager went off in Renshaw's pocket. He took it out, went to an extension phone on the wall by the door, and spoke briefly, his back to me. When he hung up and turned, he asked crisply, "Sharon, do you want in on this or not?"

His cut-to-the-chase tone alerted me that something big had happened. I stood. "Yes, I want in."

"Then let's go."

"Where?"

"Azadi Consulate. There's been a bombing attempt, and one of our operatives is injured."

Two

The police had barricaded Jackson Street between Octavia and Laguna, so we parked around the corner from the consulate. The pavement there was at a steep grade, but Renshaw neglected to curb the wheels and set the emergency brake of RKI's maroon-and-gray mobile unit. As he stepped down, the van lurched backwards. I grabbed the brake handle, pulled it up, then twisted the steering wheel to the left. Renshaw acknowledged his mistake with a rueful headshake.

When I joined him on the sidewalk, he muttered, "Dan would've laughed his ass off at that—and then made me pay out of pocket for the damage."

"You were preoccupied." I quickened my step to keep pace with him. "Surely Kessell could understand that."

"That's no excuse—and I wouldn't accept it either. Neither Dan nor I tolerates any margin for error."

Given their pasts, I could understand why. Renshaw had been an agent on the DEA's elite—and now defunct—Centac task force, based in Southeast Asia. When it was disbanded in the mid-eighties, he disappeared into Indochina and emerged a wealthy man several years later; I'd never had the nerve to ask him about that period in his life. I did know that earlier, in the seventies, he'd accepted finder's fees for steering important people who wished to remove themselves and their assets from the war-torn Asian countries to an air-charter service run out of Bangkok by Dan Kessell. Hy—who had been discharged from the marines after a flare-up of his childhood asthma—had been one of Kessell's pilots; guilt stemming from his actions and experiences during those turbulent, terrible years had consumed him for nearly two decades. Not so with Kessell, though; on him they had left no mark. He was, according to my lover, the same resilient and apparently conscienceless man of the early days in Thailand.

Renshaw and I rounded the corner onto Jackson. A police barricade blocked access and farther down I spotted squad cars, a fire truck, the bomb squad van, and an ambulance. Word about this latest bombing had already reached the media; reporters and camerapeople clamored to be allowed onto the scene, and the uniformed officers were having trouble controlling them. Renshaw and I pushed through the crush.

As Gage held up his I.D., a Channel Seven cameraman swung around and began filming us. I stepped back so Renshaw's body blocked view of me; already I had too high a public profile, and having my presence there broadcast could hamper my ability to investigate. The officer moved the barricade to let us pass, then shoved the persistent cameraman back when he tried to follow. Immediately he began yowling about the public's right to know. I shot him a disgusted look and trotted after Renshaw.

In front of the consulate, the excitement was dying down. The fire crew prepared to leave, the bomb squad van pulled away, and a pair of cops leaned against a black-and-white, talking in low voices. Neighbors from the surrounding houses and apartment buildings began to wander home, their hushed conversations in counterpoint to the harsh sounds from the emergency-vehicle radios. I recognized an unmarked blue Buick that belonged to the task force.

The big creamy-white house was set farther back from the sidewalk than its neighbors, surrounded by a low ornamental fence and fronted by a formal garden. To the left of the brick walk leading to its front door lay the ruins of a fountain; jagged chunks of concrete were scattered around its tiled base, and water had gushed from its piping, soaking and puddling the ground. The pipe, capped off now, leaned at a forty-five-degree angle.

I caught my breath, my skin prickling. The destruction here was nothing like what I'd seen after the bombing on the Mendocino coast, but nevertheless it unnerved me. I swung my gaze to the right of the walk and saw a pair of paramedics standing over a young woman on a stretcher. Her face was cut and abraded; water plastered her short blond hair to her skull.

Renshaw was talking with one of the paramedics. I went over and squatted down beside the RKI operative. "How're you doing?"

"I feel like dog meat." Her eyes were glazed by pain, but she sounded lucid.

Renshaw squatted down on the other side of her. "Holman," he said, "how the hell did this happen?"

Her fingers spasmed against her thighs, but otherwise she didn't react to his abruptness. As calmly as if she were being debriefed at the office she said, "I was on grounds patrol when I saw what looked like a UPS man handing over a package at the door. I checked for a truck. Wasn't any. So I yelled at him, and he took off."

"You allowed him to get away."

Again Holman's fingers tightened. "Yes. Mrs. Hamid's granddaughter, Habiba, was the one who accepted the package. Today's her ninth birthday, and I guess she thought it was a present for her. She had already started to open it, so I grabbed it and chucked it into the fountain."

"Thus triggering the detonating device."

Holman closed her eyes. Like all RKI's people, she was a tough pro, but either the pain or the accusatory tone of Renshaw's questioning was getting to her.

Renshaw swiveled around to face a stocky young man who had come up behind him. "Well, Wilson," he said, "where were you, that a kid opened the door?"

Wilson shifted from foot to foot, his round face reddening. "I . . . don't have any excuse for not being on the door, sir. But I didn't realize Habiba'd escaped from her nanny. The kid's a sly one—"

"Jesus, if they can't control a nine-year-old—" Renshaw

broke off, his lips white with anger. After a moment he turned back to Holman, briefly touched her arm. "They'll take you to S.F. General now. You've got some bad cuts and a few broken ribs, but nothing that can't be fixed."

Holman nodded, her eyes still closed. Renshaw stood and stalked off toward the fountain, ignoring the puddles and splashing his trouser legs with water and mud. After a moment I followed. He stood with his arms folded, glaring down at the chunks of concrete. "Jesus, what a fiasco," he said, more to himself than to me. "They'll both have to go, of course."

"You're firing them? I can understand about Wilson, but Holman risked her life to save the little girl."

"It's the margin for error again. The guy who delivered that package should never've gotten as far as the door. We can't tolerate slipups like that from any of our operatives."

I was silent, wondering how long I'd have lasted with RKI. Not very, I decided. Lucky for me I hadn't taken them up on their offer of a job the year before.

Now I heard Joslyn's husky voice coming from the consulate's entryway. I looked over there and saw her step outside, followed by a tall man who had the look of a federal agent, from his conservatively cut brown hair to his wing-tipped shoes. I started over there, but Adah saw me and shook her head slightly. They went down the walkway and got into the blue Buick.

"Joslyn?" Renshaw asked softly.

I nodded.

"She wonders what you're doing here."

"I'll explain to her later."

"Maybe, maybe not."

"What does that mean?"

He ignored my question. "We should talk with Mrs. Hamid now." Taking my arm, he steered me to the door; the police officer stationed there examined his I.D., then told us we'd find Mrs. Hamid in the library.

"Library" was a misnomer. True, there were bookcases on all four walls, but they contained few volumes and a great many art objects—enough porcelain and jade and ivory and crystal to stock a fair-sized gallery. The gleaming hardwood floor was partially covered by a deep blue Persian rug, and on a leather sofa in front of a leaded-glass window sat a heavyset woman in a plain black suit. She nodded and motioned for us to join her.

Nothing about Malika Hamid's demeanor suggested that she had nearly lost her granddaughter in a bombing attempt. She rose when Renshaw made the introductions, taking my hand in a steady grasp and meeting my eyes with an equally steady gaze. When she asked us to be seated, I was surprised to hear a cultivated British accent. Smiling faintly at my expression, she said, "I was educated in England, as are most members of my family."

As we sat down, Renshaw and I on chairs flanking the sofa, I took the opportunity to study the consul general. She was tall, with thick gray hair fashioned in a plain knot; the severe style emphasized the square shape of her face. Her eyes were so dark that it was difficult to tell where the pupils left off and the irises began, harder yet to read her expression. She wore no makeup, no jewelry, no polish on her blunt fingernails. Malika Hamid cared nothing at all for artifice, and I sensed a strong will and singularity of purpose beneath her gracious manner.

She immediately confirmed my feeling by saying to Renshaw, "I assume you are about to offer excuses for this breach of security. None are welcome—or acceptable."

"No excuses, no explanations," he replied easily. "It was error on the part of my operatives. Of course they'll be dismissed. Before I left the office I requested replacements, and they'll be on duty shortly."

"What reassurance have I that these replacements will be more efficient than the previous ones?"

"You have my personal guarantee."

"Mmm." The set of her mouth conveyed how little his guarantee was worth at the moment.

Renshaw slouched in the chair, seeming unruffled. "You spoke with members of the task force?" he asked.

"I did. An Inspector Joslyn and an Agent Morland."

"Did you tell them about the messages you've received?"

"I did not."

"Do you intend to?"

"No."

"Perhaps," Renshaw said after a moment's reflection, "it's time to confide in them."

She shook her head. "We have discussed this before, Mr. Renshaw. No one is to know about those messages."

"Have you also discussed it with Ambassador Jalil?"

"The ambassador—my second cousin—is in agreement with me."

"Oh?"

The syllable seemed to hang between them. Hamid cocked her head slightly, watchful.

Renshaw added, "I spoke with Ambassador Jalil this morning. He's concerned about withholding evidence and confesses to being perplexed as to your insistence on doing so."

"My second cousin has been perplexed since his birth."

Renshaw raised his eyebrows, waiting. Mrs. Hamid didn't elaborate.

I said, "Perhaps if there was some way to bring the messages to the attention of a discreet member of the task force, who would hold the information in confidence until she was sure the other members would do the same . . ."

"Yes?"

"As Mr. Renshaw mentioned, he's enlisted my help because I have a close connection on the force, who can be trusted."

She made a chopping motion with her right hand. "In this case, no one can be trusted."

Her insistence on privacy bordered on the pathological, I thought. Unless she had something important to hide. . . .

"Mrs. Hamid," I began again, "if you could give me . . . us some idea of why you feel so strongly about keeping the subject of the messages to yourself—"

"I have gone into that with Mr. Renshaw. We are a conservative country; we do not care for sensational publicity of any sort. In addition, our largest oil company is about to negotiate a major contract with your Chevron. Any indication of political instability in Azad would jeopardize those negotiations."

"*Are* the messages and today's bombing evidence of political instability? Do you suspect an extremist group of being behind them?"

"I mentioned political instability as an example of what

the public might think." Hamid transferred her attention to
Renshaw. "I do not appreciate you bringing in an outsider."

He still slouched in the chair, looking as if his mind were
on something else, but I knew he'd heard every word, noted
every nuance. "Ms. McCone is an excellent investigator," he
said.

"I do not want an investigator. I merely want efficient and
effective security."

"Well, that you will have." Abruptly he got to his feet and
motioned to me. "I'll check on my replacements, and then
we'll be on our way."

I took my cue from him, said good-bye to the consul general,
and followed him to the tiled reception area. When I glanced
back into the library, I saw she hadn't moved, except to clasp
her hands together on her lap. Even at a distance I could tell
her knuckles had gone white.

Renshaw crossed the foyer and spoke with a guard wearing
the maroon-and-gray RKI blazer. I started over there, but
turned when I heard a noise behind me. An enormous rose
marble urn stood in the far corner, and above its lip protruded
a forehead covered by floppy black bangs; a pair of huge dark
eyes regarded me solemnly from beneath them.

How on earth had the child managed to squeeze inside that
urn?

The eyes blinked, then disappeared; only tufts of hair
springing from a cowlick remained in view. I waited. After
a moment the eyes reappeared.

I smiled.

They studied me.

I winked.

After a moment the right eye winked back.

It was my first encounter with Habiba Hamid.

I said, "Hamid's a liar, Gage."

"I know that." He eased the van from its parking space.

"She's also a lot more nervous about the reason for these
messages and the bombing attempt than she lets on."

"I know that, too."

"So why don't you call her on it?"

"Wouldn't do any good."

"The ambassador, Jalil—can't he exert some pressure on her?"

Renshaw sighed and turned left toward Van Ness. "Malika Hamid's assessment of Jalil is correct: the man doesn't have a clue."

"Then why did the Azadis make him an ambassador?"

"Azad is literally owned and ruled by the Jalils and Hamids. Idiot relatives who have large holdings in oil-rich lands are kept happy by the award of political plums. Jalil wanted to come to America because he's a theater buff, loves Broadway shows."

"So why didn't they send him to New York? Surely there must've been a job suitable for an idiot with the United Nations delegation."

"At the time there wasn't anything appropriate to Jalil's station, but the ambassadorship was open."

"Strange system for conducting international relations." Then I smiled, thinking of some of our own diplomats. "Well, on second thought, I guess they aren't the only country that exports its fools."

"No, but they do surround their fools with astute advisors."

We were inside the Broadway Tunnel now; I watched its tiled walls slip by the van's windows. After we emerged onto the edges of Chinatown I commented, "Malika Hamid doesn't seem to need astute advisors."

"No, she's a sharp woman, but she has them, too. I'll arrange for you to meet one tomorrow, if you like."

"And that is . . . ?"

He shook his head. "I can't go into this any farther until I'm sure you're with us. We need to hammer out terms and sign a contract."

"Okay—the terms?"

"Nothing I reveal to you about the Azadis—including the existence of those messages—goes back to Joslyn or anyone else on the task force, unless Hamid changes her mind and gives her consent."

I frowned, not liking his terms already.

Gage saw my expression and added, "Of course, we'll compensate you handsomely. How does fifty percent over what we paid you last spring sound?"

That sounded handsome indeed, but I still didn't respond. "You'll also have free access to our resources and our personnel."

"I'd need someone from your data-search section assigned to help me—Charlotte Keim, if available. She did some work for me last fall, and I like the way she operates."

He hesitated, then nodded.

"And I'd have to be given a free hand—no briefings, debriefings, or instructions."

"You'd report only to me."

"And only when I felt I had something to tell you."

He smiled thinly. "I can't imagine you working any other way."

"We have something else to settle, Gage. As I asked you before, why such largess?"

His hands tightened on the steering wheel as he negotiated around a double-parked truck in front of a Chinese produce market. "All right—my reason's really quite simple. When the bomber moved his activities to San Francisco, I realized he was stepping up the pace. For whatever reason, he's got it in for the Azadis, and he's going to get his revenge. I'm not sure if the other bombings were a smoke screen for his real intentions, or related, or what. But I knew he'd strike at the consulate soon, and I know he'll strike again. He's damned serious—so serious that he thinks nothing of taking out a nine-year-old girl."

I nodded.

Renshaw added, "We held him off today, but we can't hold him off indefinitely. Unless we find out why he's after them and who he is, one of these days he's going to get past us again and take out a lot of people—including some of our own."

I nodded again.

"So there you have it. RKI can't afford that. We *can* afford you. Are you with us?"

In theory I was, but I still wanted to think it over before I signed a contract. "What about the feds' reward?" I asked.

He scowled.

"Well?"

"The reward will be split fifty-fifty."

"Seventy-five to me, twenty-five to you."

"Sixty-forty."

"Sixty to me?"

"Goddamn it, yes!"

"Okay, I'll think on it. You'll have my answer by noon tomorrow."

"Think on it?"

"Until noon, Gage."

"Sharon, you are the most stubborn, aggravating—"

"Save it. I've heard it all before."

He glanced at me with interest. "From Ripinsky, too?"

"Never."

"Why not?"

Why not? Well, it had to do with the nature of the relationship. I could have tried to explain that to Renshaw, but I didn't bother. It simply wasn't within the range of his comprehension.

Three

      I'd planned to deliver a final report to an architect who had his offices in one of the renovated piers off the Embarcadero at four o'clock, but by the time Renshaw dropped me at my car it was closer to four-thirty. I used my mobile phone to call the client, and he told me to come over anyway, so I left the MG where it was and walked there. After we discussed the report, I collected a check from him and strolled back along the shoreline boulevard. At the municipal pier next to the Waterfront restaurant I turned and took a detour.

It had been one of those brilliantly clear days that almost make San Franciscans believe a dreary fog-socked summer isn't going to happen after all. At five o'clock the streets were clogged with cars and buses, and the sidewalks teemed with pedestrians taking their time on their way home. After-work joggers pounded past me on the pier, and less active types sat on the benches facing an iron railing that was crowned with old-fashioned streetlamps. The chimes in the tower of the nearby Ferry Building played "Oh, What a Beautiful Morning," and then a melody whose words I remembered as having something to do with the evening breeze. I smiled at this typically San Francisco version of taps.

When I reached the end of the pier, I leaned on the rail,

watched a ferry ply its way toward Marin County, and listened to the swash of its wake against the pilings. I thought about Gage Renshaw's proposition, about the Azadis, about Adah Joslyn.

I wasn't sure whether in good conscience I could keep from Joslyn what I knew about the messages the consulate had received. Whenever possible I tried to cooperate with law-enforcement agencies and besides, Adah was a friend. By withholding information I could hamper the one official body that was capable of putting a stop to the bombings. On the other hand, if I turned down Renshaw's offer I'd relinquish following up on one of the most promising leads in the case so far. And even if I went to Adah with the information, I was certain Malika Hamid would deny my story and refuse to cooperate with the task force.

I looked at the situation pro and con. Tried several approaches, discarded most of them, tried some more. I thought about my fear of becoming too much like Renshaw and his cohorts. Realized that if I accepted the proposed contract I would have taken one more step toward the line that separated us. But even as I fought the notion, a compelling image kept intruding.

An image of big shiny dark eyes staring at me over the lip of an enormous marble urn. Big shiny dark eyes that—had it not been for the quick actions of a brave young woman—might now be staring blank and dull from a steel drawer in the morgue.

Habiba Hamid tipped the scales in favor of Renshaw's offer. I turned and retraced my route along the pier.

I wanted to go over my files on the case and check some things before I spoke with Renshaw, so I ate a quick sandwich and called my office as I headed across town. Mick Savage, my nephew and temporary assistant, had gone home and forgotten to turn on the answering machine.

I slammed the receiver into its base unit. Cursed and for the thousandth time vowed to find a permanent replacement for Mick. But—as Hy frequently reminded me—although Mick would forever be temporary in my mind, in actuality he was there to stay. The kid—he'd just turned eighteen—

was a computer genius, had a natural talent for investigation, and was usually a delight to have around. Besides, I couldn't fault him for rushing home tonight; he'd told me that this was the eighth-month anniversary of his meeting Maggie Bridges, the bright and pretty USF student with whom he lived. A romantic evening was in the works.

I'd just have to pull up the files and run the computer scan myself. God help me if I screwed anything up; Mick would never let me hear the end of it.

When I rounded the triangular park across from All Souls Legal Cooperative, I was surprised to find a parking space right in front. During the years I'd worked as the co-op's chief investigator, I'd spent an inordinate amount of time hunting for spaces and then wrapping the MG around corners next to fireplugs, but recently I'd found convenient spaces with great frequency. Perhaps an easy park job was cosmically included with the rented one-and-a-half rooms that I grandiosely referred to as an office suite.

I hurried up the steps of the big gray Victorian, pushed inside, and inadvertently let the door slam behind me. The TV was on in the otherwise dim parlor, the changing light patterns of the evening news flickering off the blue walls. Two heads turned toward me—Ted Smalley, the co-op's office manager, and Rae Kelleher, my former assistant and now chief investigator. Two hands waved in greeting. I waved back and went upstairs to the big room at the front of the second floor.

The first thing I did was to dump my jacket, bag, and briefcase on the sofa. Then I rushed down the hall to the unheated cubicle next to the bathroom that contained the toilet—a less-than-charming arrangement found in most of the city's Victorians. Recently someone had mounted a full-length mirror on the back of the door. As usual I grimaced and closed my eyes against a most unflattering image of myself. No wonder I avoided having clients come to the office! What if one asked to use the john?

Actually, a lot of things about All Souls were beginning to pale for me. If it wasn't for the relatively low rent and the live-in presence of Rae and Ted, plus the daily presence of my oldest and dearest friend, Hank Zahn, I'd have seriously considered moving the office. Trouble was, I didn't know where I wanted to go; I'd been working out of this building for so long that it felt like a second skin. But All Souls had changed, and so had I. The days whose memory I cherished, when the co-op had been a laid-back, unconventional institution where the old me fit perfectly, were gone forever.

Can't turn back the calendar, McCone, I told myself. And you don't really want to, anyway.

I spent the next few hours scanning the data on the bombings that Mick had entered on disk. First I looked for commonalities: among the nations whose diplomatic missions had been hit; among the members of those missions who had been the apparent targets. None applied across the board. Next I scrutinized each file for references to messages other than the ones that arrived after the bombings. There were none. None of the countries had a significant relationship with Azad, hostile or peaceful. My analysis of the dates and times of the incidents revealed no pattern.

By the time I switched off the machine I'd developed a headache. I helped myself to three aspirin from the bottle on Rae's shelf in the communal bathroom's medicine chest, then went back to my desk and made a list of things I wanted Mick to research: Azad; its consulate here; the staff of that consulate; similar background on each of the other countries that had been bombed, going back ten years. Was that far enough? Yes, for now.

I had a court appearance scheduled for tomorrow morning that would keep me away from the office, so I briefly considered calling Mick and explaining the list. No, I decided, bad idea to intrude on his romantic evening with Maggie. My nephew was fairly easygoing, but he had his limits; if I bothered him tonight he was likely to retaliate in some bizarre and unpredictable way. I'd write a detailed note and, if necessary, call him from City Hall tomorrow.

I weighted down the note in the middle of his desk with a volume titled *How To Make Your Own Professional Lock Tools* by one Eddie-the-Wire. Mick's taste in what he called professional reading ran to the lurid, and some time ago I'd decided it was best not to think too much about what skills he might be developing. He had a checkered past as far as the uses to which he'd put the computer and considering that, I supposed his interest in electronic eavesdropping, con artists, disguises, and the driving of getaway cars was only natural. Until I actually caught him picking a lock or fashioning a bug, I'd leave him to his somewhat suspect pastime.

It was now close to nine, but I felt too restless and wound up to go home. I went back to my desk and made a list of conditions I wanted in my contract with RKI, adding to those Renshaw and I had already discussed a generous advance against expenses and a limitation on how frequently I'd have to report. Then I straightened the papers in my In and Out boxes, went through my pen holder for felt-tips that no longer worked, discarded three stubby pencils and sharpened two more. After I'd checked the spindled message slips for calls I'd failed to return, I slumped in my chair and contemplated the velvety blackish-red petals of the rose in the bud vase on the desk's corner. A single rose arrived every Tuesday morning, courtesy of Hy; although the color had changed over the time we'd been together, deepening along with the relationship, it was a constant I'd come to depend upon.

Impulsively I picked up the phone receiver and dialed Mendocino County.

Hy answered after several rings, sounding groggy and oddly subdued. "Did I wake you?" I asked.

"No, I'm just feeling feverish. I think I picked up a bug in Managua." He had conducted a hostage recovery there a few weeks before—his area of specialization, and a service he provided RKI in exchange for autonomy on his own projects in the human-rights area.

"Have you seen a doctor?"

"I will, as soon as I get back to the ranch. So what's happening?"

"I spent the afternoon with your buddy Gage Renshaw."

"Not in the sack, I hope." A few months ago Renshaw had mentioned to Hy that he found me sexy; my lover still teased me, knowing I considered Gage as sexually interesting as a banana slug.

"Bite your tongue, Ripinsky!"

"So what *were* you doing?"

I explained about the Azadis, the bombing attempt, and Renshaw's proposition.

When I finished, Hy asked, "McCone, you sure you want to contract with him?"

"Why not? I've dealt with him before—under extremely stressful circumstances, as you remember—and held my own."

"You holding your own is the last thing I'm concerned about."

"What, then?"

". . . Nothing, really. I suppose I'm projecting the uneasy quality of my own relationship with Gage onto your situation."

"Well, uneasy describes how I always feel about him, but I can handle it."

"Good." Then he changed the subject. "What time'll you be up here tomorrow?"

"I'm not sure. It could be a long day."

"Why don't I fly down and get you, then. Save some travel time."

"No, I'm bringing some stuff along, so I have to drive."

"For the cottage? What this time?"

"Some more pottery. New towels. A mirror I found at a garage sale."

He laughed. "Nest feathering again, huh?"

Ever since he and I had acquired the cottage, I'd found myself irresistibly drawn to objects: rugs, linens, kitchen gear, furniture. I'd begun scouring the flea markets and garage sales for brightly glazed pottery from the thirties, forties, and fifties—even though Hy had pointed out that we'd have to wash it by hand since it wasn't dishwasher-proof. Of course, that hardly mattered, since we hadn't yet bought the dishwasher. . . .

I smiled at how the thought triggered an urge to order one first thing tomorrow.

"Kind of strange, isn't it?" I asked.

"Not really. You must know why you're doing it."

"And why am I, Dr. Freud?"

"That's easy. You're surrounding yourself with things that'll give the illusion of keeping the craziness of the world at bay. It's pretty goddamn wild and lonely out there nowadays."

It made sense. "You ever feel that way?"

"God, yes. Why do you think I wanted this cottage?"

"But you've got your ranch, your stuff. I've got my house here, my stuff. Why do we need more?"

"Somehow the craziness keeps its distance better when we're in our place, surrounded by our stuff."

My eyes stung; I swallowed. "Then I'll see you tomorrow night with another carload of it."

When I got home half an hour later, I found the craziness had invaded my earthquake cottage. W. C. Fields was lying mutilated on my sitting room floor.

I let out a howl of dismay and scooped up the seventy-five-buck silk parrot. He'd been dragged from his perch by the window, and his colorful tail hung in tatters. One talon was severed, and both beady eyes hung by threads. His formerly crotchety expression looked woeful. I didn't know whether to try to repair him or bury him in the backyard.

"All right!" I shouted. "All *right*! Who did this?"

From the kitchen door two pairs of feline eyes watched me warily. I set W.C. on the coffee table and advanced upon my orange tabby, Ralph, and his calico sister, Alice.

"I have warned you—that parrot is not for you! But did you listen? No, you did not."

Surprisingly, both cats held their ground, looking defiant and not a little smug. They'd hated W.C. since the day I'd brought him home, and apparently felt fully justified in their attack.

I leaned down and studied them carefully, hoping to spot a telltale scrap of silk hanging from a mouth or a claw. No clues.

"We have ways of making you talk," I told them.

Ralph glanced at Allie.

"And I will offer immunity to the accomplice who's willing to testify against the other."

Allie looked at Ralph.

"I'd read you your rights, but you have none."

They whirled and galloped toward their pet door.

"Don't leave town without informing me!"

The pet door flapped and clattered shut.

"I must be losing my mind," I said.

Adah called at quarter after eleven. I'd been soaking in the bathtub, alternately contemplating the feasibility of repairing W.C. and trying to decide how much to tell Joslyn about my deal with RKI. When the phone rang I got out of the tub, pulled on my white terry-cloth robe, and padded into the kitchen, dripping water in my path.

"So," she snapped, "what were you doing at the Azadi Consulate with the head of their security firm?"

"That's a pleasant greeting."

"Just answer the question."

"What the hell's the matter with you?" I took the cordless into the bathroom, slipped out of my robe, and slid back into the tub.

"One thing, I'm still at the office and likely to be here all night. The others—ah, shit, you don't want to know. Now will you tell me . . . please?"

I settled on a half-truth. "After I left you, I ran into Gage. We were having coffee when he got the call about the bombing, so I went along for the ride."

Joslyn snorted. "Cut the crap. You can't stand Renshaw; you wouldn't have coffee with him if you were going into caffeine withdrawal. Besides, why was Renshaw hanging around task force headquarters?"

"I didn't say he was."

"Craig Morland, the FBI guy I was with at the scene, told me he saw the two of you getting off the elevator at Eddy Street."

"Oh."

"Well?"

"All right—I may be onto something, but I can't talk about it yet."

"Can't, or won't?"

"Both."

Her voice rose now. "McCone, what're you trying to pull on me?"

"I'm not trying to 'pull' anything. We agreed I'd help you

with this case, but you've got to let me do it my own way. Give me some room to operate, will you?"

"Room to operate?" She sounded downright shrill. "Give you room, so you can fuck me over just like the feds—"

"Adah, take it easy. You've had a long day, a bad day. Why don't you go home—"

"I don't need advice from you. I don't need advice from anybody!" She slammed the receiver down, hard.

I held the cordless away from my ear and stared at it, as if I could see along the electronic waves to my friend's face. Then I flicked it off and set it on the floor next to the tub. I'd never heard Joslyn so out of control.

After a moment I added more hot water and bath oil, slid down till my chin was immersed and the ends of my hair trailed out around me, and thought about the nature of my friendship with Adah.

We'd met a couple of years before when a client of mine was murdered. I'd broken that case, in cooperation with her and her then partner, Bart Wallace. Afterwards we'd started hanging out together: she'd meet me after work at the Remedy Lounge down the hill from All Souls, or I'd pick her up at the Hall and we'd go out for dinner. We'd ride our bikes in the park—yet another of my schemes to get more exercise— or drive up into the wine country on weekends. Recently she'd even talked me into joining her health club. But while we were doing all those things, we also talked about her cases.

Adah used me as a sounding board. She'd fill me in on the details of a given case, run her theories by me; she'd note my reactions, draw out my ideas. I didn't mind; if anything, I felt as if I was contributing something to the effort to get criminals off the streets. But now that I thought about it, I began to see a pattern that I didn't like.

My input often helped Joslyn make her collars. But once made, they were strictly hers; she never acknowledged my help, not even to say a private thank-you. One time I'd casually mentioned my efforts, and her reaction startled me. What did I want, she asked, a citizen's commendation? My name engraved on the cornerstone of the new jail?

Well, no, but a few words of appreciation wouldn't have hurt.

Now I began to wonder why I'd spent the past two weeks brainstorming with her about the Diplo-bomber. Why I'd put in long nights poring over files that had to be back on her desk first thing in the morning. Given her past pattern, if I helped her solve the case Joslyn would take all the credit and, promise or no promise, neglect to recommend me for the reward.

I wasn't going to allow that prospect to stop me, though. The bomber was still walking the streets of the city. And now that I'd seen Habiba Hamid's shiny dark eyes, I was in this for the duration. I'd find a way to handle Joslyn, just as in the past I'd found a way to handle Renshaw.

But, damn. I hadn't expected that I'd need to play manipulative games with a woman I regarded as my friend.

Four

Kahlil Lateef, trade attaché to the Azadi Consulate, was rotund and bore an unfortunate resemblance to the late Richard M. Nixon. He glared down at the plates of tapas on the table between us and prodded the *ropa vieja* with his fork. Lateef had chosen the Mexican restaurant near Valencia Street in the Mission district because he'd read about it in a food magazine, but now he seemed displeased.

"What did the waiter say the name of this dish translates to?" he asked me.

" 'Old clothes.' "

"Why would they call it such a thing?" His Oxbridge accent would have sounded haughty, were it not underscored by the softer cadences of his native tongue.

"I suppose because it sounds more interesting than 'shredded beef.' "

Lateef set down his fork and sipped water, frowning.

"Try some of that chicken in peanut sauce," I suggested, glad we'd ordered a large variety of the tapas.

He examined the chicken suspiciously, even though it had been his choice.

The restaurant was one of my favorites—bright and homey, with excellent food and a lively staff who made every meal a festive occasion, but I was surprised Lateef had wanted to eat there, given the dietary restrictions of Islam. I suspected he'd chosen it solely for its location—near my office and about as far from the consulate as he could get. When Gage Renshaw had asked the attaché to meet with me, he'd expressed concern about Mrs. Hamid finding out he'd done so. Even now he glanced around furtively, as if afraid she'd stationed spies in the heart of the Mission.

I'd been able to negotiate my contract with Renshaw and set up this lunch because at the last minute the civil case in which I was supposed to testify had been settled. Renshaw was anxious for me to talk with Lateef; the attaché displayed no strong loyalty to Malika Hamid and might be willing to pass on useful information. Lateef, Gage said, had once remarked to him that the consul general possessed the temperament of a dyspeptic camel.

The attaché unbent and sampled the chicken, pronounced it good and helped himself to a tacquito. I relaxed, glad he'd finally eaten something, and redirected our discussion. Since we arrived here Lateef had talked about San Francisco's diplomatic community: its relatively small size, some fifty consuls general at last count, and many of merely honorary status; of consular duties ranging from issuing new passports to citizens residing in the U.S., to making loans to stranded travelers from the homeland, to negotiating trade agreements with large American corporations; of rivalries and enmities among the various missions, none of which seemed to involve Azad; of diplomatic entertainment which, he said regretfully, was not nearly as lavish here as on the East Coast. Now I steered the conversation to Azad.

"I met with Mrs. Hamid yesterday and found her a most interesting woman. I'd like to know more about her."

Lateef's small eyes gleamed—whether in enjoyment of his second tacquito or in anticipation of the dirt he was about to dish, I couldn't tell. "Malika Hamid is an unusual woman," he said. "Very forceful. Very single-minded. She always arranges to have things her way. Her grandmother was English, did you know? One of those terribly gallant impoverished gentlewomen who came out to the less civilized parts of the world during the latter years of the century, determined to do good works. You've read about them in historical novels, of course. She was hired to educate the emir's children, but decided to reeducate him as well. One day he had three wives and his freedom, the next he was bound in wedlock to the honorable Sarah Abernathy. Those early marriages were not valid according to her, you see. Poor emir! Sarah then set about reforming him, and when she finished, she set about reforming the country."

"I assume she succeeded."

"Most assuredly. She was not a woman to be stopped. Azad owes its present-day progressive status to her. Our women haven't worn the *hijab* for decades; they are educated in the same manner as our men, they drive automobiles, they hold responsible jobs. Sarah, much to her sorrow, never succeeded in making us Anglicans; we do follow the precepts of Islam. But, except for a few fundamentalist factions, we interpret our faith in ways that apply to the modern world. And we are a peaceable country. Of course"—he smiled—"it helps that we are also a prosperous country. Full bellies breed peace."

"And what about Malika Hamid? Does she take after her grandmother?"

"Oh, definitely. She was educated in England, as is the tradition with our leading families, took her final degree at the London School of Economics. Very well traveled, very well read. Never went in for jet-setting and all that sort of frivolity. Afterwards she returned home and worked on various highly placed government commissions. She also found time to marry—a distant cousin on the Hamid side, who gave her one son. The husband is still alive, you know."

"In San Francisco?"

Lateef shook his head, malice showing in his thin-lipped smile. "No, the south of France, I believe. There was a scandal some fifteen years ago involving Hamid and not one but two young boys. He went abroad, and his injured wife requested a permanent diplomatic posting to America. She preferred San Francisco, so the former consul general here was called home. Mrs. Hamid departed Djara, our capital, with her son, Dawud, and has never again set foot on Azadi soil."

"Dawud is Habiba's father?"

"Yes."

"And he's still living at the consulate?"

"No. Dawud—Dave, as he insisted on being called—disappeared a number of years ago. Five? Six? I am sorry, I don't recall. He was in his late twenties at the time. Mrs. Hamid was heartbroken; she adored her son and would have done anything for him. To compound matters, it appeared that his disappearance had to do with his involvement in illegal gambling."

"He owed gambling debts?"

"No, nothing like that. He was in charge of a high-stakes gambling operation of some sort. I must hasten to add that this is merely idle gossip. Mrs. Hamid works to keep family affairs within the family, as is the Azadi way. Most of her staff do not care for her, so they distort what little they do hear."

Including you. "Do you know whether Dawud's disappearance was voluntary or involuntary?"

Lateef shook his head and speared another piece of chicken.

"Were the police called?"

"Not to my knowledge."

"What about his wife? Is she still living at the consulate?"

He set down his fork and pushed the plate away, seeming to lose his appetite. "The younger Mrs. Hamid lives with her mother-in-law, yes."

Something wrong there. "Tell me about her."

"She is American. Dave met her at UCLA before he was asked to leave because of academic deficiency."

"Her first name is . . . ?"

"Mavis."

"What does she do for a living?"

"Nothing, now. She was a poet, a very gifted one; she was awarded many prizes. And she is still a beautiful woman, only in her early thirties."

"Why did she give up her poetry?"

He sighed. "She drinks."

Social drinking away from the consulate? She wouldn't be able to indulge in an Azadi household where, according to Islamic law, alcohol was prohibited. "How much does she drink?"

"Steadily and constantly."

"An alcoholic, then."

"Yes."

"Is her mother-in-law aware of the problem?"

"Oh, yes."

"Has she tried to get Mavis into treatment?"

"No."

"Why not?"

He shrugged.

"I don't imagine liquor is kept in the consulate. Does Mavis bring it in over Mrs. Hamid's objection?"

"As I mentioned before, Mavis Hamid is a beautiful woman, a wounded and vulnerable woman. Her name means 'song-thrush,' you know, and it suits her. For such a person, others will do things—even things that go against their better judgment and the precepts of their religion."

Meaning the staff supplied the booze for her. Because she was a beautiful, wounded, vulnerable woman? I didn't buy that. But I could imagine a desperate woman paying them, even trading sexual favors for a bottle. I was about to probe some more when I noticed the raw pain in Lateef's eyes.

He's in love with her, I thought, and he's supplied many a bottle himself.

I said, "So Mavis just stays at the consulate and drinks."

"She stays in her room. Occasionally she wanders through the house late at night when she thinks everyone else has retired."

The way he phrased it told me he'd encountered her on those wanderings; had perhaps become her lover, or at least a confidant.

"Do other people in the diplomatic community know about her problem?"

"There were a number of embarrassing incidents when the elder Mrs. Hamid was entertaining last year, that necessitated sedating Mavis, but of late she has become very reclusive."

"In your opinion, was her husband's disappearance the cause of her drinking?"

"She always drank. So did Dave. A great many more of us do than you would suspect. But I would say that it became more extreme afterward."

"I still don't understand why Malika Hamid refuses to get Mavis into treatment. If it's negative publicity she's afraid of, she could always send her to one of those discreet European clinics."

Lateef had been turning his knife over and over on his plate; now he grasped it like a weapon.

I said, "Let me ask you this: does Mrs. Hamid abet Mavis's drinking?"

"Yes."

"Why?"

"Mavis hates Malika. She has since their first meeting. If she were well and strong, she would take her daughter and leave the consulate. She would cash in the securities she inherited when her parents died several years ago and go far away. Malika would never see Habiba again."

"Mavis has said so?"

"Many times—and in her mother-in-law's hearing. Malika will never permit it. Since she lost her son, Habiba is everything to her. She will not let her go, and anyone who attempts to take her is expendable."

"Gage, I need to get inside that consulate and talk with Mavis Hamid."

"Malika won't allow that. And anyway, Mavis is so zoned out most of the time that nothing she says makes any sense."

"Still, I've got to try."

"Impossible."

"How can you say that? You control the security there!"

"If Malika found out I set up a meeting between you and her drunken daughter-in-law, she'd cut off my pecker."

"That's nothing."

There was a silence. Then Renshaw recognized my reprise of his earlier comment about my self-respect and laughed. "Shows what you know," he said. More soberly he added, "You'll have to prove to me that it's necessary you talk with Mavis."

"I can't *prove* anything. But you ought to realize that any bit of information, no matter how irrelevant it seems, can prove crucial to an investigation."

Renshaw was silent again. I cradled the receiver against my shoulder and glanced at the door that connected my office with Mick's. He hunched at his desk, sandy blond head bent over the computer keyboard, stocky body dwarfing the posture chair. His fingers tapped furiously. Suddenly he peered up at the VDT, said "Uh-huh," and recommenced tapping.

"Gage?"

"Hang on, I'm checking Hamid's schedule."

More silence. Mick said, "Uh-*huh*!" I tried to catch his attention, but he was enrapt with whatever had appeared on the screen.

"Okay," Renshaw said, "the old dyspeptic camel—I like that, don't you?—is off to dinner with the head of the Saudi Trade Commission tonight; they'll probably plot to raise world oil prices. She'll leave the consulate at seven; I'll take you in to see Mavis at nine when our shifts change—less conspicuous that way. By then the younger Mrs. Hamid will be shit-faced and puking on the rug, but if you insist . . ."

"I insist." Then I thought of my plans to arrive at the cottage tonight with another load of possessions designed to ward off demons. If I didn't get there Hy, unlike other men with whom I'd been involved, would understand. But the interview with Mavis Hamid probably wouldn't take long. I'd nap before I went to the consulate and be fresh for the four-hour drive.

Renshaw said, "One of our mobile units is parked around the block from the consulate on Laguna Street by Lafayette Square. I'll meet you there."

I agreed, broke the connection, and motioned to Mick, who was standing in the doorway. "What had you so interested?" I nodded toward the computer.

"The feds're using the TechnoWeb to solicit information about the bomber."

"The TechnoWeb?" It was one of the on-line services he insisted we subscribe to, but I couldn't for the life of me keep them sorted out.

"Shar, I guided you through it just last month."

Mick found my inability to internalize computer-related information so irritating that sometimes I perversely simulated ignorance in order to get a rise out of him. I was feeling perverse now. "Refresh my memory."

He sighed. "The Web is a nationwide service with over two million individual users. It offers news, sports, and weather; educational and reference services; games, shopping, and travel arrangements; investment and real-estate advice; bulletin boards, E-mail, and live discourse."

"Those boards—"

"Each board is devoted to a specific interest; you post notes that everybody using them can read, and anyone can respond to you by note. E-mail is private communication with an individual, again by note. Live discourse is like talking, only it's via computer terminal. The feds're smart to tap into the Web, and I'll bet they're using the other services like Prodigy and CompuServe and America Online, as well as the Internet."

"The Internet—that's the monster one you need a road map to use?"

Mick smiled smugly. "*Some* people need a road map, but not this kid."

"Okay—the task force posted on a bulletin board?"

"Three that I've found so far: Law Enforcement, Crime and Criminals, and Famous Criminals. Basically the note was a recap of what anybody who reads the papers already knows about the case. It asked people to come forward with information, either on the boards or the task force's eight hundred number, and mentioned the reward."

"You think they'll get anything that way?"

He shrugged. "You never know. People who use the on-line services are generally pretty intelligent, and a lot of the ones I communicate with tend to get caught up in what you'd call amateur sleuthing. But here's what I'm thinking: this is an unusual item; people'll be posting about it all over the boards. If I monitor them, maybe we'll learn something before the feds do."

"Go ahead, then. But I'll tell you, I don't have too high an opinion of this mania for the boards. The computer puts distance between people, allows them to conceal and lie outright. Look what happened to Rae when she fooled around on the boards on Wisdom."

The previous fall Rae had become involved with two men through Wisdom's Frank Conversations board. I wasn't clear on the exact nature of the involvement because, try as I might, I could never figure out how one could have what Rae termed "an incredibly sensual experience" via computer terminal. Computer sex, I suspected, had evolved into phone sex, and

Rae had gone about her business in a blissful if somewhat glassy-eyed condition until New Year's Eve, when the two had traveled from their respective homes in Kansas City and El Paso to escort her to All Souls's traditional party. Unfortunately, the evening ended badly when they recognized a mutual attraction and left together. Rae immediately swore off the computer as a recreational device and gave up on men in general. She now spent the majority of her free time watching old movies on TV or playing pinball down at the Remedy.

Ted, who had recently taken a volunteer counseling position at a Noe Valley gay/lesbian crisis center, kept trying to convince Rae that such behavior was unhealthy, but she either barricaded herself in her office or used the TV's remote control to turn up the sound and drown him out. Last week he'd asked me to reason with her, but I declined. I'd advised and consoled her during too many emotional disasters; my few words of wisdom had begun to sound like platitudes, even to me. Besides, Rae was an adult; if she felt she needed help, she'd ask for it.

Mick interrupted my thoughts. "That call on the other line, it was Adah Joslyn again. Makes ten altogether today."

"How does she sound?"

"Burned out and seriously mean. She said, 'Where the fuck is McCone and why the fuck hasn't she returned my calls?'"

I sighed. "What did you tell her?"

"That you were still out of the office and hadn't called in. I didn't think you'd want to deal with her."

"I don't. If she calls again, you can tell her I've left for the weekend. In fact, I'm going home right now to pack the stuff I'm taking along. And then, you know what? I think I'll relax for a few hours."

"I'll believe that when. Are Maggie and I still supposed to look after the cats while you're gone?"

"Yes, but don't coddle them. One of them assaulted W.C. yesterday, and the other's refusing to turn state's evidence."

Five

At a few minutes before nine I parked down the block from the consulate and walked up Laguna Street through the gathering shadows. RKI's van sat inconspicuously under an olive tree at the northwest corner of the hilly park called Lafayette Square. As I approached, Renshaw stepped away from it.

"Electronic surveillance on the consulate?" I motioned at the van.

"We've tightened security. So far, everything's quiet. Hamid left on time, ordered the car to pick her up again at midnight. All the same, you'd better be quick about this. We'll go in by the service entrance, and I'll take you upstairs. You've got half an hour."

As we started downhill I asked, "Does Mavis Hamid know I'm coming?"

"I dropped in on her earlier and asked if she'd like a visitor. The idea seemed to please her. As far as she's concerned, you're one of our operatives, making sure she's comfortable with the security arrangements."

Renshaw led me through an automobile gate and down the consulate's driveway; a door opened onto a graveled parking area in front of the three-car garage. He knocked, spoke softly to the guard on duty there, and we went inside, past a laundry room and a pantry to a steep uncarpeted stairway. The big house was silent; our footfalls seemed to thunder. The noise faded to a whisper on the Oriental rugs in the upstairs hallway. Renshaw went to a door, tapped lightly, and said, "You're on your own now."

A woman's voice called out something unintelligible. I took it as an invitation to enter and opened the door. The room beyond was lit only by the flames from a gas fireplace. Dark draperies masked the high windows, and it felt overly warm. There was a stale odor trapped within its walls—the kind you find in houses that have been closed up for a long time but shouldn't exist in an inhabited place. I could make out very little except for the figure seated Indian-style on the floor in front of the marble hearth.

Mavis Hamid was not beautiful, as Kahlil Lateef had claimed. She had dingy brown hair that cascaded over her shoulders and back; it looked thin and uncared for. She wore a black bathrobe with white piping, and her feet were bare. As she turned my way in the fire's light I saw a pale oval face, its features puffy, its skin blotchy. In her hand she held a deck of cards, and a game of solitaire was spread out in front of her. I didn't see a bottle or a glass, but as I got closer I could smell the alcohol; she wore its scent like perfume.

"Mrs. Hamid?"

"Call me Mavis. I don't like that name; it's my mother-in-law's, not mine. Mr. Renshaw said you want to talk to me about something?"

"Yes. We want to make sure you're okay with the security arrangements. They've been tightened since the bombing attempt."

"Security's fine," she said vaguely and waved toward a love seat arranged at an angle to the fireplace. "Sit, please. Do you want a drink?"

I didn't, but she obviously did, so I said, "Yes, thanks."

She got up, stumbling slightly on the trailing hem of her robe, and hurried to a door that probably led to a bathroom. My eyes were accustomed to the gloom now, and I looked around. The room was large and overdecorated with gilt-framed wall mirrors and floral wallpaper that matched the valances over the dark blue draperies. The bed was buried in flounces and crowned by a canopy; a dressing table with a three-way mirror looked as if it were wearing a hoop skirt. The sitting area here by the hearth seemed crammed with furnishings: the love seat, a chaise longue, two recliner chairs. Yet Mavis Hamid preferred the floor.

She returned holding two glasses full to the brim with clear liquid, no ice. I took the one she offered and smelled it. Vodka. Why do they always think it has no odor?

Mavis said, "Cheers," toasted with her glass, and took a drink. Then she sank to the floor, set the glass down, and picked up the deck of cards. "Solitaire. It relaxes me. A couple of years ago I got bored with the regular game, so I taught myself to play it backwards—kings up first, instead of aces— and made a lot of other new rules. My mother-in-law said I couldn't do that. I told the bitch, 'I can do any damn thing I please, it's my system, it's the one time *I* get to make the rules.' "

I'd been noting her speech patterns: she slurred some words, but on the whole she sounded coherent and animated, if a little erratic. What interested me besides that was her apparent lack of emotional affect—she hadn't reacted at all to my mention of the bombing attempt that had nearly taken her child's life—as well as her undisguised hostility toward Malika Hamid. The latter could be exploited.

I asked, "What was your mother-in-law's reaction?"

"She told me I was being childish. I don't know why she couldn't understand. I mean, she makes up all the rules around here. Malika's got a rule for every occasion, and when they don't suit her anymore, she just changes them. I told her she ought to have them printed up daily and posted like a menu so people would know which set we're following. You can bet she didn't like that." She giggled, holding a card over her mouth—a naughty child.

"Tell me about Malika's rules."

Mavis looked pointedly at the glass in my hand. "You're not drinking."

I took a small sip, nearly gagging on the warm undiluted liquor. "The rules?" I repeated.

She tossed the cards on the floor, reached for her drink, and leaned back against the chaise longue. "There's the rule that I can't see Habiba—that's my daughter, do you know her?"

I nodded.

"That I can't see Habiba for more than an hour a day. Except when Habiba pitches a fit and cries for me, and then I can see her till she stops. There's the rule that I can't drive or go out for a walk, I can only go in the car with Karim— he's the driver. Only I don't have a car of my own, so I wouldn't drive anyway and, besides, there's no place I want to go. But that rule gets changed when I drink too much and take pills and they can't get Dr. Lee over here to give me a shot. *Then* they make me go out and walk and walk, but always with Karim." Her lips curled up—slowly, almost dreamily. "There's no rule about the booze, of course. I can have all I want, as long as I behave and stay in my room."

"Behave how?"

"Oh, don't wander into one of her damn dinner parties and start talking to somebody important. Don't ask to see Habiba except during her hour. I'm a bad influence on her, you know."

"Do you really believe that?"

"Oh, yes, I must be."

"So that's what you do—stay here in your room most of the time?"

"If I want the booze, I do. And I do—want the booze, I mean."

"What about Habiba's father? What does he have to say about all this?"

Her still smiling lips pulled down and her eyes sparked with anger. "Dave-the-magnificent? You see any signs of a man around here?"

"No."

"That's because Dave-the-perfect, Dave-who-Mama-claimed-could-do-no-wrong hasn't been around for years. Malika didn't think to make up any rules about sons not being able to disappear."

"He disappeared on purpose, then?"

"Of course. Who wouldn't want to get away from that smothering bitch?"

"But what about you and Habiba? Why did he leave you behind?"

"Dave and I stopped getting along the minute he brought me to live under this roof. He was as glad to get away from me as from his mother, I'm sure. Habiba ... that I don't understand. He adored her." Briefly her eyes grew soft with some memory, then turned hard and angry again. "But if he really adored her, he'd've never subjected her to this household, now would he?"

"I don't know. What was his reason for living here?"

"Money, what else? Dave-the-paragon was kicked out of UCLA; he claimed it was grades, but I know it was cheating. I graduated, but a degree in English lit and a flair for poetry don't pay rent or buy food, and it wasn't in Dave's scheme of things to hold down a job. So we came here. For a while Malika pulled the financial strings and Dave was her little puppet. But then he got into something else."

"What?"

Mavis shrugged and went to refill her glass. When she came back she flopped on the chaise. "What did you ask me?"

"What did your husband get involved in?"

"Oh, that. I don't know. By the time I realized he had something going we were living in separate rooms and barely speaking. I supposed it was another woman—somebody with money, because all of a sudden he had plenty and was taking absolutely no shit off Malika. But if there was somebody, why didn't he divorce me and take Habiba? Divorce is no big deal in the Muslim community, and Malika would've made sure he got custody."

"How?"

"By making me out to be an unfit mother. I was already drinking a lot at the time and I'd ... had some affairs."

"But your husband never mentioned divorce?"

"No. And then all of a sudden, no Dave."

"When did that happen?"

"February of ... ninety. Dave didn't come home all night. That wasn't unusual, he stayed away a lot that last year, but he always came back in the morning to change clothes. After three days and still no Dave, Malika called in private detectives."

"Not the police?"

"No way."

"Do you recall the name of the detective agency?"

". . . No. I don't know if I was ever told. Frankly, my memory isn't all that good."

"Did the detectives find out anything?"

"Not that anybody ever said."

"Why do you suppose your mother-in-law didn't want the police involved?"

"It was too soon after—"

"After what?"

"No. That's got nothing to do with it."

"Mavis—"

She sat up straighter and looked sharply at me. "I'm sorry, why did you say you were here?"

"To make sure you're satisfied with the new security arrangements we instituted after the bombing attempt."

She frowned. "What bombing attempt?"

My God. Mavis Hamid was so disconnected from the household that she didn't know her daughter had nearly been killed the previous afternoon. I didn't dare enlighten her; there was no telling how the news might affect her, and I'd risk her mother-in-law finding out about our meeting.

Quickly I said, "At another consulate."

"Oh."

"As you were saying about Dave's disappearance—"

"I don't want to talk about him anymore." Then she made another erratic conversational detour and began a monologue about poetry. I hadn't read much of it since high school and the few lines I'd once penned for a class assignment made Hallmark verses look like Shakespeare, but I couldn't help being intrigued by Mavis's talk about shaping ideas and emotions into poetic image. Intrigued, too, by the pleasure and excitement she displayed and how her hand never once strayed toward her glass of vodka. When I finally told her I had to leave and went to the door, she hurried after me and pressed a slender volume into my hand. *Laments and Victories*, by Mavis O'Donnell Hamid.

"Thank you for listening," she said. "I haven't talked about my work for such a long time."

Impulsively I hugged her before I stepped into the hallway. Renshaw was leaning against an armoire by the far wall.

As I closed the door he said, "What a touching display of sisterly affection."

"Listen, somebody ought to be a sister to that woman. This"—I gestured at Mavis's room—"is a criminal situation!"

"And not ours to interfere with."

"Probably not, but it makes me furious!" I clutched Mavis's book tightly while we left the consulate, as if by protecting it I could somehow protect its author.

We parted on the sidewalk, Gage heading toward the mobile unit up the hill and I to my nearby car. When I turned the key in the door lock I realized I'd left it open. Careless, McCone, too damn careless.

As I slid behind the wheel and reached for my seat belt, a voice said, "Take me for a ride . . . please."

Even though it was a child's voice, I briefly froze. Then I turned toward Habiba Hamid. She sat in the passenger's seat, all buckled up and ready to go.

"How did you get out?" I asked sternly.

"I know lots of ways." In the dim light I made out a sly grin that resembled her mother's. She was a thin little girl— too thin, really—with shoulder-length black hair that curled under like mine and a slash of bangs across her forehead.

"I'll bet you do," I said, "but it's not too smart, particularly at night. And why are you in my car?"

"I like red sports cars. My father used to have one. And you were nice to me yesterday. So tonight when I saw you drive up and you came in to see my mom, I snuck out."

I was nice to her. I'd winked, that was all. My God, the child's life must be as empty as her mother's.

As if she knew what I was thinking, Habiba added, "Yesterday? When you winked?"

"Yes?"

"That used to be my mom's signal when she wanted to see me for some special time together. She'd wink and say something like, 'The flowers down at the gazebo are lovely this year,' and then I'd know she'd be waiting there for me in an hour."

"You said 'used to be.' Doesn't she do that anymore?"

"Not for a long time, she hasn't. She doesn't even notice me . . . or anything very much. She's awfully sad and sometimes I hear her crying. That's why I'm glad you came to see her." She twisted around and looked into the rear carrying space where I'd set my bag and Mavis's book. "She gave you her poetry collection. That means she was happy. When she's sad she won't even talk about the poems."

"She did seem sad at first. Do you know why?"

She shrugged, looking down and fiddling with the seat belt.

"Are you sad, too, Habiba?"

". . . Most of the time. Lonesome, too."

"Do you miss your father?"

"Sort of, but I don't really remember him."

"No? You must've been around four when he went away; that's old enough to remember something about him."

She pursed her lips, as though she was making a difficult decision. "Okay, I lied. I remember him; I saw him just last month. Grams says I can't tell anybody about his visits because if my mother found out she'd put a stop to them."

Was the child making this up? Hamid had supposedly vanished years ago. "How often does he come?"

"Two or three times a year. He always brings presents."

"Where does he live?"

"I don't know. He says he travels a lot."

"Well, what kinds of presents does he bring you?"

"The last time it was this wooden bracelet with parrots carved on it." She pushed up the sleeve of her sweatshirt and held out her arm. The bracelet was white, girded with brightly painted birds, and looked like a cheap tourist souvenir. Hamid—if Habiba's story was true—must have been traveling in the Tropics.

I tapped my fingers on the steering wheel, wondering if the gift-bearing father wasn't only a wishful fantasy created by a lonely little girl. Two of my nephews had suffered through their parents' bitter divorce, and my youngest sister's three kids had never even known their respective fathers. From observing them I knew how yearning for an absent parent could create a rich imaginary life.

"Please take me for a ride," Habiba said again.

"All right, but only a short one." I started the MG and edged out of the parking space. Drove down the block and made the first in a series of right turns that would eventually take us to RKI's mobile unit.

"Tell me more about your father's visits," I said.

"Well, he only stays for a few hours. Beforehand Grams sends everybody away except Aisha—that's my nanny who she trusts 'cause she's been with us forever. First my father and Grams talk in the library. Then they come out and Aisha serves us lunch." Frown lines appeared between her eyebrows. "He really doesn't know what to say to me. He asks all these questions about school and my lessons and what I've been doing, but I can tell he's not listening to my answers because he's too busy trying to think up the next question. Sometimes Uncle Klaus comes with him; then it's better."

Kahlil Lateef had said Dawud was an only child. "Is Uncle Klaus your mother's brother?"

"No, he's not really an uncle, that's just what Grams told me to call him. He's my dad's business partner."

"What kind of business are they in?"

"Well, it's got to do with managing money and they both travel. Dad said he'd explain it to me when I'm older. You see what I mean about him not knowing how to talk to me? He acts like I'm about three!"

In some respects Habiba did seem younger than nine; she'd led a very sheltered life within the confines of the consulate. On the other hand, she'd demonstrated a fairly adult insight about both her parents. "Klaus," I said, "that's a German name."

"Yes, he told me once that he was born there, but he left when he was a teenager."

"Your grandmother—"

Habiba leaned forward suddenly, peering through the windshield. "Oh, no, it's Mr. Renshaw!"

We'd rounded the last corner and were approaching the mobile unit. Gage stood behind it, scowling and motioning for me to pull over.

"He'll tell Grams I snuck out!" Habiba's hand clutched at my arm.

"I don't think so." I stopped the car. Renshaw leaned down, saw Habiba, and scowled.

I reached across her and rolled down the window. "Hi,

Gage. Habiba needed to get out for a while, so I suggested we go for a drive. I told her you wouldn't mind."

Renshaw covered his annoyance quickly. "Well, her nanny's upset, so I guess we'd better get her back home." He opened the car door and bowed from the waist. "May I escort you back to your castle, my lady?"

I stared; in all my dealings with him, Renshaw had never exhibited so much as a shred of whimsy. Habiba giggled.

I said, "The lady would prefer the queen not know about this excursion."

"Understood."

The little girl turned to me. "Thank you," she said softly. "And thank you for being nice to my mom." Then she added, "What's your name?"

"Sharon."

"Sharon." She seemed to savor it, forming the syllables slowly.

Renshaw said, "Your escort awaits you, my lady."

Habiba got out of the car.

"Wait," I said. "That signal you and your mother used to have? The wink? How would you like it if it was ours—yours, mine, and Mr. Renshaw's? If you need to talk privately to either of us for any reason at all, just wink and say something about the place where you want us to meet you and when to be there."

"Could we? I'd like that."

"Just remember—for any reason at all. And we'll do the same with you."

Renshaw smiled at me and made a circle with his thumb and forefinger above Habiba's head. He didn't realize that I hadn't set the game up for the sake of the investigation. I'd done it for her.

Six

So what did I have?

A lot of facts and events that might be relevant to the bomber's activities and might not. A lot of behavior on the part of Malika Hamid that didn't add up. A badly damaged woman and a love-starved little girl who were virtually prisoners in a house that technically was considered part of a foreign nation. A man who seemed to have disappeared but hadn't.

And where was I going with all this?

Nowhere except home to pick up the boxes I'd packed that afternoon, then straight north on Highway 101 to the Anderson Valley cutoff to the coast.

Still . . .

While stopped at a light on Market Street I called my office. Friday and Saturday nights Mick could usually be found there while Maggie—a premed student—worked the late shift at a nursing home. When my nephew picked up, he sounded relieved to hear my voice. "I've been trying to reach you all evening. You should think about getting a pager."

Then he'd really have me where he wanted me—on a short tether. "I'll think about it," I lied. "What's up?"

"Don't go home."

"Why not?"

"Joslyn called; she's camped on your doorstep. She doesn't

believe you've left for the weekend, and she sounds like she's ready for an ugly face-to-face."

"Damn!" I'd thought she'd have calmed down by now. It didn't matter that I couldn't go home to pick up my things; I kept weekend clothes and extras of everything else I needed at the cottage, and the boxes could wait till the next trip. But I'd hoped to ask Adah to access some information for me before I left town.

"Well, thanks for the warning," I told Mick. "Are you checking the bulletin boards?"

"Yeah. So far there hasn't been anything worthwhile."

"What about that research on Azad that I asked for? How's it going?"

"Done."

"Printed out, too?"

"On your desk."

"Good. You willing to work tomorrow?"

"Might as well. Maggie's cramming for exams." He sounded glum.

"Okay, here's what I need." I explained it in detail. "Fax it to me at the cottage." Then I pulled into the left-turn lane at Church Street, correcting course for Bernal Heights.

Mick had gone by the time I got to the office. I looked at my watch: after eleven. Hastily I bundled the stack of printout he'd left on my desk into my briefcase, but something nagged at me and I sat down to think. After a few minutes I moved my chair closer to the desk and dialed Captain Greg Marcus's extension at the Hall of Justice. My old friend was now on Narcotics and by virtue of rank should have been off duty at this hour, but he'd recently told me he'd been putting in double shifts because of a severe manpower shortage. Tonight he was still at his desk.

"This is a surprise," he said. "I take it you want something."

Greg's and my relationship has always been abrasive, even when—eons ago—we were lovers. Something about our personalities, which doesn't allow us to blend our strengths and dilute our weaknesses. With us there's always a competitive edge—and not the sort that allows us to be the best we can.

Over the years we've both mellowed, but I still don't know how things will go when I contact him.

That night we must've both been in a very mellow phase; his voice was playful, and the remark simply amused me. "Yes," I said. "I want to buy you a drink."

He laughed. "As I recall, you buying me a drink usually leads to me doing you a favor. Where are you? Your office?"

"Yes."

"Then I'll see you at the Remedy. Half an hour, max."

I closed up the office, stowed my briefcase in the MG, and walked downhill to Mission Street. The usual Friday-night crowds were out; the usual sex and drug deals were going down. I spotted one of my informants, Frankie Cordova, leaning against an iron-grated storefront, beer in hand, his arm draped across the shoulders of a stoned young Latina. When I nodded, he toasted me with his bottle.

The Mission had long ago lost its charm for me. Years before, when I lived in a tiny studio apartment near Twenty-second Street on Guerrero, it was a hospitable area, if a little rough at the edges. I had good neighbors in the building, good neighbors across the street at Ellen T's, my favorite bar-and-grill. But then one of the tenants on the floor above me was murdered and my investigation into her death showed me the ugly underside of the district. As soon as I could afford to, I bought my house and moved away. In the intervening years gangs and pushers had moved in. Ellen T's husband, Stanley, was shot to death in a holdup, and Ellen sold the bar and moved back to Nebraska. Now parts of the Mission came close to being war zones. Drug dealers terrorized residents on their own front steps; gunshots were commonplace. Parents were afraid to let their children walk to school alone; the ever present gang members looked nothing like the highly romanticized figures I'd cynically viewed during a recent rerun of *West Side Story*.

Some of the Mission's residents hadn't caved in to the criminal element. Frustrated by the lack of police protection, they banded together with merchants to organize and fund citizen patrols. Women and men stood guard at such trouble spots as the Sixteenth-and-Mission BART station. Armed only with nerve and wits, they were determined to take back their neighborhood. I wished I could believe they'd succeed. The McCone who had inhabited that tiny apartment on Guerrero would have naturally assumed so, and probably joined in. But she was someone I hardly knew anymore, distanced by a number of eye-opening years.

Noise greeted me as I pushed through the door of the Remedy Lounge; patrons crowded around the bar and jammed the booths and tables. When I finally got to the bar, I ordered an espresso from Brian, the owner, then settled down in a booth that had just been vacated.

After twenty minutes the crowd began to thin. I went back to the bar, got another espresso to fortify myself against the long drive ahead, and ordered a glass of red wine for Greg. I'd just sat down again when he came through the door—a big man with sandy blond hair that was now shot with white and a body that as yet showed few signs of middle-age spread. He grinned when he spotted me, quirked one dark blond eyebrow when he saw his drink was already on the table.

"Service with a smile, even," he said, planting a kiss in the vicinity of my right ear. "Thank you, ma'am."

"It's about the only service you'll get in this place." The Remedy has never been able to keep a waitress or waiter longer than a week, and Brian refuses to extend table service to anyone but Rae, who reminds him of his dead sister.

Greg sat opposite me, took a sip of wine, and said, "You're looking as good as ever."

"What, did you think I'd fallen apart in the last few months?"

"You never know, in your business. You still seeing that terrorist with the airplane?"

"Hy specializes in counter-terrorism, and you know it. You still seeing the fry cook?"

"Lynda's a chef at a four-star restaurant—and you know it."

We smiled, the seals of our friendship intact.

"So what do you want this time?" he asked.

"First of all, confidentiality."

"I'm not your lawyer. Or your priest."

"This is serious. Can I count on you?"

He ran his hand over his stubbled chin, eyes thoughtful—

probably remembering the other times he'd trusted me and I hadn't disappointed him. After a moment he nodded.

"I've been working with Adah Joslyn on the Diplo-bomber case. She's out of control."

"So I've heard."

I'd suspected word of Joslyn's uncharacteristic behavior had gotten back to the department. "How bad do they say it is?"

"She's riding for a fall."

"That's why I can't ask her for what I need—access to NCIC and CJIS. There're a couple of other ways I could get it, but I'd rather go through official channels."

"Right. Your nephew's a nice kid, you don't want him in trouble. But then there's RKI; they abuse the system all the time. Tell me, Sharon, what's it like to be in bed with them?"

I didn't flare up because I sensed a real concern for me behind the question. "I use RKI. They don't use me."

"Yet."

"Ever."

"Your boyfriend's one of them."

"But cut from an entirely different bolt of cloth."

"So you tell yourself."

"So I know."

"I've never heard you sound so sure about anyone. Certainly you never did about me." He thought for a moment, turning his wineglass round and round on the table. "Okay, I guess I should let it go. Can't help feeling protective toward you, though. So tell me what you need."

I repeated the mental list I'd made back at the office. Greg jotted down items on a notepad. When I finished he said, "I'll get started on it first thing tomorrow. Where can I reach you?"

I gave him my phone number at the cottage, then asked, "What else are they saying about Joslyn?"

"She's going to crash and burn, and it's a damned shame."

"But if she gets it together and collars the bomber—"

"You going to do her work for her again?"

So the departmental brass was aware of that, too. I shrugged. Greg finished his wine. I asked, "Where're you off to now?"

"The fry cook's. You?"

"The home I share with the terrorist."

He looked surprised at the mention of a shared home, but only said, "Give him my regards."

The two-lane road through the Anderson Valley was dark but well paved and easy. I sped past the closed-up wineries and through the little hamlets. Toward the coast the pavement narrowed and snaked through heavily forested hills. I felt wired from the espresso and pushed the MG to its limits, downshifting at the ends of the straightaways, accelerating on the curves. Then I glided down the coast highway and turned north to where our cottage sat on the cliff above Bootlegger's Cove.

Soon I could see our security lights across the rocky land between the road and the sea cliffs. The cottage itself was dark. I followed the blacktop past the place where our friends' home once stood, reminding myself that someday Hy's and mine would rise on the site. My headlights washed over the little stone-and-timber structure nestled in a cypress grove at the land's edge. When I got out of the car, the sea wind assaulted me, the sea smell stung my nostrils.

I stood there for a moment listening to the surf, feeling the serenity. Tonight I sensed none of the violent ripples beneath its surface, heard no sounds of grief and loss in the waves. This was not a gentle land; its edges were jagged and sharp. But it was a land of strength, vitality, and resilience, and it suited Hy and me. We'd renamed the property Touchstone, after the siliceous rock used by metallurgists to test the purity of silver and gold. Hy and I were one another's touchstones, each continually testing the purity of our actions, motives, and decisions. Like the land, the interface between us was often jagged and sharp, but we always meshed.

I went to the door, disarmed the security system, and stepped inside. Rearmed the system. Embers glowed on the hearth, but the two rooms were silent. I looked through the bedroom door and saw my lover lying long-limbed beneath the down comforter. He had wrapped his arms around his pillow, and his dark blond hair was tousled. Quickly I slipped into the bathroom, weariness overcoming my caffeine rush. I shed my clothes, gave my teeth a cursory brush, my face an even more cursory wash.

Sleep, I thought. Hours and hours of blissful sleep.

In the bedroom I moved cautiously, sliding beneath the comforter with extreme care. Hy's wake-up mechanism had a hair trigger; while it had been many years since he slept with a gun under the pillow, any sudden movement would make him reach for the .44 he kept in the nightstand.

In spite of my caution he stirred. Pushed the pillow away and reached for me instead of the gun. "McCone," he said, "about time."

No blissful sleep—for a while, anyway.

But who was complaining?

Seven

Except for a long walk on the fog-shrouded beach we spent Saturday lounging in front of the fire. Hy lay on the couch studying reports on the military situation in Haiti; with his dark-rimmed reading glasses perched on the bridge of his hawk nose he looked more the college professor than a specialist assessing the feasibility of bringing a Haitian dissident over the frontier into the Dominican Republic. Word of the well-financed one-man crusade he'd embarked upon last fall had spread quickly among human-rights organizations; this was the second rescue attempt referred to him by a group in Miami.

I curled in the big cushioned rattan chair reading through the printout of Mick's research. Every now and then Hy would mutter something and I'd look up and see he was making notes. When I burst out laughing, though, he stopped and took off his glasses. "What's so funny?"

"Mick. Whenever he does a complicated report for me, he goes overboard with the prose. I swear that if he falls out of love with investigation he could become one of those terribly snide and irreverent columnists. Listen to this: he's writing about the emir of Azad, Sheik Zayid bin Muhammad al-Hamid.

" 'The sheik is a real piece of work. His thing is flowers, and he's blown millions trying to grow an English garden in the middle of the desert. When his old man died, his brother was first in line to take over, and Zayid wasn't too happy about that. So what does he do? He invites the bro over to look at his new rose bushes and shoots him in the back. I guess afterwards he felt guilty, because he turned into a born-again; they've got them there, too—Islam style. He's big on morals and family values, has reinstated the death-by-stoning penalty for rape and murder. They say he's trying to take Azad back into the nineteenth century, which is probably why a lot of Azadis like to live abroad. Frankly, it sounds like a pretty boring place.

" 'The sheik's life is anything *but* boring, though. In the seventies his father built up the capital city, Djara, in a major way. Only the old man was cheap and always took the lowest bids, and now everything's falling down—including the sheik's palaces, so he keeps having to move. He's got this family you wouldn't believe, they make *ours* look normal. There's this brother he keeps having to ship off to a nuthouse in Switzerland. Another brother gets off on hanging his servants when they piss him off. So far none of them have died because the bro doesn't know his knots. Zayid's daughter is rough on servants, too—she's always trying to lay them, and if they don't cooperate she drops them off in the desert, naked. No wonder the royal family can't get decent help these days. Zayid's wife is hooked on tranquilizers—who wouldn't be? And they all drink on the sly, except for the sheik. The *whole country* drinks. The capital city's got a pop of fifty thousand, and ten thousand are certified alcoholics. And a lot of the men prefer their poker buddies over their wives as bed partners. All this came out of a report commissioned by their ministry of health and welfare. The Azadis are so dim they actually *published* the thing.' "

Hy was laughing and shaking his head. "Jesus, the kid's good."

"How much of this d'you suppose is true?"

"Well, the stuff about the royal family may or may not be an exaggeration—he couldn't've gotten that out of a government report—but the rest fits with the Middle East that I remember."

"Oh?" He'd mentioned flying in supplies for the oil fields when he worked for Dan Kessell's air-charter service.

"Uh-huh. Repression pushes them over the edge into sheer insanity, and alcoholism really is that common. Back in the mid-seventies one of our people—hotdog pilot named Ralston—got his ass thrown in jail in Qatar. The son of a bitch was importing alcohol on the side, and the natives were making him rich, but when he got caught it was a potential life sentence. Dan and I flew in, delivered a load of pipe fittings, and then spread a lot of U.S. dollars around to the jailers. When we left we had Ralston in the skin of the plane. That was when we more or less developed that method."

The skin-of-the-plane method involved wrapping an individual in as much insulating material as possible and hiding him between the inner cabin wall and the outer wall of the aircraft, where he would escape detection by police and customs authorities. At high altitudes for prolonged times, temperatures in that space can cause frostbite or death, and even with the best of precautions things can go wrong—as Hy had found out after a mission in Laos.

Momentarily I was silent, remembering the pain in his eyes when he told me about finding the frozen bodies of the Laotian government official and his young family whom he was transporting to Hong Kong. They hadn't understood his instructions, had removed their protective layers once aboard and weren't able to put them back on in the confined space.

Hy said, "Hey, McCone, it's okay. I've come to terms with all that old garbage."

I nodded and set Mick's report on the floor. "Look, do you want to take a break? I need to run some things by you."

"Sure." He got up and closed the blinds against the darkening bank of fog outside the seaward windows. "I don't know about you, but I could use a beer."

"Red wine, please."

He went to the tiny kitchen area and returned with our drinks. I moved to the couch, nestling in a corner, my stockinged feet against his blue-jeaned thigh.

"So what's the problem?" he asked.

"My approach to this case isn't working. The task force has been concentrating on the bomber—profiling him, trying to get people who may know something to come forward. They've also put together profiles of the victims, as well as the diplomatic missions that were hit and the countries they represent, but they haven't had time to do more than scratch the surface. So first I did a more in-depth profile of each, then looked for commonalities among them. There weren't any."

"And now because of what Gage told you, you've shifted your focus to the Azadis."

"For a while I thought I was really onto something, but none of it hangs together."

"Well, you haven't gotten the information you asked your friend Greg for yet."

"No, and that probably means he hasn't come up with anything, since he said he'd get on it first thing this morning. NCIC used to take a long time to reply to requests for information, but they're fully automated and on-line now; you can access their criminal history database in a matter of minutes."

"Strange, since one of the people you asked him to check out is supposed to've been involved in organized gambling."

"Yes, but there's a hitch with that. I thought of it last night and asked Mick to check it out—that's what the information he faxed here was about."

"And?"

"The hitch is diplomatic immunity."

"Aha!"

I reached for Mick's fax and read, " 'According to Article Thirty-one of the international treaty adopted by the Vienna Convention on Diplomatic Relations of nineteen sixty-one, ambassadors and other diplomatic agents *and their direct families* have complete immunity from all criminal prosecution and civil suits in the host country. Courts have ruled that the direct family includes both spouses and children. Although these rulings have been challenged in specific cases, they've generally been upheld.' That means that Dawud Hamid could've been caught red-handed running the biggest gambling operation in the country, and he'd've walked within the hour. So there isn't going to be any criminal history on him."

"Above the law, all the way."

"Dammit!" I tossed the fax on the floor. "There's got to be *some* way of finding out what he was involved in. I'm pretty sure he had at least one run-in with the police; Mavis Hamid said her mother-in-law wouldn't call them in when he disappeared because it was 'too soon after . . .' And then she said that—whatever it was—couldn't've had anything to do with it, and changed the subject. Too soon after *what*? And how the hell can I find out?"

Hy sipped beer silently, stroked his droopy mustache. I nibbled on my lower lip, reviewing the possibilities. Then, at the same time, we said, "The newspapers!"

Of course. Diplomats are granted immunity from prosecution, but not from media coverage. "God, I must've been in brain stall not to think of this earlier," I said.

Hy was still looking thoughtful. "When did you say Hamid disappeared?"

"February of ninety."

"A month before the first bombing. You ever think he might *be* the bomber?"

"I've thought of it. I'm going to try to get a photo of him to see how closely he fits the physical profile."

"Which is?"

"Sketchy. Medium to dark complected, medium height and weight. No information about hair color because he always wears some kind of hat. No information about eye color because he always wears aviator-style sunglasses. Conflicting descriptions of his voice. No noticeable scars or defects."

"Where'd they get that?"

"It's based on the descriptions of the messengers who delivered the bombs that weren't sent through the mail. They all sound like the same man, and the task force assumes they're only dealing with one perp, because the psychological profile of this kind of bomber indicates he works alone."

"What's his signature?"

Every bomb maker leaves a "signature" on the explosive device, whether intentionally or otherwise. Subtle details identify him or her, much as brushwork and palette identify the creator of an oil painting. "That's the detail the task force has held back from the public. It's the device for completing the electrical circuit—a spring that looks like a pair of praying hands, held together by a twisted ring."

"Odd."

"It's the same every time. He's precise; the bombs are well crafted. He doesn't get fancy; he uses ordinary black powder that can be bought at sporting-goods stores. He's cool; he walks into post offices and mails the packages without calling attention to himself. And he probably enjoys a certain amount of danger, since he delivered some of the bombs personally. The task force knows all that, yet they're no closer to identifying him than before."

Hy finished his beer and went to the refrigerator. "Well, maybe you'll come up with something about Hamid from the newspapers that'll give you the break you need. When're you going back to the city?"

"Tomorrow night. Renshaw's assigned Charlotte Keim in Data Search to help me, and I want to get her working on this first thing Monday."

Hy began to take paper-wrapped packages from the fridge: oysters, some smoked salmon, a crab. We'd decided on an easy-to-prepare cold seafood-and-sourdough supper tonight. "Keim's a good choice. She helped me out before I went to Managua." His voice was muffled as he hunted for a package of shrimp that had found its way into the fridge's depths. "Not only is Charlotte bright and a real pro, but she's cute and has a hell of a sense of humor—something you don't find in too many of our operatives."

"Hmm." I pictured the young, attractive brunette.

Hy backed out of the fridge, grabbed an apron, and tossed it to me. "Quit being jealous and start dismantling that crab while I shuck these oysters."

"Me, jealous? Never."

"Oh, yes, you are."

"And I suppose *you're* never jealous?"

"Never. By the way, how come it took you so long to get up here last night after your so-called business meeting with your former lover?"

I smiled serenely at him and donned the apron.

Sunday morning dawned clear, the sea glassy and gentle. We finished off the previous night's leftovers in an enormous omelet, then climbed down the stairway that was anchored to the cliff face to Bootlegger's Cove. For a couple of hours we walked, collecting shells and driftwood and exploring the caves that had served as stashes for illegal liquor during

Prohibition. It was after one when we returned to the cottage. The phone was ringing, and I ran in to answer, my wet and sandy athletic shoes skidding on the hardwood floor.

An unfamiliar voice said, "Ms. McCone?"

"Yes?"

"Sorry to bother you on the weekend. This is Craig Morland. I'm one of the FBI's representatives on the Diplo-bomber Task Force."

Morland—the rather colorless man who had been with Adah at the consulate after the bombing attempt. "Yes, Mr. Morland?"

"We've got a problem here, and Adah Joslyn asked me to call you."

A nervous prickle skittered up my spine. "Is she all right?"

"She's not injured, nothing like that. Sorry to alarm you, ma'am." Now I caught a faint touch of the South in his voice, as though he'd been born there but left long ago. "The problem is, Adah's been put on administrative leave. There was . . . a bad incident yesterday, and our task force head and her chief agreed she'd better take some time for herself."

A bad incident. Morland's tone had been hesitant; I decided not to ask for details now. "Where is she?"

"At her apartment. That's where I'm calling from. I dropped in this morning to see how she was doing and, to tell you the truth, I don't feel easy about leaving her alone."

"Why not?"

". . . Well, she's not herself."

"In what way?"

"She's very withdrawn. A while back she was crying and now she's barricaded herself in her bedroom. I've taken charge of her revolver."

Adah, suicidal? "What about the nine-millimeter automatic?"

"I didn't know she had one; I'll check around for it. But the reason I'm calling you—she says that if you could stop in and talk with her later, it'd be a big help."

"The last time I tried talking with her, she hung up the phone on me."

"Apparently she's changed her mind since then. She asked me to make this call."

I hated to leave the coast early, but this sounded serious. "I can be there in about four hours. Can you stay with her till then?"

"I can stay all night if I have to."

I said good-bye and hung up, trying to imagine what relationship the bland-looking FBI man might have with Adah, that he was willing to play nursemaid to her all night.

Hy had come in behind me and caught the tail end of the conversation. When I turned he smiled regretfully. "There's never enough time, is there, McCone?"

I shook my head, feeling keenly the loss of my afternoon with him.

"You have to leave right away?"

"Adah needs me; she's been put on administrative leave and is taking it badly."

"Well, I've got an idea that might buy us some time."

"Oh?"

"Uh-huh. You take the Citabria. I'll drive down in the MG tomorrow."

I blinked in surprise. "Take the Citabria—solo?"

"Sure. I'd go with you, but I've got to finish going over those reports and, besides, we can't just leave your car at the airport. You can do it. Since you soloed last winter you've been zipping around the block just fine."

Zipping around the Bay Area and the little airstrip in Mono County wasn't the same as flying alone from Little River to Oakland.

All of a sudden I couldn't wait to leave.

1,500 Feet Above The Mendocino Coastline

May 21, 3:33 P.M.

It was a high, beautiful world up there and not the least bit lonesome. The little white plane and I skimmed south along the coast as if together we'd made the journey many times. Double-luck-two-eight-niner—her registration number was 77289—responded to my touch as a racehorse to a jockey's.

I'd felt somewhat uneasy when I waved good-bye to Hy at the Mendocino County Airport at Little River, but a rush of exhilaration on takeoff cured me. By the time I made my turn over the sea, I was confident and in control, and for the first time I really understood what it is about flying solo.

You lift off the ground—a triumph over gravity and human limitation. As you gain altitude you become single-minded and precise. You check this, you adjust that. It's just you and your aircraft; anything else becomes far away and inconsequential. You can rely only on your skills and instincts.

By the time I reached Bodega Harbor, I realized my world had narrowed to the elemental. Below was all manner of chaos and complexity, but here none of that mattered. My thoughts were clear, my movements sure. I was in perfect balance with the very real danger of dropping from the sky to my death.

And that's exactly what it's about, I thought. Placing yourself at risk and overcoming it.

I'd always had a love-hate relationship with danger. I'd run from it, balanced on its thin edge, plunged in headlong. Now we renewed our affair.

As I corrected course for Oakland Airport, I knew that I'd never before felt so alive—or so free.

Eight

My cab dropped me off at Adah's building at six-twenty. It was a wonderful old Spanish-style apartment court on North Point Street, not far from the Marina Green and the yacht harbor. A Moorish arch in its white stucco facade let onto a mosaic-tiled courtyard where roses bloomed around a fountain; the units were set at various levels, up private stair-cases and fronted by tiny wrought-iron balconies. I climbed to Adah's and knocked on the thick paneled door.

The judas window opened and Craig Morland looked out. His pale, slender face was honed sharp by vigilance. "Ms. McCone?"

"Yes."

"May I see some I.D., please?"

Federal agents! I took my I.D. folder from my purse and held it up. Almost immediately Morland stepped back and worked the dead bolt. "Sorry about that," he said as he held the door open. "I've only seen you a few times, and then you were dressed up, so I didn't recognize you. My training kicks in at the damnedest times."

"That's okay." I bent to pat Adah's white cat, Charley, who was rubbing around my legs. Like my first cat, Charley had once belonged to a murder victim; Adah had adopted him at my urging. "How is she?" I asked, motioning at the closed bedroom door.

"Asleep."

As Morland relocked and tested the dead bolt, I looked him over. In spite of it being Sunday, he wore a dark suit, conservative tie, white shirt, and wing tips. The FBI uniform was spoiled by a dusting of cat hair; Charley loved any kind of fabric to which his hairs would adhere.

"Did you find the other gun?" I asked.

"Yes. Thanks for telling me about it."

"Fill me in about this bad incident you mentioned."

Morland motioned at the couch, which was upholstered in flamboyant splashes of primary colors. The fabric was expressive of Joslyn's personality—and immune to white cat hair—but when the FBI agent perched at its end he looked horribly out of place. Charley jumped up and tried to crawl on his lap; he pushed him away, lips tightening. I made a clicking sound with my tongue and the cat came over and began kneading my thigh with his paws.

I asked, "So how come you're not in there comforting Adah, dude?"

Morland looked alarmed, then grinned weakly. He'd thought I was talking to him. "I didn't know if the cat was allowed in the bedroom or not."

"This cat is so spoiled he'd be allowed at the table if he could handle a knife and fork." I pushed Charley flat so he'd stop kneading. "Tell me what happened with Adah."

The agent relaxed somewhat, resting his closely clipped head against the high back of the couch; I supposed he felt more comfortable addressing official matters. "Last night Ed Parkhurst—he's FBI, head of the task force—called an emergency meeting. There had been a leak of information on the TechnoWeb, something only members of the force or the bomber himself could know. You're pretty close to Adah, aren't you?"

I nodded.

"Well, then she's probably told you that she's been feeling shunted aside on the investigation. In a way I don't blame her. Parkhurst thinks the Bureau should be running the show; he particularly didn't like the SFPD demanding to be represented on the force. But Adah's not the only one who's been slighted; the ATF and USPS people feel it, too. She just takes it more personally."

"She's been unusually sensitive lately," I admitted.

"And somewhat out of control. No, a whole lot out of control. Parkhurst's been keeping an eye on her. Anyway, at the meeting Adah realized that she hadn't been told the detail that was leaked on the Web. I doubt that's true. A memo went to all members. My guess is that she didn't read it and then misplaced it. Anyway, she snapped, got into it with Parkhurst."

"Uh-oh." I'd never seen Adah lose it, but it didn't tax my imagination to picture how awful the scene must have been.

"First she accused Parkhurst of deliberately shutting the SFPD liaisons out of the investigation. Wells, the bomb squad guy, tried to tell her otherwise, but she told him to shut up. Then she told Parkhurst that he couldn't run a task force any better than he could find his ass with both hands. And then . . ." Morland closed his eyes. "And then she called him a macho, elitist asshole."

"Jesus!"

"You can understand why they placed her on leave."

I was stunned. She'd crashed right over the edge—and taken her career with her.

Morland got up and began to pace, hands locked behind his back. "I couldn't fucking believe it. I just sat there and watched while she trashed her life. I've been spending a lot of time with her; I suppose I should've seen this coming. I care about her; I suppose I should've gotten her out of there. But I just couldn't fucking *believe* it."

"Not your fault. She did this to herself. Any chance she can turn it around?"

"Not if I know Adah. They're going to make her see a shrink, and you can be sure that'll go badly. She's too damn proud and stubborn to crawl into Parkhurst's office with an apology, and I doubt he'd accept one, anyway. No, she's really done it this time."

I stroked Charley, sinking my fingers deep into his fur—and into his fat roll. Adah feeds the cat too much, I thought. He's like a child to her, a substitute source of love.

Well, it was only natural. My friend received little enough

in that line. Her parents, Rupert and Barbara, were also like children to her, but problem children—eccentric, self-absorbed, willful. She had no siblings to help her shoulder the responsibility, and for as long as I'd known her she'd had no romantic interest to brighten her life. No wonder she overcompensated Charley for his comforting purrs.

My fingers prodded the cat's well-nourished hide until he wiggled and emitted a sound that was a cross between a growl and a burp. I stood, tucking him under my arm like a struggling sack of potatoes, and said to Morland, "I think I'd better look in on Adah now."

She lay on her stomach beneath a lurid jungle-print comforter, her head buried under the orange-and-green pillows. When I shut the door her body tensed slightly. I went over to the bed and deposited Charley on the small of her back.

"Cat delivery," I said. "That'll be eleven dollars and fifty cents, plus tip."

Slowly she pushed the pillows away and looked over her shoulder at me. "Is he gone?"

"Morland? No, he's still out there. In a few minutes he may actually loosen his tie."

"Shit." She flipped over onto her back, sending Charley rolling. He dug his claws into the comforter to keep from falling to the floor.

"I've tried everything, McCone, but he won't go. I yelled at him. He made tea. I pretended to cry. He brought me a box of Kleenex. I told him I was going to take a sleeping pill. He confiscated them and took my thirty-eight. I asked for you. He made the call and then started pussyfooting around. By now I suppose he's got his paws on the automatic. I've been pretending to be asleep and praying you'd get here quick."

"He hinted you were suicidal."

"I did consider hanging myself if he didn't leave."

"He also told me what happened last night."

"Oh, yeah?" She reached for the cat, who was tearing at the covers, and pushed him under them. He wriggled down by her feet, then lay still, purring loudly.

"What made you snap like that?" I asked.

"What the hell makes anybody snap?" She glowered at me,

then relented. "Okay, I've been letting the stress build. Maybe I can't control it like I used to. Maybe I do need help. But for God's sake, McCone, first *you* help me by getting Craig out of here! And please don't let him make off with my guns."

I studied Adah. She seemed too calm for someone whose career had just crashed and burned. Shock? No, probably relief at having taken the edge off the stress by ventilating. "Okay," I told her.

But I'd take charge of the guns.

Morland didn't want to leave. I must be tired, he said. Why didn't I go home and let him watch over Adah? I could talk with her tomorrow, when she also was rested. When I finally convinced him he wasn't needed, he wanted to retain custody of the guns. I had to show him my carry permit before he'd concede that I was a responsible guardian. Finally, mercifully, he went.

I returned to the bedroom. Adah lay on her back now, a Charley-sized lump on her stomach. When I gave her a thumbs-up sign, she sat up and the cat oozed out from beneath the covers and hit the floor with a thud.

"Jesus, what a relief!" she exclaimed. "I got more mothering from Craig today than I did my entire childhood with Barbara." She got out of bed, shaking the wrinkles from her striped caftan, and stalked into the living room, looking around as if she expected to find some noxious residue of the FBI man. "You want a drink?"

"Yes."

"Beer, wine, or hard stuff?"

For a moment I seriously considered a double shot of the hardest stuff she had. Then I cautioned myself against doing something that would only make the situation more bizarre and scaled back my request to white wine. Adah started toward the kitchen, Charley following hopefully, but she paused to say, "Let's sit out on the deck, huh? I need some air."

I nodded and went back through the bedroom to a sliding door that opened onto a deck that Adah shared with the residents of the adjoining apartment. It overlooked a narrow alley and then the backyard of a peculiar-looking Bavarian-style building on Fillmore, the street that ran perpendicular to hers.

A tangle of vines and old rosebushes forced its way over the high fence toward the sun and spilled down onto a garbage dumpster beside its gate. I flopped onto a green-and-white ribbed lounge chair and listened to the conversation that floated through Adah's kitchen window: a debate on the merits of kitty mixed grill versus sliced veal with gravy. Naturally the food with the gravy won.

What the hell was going on here? I wondered. Morland's call had made Adah's emotional condition sound so serious that I'd cut short my weekend with Hy and made my first long solo flight. Now I found my supposedly desperate and suicidal friend well on the road to recovery—and felt both defrauded and guilty for feeling that way. I'd better get some answers out of her, and damn quick.

She came outside, a glass of wine in either hand. "I took the liberty of ordering from Mama Mia's. I'm starved, and you must be, too. Meat combo with olives and mushrooms, anchovies on your side. Okay?"

I took the wineglass, frowning.

"What, you're off anchovies?"

"Anchovies are fine."

"Then what the hell's wrong with you?"

"Wrong with *me*? What's wrong with *you*? You trashed your life, and you're ordering pizza?"

She sat down in a basket chair, tucking her long legs underneath her. "Ah, McCone, I did my breast-beating last night. All night, and if it wasn't for this nifty herbal cream I've got, my eyes'd be swollen shut from crying. But then I got over that and started thinking of the possibilities—and they are absolutely infinite!"

Still out of control, I thought, but on the other end of the spectrum. "Okay—what are they?"

"Well, for one thing, you and I are going to nail the Diplo-bomber. And collect the million-buck reward."

Humor her. "Sounds good to me."

"You remember the other day, when I told you the shield had gotten kind of tarnished?"

I nodded.

"Well, the way I see it, disasters like yesterday are a sign that things've got to change."

"So you're glad that you'll probably be thrown off the task force and out of the department?"

"I'm ecstatic. All my life, McCone, I've been going by the book. Probably a reaction to Barbara and Rupert, who don't even know there *is* a book. Now's my chance to fly."

"And do what?"

"I'll figure that out later. Right now we've got to get to work on the Diplo-bomber."

"Adah, we have *been* working on the case. And with very little success."

"Well, thanks to last night's meeting, we've got one more piece of information. The detail that was leaked to the Techno-Web? It was a second signature that appeared for the first time on the bomb that went off at the Azadi Consulate: the letters C.L. incised on its metal base."

"Initials?"

"Looked like."

"C.L." I reviewed the names of the people connected with the consulate. None matched. "The bomber's?"

"Could be."

I was silent, sipping wine.

"Adah, this leak—do they think it might have come from a member of the task force?"

"No."

"The bomber, then."

"Uh-huh. They're trying to get a court order for a list of the Web's subscribers. But even if they do—and given the privacy laws, it's dicey—it'll take an enormous amount of time and manpower to track him down."

"And you think we can? Especially now, when we no longer have access to task force files?"

"Don't we?"

"Do we?"

"Yes."

"How?"

"Leave that detail to me."

Morland, I thought. He cares about her, and she's going to use that for all it's worth.

"By the way, McCone," she added, "I'm sorry about how I acted on Friday."

"Apology accepted. I've got to tell you, though—I didn't appreciate the barrage of phone calls, to say nothing of you camping out on my doorstep."

She moved her shoulders in a manner that was usually a prelude to a difficult admission.

"What?" I asked.

"It's, uh, about Friday night."

I closed my eyes, waiting for the other shoe.

"I was pissed to begin with, but when you didn't come home, I got *really* pissed. So I used the spare key you gave me when I stayed at your house while this place was being painted last winter."

"And did what?"

"Uh, you know that bottle of ninety-three Deer Hill Chardonnay that you were saving?"

I opened my eyes and frowned at her.

"I drank it."

"You *what*? That wine cost fifty-five dollars! I was saving it for my fortieth birthday!"

"Yeah, I know. And that's not everything. Afterwards I got into the hard stuff and passed out on your couch. I think I broke one of those nice crystal glasses your sister gave you."

"You think?"

"Well, I did."

"Is that all? You didn't throw up on something? Wreck the furniture? Terrorize my cats? Uproot my houseplants?"

"What do you think I am?"

"You don't want me to answer that."

"I feel bad enough about this, McCone. Don't make it any worse. I'll pay you for the wine, I promise."

"Damned right you will!" Inside the apartment the doorbell chimed. "And you're also paying for the pizza."

She stood. "It's fourteen bucks. Two-buck tip makes it sixteen. Your share's eight, so that's fifty-five less eight. Forty-seven I owe you."

"What about the glass?"

"You told me you never liked that pattern anyway."

I sighed and went to the kitchen to refill my wineglass before she decided to start charging me.

When I went back outside with the wine and a handful of

paper napkins, Adah was sitting beside a low table on the deck, ripping open the pizza box. As usual, Charley was sucking around for more food. I sank down across from her, reaching for a slice with anchovies.

"Look, McCone," she said, "don't be mad about the wine. Let's get serious about the Diplo-bomber."

I chewed, looking inquiringly at her.

"I'm dead certain that the guy on the TechnoWeb was him. I had plenty of time to dope that out while I was hiding in bed from old Craig—who, incidentally, has a hot thing for me, in spite of his tepid appearance."

I'd been right about how she planned to get access to task force files. "Have you . . . ?"

"God, no! And he's too worshipful to expect anything. But listen: according to the profiles, a lot of guys who mess with explosives are also computer geeks. Computers're an impersonal way to relate to people; bombs're an impersonal way to kill them. Get the correlation? So now we know this: the guy subscribes to the Web, or he knows a way to get other subscribers' passwords. He's playful. Confident, too. He's toying with us."

I nodded, mouth full again.

"And here's something else that I haven't told you: I was on duty at the Azadi Consulate when the mail came on Friday. I intercepted a note that was meant for Malika Hamid. Guess what it said."

Be forewarned, I thought. I kept silent, though; my contract with RKI bound me to say nothing about the earlier notes the Azadis had received.

"Well, the lettering was the same as in the ones he sent after the other bombings. Same stationery stock, too. Mailed at the Lombard Street post office. But it didn't say 'Vengeance is mine.' It said, 'Warning Number One. Remember C.L.'"

That *was* a departure. "Did you question the consular staff to see if it meant anything to any of them?"

"Spoke with Mrs. Hamid. We're only supposed to deal with her, and at the time I was still following orders. She claimed she hadn't a clue, but that she'd question the staff and bring it to the attention of the security people."

"You believe her?"

"No."

"You bring it to the attention of Renshaw or his people?"

She shook her head. "Like I said, Hamid told me she'd take care of that and somebody would get back to us."

And, I was sure, she'd conveniently neglected to do anything.

I looked at the fresh piece of pizza I'd just picked up and set it back in the box, my appetite gone. "This is only the first in a series of bombing attempts—I'd stake my license on that."

Adah grimaced. "And I'd stake my career—if I had one."

I said, "I think I'd better get hold of Gage Renshaw."

Nine

Renshaw had flown back to Southern California, but I couldn't reach him at his home. I called RKI's headquarters in La Jolla and used the emergency code number he'd had assigned to me on Friday to get the night operator to track Gage down. By the time he called back, Adah had been badgering me for close to half an hour to tell her what I knew about the Azadis.

"Where are you?" I asked impatiently.

"Orange County. What's happening?"

I explained about the note Adah had intercepted. "Hamid didn't mention it to you, did she?"

"No." Renshaw hesitated. "Let me call you back. I want to order tighter security there."

I set down the cordless phone I'd fetched from Adah's bedroom and looked sternly at her. "If you ask me one more question, I'll take the phone and lock myself in the bathroom."

She shrugged sulkily and carried the remains of the pizza inside. The evening was still warm, warning that we might be headed into one of those heat waves with which San Francisco is ill equipped to cope. I moved back to the chaise longue; when Adah returned she pulled the basket chair over by the railing and sat with her feet propped on it.

"I love this deck," she said in a studiously conversational

tone that told me she'd decided it was in her best interests to keep off the subject of the Azadis. "Times when I'm too wiped out to read and the TV programming is too gruesome, I come out here and people-watch. Sometimes I feel like the Jimmy Stewart character in *Rear Window*."

"Oh? See anything interesting?"

"That apartment building across the fence? I've named all the tenants, just like Stewart did. There's Mrs. Cookie Monster—big fat woman who sits in a BarcaLounger and does nothing but eat Oreos morning, noon, and night. Takes them apart and licks off the frosting first. Then there's Mr. Duck. He drives down the alley in one of those funny European cars and parks it by the dumpster. Waddles in, stays a couple of hours, waddles out again, dropping off his trash as he leaves. Fascinates me: those apartments aren't very big, and he's not there often, but he sure makes a lot of trash. Fascinates Ms. Feather, too."

"Ms. Feather?" In spite of my anxiety about the situation at the consulate, I was interested in Adah's ramblings—mainly because they revealed an imaginative side to her that I hadn't glimpsed before.

"Ms. Feather lives in the building, but she acts like a homeless lady, always going through people's trash. She's got a whole collection of fancy feathered hats, and she gets dressed up before she checks out the dumpsters. She seems to prefer Mr. Duck's trash to anything else; someday I'm going to pick through it, just to see what's so fascinating. And then there's Mr.—"

The phone rang. I picked up and Renshaw said, "It's taken care of. You have anything else to report?"

"No, but I'm wondering if you shouldn't get the little girl out of there. Her mother, too."

"I just suggested that to Hamid. She refused."

"She'd rather jeopardize their lives then give up a little control? That's insane!"

"You and I know that, but she's within her rights. The child's a minor, and the mother's in no condition to take care of her. I don't know if they're Azadi citizens, but technically they're living on Azadi soil."

"Very technically; the principle of extraterritoriality of diplomatic missions hasn't always been upheld by the courts. Besides, Hamid's rights shouldn't take precedence over their safety. Maybe somebody should lay some hard facts on her—such as how helpless Mavis is. Such as what nasty things a bomb can do to the body of a nine-year-old!"

"Sharon, calm down. I'll try to talk sense to her when I get back there. You making any progress at all on this?"

I didn't reply immediately; anger had made me tongue-tied. The situation at the consulate had become untenable. There had to be a way to persuade Hamid that Habiba and Mavis should be moved to a safe location; there had to be a way to persuade her to share the bomber's earlier communications with the task force.

"Sharon?" Renshaw was impatient.

"I need to meet with you. When're you coming back here?"

"Not till Tuesday. I'm tied up in meetings with a major client in Irvine all day tomorrow."

"Tuesday might be too late."

"So come down here. There's a seven A.M. flight from SFO that'll put you into John Wayne at eight twenty-eight. I'll buy you breakfast at the airport."

Awful hour. "Will do. Have my coffee waiting for me."

As I hung up, Adah said, "Well?"

"Tomorrow afternoon we'll talk some more. Where're your Yellow Pages?"

"Living room bookcase."

I went inside, paged through one, and called for an airline reservation. Then I dialed Mick.

"It's about time you got home," he said. "I tried to call you at the cottage to warn you, and Hy said you'd left early. Where've you been?"

"Warn me about what?"

"Somebody got into your house while you were away. There was an empty wine bottle and an open bottle of bourbon on the table in the sitting room. A broken glass on the floor. And it looked like they slept on the couch."

"Don't worry about it." I glanced at Adah, who had followed me in. "It was a benign burglar with alcoholic tendencies."

The burglar glared at me.

I said to Mick, "Grab a pencil and paper, would you, and

take down this list." Turning my back to Adah and lowering my voice, I told him what information I wanted from the newspaper files; it was a long list, and I added items as I went. "First thing tomorrow I want you to call Charlotte Keim at RKI and get her working on this."

"Shar, why can't I do it?"

"We can't let down our regular clients just because I've taken on too much. I'm counting on you to keep the agency running smoothly."

He gave me no further protest, just read the list back to me and said good night. I hung up and turned to Adah. She was looking sulky again, but agreed to give me a ride home. When she dropped me in front of my house, though, she couldn't resist a parting shot: "McCone, if you can afford fifty-five buck bottles of wine, you really should start thinking about buying better bourbon."

I didn't reply. She'd get her comeuppance soon enough when she got home and realized I'd taken her guns for safe-keeping.

John Wayne Airport had palm trees in the center of its indoor concourse. A friend who lived in nearby Newport Beach had told me they were embalmed. Literally. Just how it was done, she didn't know, but the trees looked fully lifelike, and it was eerie to know there wasn't a single living cell among them.

Another thing that was strange about the airport was that nobody would call it by its official name. The reservations people, the ticketing agent up north, and the locally based flight crew all referred to it as Santa Ana. I mulled that over as I looked for the restaurant, and decided that they must be resistant to the airport being named after a movie actor. As far as I was concerned, the attitude made no sense. After all, hadn't the state twice elected a far worse actor as governor? And then hadn't the entire country put same in the White House? At least the airport commission had honored Wayne after his death, rather than putting him in charge of the control tower.

I spotted Renshaw in a booth toward the back of the restaurant, hunched over a cup of coffee. In his natural Southern

California habitat he dressed casually in a sport shirt and slacks, but they looked as rumpled and shabby as the suit and tie he wore up north. Gage was reputed to be a millionaire many times over, and Hy had told me he displayed good taste in other areas. The clothing, I concluded now, was an affectation designed to soften the image of a very ruthless business.

Dan Kessell had always kept in the background at RKI, allowing Renshaw to act as the firm's front man with clients and the press. Frequently Gage gave newspaper and magazine interviews in which he essentially said, "Oh, gosh, we're just this little company that teaches executives self-defense tactics and creates corporate security systems. Do we operate outside the law? Come on! Do I look like the kind of guy who would do something illegal?"

But illegal activity had been a constant in Renshaw's life, dating back to when he was with the DEA in Southeast Asia.

A great deal of smuggling went on across the war-torn borders in those days, and while Gage's job was to prevent drug trafficking, his sideline was to profit from moving commodities and people. As Hy had told me, "Kessell would get at least one referral a week from Gage. Along with his official work, he was out there hustling and making contacts. People wanted to move stuff fast—firearms, gold, jewelry, artifacts, uncut stones, currency. Drugs, too, although Gage pretended not to know about that. They wanted to move themselves and their families, and didn't care what it cost. And it cost plenty, because before Kessell gouged them, Renshaw had his hand out for his finder's fee."

Those were dangerous times, violent times. A lot of people got rich, and everybody else—including Hy—profited nicely. But, like my lover, many brought away more than the numbers of Swiss bank accounts: nightmares, tightly boxed demons, enough regrets to last ten lifetimes. As I approached Renshaw's booth I wondered about the quality of his sleepless nights. If he was human—and the jury was still out on that— they must be nights of which I hoped never to experience the equal.

Gage rose and motioned for me to sit across from him. I nodded to the waitress who had appeared with a coffeepot, then scanned the menu. As a consequence of getting up before five I was starving, so I ordered corned beef hash with poached eggs, an English muffin, and tomato juice. Renshaw looked astonished and faintly disgusted.

He said, "Am I to assume you'll be able to talk while you shovel all that in?"

"No problem. But we do have a problem with the Azadis. First, Hamid's got to allow Habiba and Mavis to leave the compound. I suggest stashing them in the hospitality suite at your San Francisco building; God knows it's got everything you'd need to keep a kid amused, and I'm sure at least one of your operatives has enough of a maternal or paternal streak to baby-sit both of them."

"I agree."

That surprised me. "Can you talk to Hamid, or do you want me to do it?"

"You're the likely candidate for the task."

"I thought she'd refused to deal with me."

"She did, but she will." The set of his mouth was grim.

"Will you call her and set up an appointment for me?"

"I'll do more than that—I'll insist she see you."

"Good. Now, there's something else I've got to take up with her: the messages they've received from the bomber. This secrecy has got to stop; she's got to show them to the task force."

"I agree," he said again.

I eyed him speculatively. He seemed unusually subdued this morning, and I couldn't remember him ever agreeing with me twice in the course of any given conversation. "Has something happened that I don't know about?"

He signaled for a coffee refill. When the waitress departed he said, "Within the past hour a bomb arrived by mail at the Azadi Embassy in D.C. and the apartment of their U.N. ambassador in Manhattan. Fortunately, they didn't get past our people, and the bomb squads were able to disarm them. I got off a conference call with the heads of those squads just before you got here; the signature C.L. appeared on both devices. I suspect there'll be a follow-up message before long."

My breakfast arrived. I looked down at it, wondering how I'd thought I could eat. "Where were the bombs mailed from?"

"San Francisco, Van Ness branch post office."

"He's staying close to the consulate, then."

"Uh-huh. Aren't you going to eat?"

"You take it. I've lost my appetite."

Renshaw looked at the plate as if I'd offered him something with mold growing on it.

"So what do we do—just wait for the message?" I asked. "Just wait for him to strike again and again?"

Renshaw's eyes moved, calculating. He nodded in quiet resolve. "What time's your return flight?"

"It's open. There's one in ten minutes."

"Be on it." He opened the briefcase that lay flat beside him and took out a cellular phone. "I'll call Hamid now, pave the way. When you get back to the city, here's what you do: Go straight to the consulate and tell her how it's got to be. If she won't let you take the kid, demand to see her. Play that winking game with her, and get her out of there. Our people'll assist, and I'll take full responsibility. If Hamid refuses to release the messages to the task force, get the file copies from Green Street and deliver them yourself. Then call me at this number." He scribbled on the back of one of his cards and passed it to me.

I slid out of the booth and headed for the boarding gate.

Malika Hamid was furious. She stalked around her library, railing about Renshaw's high-handedness and clapping her hands for emphasis. He had no right to ring up and make demands, she said. She had told him in no uncertain terms that she would tolerate no interference on my part, so why was I here? And how dare I demand to see her granddaughter?

I let her rant.

I was to leave the premises immediately, she said. She would contact her cousin the ambassador and demand he dismiss RKI from their employ. She would sue Gage Renshaw for harassment. She would . . .

I glanced at Kahlil Lateef. The trade attaché perched on the edge of the sofa, his nervous gaze following the consul general. She'd already sent him from the room on two errands;

he looked as though he'd welcome a third. Every time she clapped, he winced and jumped. The claps grew more frequent; Lateef's jumps grew higher. Pretty soon he would spring off the sofa like a demented jack-in-the-box and run amok through the halls of the consulate.

Finally Hamid's voice stopped. I realized she must have delivered some dramatic ultimatum, but I'd tuned her out. I said, "Frankly, we're wasting valuable time here. The situation boils down to this: do you want your granddaughter to die? I don't think so. You may not care about your daughter-in-law; you've demonstrated that by abetting her drinking—"

"I have never—"

"You have, and we both know it. Alcohol is your hold over Mavis—and, by extension, Habiba. You must love her very much to go against your religion. You don't want to lose her."

She turned away, hands locked behind the back of her dark suit jacket, and continued pacing, fighting for control. After three passes up and down the Persian carpet she said, "You seem to know a great deal about the inner workings of this household."

"Once you grasp certain facts, the rest isn't too difficult to figure out."

Lateef shot me an alarmed look, eyes pleading with me not to reveal where I'd learned those facts. I gave him a reassuring nod and he relaxed some.

"As I said earlier," I went on, "one way to minimize risk to Habiba is to remove her to the hospitality suite at RKI's building. It's completely secure, has closed-circuit monitors that allow the occupants to watch all entrances to the building, as well as the elevators and hallways. The combinations to the locks are changed daily, and I'm sure Mr. Renshaw will authorize additional guards if you'd be more comfortable with that arrangement. There's plenty of room, so Habiba's nanny could go along to look after her and Mavis—"

"I cannot allow my granddaughter to be exposed to her mother for a prolonged period."

"Habiba loves her mother; she'd be upset if Mavis remained behind."

Malika Hamid had been standing with her back to me.

Slowly she turned. "How do you know what Habiba feels for her mother?"

"Your granddaughter is very clever at escaping the people who should be watching her."

Hamid took a quick breath and strode to a window, pulling the drapery aside and looking out at the garden. What did she expect to see? I wondered. Habiba escaping the compound?

When she didn't speak I added, "Another way to reduce the risk to your granddaughter—once she's safely off the premises—is to take the messages you've received from the bomber to the task force. As it is, your secrecy has played straight into the bomber's hands."

"That is enough, Ms. McCone!"

Now Lateef did leap off the sofa. Mrs. Hamid turned from the window and gave him a scornful look. He smiled weakly and inappropriately, then tried to cover by leaning casually against a bookcase dominated by a bronze sculpture of a horse's head. It leered over his shoulder, putting me in mind of Mr. Ed.

Hamid transferred her haughty expression to me. I met her gaze and asked softly, "What are you afraid of?"

"Afraid! That is the most absurd thing you've said yet."

"It has to do with Dawud, doesn't it?"

Her face paled and she put a hand to her throat. Seconds of silence ticked by. Then she ran her tongue over her lips and moved toward the sofa. Her unsure step and the fragile way she seated herself gave me a preview of how she'd move as an elderly woman. In a brittle voice she said, "My son has been missing for many years."

"Except on the days when he visits you and his daughter."

Lateef's eyes narrowed with interest. We both watched the consul general closely. She didn't speak, just closed her eyes and leaned back heavily.

"Mrs. Hamid," I said, "please let me take Mavis and Habiba away from here."

Her eyes remained closed; she shook her head.

"We'll table any further discussion until Mr. Renshaw returns—providing you allow the two of them to leave."

She shook her head again.

"Of course," I added, "if you don't allow it, I'll have no

choice but to hand deliver RKI's file copies of the messages to the task force. They'll question me thoroughly, and I'll be obliged to tell them about the situation here. And about Dawud. And Klaus."

Suddenly her eyes opened, full of shock that flared into rage. They fixed on me for a moment before she said to Lateef, "Kahlil, please ask Aisha to pack Mavis's and Habiba's things. Tell her she's to go along as well. They must be ready to leave in fifteen minutes."

Lateef hurried from the room, a sly, malicious smile on his lips.

Hamid watched him—marking down that smile on a mental balance sheet. When she turned back to me, her face was composed. "You will wait in the reception hall for them. Do not return here. Any further communication between my country and RKI will be brief and final."

I nodded curtly and went out to the reception area, where I sat down on a small velvet-cushioned bench. Ten minutes passed. Fifteen. Twenty. I was growing impatient when a gray-haired woman dressed in a white uniform hurried down the wide staircase, followed by Lateef.

Habiba was nowhere to be found, they told me. Her mother had vanished, too.

Ten

All at once the reception area was full of people, most of whom were yelling. I remained by the bench, watching RKI's shift supervisor attempt to restore order and waiting for Malika Hamid to make her entrance. The door to the library stayed closed, and after a minute Kahlil Lateef went in to her.

Curious.

Nobody was paying any attention to me, so I moved toward the rear of the house, past archways opening onto formal rooms to a swinging door that led to the service area. I slipped past the laundry and pantry and took the back stairs to the second floor.

The door to Mavis's room stood open. I stepped inside and surveyed the disorder. A vodka bottle lay on its side on an end table, clear liquid puddled beneath it; a glass and a lamp were in pieces on the floor. Mavis throwing a tantrum, or Mavis being forcibly removed? Impossible to say.

Quickly I went back to the hall and moved along, opening doors until I came to a yellow-and-white child's room. Habiba had been subjected to the same overdone decor as her mother: canopied bed, skirted dressing table, organdy curtains, reproductions of Degas ballerinas. A bookcase held dozens of insipid-faced dolls that looked as though they'd never been played with; the bed was mounded with too-cute stuffed animals. I'd have thought the pathologically neat room uninhabited, perhaps a shrine to a long-grown girl, had it not been for the area by the window bay.

Books were stacked on the floor around the window seat, as though Habiba had forted herself up there. I went over and examined them: some school texts, bearing the stamp of an exclusive private institution nearby; a few Nancy Drews and Judy Blumes. But mostly they were adult nonfiction on a variety of subjects ranging from oceanography to ecology to natural history. Beside them was a stack of *National Geographics* and a pile of jigsaw puzzles depicting foreign scenes. Imaginary travels to relieve the tedium of Habiba's restricted life.

I moved around the stacks to the window. It overlooked a backyard that fell away in terraces to the rear of the house behind it, which appeared to be an annex to the consulate. In between was the old-fashioned gazebo where Habiba used to meet secretly with her mother. A stout wisteria vine scaled the wall not two feet from the window—the perfect escape route for an agile little girl, and why hadn't anyone recognized that?

As I turned, something brushed my leg. A telltale piece of paper protruded from under the seat cushion. When I pulled it out I saw it was a math test with an A+ penciled in red at the top. The bench was actually a chest with a hinged lid; I lifted it and found Habiba's treasure trove.

It contained the usual things kids save: report cards and more school papers; birthday cards and wallet-sized pictures of classmates and souvenirs of field trips. Ticket stubs and theater programs and a Forty-niner pennant. In one five-by-seven photograph a younger Habiba posed shyly with Donald Duck at Disneyland.

In a gift box decorated with jungle animals I found more interesting items: a picture of Mavis showed her smiling broadly and holding up her book of poetry; she had been almost beautiful before the booze exacted its price. In another photo she held hands on a beach with a darkly handsome man, presumably Dawud Hamid. A posed studio portrait of the young family when Habiba was a toddler confirmed his identity. Hamid had a high brow, thick sensual lips, and a wavy mane of dark hair; the square shape of his face and the stockiness of his body were his mother's. The way he held his head was highly stylized, as though he'd practiced it many times in front of a mirror; his eyes held a brooding intensity. In both pictures he looked directly into the camera lens, communing with it while Mavis stared at him with frank admiration.

The way a person poses for a photograph can tell you a great deal about him and how he relates to others. Hamid's told me that he was proud of his good looks, aware of their impact on both men and women, and would use them to get whatever he wanted. It also said that he placed his interests well ahead of his wife's and child's.

After memorizing Hamid's features, I returned the pictures to the box and shut the window seat.

Before I left the room I checked a few more things. Nothing seemed to be missing from the closet, but it was so jammed with clothing—including a large number of frilly pastel dresses that I was willing to bet Habiba hated—that I couldn't conclude anything. In the adjacent bathroom I found a still-damp toothbrush and a nightgown on a hook behind the door. I looked in all the usual hiding places, hoping to find another cache of treasures, but came up empty-handed.

Time to see what was going on downstairs.

The only person in the reception area was the RKI operative on door duty. I identified myself and asked for his supervisor. He pointed me toward the library. I went over there, knocked, and stepped inside without waiting for an invitation.

Malika Hamid sat on the sofa, her posture rigid. The air in the room was charged with anger. A man in an RKI blazer with a nametag that said "S. Long" stood behind one of the chairs as if he were using it as a shield against the consul general's wrath, and Kahlil Lateef had resumed his position in front of Mr. Ed. When she saw me, Hamid's brows pulled together as though I was one more cross she had to bear. If I hadn't seen her genuinely enraged, I would have bought her act.

I told Long who I was and asked, "Have you been in touch with Mr. Renshaw?"

"He's winding things up in Irvine, and the company jet is standing by at John Wayne. He should be here in"—he consulted his watch—"approximately two and a half hours."

"What about the police?"

"No police—standard operating procedure. We're waiting for a ransom demand, and when it arrives, we'll meet it and make a recovery."

Unlike other international security firms—who were required by the insurance carriers who underwrote their clients' antiterrorism policies to immediately report kidnapings to the FBI—RKI had more leeway. Their clients tended to be marginal or very vulnerable or to prefer to rely on their security firm's protection rather than insurance. RKI operated independent of the authorities, taking advantage of a legal loophole that provides no penalty for either failing to report a kidnaping or making a good-faith attempt to recover the victim. I didn't wholly approve of their method—it involved too much risk for my taste—but I had to admit that more often than not it worked.

Long added, "We've already got our monitoring equipment in place, and our top man in that line is flying in from Denver. Our operatives are canvassing the neighbors to see if anyone noticed anything. Everything's under control."

Everything was under control, but it didn't matter. There would be no ransom demand and no one in the neighborhood would report having seen Mavis and Habiba leave the consulate. Their disappearance had the feel of an inside job—probably engineered by Malika Hamid in order to retain custody of them.

The consul general was looking at Long and me, eyes watchful. I looked back, taking in her body language and facial expression. For a moment she met my gaze as if daring me to speak; then she lowered her eyelids in feigned weariness. Hamid knew what I suspected.

I turned to Long. "When Mr. Renshaw gets here, tell him I need to talk with him. I'll be at Green Street, Charlotte Keim's extension."

Keim said, "Your assistant's as cute as a bug's butt."

The saying had to be straight out of Texas because she

spoke it with a trace of the drawl that she'd once told me she'd worked to lose after leaving home. "You've met Mick?"

"Uh-huh. He stopped by this morning on the way to the office and left off your list." She swiveled away from her desk, tossing her long brunette curls. "How old is he, anyway?"

"Eighteen." I parked myself on the straightbacked chair that was sandwiched between the desk and the wall of the cubicle. RKI's data-search people didn't labor in spacious surroundings.

"Well, he plays older. He involved with anybody?"

"Living with someone, yes. Don't tell me you're interested?"

"Why not?"

"The age difference."

Keim threw back her head and laughed—a deep, uninhibited sound. "Christ, Sharon, I'm only twenty-five. And younger men, they're so adoring—and so grateful."

I was about to warn her off Mick, but then I told myself to mind my own business. Last fall I'd made a promise to cut the already frayed apron strings, and so far I'd kept it. Besides, with her upturned nose and wickedly sparkling eyes, Keim didn't fit the role of evil temptress.

"Well, just don't break his heart," I said. "You mind if I make a few calls?"

"I'll be gentle with him." She motioned toward the phone. "While you're doing that, I'll print out the info I've got for you."

I thanked her and dialed Greg Marcus. There had been no message from him on either of my machines; I assumed the checks he'd made for me had turned up nothing, but I wanted to confirm that. Greg, however, was out of the office. Next I called Mick. Business was slow, he said, and he was bored. My only call had been from Hy, who was at my house and waiting to hear from me.

"Thanks," I said. "I probably won't be in today."

"No problem. It's so quiet here that I'm playing solitaire on the computer. By the way, I took the list of stuff you wanted to Charlotte Keim in person."

"I know; I'm calling from her office."

He lowered his voice as though he thought I was calling from a speakerphone. "Uh, how old is she?"

"Twenty-five." I threw an amused glance at Keim, who abruptly looked over her shoulder, eyebrows raised. "Why?"

"Just curious."

"Uh-huh. Roving eyes so early in your relationship with Maggie?"

"Shar, I hardly ever see Maggie, she works such long hours. I've got to look at *somebody*."

"Your secret is safe with me."

He snorted and hung up on me.

"One more call," I told Keim, dialing my home phone.

When he heard my voice Hy said, "Okay—what did you do with them?"

"Do with what?"

"The keys to the Citabria."

"Oh, God." I could picture them resting at the bottom of my purse.

"I thought as much. One loan of my airplane and you appropriate it. And I went to the trouble of leaving the MG at All Souls and taking a cab over here."

"Hy, I'm sorry. Are you in a hurry to leave?"

"Not really. I'm feeling kind of feverish again, so I'm wrapped in an afghan on your couch with Ralph lying on my chest. In a minute I'm going to send him to the kitchen to make a hot toddy."

"You really should see a doctor."

"It's just a bug; I'll get over it. What time d'you think you'll be home?"

I explained about the new developments in the case. When I finished he said, "Sounds like you've got a full plate. Speaking of that, I found the lasagna you've been promising to make me in your freezer. If you want, I'll make a salad and we can heat the lasagna up in the microwave when you get here."

"Great. There're plenty of salad things in the fridge, and I'll pick up some sourdough. See you whenever."

As I hung up Keim commented, "A man who can make a salad—all right!"

"And a decent one, no less. Both the salad and the man, I

mean." I motioned at the printout that she'd spread on her desk. "So what have we got here?"

"Well, I'm not coming up with anything on this Dawud Hamid or any of the other Azadis, except for the usual society-column stuff. But I ran a year's search to either side of the date he disappeared for the first name Klaus. What I got was Klaus Schechtmann—Speed Schechtmann, to his friends."

"That sounds vaguely familiar."

"Ought to. Up till six months before your guy disappeared Schechtmann operated a high-tech sports book out of his German restaurant on Vallejo above the Broadway Tunnel. The whole second floor of the building was given over to operators answering toll-free lines and taking bets on everything from college football to the Kentucky Derby. Speed was raking in over a billion a year, plus his restaurant was *the* in spot for the international set."

"Meaning diplomats?"

"Diplomats, Eurotrash, any fast-living foreigners."

"What was the name of the place?"

Keim grinned. "Das Glücksspiel."

"What's so funny?"

"It translates to 'game of chance.' "

"Talk about red-flagging the place!"

"I've got a hunch old Speed suffers from the typically Teutonic ailment of thinking he's a superior creature and thus untouchable. I had a couple of uncles who thought the same way—till they got sent to the slammer for embezzlement. Speed learned the same lesson when his crowd was infiltrated by a couple of undercover inspectors from Vice; the week before the D.A. took the case to the grand jury, he closed up shop and ran."

"Where to?"

"The Caribbean, initially. In November of eighty-nine he was spotted on St. Maarten, the Dutch side of one of the Leeward Islands. They've got legalized gambling there, but it's tightly controlled. Nothing flashy enough for the likes of Speed. After that he dropped out of sight."

Except for occasional appearances at Malika Hamid's luncheon table.

I gathered the printout and read through it slowly. There

was no mention of Dawud Hamid in connection with Klaus Schechtmann, but the sports book must have been the scam he became involved in. After I thought about it for a few minutes, it was easy to imagine the chain of events: Hamid frequents Das Glücksspiel and becomes friendly with its proprietor; Schechtmann's rich, fast lifestyle is seductive to a young man whose domineering mother keeps him on a short leash. Schechtmann recognizes Dawud as an easily manipulated personality who lacks scruples, needs money, and has enough talent to manage the fast-growing gambling operation for him. And in addition Hamid possesses one invaluable asset that Schechtmann does not—diplomatic immunity. If Speed shows Dawud the ropes and brings him on board, he can distance himself from the operation, leaving it in the hands of a man who cannot be forced to testify about his activities or prosecuted for them. And the billions will keep pouring into Swiss and offshore bank accounts. . . .

And then, I thought, it all fell apart. Before Schechtmann could fully implement his plan, he realized his operation had been infiltrated and the D.A. was about to move on him. He sold the restaurant and fled the city, abandoning both his fiery-tempered Argentinian wife, Leila, and his young protégé. A month after he left the grand jury handed down an indictment on nine felony counts, including conspiracy and running an illegal gambling business. A warrant was issued for him, and Leila started telling their mutual friends that she'd bought a Beretta and was prepared to shoot him on sight. Schechtmann's return trips to the city to break bread with Malika Hamid, even if he was traveling under a false passport, were hard evidence that he did indeed suffer from the Teutonic illusion of invincibility.

I asked Keim, "What about Leila Schechtmann? Is she still in the city?"

She grinned smugly. "I knew you'd ask, so I tracked her down. She's living on Russian Hill with a rich Brazilian, Alejandro Ronquillo—Sandy, they call him."

"Diplomat?"

"No, what they used to call a remittance man. He's supposedly in the country to work in the trust department of Banco do Brasil—my sources say his father owns a big block of their stock—but he hardly ever shows up there. Where you'll find him during the day is Tanforan or Golden Gate Fields or various private gambling clubs around the city. At night he's wherever it's currently trendy to be."

"And Leila? What does she do?"

"Hangs out with the wives and mistresses of other men in Ronquillo's set. They lunch, hit the shops and the beauty salons—you know the type." She passed a piece of scratch paper to me. "Here's where you'll find her."

The address was on Francisco Street near Leavenworth, high above the tourist hustle in the Fisherman's Wharf area.

"Way ahead of me, aren't you?" I said to Keim.

"I'm paid to be."

"Any chance I can hire you away from these guys?"

She pursed her lips thoughtfully. "Well, I doubt you can afford me now, but from what I hear about you, that'll change. When it does, who knows?" She grinned, nose crinkling. "I'll tell you this—I sure wouldn't mind working at close quarters with that darlin' Mick."

Eleven

The building where Leila Schechtmann lived with her Brazilian lover was a prime example of the moderne style of architecture popular in the thirties. Four stories of white concrete with plainly framed windows and a minimum of ornamentation, it had a recessed entrance flanked by pale marble slabs and sheltered by a cantilevered canopy; the lobby was floored with large black and white tiles in a checkerboard pattern.

I'd taken a cab to All Souls and picked up the MG, then called Schechtmann and asked if I might stop by and talk with her about her husband. She sounded intrigued and a bit amused when she replied, "I am always happy to talk about Speed. I can tell you many dreadful things." There was a burst of female laughter in the background before Schechtmann added, "Don't bother to ring, the lobby door will be open. The building is only two units, we have the top, so take the elevator to the third floor."

The elevator opened directly onto a foyer tiled in more black and white checkerboard. A uniformed maid met me there and took me up a stairway to a big blue-and-white living room overlooking a terrace that faced the Bay. I heard female voices, but they came from above. When I looked questioningly at the maid, she indicated a spiral staircase, and I climbed it to a greenhouse room on the flat roof.

All four walls were glass, reinforced by steel crossbeams; its retractable roof was open, and flowering plants swayed on hangers in the breeze. Other plants grew in tubs along the perimeters, and in the center was a grouping of brightly cushioned wicker chairs on which five women lounged. None was over thirty; all were fashion-model thin, dressed in expensive chic. They'd discarded their costly shoes and jackets, hiked their skirts up and propped their legs on hassocks to sun. At least a half dozen open wine bottles sat on the glass-topped table, and two more chilled in ice buckets. A sixth woman with long dark hair lay on her back on the Berber rug, stripped to her lacy red bra and panties, a wineglass propped on her flat stomach. They were all drunk as skunks.

Years before I would have been intimidated by walking into such a gathering. I'd have felt naive and poorly dressed next to these beautiful people. But in the interim I'd met too many genuinely beautiful people, who used their wealth and leisure time to finance literacy programs and organize AIDS benefits and raise funds for the arts, to be impressed by cheap people with money. A not-so-subtle scent of corruption wafted on the breeze. I breathed it as I waited for someone to notice me.

Finally a redhead at the opposite side of the room said, "Company, Leila."

The woman who lay on the rug pushed up on one elbow and looked toward me, shading her eyes with the hand that held the glass. "You must be the lady detective," she said in a lilting Spanish-accented voice. "I have always wanted to meet a lady detective. Come enjoy a glass of wine with us and tell me what terrible, terrible thing Speed has done now."

I recognized Leila Schechtmann's voice from our phone conversation. Recognized a quality in it that told me that more than wine drinking had been going on here. A few lines of coke, perhaps, to counteract the alcohol and the sun's effects. As the other women turned curiously toward me I said, "No wine, thanks. Can we talk downstairs, please?"

"These are my friends." Leila gestured expansively with

her glass. "Anything you have to say can be said in front of them."

"I'm not sure you want that." I put a warning note behind the words, just enough to instill some unease.

Schechtmann hesitated, pouting. This visit wasn't going to be as much fun as she'd anticipated. After a moment she shrugged and got to her feet, stretching to show off her sleek body. To her friends she said, "Enjoy. I will not be long." To me she added, "This way," and moved toward the staircase.

Downstairs she led me to a blue sofa that faced the terrace and curled in one corner. I sat at the far end and let the silence lengthen. Schechtmann worked on her wine and finally said snappishly, "Well, what is it? What has Speed done now?"

"He may be in worse trouble than the last time, but in order to confirm that, I need some background information from you. Tell me about him."

"How can I start? He is a pig, an absolute pig. Do you know he abandoned me? Without so much as a cent? One day everything was fine, and the next . . ." She shrugged.

"You knew about his gambling operation?"

"Of course. It was not amusing—all those phones and little men and women taking calls—but it made us a nice living. Speed worked too hard at it, though. We never went anywhere, we never traveled at all, I was quite bored and fed up. So that year, the year he abandoned me, he found a young man and was training him to take over. Now *he* was amusing." She giggled.

"The young man was Dave Hamid?"

"Oh, yes, now there was a man. Very handsome, he had the machismo, you know." She set her empty glass on the end table and looked around irritably. The maid materialized with a bottle, refilled the glass, and departed. "Oh, yes, Dave Hamid was something. I ought to know."

"Oh?"

"Ah, you're curious. Well, a couple of times I had him, when Speed was otherwise occupied. It should have been more, but he was a strange one, he couldn't see anybody but Chloe, not that she could be bothered with Dave."

"Who's Chloe?"

"Chloe Love, she was one of the chefs at the restaurant."

Schechtmann wrinkled her nose as if she'd smelled something bad. "The staff and the customers all thought she was so wonderful, I never did understand why. Oh, she was pretty enough, if you like those Nordic blondes, but nothing special. And why was she a chef, anyway? Woman are cooks; men are chefs."

Chloe Love. C.L. Coincidence? Maybe, maybe not.

"How did your husband feel about Chloe?"

"How else? He is a man, and like all men, a fool."

"And her feelings for him?"

"Oh, I see, you think I speak the way I do of her because I'm jealous. Well, no, it wasn't like that at all. She couldn't be bothered with Speed, either. Like Dave, he couldn't understand why."

"Why do you think she wasn't interested?"

"Maybe she is a dyke, who knows?"

"What happened to Chloe after your husband sold the restaurant?"

"Why do you want to talk about her?"

It was the first curiosity she'd displayed about my questions or the reason for my visit, other than a mild interest in finding out if Speed had done something terrible; she'd be satisfied with a vague reply. "Just interested, that's all."

"Oh, well, I guess she got another job, or maybe she didn't, maybe she left town. I don't give a damn."

"Let's get back to when your husband left town. You said one day everything was fine, and the next it wasn't. I gather you didn't suspect what he was going to do."

"Not at all." She curled her body deep into the sofa's cushions and shivered. Her lacy bra and panties were scant protection against the late-afternoon chill that was gathering in this sunless room. The maid reappeared with a loosely woven wrap and draped it over her, then topped off her wineglass.

Impeccable service, I thought, but beneath the surface of the woman's impassive expression I sensed strong disapproval. She was a Latina who looked to be around fifty: plain, running to plumpness, wearing a wide wedding band, she was probably a good Catholic wife and mother who would give up this job in an instant if she didn't need the money.

Schechtmann didn't even thank the woman. She snuggled under the wrap, sipped wine, and began her tale of woe. "That day, I remember it so well, Speed and I were living on Tel Hill near that tower. I love the tower, don't you, so very phallic. I was out late the night before, a party with some friends, he couldn't go, some problem at the restaurant. When I came home he was asleep. In the morning he kissed me good-bye, left at the usual time, nothing was different.

"Well, I had a lunch date at Stars, you know Stars? Some people say it may have had its day, but I don't know, to me it's as good as ever. Then a manicure and pedicure, some shopping, and at five o'clock time for drinks at a friend's place in Sausalito. I tried to call Speed on his portable phone, to tell him to join me there, but he didn't answer. You can imagine what I thought."

I shook my head.

She looked at me as if I were incredibly stupid. "I thought he was making it with some woman. You know, the phone in the jacket pocket, the jacket on the living room floor, and Speed in the bedroom." Again she giggled. "I ought to know how that goes."

"So you went to Sausalito for drinks," I prompted, anxious to hurry her through this recitation of her activities.

"And dinner. There's a marvelous restaurant . . . no, there's not, it's gone now. We had dinner and more drinks, and when I got home to Tel Hill Fig Newton was waiting for me."

". . . Fig Newton?"

"His real name is Langley, but who wants to be called that? And the nickname is so clever, don't you think?"

I hadn't had a drop to drink, but I felt as if I'd been imbibing along with her. "Who is he?"

"He was manager of Das Glücksspiel. Stupid name for a restaurant, don't you think? Speed thought he was being so clever, and look what happened. Anyway, Fig told me everything."

"And that was . . . ?"

"While I was having a perfectly nice day, Speed sold the restaurant to one of his gambler friends, sold the condo to another, emptied all our bank accounts, and caught a plane for Miami. Fig went to the restaurant as usual that morning,

Speed sent him on an errand to Oakland, and by the time he got back the new owner was there taking inventory. He'd turned all the phone people out of the second floor, ripped out the lines, fired the restaurant staff, and then he fired Fig. And he told Fig about the condo, the bank accounts, and the flight to Miami."

"Did you try to trace your husband in Florida?"

"Of course, but it was too late, he disappeared with every cent we had."

"What about Dave Hamid? Did you see him after that?"

She laughed cynically. "Oh, no, Dave was too busy keeping a low profile."

"Did the police question him?"

"I don't know. They may have tried, but of course it would have done no good, Dave had diplomatic immunity, he couldn't be prosecuted, didn't even have to testify before the grand jury. That was the reason Speed brought him into the business in the first place. Not that it helped Speed. Do you know there's still a warrant out for him?"

"Yes. How come Hamid's involvement in the operation didn't come to the attention of the media?"

"Have you met that mother of his?"

"Yes."

"Well, I have, too. One of the most *boring* evenings of my life, dinner at that wretched consulate, her talking international relations as if anything like that matters. The woman is filthy rich, I'm sure there were payoffs, ask anybody in the diplomatic community how that works."

A voice from above sang out, "Lei-la! We're out of wine!"

Leila snapped her fingers. "Wine, Blanca. Better yet, give them champagne."

I felt a slight movement behind me as the maid left her station.

"She's very attentive, your Blanca," I said.

"A real treasure." She smiled insincerely.

I'd known other people like Leila Schechtmann and her friends but—thank God—had never had many dealings with them. With any luck, my dealings with Leila would soon be over. "This Fig . . . Langley Newton, do you know where I can find him?"

"What do you want with Fig?"

"To get his story about the day your husband left town."

"I see." She frowned in concentration. "Someone said . . . Sandy, maybe? Yes, Sandy said he saw him. Where? South Beach? No, too upscale. More likely it was south of Market, but not the good part of SoMa."

Blanca passed through the room with two magnums of champagne in ice buckets and climbed the spiral staircase, balancing carefully. When she reached the top there were cheers and applause.

"Mrs. Schechtmann—"

"Leila."

"Leila, the morning before your husband—"

"Robbed and abandoned me."

"Yes. Was that morning the last time you had contact with him?"

A secretive look stole over her face. "Why?"

"I understand he's made trips back to the city—"

Male voices came from the entry level below. Schechtmann's head whipped around and her face became animated. The voices came closer as the men climbed the stairs. Leila shrugged off her wrap, and as they reached the top, stretched the way she had earlier for her women friends.

There were three of them: Hispanic, handsome, expensively dressed. They greeted Schechtmann as if she were fully clothed and began loosening ties and taking off jackets.

"*Queridos,*" Leila said, "this is a lady detective, I've been telling her such nasty things about Speed. The others are upstairs, we've had such a lovely afternoon in the sun, and Blanca has just taken up champagne."

The men cast disinterested glances in my direction and moved toward the spiral staircase, stopping to let Blanca by, her arms full of empty wine bottles.

Leila turned to me. "The man in gray, he is my lover, Sandy Ronquillo. Very jealous, he doesn't like to hear about Speed. Please, you must go now."

"About your husband's visits to the city—"

"I know nothing of them, I must get back to my guests. Blanca will see you out." She threw me a brilliant, false smile and skipped toward the staircase; caught up with the last man—who was not her lover—and playfully grabbed his ass.

I waited till they were all upstairs and then went looking for Blanca.

I found her in the kitchen—a large white room whose thirties ambience had not been spoiled, merely updated with new appliances cleverly concealed within the original cabinetry. The one window opened onto a light well; filtered sunshine spilled through it and across the sink where Blanca was washing out the empty bottles. A small cassette tape recorder sat on the counter, and as she worked she hummed along to my brother-in-law Ricky Savage's current country-and-western hit, "The Broken Promise Land."

I let the swinging door close behind me and cleared my throat. Blanca stopped in the act of setting a bottle in a plastic recycling tub and glanced up in surprise.

"Mrs. Schechtmann's rejoined her guests," I said. "I thought you might be able to answer a few questions she couldn't."

The maid regarded me warily, then shrugged.

"Do you like that song?" I motioned at the tape recorder.

"I like all Ricky Savage's songs. He is my very favorite singer."

Convenient. I sensed an opportunity for building rapport here. "Mine, too. Of course, I'm prejudiced—he's married to my sister Charlene."

Blanca's face flushed with pleasure. "Really?"

"Really. I've known Ricky since he was eighteen and came through San Diego playing backup for a crummy band. One of their gigs was a high-school dance, where he saw Charlene. He stayed on, and they were married within three months." I didn't add that Ricky had gotten her pregnant on their first date.

"Your sister is a very fortunate woman."

"In many ways. She and Ricky have a lot of money, like these people." I hooked my thumb at the door. "But they're still just plain folks. None of this drinking and doing drugs, and they've raised their kids right." Don't lay it on too thick, McCone. "A lot wrong in this household, isn't there?"

Again Blanca shrugged, and turned back to the sink.

"Blanca, I really need some information about Leila's husband, Klaus Schechtmann."

"I cannot help you with that."

"Not even if it would save a little girl who's in serious trouble?"

She paused in her rinsing. Shook her head. "This job is very important to me."

"I promise complete confidentiality."

At that point Ricky belted out the phrase "broken promise land." Thanks, guy, I thought.

The irony was not lost on Blanca. She shut off the water and turned to face me, a faint smile on her lips. "I do not even know you are telling me the truth about being related to him. How can I trust you?"

"Look." I dug in my bag, pulled out a photo folder and showed her a snap of Ricky, Charlene, and their three youngest sitting on the foundation of a house. "That's the place they're building in the hills above San Diego."

She studied it, shook her head again. "I am not supposed to talk about Mr. Schechtmann."

"How would you like Ricky's autograph and his new release? I can get you a tape, a record, or a CD."

"You are offering me a bribe, I think."

"Yes, I am."

"Then you must be desperate." She hesitated. "You say a child is in trouble?"

"Yes. She's only nine years old."

For a moment her gaze wavered, then firmed and met mine. "All right. And I accept your bribe. I would like a tape, please."

"Done." I dug in my purse and handed her a notebook so she could write down her full name and address.

"So," she said, handing it back, "what is my part of our bargain?"

"Leila's husband, Klaus Schechtmann—or Speed, as she calls him—has he ever visited here?"

She nodded. "Twice, that I know of. A few months after she moved in last year and again in December, the week before Christmas."

So Schechtmann—and possibly Dawud Hamid—had been

in the city the week the Libyan Trade Commission had been bombed. Interesting. "Tell me about the visits."

"The first time, she was very angry with him. There was an argument, a physical argument. Then silence. They went to the bedroom, of course. The second time, she welcomed him. There was caviar, champagne, music. And, of course, the bedroom again. After she had me change the sheets she cautioned me to say nothing to Mr. Ronquillo, and there was extra money in my Christmas bonus. I think her husband gave her money, because for months she shopped more than usual."

"Have you ever heard Leila or Speed mention Dave Hamid?"

"The first time I heard that name was when you and she were talking."

"What about the country Azad, or their consulate?"

"No."

"Chloe Love?"

"No."

"A man named Langley Newton—Fig, for short?"

"Oh, yes. Fig does things for Leila—takes her car to be serviced, runs errands. She gives him little jobs because he is having a hard time. He comes by at least once a week."

I'd thought there was a false note in Leila's denial of knowing Fig's whereabouts. "Why do you suppose she told me she doesn't know how to contact him?"

"Perhaps she was afraid you meant to harm him. Leila likes Fig, without any of the usual woman-man things."

"Why?"

Blanca shrugged. "Maybe because he went to her when her husband left and told her what Speed had done. Maybe because Fig does not judge her. And Fig would never hurt her, not like Mr. Ronquillo. *He* has violence in him, and Leila often has the bruises to prove it."

"Do you know where I can find Fig?"

"I am sorry, I don't. His mother died last year and left him an apartment building somewhere in the city, but he doesn't live there. There are problems with it, and he is having trouble selling it. In the meantime he stays down on the Peninsula, but I am not sure where."

"Do you know when he'll come to see Leila again?"

"I believe he was here yesterday making some repairs, but I am not sure because it was my day off. The next time he comes I will ask him to call you."

I thought I could trace Newton by other means, but I gave Blanca one of my cards. "Will you also call me if Speed Schechtmann visits Leila again?"

She nodded and tucked the card into the pocket of her uniform.

A bell in an old-fashioned call box mounted above the door rang. Blanca looked at the box and sighed. "They want more champagne. No food—the drugs kill their hunger."

"Blanca, why do you continue to work here?"

"I am well paid and my salary helps with my daughter's college tuition. She is at U.C. Davis studying to be a veterinarian. When she opens her practice I will quit this job and work for her." She grinned wickedly. "I think I will enjoy working with the animals. By then I will have had much experience."

Twelve

       Back in my car, I phoned Mick at the office and
asked him to call his father about Blanca's autograph and
tape. He said he would before he closed up for the day.
"Nothing's happening—here or on the bulletin boards. You
haven't even had a phone call."

"What, no messages from Adah Joslyn?"

"No, thank God."

"Odd." After the way she'd badgered me about the Azadis
the night before, I'd expected a string of them.

Next I called Keim's extension at RKI. "Anything?" I asked
her.

"No. This Hamid's a tough one to pin down."

"Well, put him aside for now. You feel like logging some
overtime?"

"Sure. What do you need?"

"Current addresses for two people: Langley Newton, aka
Fig, and Chloe Love. They both worked at Das Glücksspiel;
he was manager, she was one of the chefs."

"I'll get on it. Anything else?"

"Did Renshaw call?"

"Yeah, didn't he get hold of you? He's at the consulate;
here's the line you're to call on."

When I reached Renshaw he said he'd have to get back to

me. I stayed where I was, watching tendrils of fog slip in from the Bay to end our stretch of fine spring weather. We would have an early dusk and a chilly evening—a good time to curl up with Hy in front of my fireplace. The idea was immensely appealing, but still I felt the edgy need to keep moving.

The phone buzzed. Renshaw. So far, he said, there had been no ransom demand.

"And there won't be, either," I told him.

"You figure this the same way I do."

"Hamid was too cool by far. If she didn't arrange the snatch, she knows who has them, and she isn't worried. What's she been doing since you got there?"

"Staring out the library window at the garden. What're *you* doing?"

"Working on a lead. You'll be there for a while?"

"I'll be here till this situation is resolved one way or the other."

Next on my list of calls was Joslyn. Her answering machine promised she'd get back to me. Last call: Greg Marcus. He was in his office, and he confirmed that he'd been unable to come up with anything on Dawud Hamid or the other Azadis. I asked him to run checks on Klaus and Leila Schechtmann, Sandy Ronquillo, Langley Newton, and Chloe Love. He grumbled for form's sake, but I could tell he was interested enough in what I might be coming up with to expedite them.

As an afterthought I asked, "You seeing your chef friend tonight?"

"Later on, yeah."

"Will you ask her if she knows anything about Love, seeing as they're both members of the city's culinary community?"

Greg promised he'd call if Lynda knew anything.

I was about to turn the ignition key when the phone buzzed again. Keim said, "I've got your cookie."

"You what?"

"Fig Newton. He lives in Brisbane."

"How'd you find out so fast?"

"Phone book."

"Oh," I said weakly. Already I'd come to rely so heavily

on assistants with technology at their fingertips that I'd forgotten to let *my* fingers do the walking.

Keim read me an address on Manzanita Lane. "It's one of those little streets on San Bruno Mountain," she added. "Borders on the county park. You want to take Bayshore Boulevard down there, turn right on San Bruno Avenue, and head uphill. After that you're on your own."

I certainly was on my own; even my Rand McNally Streetfinder couldn't help me. The streets scaled the humpbacked hill in curves and switchbacks, crossed and separated, and recrossed. As I neared the open space that stretched between Brisbane and Daly City, they became narrow lanes lined with small rustic dwellings and overhung with eucalyptus trees. Fog had crested the hilltop, was spilling down now. To the east the Bay still shimmered under blue sky.

I turned right on an unmarked road, snaked through a switchback, thumped in and out of potholes. In moments I reached a dead end. The land banked steeply on the uphill side, thick with wild vegetation; on the other side it fell away to the backs of the houses on the street below. I U-turned and crept along, looking for mailboxes. One finally appeared on the uphill side, its post leaning crookedly, its door hanging open. With difficulty I made out the name Newton. I stopped the MG next to it and got out.

Two wide, sagging planks bridged a declivity where a little creek trickled. I crossed on one of them and followed a well worn car track through a eucalyptus grove. The trees' silvery green leaves shivered in the drifting mist. When I came out of the grove I saw faint light shining in the front window of a small brown-shingled bungalow nestled at the bottom of the slope. Its porch was crowded with junk—a wringer washing machine, some wooden crates, a lawn mower, three straightbacked chairs. A pair of old pickups and a dusty black Citroen hulked in what could loosely be called a yard. A broken flowerpot lay at the foot of the steps, dirt and a withering geranium spilling onto the ground.

I felt as if I'd stepped back in time to the days when Brisbane's residents kept goats and chickens and eked out their livings farming the hillside. Present-day San Francisco seemed remote as I walked through the late-afternoon fog. I didn't allow nostalgia for simpler times to ease my caution, though; instead I reached into the outside pocket of my shoulder bag and rested my hand on the .38 that I'd removed from the strongbox in the trunk before driving down here. For years I'd resisted carrying it, in spite of my permit, but after a near-fatal incident the previous October I'd overcome my reluctance on the grounds of better-them-than-me.

I approached the bungalow warily, keeping an eye out for watchdogs. None growled in warning, none rushed out to investigate my presence. In the house a medium-sized shape crossed behind the drawn shade on the lighted window. I mounted the shaky steps and knocked. After a few seconds footsteps approached within.

The man who opened the door had a bald egg-shaped dome that gleamed above a ruff of curly silver-gray hair. His body was suety-soft, clad in a threadbare maroon bathrobe. His feet, in equally threadbare black socks, turned out like a ballet dancer's. His brown eyes took a long time to focus on me, as if his mind was on something remote and preoccupying. When he greeted me cordially I relaxed my hold on the .38.

I identified myself and verified that he was Langley Newton. Mentioned both Leila Schechtmann and Blanca and asked if I might come in. Newton looked uneasy, as if he didn't have many visitors and wasn't sure how to deal with me. He wasn't dressed, he said. Could I wait a minute?

I waited, watching the fingers of fog reach downhill toward the Bay. They were claiming the marinas on its western shore when Newton returned, wearing jeans and a blue pullover sweater, and invited me inside.

The front room of the bungalow ran the entire length of the structure and was as shabby as its exterior. An old darkwood hutch stood in shadow at one end, its shelves filled with dusty commemorative plates and floral-patterned teacups. At the other end sat a potbellied woodstove, and in between a high-backed Victorian-style sofa upholstered in faded red velvet. A card table on which a half-finished jigsaw puzzle was laid out stood in front of it. The only light came from a floor lamp near the window, and the room was very cold.

Newton went to the stove, crumpled some newspaper that

lay in an untidy pile on the floor, and lit the fire. He turned to me with an uneasy smile. "The fog came in so quickly that I didn't notice how cold it had gotten. I seldom use this room except for company. It'll warm up soon."

"It's not that bad." I looked at a round table flanked by two chairs with needlepointed seats. Atop a crocheted doily on the table sat a dozen or so Hummel figurines; a finger-smudged glass stood incongruously among them.

"My mother's collection," Newton said, motioning for me to sit on the sofa. "This was her home. She died last fall, and I haven't gotten around to clearing out her things." He regarded the figurines disapprovingly, as if seeing them more clearly than before. "I really should do something about those. I find them quite ugly."

"I'm not too fond of them myself, but they're probably worth something. You might try selling them."

"Really?" He looked at them speculatively and with greater tolerance.

When I sat on the sofa a telltale puff of dust rose around me. What, I wondered, had the man been doing since last fall, that he'd neither cleaned nor gotten rid of objects that offended him? Perhaps he simply didn't see the dust and grime, didn't notice the knickknacks unless someone directed his attention to them. His capacity to connect with his surroundings did seem somewhat limited; his gaze had become remote again, barely acknowledging my presence.

I asked, "You've lived here since your mother passed away?"

He nodded slowly, coming back from wherever his mind had taken him. "I suppose Leila's told you that I'm having a hard time of it. Since the bungalow's paid for and the taxes and upkeep are low, I have no option but to stay here."

"You sound as though you're not too happy about that."

"Oh, it's all right here, I guess. It's private and quiet. But there are inconveniences: no garbage pickup, and it's a long drive for groceries."

"Blanca told me you also inherited an apartment building in the city. Why not live there?"

"I don't really care to live at close quarters with other

people and, besides, the building's got problems. It's for sale, if you know anyone who's in the market for rental property."

I didn't, so I continued a line of questioning that would gradually lead up to the subject of Dawud Hamid. "When I spoke with her, Leila went into great detail about how Speed sold Das Glücksspiel. Was it really as sudden as she says?"

"Yes." He took a box from beneath the card table and swept the puzzle pieces into it, carelessly undoing his time-consuming work. "She's bitter, and she's got a right to be. I at least was employable. Although having worked downstairs from an illegal gambling operation didn't score me too many points on job interviews."

"You must've known about the sports book."

"No, I didn't. Speed kept the two businesses strictly segregated. I thought he was running some sort of mail-order outfit up there."

I must have looked skeptical because he added, "Hard to believe, isn't it? The D.A. didn't credit it, either, but the other employees backed me up."

"What did you do after you were fired?"

"Nothing very impressive." He stowed the puzzle box in a small bookcase, then sat down on one of the needlepointed chairs. "Speed sold the restaurant in eighty-nine. For a few years I worked for a government contractor setting up management systems for food services on military bases, but with the closings . . . For a while after that, I worked abroad for a franchise that was establishing itself in Europe. But now I'm down to scrounging odd jobs. Did Leila send you to me about one?"

"Actually, I'm trying to trace some people you might've known when you worked for her husband. Dawud Hamid— is that name familiar?"

"Hamid." Something indefinable flickered beneath the surface of his remote gaze, but he simply said, "There was a Dave Hamid who ran with the diplomatic crowd. I believe he and Speed were close friends."

"That's the man. He ran the sports book."

Newton nodded thoughtfully. "That makes sense. At the time of the indictments there were rumors that one of the major players had gone unnamed because he had diplomatic immunity, but his identity never came out."

"You didn't know Hamid, then?"

"Hardly at all. I didn't run with Speed's crowd; they were too rich for my blood—and too corrupt."

"What about Chloe Love?"

"Chloe?" He seemed startled. "What about her?"

"Leila said Hamid was interested in her. Is there a possibility they might still be in touch?"

"That I very much doubt." Newton glanced at the woodstove, which had begun to smoke, and got up to tend it.

"Do you have any idea where Chloe Love might be living now?" I asked.

"Living? No, I don't." He prodded at the logs with the poker, then set it down and dusted his hands off. "But I do know you won't find her with Hamid or any of that crowd."

"Why not?"

"Because Chloe was a nice person, through and through. She was intelligent and she wasn't taken in by money or appearance." He returned to his chair. "Men from the diplomatic crowd were always visiting her in the kitchen and hitting on her, but she'd have nothing to do with them. She was . . . an impressive woman."

"You sound as though you were fond of her."

"I was. She was probably the most kind and genuinely decent person I've ever known. She went to bat for me with the D.A. when he didn't believe I hadn't known about the sports book. I owe her a great deal for that."

"And yet you lost touch with her."

He shrugged. "After the restaurant closed, we all went our separate ways. The industry was in a bad recession, and we had to scramble for jobs, thanks to Speed."

"Tell me about Speed."

"As Leila's fond of saying, he's a pig."

"Leila's no saint herself."

"She's a naughty little girl and none too bright, but that doesn't mean she deserved to be abandoned that way."

"And yet she welcomes Speed back into her bed whenever he's in town."

"Oh?" The questioning syllable came too quickly.

"She's told you about his visits, hasn't she?"

". . . Yes."

"How does Speed get back into the country—on a false passport? And why does he come back?"

Newton was silent.

"Mr. Newton, I'm not acting in an official capacity. I don't care if they ever bring Speed Schechtmann to trial on the gambling indictment. But I do need to locate him."

"Why?"

I explained about the ongoing relationship between Schechtmann and Hamid, about the Azadi Consulate being the latest target of the Diplo-bomber, and about Mavis's and Habiba's earlier disappearance. "The consul general seems curiously unworried, so I assume they're in a safe place, but I want to make sure that they're not with Hamid or on the way to him."

"Why should you concern yourself? They're his wife and child."

"Because I think the Azadis are more than a target of the bomber; I think they're the primary one. My gut-level instincts tell me that Dave Hamid's involvement in the sports book and his later disappearance are at the very root of these bombings. If that's the case, you can understand the danger his wife and child will be in if they're anywhere near him."

"But they were in danger at the consulate."

"Yes, and I was about to remove them to a secure place when they disappeared."

Newton picked up one of the figurines and turned it round and round in his hands, studying it. "What would you do if it turned out they were with Hamid?"

"Go after them and bring them back—forcibly, if necessary." I hadn't thought that far ahead, but now the answer seemed obvious.

"And take them to that secure place you mentioned?"

"Yes."

"What if Hamid came after them?"

"I certainly hope he would. I'd like to get him back here, where the Diplo-bomber Task Force could question him about his involvement in what's going on."

"Not likely—given his diplomatic immunity."

"Then maybe I'll just have to question him myself, using

my connection with the consulate's security firm. At any rate, to do that I need to find him, and to find him I need to locate Speed. You can help, Mr. Newton."

He hesitated, then sighed and set the figurine on the table. "All right, I don't know where Speed has been living. Leila does, I think, but you'll never force her to reveal it—she likes the money he gives her too much. I do know that Speed moves in and out of the country on a yawl that one of his gambler friends, Eric Sparling, keeps berthed at Salt Point Marina. He has his crew pick Speed up at an offshore ship and bring him back to the city."

"This yawl—what's her name?"

"The *Freia*."

"And Salt Point Marina is one of those between Candlestick Park and the airport?"

"Yes." For the first time Newton's eyes connected with mine; there was something else he wanted to tell me.

"What?" I asked.

". . . Yes, all right. Speed visited Leila yesterday. I went there to put up some towel racks for her, and he was just leaving. I heard him say he'd be returning home today."

Salt Point Marina nestled in the curve of land that bowed out just south of the San Francisco–San Mateo County line. Strong winds are a given there in any kind of weather; tonight they blew the fog like snow and chilled me to the bone. The marina was fronted by a mostly empty parking lot and surrounded by a high electrified fence. I left the MG next to an empty boat trailer and crossed the ramp to the gate. It operated on a key card, and there was no guard or any way of summoning someone. I peered through the eerily blowing mist and saw cruisers and sailboats of all sizes moored in their slips; faint lights shone in the windows of a few.

Security lights, or evidence of people living aboard?

The hum of rush-hour traffic on the Bayshore Freeway was at my back; the only sounds in the marina were the water's gentle swell and the creak of lines. After a moment I got back in the car and sat in the gathering darkness, drumming my fingers on the wheel as I tried to decide what to do next. Headlights flared behind me and I watched a dark-colored

Porsche pull up on the other side of the boat trailer. A man in a business suit got out, locked the car, and headed toward the gate.

People living aboard, then.

I was out of the MG immediately, but before I could get to the gate the man used his key card and shut it behind him. Chances were he wouldn't have let me in, anyway; when he locked the Porsche he'd activated an alarm—the security-conscious type. I needed to create the impression I belonged here.

I got back into the car and drove into Brisbane, avoiding the clogged freeway. There I found a market and bought a sack of groceries, including the sourdough I'd promised Hy I'd bring home. When I returned to the marina a few more vehicles were parked in the lot. I waited.

After about ten minutes a Mustang drove in and parked a few spaces away from me. A tall woman in a tan suit got out and hurried toward the gate, hugging her jacket around her. I followed, pretended to stumble on the canted ramp, and dropped the grocery bag.

"Oh, no!" I fell to my knees and began running my hands over the ramp.

The woman turned. "Your groceries! Let me help you." She squatted and started gathering up apples that had rolled from the bag.

"It's not the groceries I'm worried about," I said. "I dropped my key card. Oh, dammit, you know what? I think it fell in the water."

She put the apples in the bag and set it upright. "Well, you can get a new one from Evans tomorrow. I'll let you in."

"Thanks, I really appreciate your help. I just couldn't see where I was stepping."

"Who could? It got dark so early tonight, and it looks like nobody thought to turn on the pierside lights." She shivered as she held the gate for me. "Damned fog. I knew that stretch of good weather couldn't last."

I thanked her again and waited till she started off to the left. Then I went to the right and turned down one of the finger piers, checking the names of the boats that were berthed there, looking for the *Freia. Lazy Daze, Marguerite, The Money Pit, Roger's Jolly, Ms. Freedom*—

A high keening scream cut through the mist. Cut through me and set my flesh to rippling.

I slued around and ran back along the dock. The scream was a woman's and it came from the direction that my Good Samaritan had gone. The dock swayed beneath my feet, throwing my balance off. I dumped the cumbersome sack of food, spread my arms to steady myself.

Now I heard voices, excited and distressed. A line of lights on the main pier had come on, and under one of them I saw the woman. She leaned against a tall man, her face pressed against his brown leather jacket, rolling her head back and forth in denial. A second man was looking into the water.

I ran up to them. "What's wrong?"

The second man motioned down, looking sick. "Rosalie turned on the lights and saw it."

It. I went to the edge of the pier, squatted, and scanned the shiny blackness.

A body floated face down, bobbing on the slight swell, one bare foot caught by a loop in a mooring line. A small body, a woman's, clad in a loose garment that billowed out around her. A black garment with white piping on the sleeves and collar. Dark tangled hair swirled across her shoulders.

I moaned. Dropped my bag, shrugged out of my jacket, toed off my athletic shoes.

"Hey," the man said, "don't—"

I braced myself for the shock, took a breath, jumped in feet first.

Cold! Heart-stopping cold and deep, I keep sinking. Air, I need air—

My feet touched bottom. I pushed hard, shot up, and broke the surface. The body was about four yards away. I thrashed over, grabbed its shoulders. Turned it on its back and got it in a lifeguard's hold.

Heart-stopping cold for her, too. But her heart's stopped for good. I'll never forget this cold. I'll feel it in my nightmares to my dying day.

I began towing her toward the dock. Death made her slight frame heavy and ungainly.

Cold and still and God those blank forever eyes. She ought to be at home in front of her fireplace with her solitaire game spread out and her glass of vodka to hand. Even that's better than this. No, she ought to be talking about her poetry, forgetting the booze for a little while—

Stop it, McCone!

More people on the pier now. Hands reaching to lift the body. Somebody was saying that he knew CPR. They hauled her up and he set to work. I supposed he had to try, but it wouldn't do any good. I'd been too late to save Mavis.

The hands reached for me now. I grasped them. Gained the dock but fell to my knees. Somebody wrapped me in a blanket.

Too late to save Mavis.

And where, oh God *where*, was Habiba?

Thirteen

When I made my statement to a San Mateo County sheriff's deputy some thirty minutes later, I knew that my fears of becoming like Gage Renshaw and his cohorts were one step closer to being realized. I said nothing about Klaus Schechtmann, Dawud Hamid, or Habiba. I denied knowing Mavis's identity. I did not admit to being a private investigator. I did not mention Eric Sparling or the *Freia*.

One of the men on the pier had called 911 and then contacted the marina's manager, a Mr. Evans. When Evans arrived and saw me wet and shivering in the borrowed blanket, he offered me the loan of his office to change into the emergency clothes I kept in the trunk of the MG. But by the time I'd changed, Evans had thought the situation over and realized I was on the premises without authorization. Quickly I confessed to employing subterfuge. I'd planned a dinner to surprise a friend who berthed his yawl there, so I'd tricked Rosalie into letting me through the gate. The friend's name? Eric Sparling.

"Mr. Sparling don't live aboard," Evans said.

"I know, but I thought he'd be here tonight."

"Well, the *Freia* set sail late this afternoon. I know, because the crew was getting her ready at three-thirty when I went home."

"I must've got my dates mixed up. You didn't see Eric . . . Mr. Sparling?"

"Just the crew and a fellow who's used the yawl before— blond-haired man with a German accent."

Klaus Schechtmann. "He have a woman and a little girl with him?"

Evans frowned; I was asking too many questions. "I didn't see no woman or kid, no. And listen, you, don't go sneaking in here again, surprise or no surprise. That's why we got the gate—to keep out potential insurance problems like yourself."

I promised not to commit future trespass, and Evans left me alone. Then I gave my brief duplicitous statement to the sheriff's deputy and got out of there. I consoled myself both for my sins of omission and commission by telling myself that the deputy wasn't really interested in my story anyway. Twice he'd referred to Mavis as the victim of an accidental drowning, and he seemed to find nothing unusual about me leaping into the Bay to recover the body of a total stranger. Perhaps he thought I got my kicks by courting pneumonia.

From the MG I called Renshaw at the consulate and broke the news. When I finished he asked, "Murder?"

"Hard to say. So far, the sheriff's department is leaning toward accident."

"You didn't tell them anything, then."

"I thought about it, but I was afraid they'd send the Coast Guard after the *Freia*. Schechtmann's a fugitive and, however she ended up there, I'm sure he's the one who left Mavis dead in the Bay. I doubt he'd allow himself to be taken. If Habiba's aboard that yawl, I don't want to jeopardize her."

"Good judgment call."

"You'd better get on to the sheriff down here with whatever cover story you can think of. I don't like the idea of Mavis lying unidentified in the morgue. And you'd better break the news to Mrs. Hamid."

"Yeah. If I know her she'll take it stoically, no matter what she feels. And explain nothing."

"Well, good luck."

"What're you going to do now?"

"Find out where Schechtmann's headed."

* * *

The fog completely blanketed San Bruno Mountain now; it dimmed the lights of the small dwellings to faint glows, wrapped thick around the trunks of the eucalyptus. Once again I left my car by Langley Newton's mailbox and crossed the plank bridge. Once again my hand rested on the .38 in my purse. Newton might be a remote, harmless-appearing recluse, but he was also a man with a secret.

When I knocked on the bungalow's door, it took him well over a minute to answer. Footsteps came from the rear and an overhead bulb flashed on. Newton looked out; surprise flared in his eyes and he recoiled.

I pushed past him into the front room. The finger-smudged glass still stood on the table among the Hummel figurines. I went over, picked it up, and smelled it. Vodka.

Newton didn't ask what I was doing; he knew.

"Who brought them here?" I demanded. "Speed?"

His gaze slid away from mine. "Brought who?"

"You know—Mavis Hamid and her daughter."

"I don't understand why—"

"Yes, you do. Look, Newton, you told me you never use this room except for company, but this afternoon it had a lived-in feel, as if somebody'd been here before it got so cold you needed to light the fire. Habiba's a jigsaw puzzle enthusiast; you had one half completed on the card table, but didn't hesitate to dump it back in its box. Mavis is a vodka drinker, and this glass—"

"I drink vodka."

"You didn't smell of vodka earlier."

"It's been there several days."

I held the glass up, let a drop of liquid slide out of it and splat to the floor.

Newton's shoulders slumped in acknowledgment of defeat. "All right," he said heavily. "Speed brought them."

"When?"

"Around noon."

So Schechtmann had probably removed them from the consulate while I was trying to persuade Malika Hamid to let them go with me. I remembered Kahlil Lateef leaving the library twice on errands for her; she'd spoken to him in their native tongue and I hadn't given it a second thought.

"Why'd he park them here, rather than on the *Freia*?"

Newton went to the sofa and sat down. "She wasn't going to be ready to sail until four, and Speed didn't want the marina manager to see them. He'd planned to take them directly from the consulate to the boat, but some emergency came up and he had to get them out of there early. So he called Leila, and Leila called me and said Speed would pay if I'd keep them amused for a few hours. That wasn't easy. The mother . . ." He grimaced.

"What about her?"

"She was drunk and upset and wanted to go home. Speed went down to the marina to check on things and in the hour he was gone she ran out into the yard and tried to get away twice. When he came back he brought a bottle; she drank most of it, but she didn't calm down."

"How was Habiba doing?"

"She was worried about her mother, but I guess she'd seen her behave oddly before. After a while she just tuned her out and worked on her puzzle. It helped that she had something to look forward to; she said Speed was taking them on an adventure, and when they arrived they'd see her father."

"Arrived where?"

"I don't think she knew."

"Did Mavis know?"

"She barely knew she was *here*."

His description of Mavis's last hours made me both sad and angry. "Well, she's nowhere now, Mr. Newton."

"What does that mean?"

"Mavis is dead, and Habiba's missing."

Something bright sparked in his eyes. "What happened?"

"She was drowned, whether on purpose or by accident, I can't say."

"Speed's fault?"

"Had to be. She was floating in the *Freia*'s slip at the marina. Even if she went into the water by accident, Speed left her there. She was drunk and helpless and she might've still been alive—but he left her to die."

Newton's facial muscles rippled, and when he spoke his

voice shook with emotion. "I begged Speed not to give her that bottle. He just laughed and said she needed to be sedated. Then he sat right here where I am now and watched her drink." He stood, took a quick turn around the room, his movements tight and angry. "I hate men who prey on women! I *hate* them!"

Then why didn't you do something? I asked silently. And left him to his recriminations.

Blanca's eyes widened in alarm when I arrived at Sandy Ronquillo's condominium. Something in my face, I supposed, plus the disheveled condition of the jeans and sweater that had long been crammed into the travel bag in the trunk of my car.

"Is she here?" I asked.

Blanca nodded, glancing across the foyer to a hallway.

"Sober?"

She didn't bother to reply to the absurd question. "She is dressing to go out to dinner."

"Get her, please."

She hurried down the hallway, knocked on a door at its end, and went inside. I paced up and down on the black and white checkerboard, trying to control my anger before it controlled me. After a few minutes the door slammed and Leila stalked down the hall, wearing a short red silk robe and a scowl. "What the hell do you want now?" she demanded.

"Where is your husband taking Habiba Hamid?"

Under her freshly applied makeup, her face paled. She glanced over her shoulder. "Sandy," she whispered. "He will hear."

"Then let's go upstairs to talk."

"No, you must leave now!" She put out her hands to push me toward the door.

I sidestepped. "Shall I raise my voice, Leila?"

"Don't! Please." She looked around in confusion, then grabbed my arm and hurried me upstairs to the living room. Apparently that wasn't far enough from Ronquillo, because she motioned toward the spiral staircase and led me up to the greenhouse room on the roof.

The room wasn't as appealing in the night mist as it had

been that afternoon in the sunlight. Its view of the city lights was blurred by moisture that streaked the panes, and the air was cold enough to make Leila shiver. She sat on the edge of one of the chairs, and I remained standing.

"Now," I said, "where is he taking her?"

"How did you find out . . . ? Fig, that rat!"

"Don't blame him. Just tell me where Speed's going."

Her eyes moved from side to side as she tried to calculate how little she could get away with telling me.

"I know you arranged for them to stay with Fig. I know about the *Freia* and the ship offshore. Now give me the rest of it, Leila, or I'll start talking very loudly. You don't want Sandy to find out everything I know."

"Everything?"

"About your husband's visits to you. About the money he gives you."

She put her fingers to her lips for a few seconds, then recovered. "That Fig is a liar, you know, that's why he can't keep a job."

I didn't reply.

"Or was it Blanca who told you? She lies, too. I have caught her stealing."

"That I very much doubt. You're lucky to have an employee like her—and a friend like Fig."

"Who, then? Speed? Speed wouldn't—"

"You don't know what Speed would do. Now—where is he going?"

She bit her lip. "Sandy will *kill* me if he finds out. All right, you want to know where Speed is taking them. All right, I will tell you. I do not know the exact location, but Speed owns an island somewhere in the Caribbean. He is operating the sports book again, but there he cannot be charged with breaking the law."

"He must be breaking the law of *some* country."

She shook her head. "The island is sovereign. I do not know why that is, something about the old man he bought it from having declared its independence from Great Britain and the British not wanting it anyway. It is a small island, and very poor."

"But you don't know its name?"

"No."

"Or its location?"

She closed her eyes. "I think it is in the Leewards."

"Near St. Maarten, perhaps?"

"I am not familiar with that area, I really do not know."

I studied her face for a moment to see if she was lying, but anxiety was all I saw. "Okay, Speed is operating the sports book again. Why does he risk making trips to San Francisco?"

"Me, of course."

I doubted that. Speed Schechtmann didn't sound like the type who would risk his freedom for any woman—particularly one in whom fidelity was so demonstrably absent. "He must do something else besides see you."

"Well, there is the check cashing."

"What about it?"

"Eric Sparling, do you know him? The man who owns the *Freia*, he has a chain of check-cashing places, mostly poor people on welfare use them."

"And?"

"Speed brings the checks he collects for gambling debts, and Eric cashes them."

"Eric launders money, you mean."

"I guess that is what it is called."

"Where can I find Sparling?"

Alarm flared in her eyes. "You can't tell him—"

"It won't be necessary for me to tell him you're involved. Where?"

"His office is in his main branch on Sixth Street near Howard."

Sixth near Howard was in the middle of Skid Row. Appropriate. "What's his home address?"

"I don't know, Speed never mentioned where he lives."

It shouldn't be too difficult to obtain. I turned and started down the staircase.

"Ms. McCone?" Leila hurried after me, frightened now. "You will keep my secrets?"

"I will, but secrets have a way of coming out on their own."

Again she covered her lips with her fingers, as if by doing so she could prevent that from happening. Like Langley Newton, Leila now had to deal with her recriminations.

Fourteen

Eric Sparling was unlisted. I called Charlotte Keim's extension at RKI, hoping she'd still be there and could pull a quick check for me, but only reached her voice mail. When I glanced at my watch I saw it was well after eight. Time was passing too fast, and every minute took a little girl who by now must be very frightened farther away from me.

I didn't leave a message for Keim, instead transferred my call to the building operator. Was anyone in, I asked, who could run an address check for me?

No, he replied, there had been a problem in La Jolla and the central computer was down. Mr. Ripinsky was in the office, though; did I want to speak with him?

You bet I did.

"How're you feeling?" I asked when he came on the line.

"Better; this bug comes and goes."

His repeated bouts with it had me seriously worried, but I knew I'd get nowhere by insisting he see a doctor. Hy tended not to give in to illness, but he wasn't irresponsible; he'd see to it in his own good time.

He added, "I spoke with Gage, and he told me what went down today, so I gave up on you and came in to access some documents. Just my luck—no computer."

"You'll be there for a while?"

"Yeah. Some of the night people in the data-search section are putting together a poker game. I thought I'd sit in on it and see if the computer comes back up."

"Then I'll stop by later. Wish me luck."

"With what?"

"I'll explain when I get there. Just wish me."

So because of a balky computer, I was walking along one of the city's roughest streets toward Eric Sparling's check-cashing establishment, caressing the .38 and feeling bad all over again about having come to depend on it. The mayor's controversial Matrix program—designed to roust the homeless from the inner city—may have worked at the Civic Center and Union Square, but not at Sixth and Howard. A man with a little dog begged for spare change in front of a closed sandwich shop; a woman with a shopping cart full of shabby possessions slept in a doorway. Poverty-stricken souls were everywhere; add to them the drunks, addicts, teenaged run-aways, pimps, and hookers, and you had the full flavor of life on the city's sad, seamy underside. I walked quickly, avoiding all eye contact.

The exterior of Ace Check Cashing flashed neon like a Las Vegas gambling casino, but the interior was a cross between a small bank and the visiting room at a county jail: a high counter, two cashier's stations equipped with automatically operated tills and microphones. Glass—probably shatter- and bullet-proof—rose from counter to ceiling. Only one of the booths was staffed, by a white-haired woman whose slate-blue eyes told me I hadn't seen the half of it. When she said, "Help you, honey?" the microphone amplified her smoker's voice.

I held up my I.D. and asked if Sparling was in.

The woman looked my license over carefully, then picked up a phone receiver, punched a button, and—turning her head so I couldn't hear—spoke softly.

"Mr. Sparling wants to know what this is about," she said.

"Tell him it's about the *Freia*."

Apparently my voice was as loud on the other side of the glass as hers on this side because she didn't relay the message, merely listened to Sparling's reply. "He says the boat's in its slip at Salt Point Marina."

"It may be now, but it wasn't at five-thirty when I fished Mavis Hamid's body out of the water."

The woman didn't react. She listened to Sparling, then motioned at a door near the end of the counter. "I'll buzz you in."

Before I was through the door, one in the facing wall opened. A silver-haired man with a sailor's tan stepped out and said, "Ms. McCone? This way, please."

I followed him into a narrow robin's-egg blue corridor. He motioned for me to go around him, latched the door, and leaned against it, arms folded across his chest. "Now," he said, "what's this about a body?"

I took a few steps along the corridor, distancing myself from him. "You *are* Eric Sparling?"

He nodded.

"Well, I'm surprised the sheriff down in San Mateo County hasn't been in contact with you. They'll want to question everyone who keeps a boat at the marina—and the body was floating in the *Freia*'s slip."

"Get to the point, please."

"The point is that the body was the woman your associate, Speed Schechtmann, kidnaped from the Azadi Consulate this morning."

"Schechtmann left the country years ago."

"And has returned a number of times, with your help."

"Nonsense. And what's this about him kidnaping someone?"

"Mr. Sparling, you don't have to cover up with me. I know all about you having the *Freia* pick Schechtmann up offshore. The marina manager has seen the two of you together. And I know about the check-cashing service you perform for Speed."

"Check cashing is my business."

"Social Security checks. Welfare checks. Payroll checks. But not checks that are in repayment of gambling debts."

His lips twitched and his eyes moved to my right hand, where it rested on the gun. He glanced along the corridor, then back at me. "Is this a shakedown?"

"Blackmail? No, Mr. Sparling. I need information."

Again he glanced along the corridor. Someone back there should have been paying attention but wasn't.

I pressed my advantage. "Look, I don't care about your connection with Schechtmann and his betting operation. I don't care what kind of checks you cash, or for whom. I do care about finding out where Speed is taking Habiba Hamid, the daughter of the dead woman."

Silence.

"You really don't want to jeopardize a pretty nice setup here by aiding and abetting a kidnaping, do you?"

"Speed didn't kidnap either the mother or the kid. He was supposed to be taking them to Dave Hamid, with his mother's blessing."

"Why?"

"These bombings—she felt they'd be safer down there."

"Down where?"

Another silence.

"It's still kidnaping; neither Mavis nor Habiba wanted to go."

". . . Was Hamid's wife murdered?"

"We won't know until after the autopsy but yes, I'd say so."

"By Speed?"

"Besides your crew and the little girl, he was the only one there. By the way, why haven't any of the crew contacted you?"

"The *Freia*'s not due back yet. And if what you say is true, my captain certainly wouldn't put out the word on the marine radio." He spoke distractedly, as though he was considering his options. There was a sound at the far end of the corridor; Sparling shook his head and by the time I glanced back there, whoever it was had gone away.

He said, "There's no proof they were on the *Freia*; my crew will back me up."

"I don't really care about proving anything. All I want is the little girl."

"Why?"

"She's in danger."

"That's ridiculous."

"Is it? You know Speed—and Dave Hamid."

"Hamid's her father, for God's sake! She calls Speed her uncle." But I'd struck a nerve, which produced a tic under his right eye.

I said, "I can find them by other means. I know Speed's running the sports book from a private island somewhere in the Leewards. It used to belong to Great Britain until the former owner declared independence; there can't be too many of those around. But going about it that way will take longer and put the little girl at greater risk. Won't you help me, so I can go there and bring her back as soon as possible?"

"You'll never get near it."

"I've got to try." I hadn't been fully committed to the idea until I saw the tic under Sparling's eye, which had grown more pronounced. He knew something about Hamid and Schechtmann that would give support to my uneasy feelings.

Sparling looked away, covered the tic with his fingertips.

"She's nine years old, Mr. Sparling. A young nine. Her mother's already been killed, and she probably witnessed it. Think about it."

He shifted uncomfortably from foot to foot, then became still, his gaze turning inward. He didn't like what he saw; the tic came faster. After a moment he said, "I have two daughters. Five grandchildren. In spite of what you might consider me and my business, I'm not an insensitive man."

"Then help me."

"You'll be taking your life in your hands if you go near that island."

"I've risked it before."

"I'm aware of that."

"Oh?"

"You're not unknown in this city, Ms. McCone."

"No, I guess not. So how about it, Mr. Sparling? Will you tell me how to get to Speed's island?"

He thought for a moment more, then pushed away from the door. "Come to my office. I'll write down the details and draw you a rough map." He paused, eyes shaded by uncertainty. "I just hope I'm not sending you to the same fate as the Hamid woman."

The nearest major airport to Jumbie Cay, Schechtmann's island, was Princess Juliana on St. Maarten. As I drove to Green Street I called Mick at home and asked him to look into flight schedules. Next I accessed both my office and home answering machines. The messages at the office were about routine matters that Mick could handle in my absence; at home was only a cryptic one from Adah Joslyn: "I stumbled onto a lead on the bomber by coincidence, and it's too damn close to home for comfort. I'm heading out now to confirm it. Sure wish you hadn't appropriated my guns. Call you later."

Now what could that mean?

I dialed Joslyn's apartment and let the phone ring fifteen times. She must've forgotten to turn on her machine when she went out. Not a good sign. Adah was the most detail-oriented person I knew.

Mick called back as I slid into a parking spot across from RKI's building. There was an American Airlines flight leaving SFO for Dallas-Fort Worth at half past midnight; at seven-thirty I could connect with another destined for St. Maarten via San Juan and arrive at three tomorrow afternoon. I told him to make the reservation.

As I passed through the security gate in RKI's lobby, Renshaw stepped off the elevator. He looked exhausted, more rumpled than usual, and furious. Obviously he'd been waiting for me; the guard must've buzzed him when I came in.

"Where the hell've you been?" he demanded. "Why haven't you reported?"

"Our agreement was that I'd report only when I had something to tell you."

"As far as I'm concerned our agreement is voided."

The guard was staring at us; he'd probably never seen Renshaw this angry. I said, "Gage, let's go someplace where we can talk privately."

He turned on his heel and stalked toward the hallway that led to the projection room. When we got there, he slammed the door and glared down at me.

I said, "We're both on edge, but shouting isn't going to accomplish a damn thing." Then I told him what I'd found out in the hours since we'd last spoken, ending with, "My flight for the Caribbean leaves at twelve-thirty."

"Why the hell're you going down there?"

"To bring Habiba back and, if possible, find out more about Dave Hamid's connection to these bombings."

"You'll do no such thing. Mrs. Hamid wants—"

"Fuck what Mrs. Hamid wants!" The rage I'd been reining in since I saw Mavis's body floating in the icy black water threatened to run wild. I gave the reins another tug and said more calmly, "This is one time that woman is not going to have her way."

"Hamid is the client—"

"And the client is *not* always right. Look, Gage, so far I've played it your way, but right now I'm sitting on a kidnaping and a probable murder."

"The sheriff's department told Mrs. Hamid a probable accident, and there was no kidnaping. According to you, she arranged for Schechtmann to take them."

"I have a witness who says Mavis wanted to go home and was restrained by force. And after seeing her mother die, you can bet Habiba isn't a willing traveler anymore. But to get back to what I was saying, it isn't going to be very long before the San Mateo Sheriff's Department figures out a few things, and then I'll be in too much trouble to be of any use to you."

"So you think running off on a Caribbean junket will solve your problems?"

"Get serious. This isn't about me, Gage. It's about a little girl whom you were ready and willing to yank out of that consulate this morning. It's about a maniac who continues to deliver lethal packages."

"You're not going to crack the Diplo-bomber case by running off on a rescue mission."

"Maybe not. But I'll bet you ten-to-one that these bombings are directly related to Dave Hamid and—yes—his mother, too. They're at dead center of what's been going on. You indulge the client's wishes now, you're setting her up for disaster. And I'll bet you that I find out something down there that'll prove me right."

Renshaw looked thoughtful. "You'll give me ten-to-one odds on that?"

"Yes."

"I suddenly feel myself becoming a gambling man. Okay, Sharon, you feel so strongly about the kid and you think you can find out something that'll crack the case, go ahead and fly down there. But on one condition: if you succeed, you get your expenses and ten times your fee. If you don't, you get nothing, and you work nine more jobs for us free of charge."

Jesus, me and my smart mouth! I was a damned fool for making such a wager at a time when I was starting a new business. But my pride wouldn't allow me to backpedal, not with Renshaw. Hoping I sounded more confident than I felt, I said, "You've got yourself a bet."

We shook on it.

After I'd made arrangements for Gage to either get hold of Habiba's passport or a false one on which she could travel, I went to find Hy. The poker game he'd mentioned was going on in one of the second-floor conference rooms. When he saw me he turned his cards face down and said, "I fold. Cash in my chips, will you, Bruce? I'll collect from you later."

As he came toward me I noticed he looked pale. He grinned easily when he took my arm, though, and we went into the corridor. "The next time you get to thinking I don't appreciate you," he said, "just remember that I folded with a pair of aces. So did my wishing you luck pay off?"

"Yes, it did." As we walked to the corner office that he seldom used, I gave him a brief rundown on my evening's activities, including my wager with Renshaw.

"My God, McCone, I ought to send you to Gamblers Anonymous!"

"Yes, I'm beginning to understand how people get in trouble. But anyway, I'm leaving for St. Maarten at twelve-thirty. Want to come along?"

"Wish I could, but I'm moving on this Haitian project tomorrow."

"So soon?"

"Situation's heating up. Foolish to delay any longer."

"Well, good luck."

"Thanks. Actually, it'll be a piece of cake."

I followed him into the office and flopped on the leather couch. Suddenly I felt beat, the prospect of two long plane flights overwhelming me. Maybe I'd be able to sleep en route—if my mind didn't get too active, if I wasn't visited by nightmares of a body floating on the black water, if . . .

Hy sat next to me, his arm around my shoulders. My gaze wandered about the office. It was expensively and tastefully furnished, courtesy of RKI's decorator, but contained no trace of its occasional occupant, save a gnarled chunk of what looked to be porous rock but actually was calcified vegetation from one of the towers of Tufa Lake near his ranch in Mono County. Hy's late wife's environmental foundation had saved the dying lake from virtual extinction.

Sometimes I wondered if my lover didn't miss the rough-and-tumble ecological wars in which he'd been a frontline soldier for many years, but recently I'd realized that his current work suited him better. The edge was off the environmental battles; the Spaulding Foundation continued its work under a white flag of uneasy truce. But there was a part of Hy that needed conflict, that courted danger in the same way I did. Harness it to the business of saving lives, and it was an asset; leave it untethered, and it could become a lethal liability.

"Where did you say you're flying into?" he asked.

"St. Maarten."

"You probably could use a contact there." He got up, consulted a Rolodex, and scribbled a few lines on a scratch pad. "Cam Connors, old buddy of mine, runs an air-charter service out of there; lives in Marigot, the capital of St. Martin, the French side of the island. I'll call him, tell him you're coming."

"Thanks." I tucked the paper in my wallet. "Do you happen to know somebody in every corner of the world?"

"Just about." He sat down again and began nuzzling my neck.

"Quit!" I exclaimed. "I've got to go home and dig out my passport. I've got to pack, and I'm not sure what shape my hot-weather clothes are in."

"Why're women always worried about what to wear?" He bit my earlobe and nuzzled some more, lower.

"I can't go down there not looking like a tourist; I don't want to call attention to myself."

"Pay attention to *this*."

"Ripinsky! I have to—Hy!"

Well, maybe I did have a half hour to spare. . . .

37,000 Feet Above The Grand Canyon

May 23, 4:49 A.M., MDT

I replaced the Airfone in its cradle on the seatback in front of me, extracted my American Express card from the slot, and began to worry seriously. I'd been calling Adah every half hour since my flight left SFO, and still there was no answer. I was half tempted to call her parents, Barbara and Rupert, but I didn't want to alarm them unnecessarily. Besides, if Barbara thought her daughter was in danger, she'd be out scouring the streets for her, and Rupert would be banging on the mayor's door, demanding to know why he hadn't made those streets safe for his little girl.

And Adah, once she surfaced, would kill me.

Their excesses aside, sometimes I envied Adah her parents. After we McCone kids fled the nest, my mother used to fuss endlessly about us, but now that her new love, Melvin Hunt, had sold his chain of Laundromats, they'd begun to travel extensively; what little news I had from her came on postcards from foreign lands. The photograph she'd recently sent of herself riding in a rickshaw in Hong Kong couldn't begin to replace the weekly phone calls she used to make from home. As for my father, even before Ma divorced him he'd spent most of his time puttering in the garage while singing bawdy ballads. Now he too had found himself a companion, a widow named Nancy Sullivan, and they were constantly on the go in Pa's Chevy Suburban, a new Airstream trailer hitched to its rear. They didn't even send postcards.

Time passes, the structure of a family disintegrates. I could accept that. You stay close to some members, as I had to my brother John and sister Charlene; you drift away from others, as I had from my brother Joey and sister Patsy. But I'd never dreamed that Ma and Pa would drift away from us.

Maybe that was why I'd embarked on such a frenzy of nest-feathering at the cottage. Create a new structure, a new shared home. That, and the fact that I sensed a number of my old friendships at All Souls and elsewhere to be fading away. My focus had narrowed to the tried-and-true: Hank and his wife Anne-Marie, Rae, Ted, Adah. And of course, Hy. . . .

My hand strayed toward the Airfone. Hy was staying at RKI's hospitality suite tonight; I could call him, relay my anxiety about Adah, ask him to check on her—

No, he needed his rest. He was leaving for the Dominican Republic tomorrow, and then he'd cross the border into strife-torn Haiti to bring out the political dissident. Piece of cake, he'd called it, and I didn't believe that for an instant.

Thinking about the danger he'd face put chills on my shoulder blades, what-ifs in my mind.

To banish them I leaned back, closed my eyes, listened to the thrum of the engines. Immediately images began to flicker against the back of my eyelids.

Habiba sitting in the passenger seat of the MG, begging to be taken for a ride—lost little girl who worried about her mother and missed her father. Mavis dealing out a hand of solitaire in front of her fireplace—lost wounded woman who missed the days when she wrote her poems. Mavis floating facedown in the water, the poems lost to her forever. Langley Newton's face when he said, "I hate men who prey on women." Eric Sparling's face when he said, "I just hope I'm not sending you to the same fate as the Hamid woman." And Habiba's dark eyes: what they must have seen at the marina, what they might be witnessing now.

I forced my own eyes open. The images were all unbearably lonely.

Maybe it was only the plane: so huge compared to the Citabria, so full of strangers. In the Citabria I'd flown through a high, beautiful world guided only by my fledgling pilot's instincts and felt not the least bit lonely. But in this 767 I felt as if I'd been abandoned on a distant space satellite.

Lonesome world up here. Down there too, sometimes.

PART TWO

THE LEEWARD ISLANDS

MAY 23–25

Fifteen

It was drizzling and muggy when I landed at Princess Juliana Airport on St. Maarten. The little yellow terminal seemed stuck in another time, the Netherlands' crown princess having long ago been succeeded as queen by her daughter. We left the aircraft by stairs rather than a jetway and crossed tarmac from which steam rose in plumes. By the time I cleared Immigration, the light Tee that I'd changed to during my brief stopover in San Juan was sweat-plastered to my back. I hurried outside and encountered a swarm of taxi drivers.

A tall chocolate-skinned man in a Dodgers cap accosted me first, speaking softly and swiftly in French-flavored English. I gave him Cam Connors's address on Rue de la Liberté in Marigot, and we agreed on a price and set out in a red Toyota Celica that had seen hard service. In spite of the fact he was taking me to St. Martin, the French side of the island, the driver—whose name was Kenny—kept up a running commentary on the hotels and restaurants that clustered near the airport. The monologue—much of it in outdated American slang—relaxed me because I didn't really have to listen and, more important, because it proved that my tourist guise was convincing. I stared out the window at the pastel high-rise hotels that rose across a silver-gray lagoon, then looked toward

the cloud-draped hills of the island's interior. After a while
the oppressive heat made me nod off.

I was a few frames into a cool dream of walking on the
beach at Bootlegger's Cove when the cab came to such an
abrupt halt that I had to grab the armrest to keep from sliding
to the floor. The Toyota's front bumper was only inches from
the back of a bus, and traffic ahead had stopped. "Philipsburg,"
Kenny said with a philosophical shrug that I took to mean it
was always congested there. "Bypass," he added, wrenching
the wheel to the left and gunning between two oncoming cars.

The side street he turned onto was narrow and potholed,
lined with pastel cinder-block houses with corrugated iron
roofs. People lounged on their porches or in their doorways,
the women clad in bright-colored shift dresses reminiscent of
the fifties, the men wearing T-shirts and tropical-weight pants.
Children played in the dirt, and an inordinate number of mangy
dogs lazed in the street. The dogs were supremely confident,
barely raising their heads at the taxi's approach; Kenny oblig-
ingly steered around them. Interspersed among the residences
were lottery-ticket stands that seemed to be doing a turnaway
business; they put me in mind of Speed Schechtmann.

For a moment I considered asking Kenny if he knew of
Schechtmann or Jumbie Cay, but decided against it. On a
small island of less than thirty thousand population, word of
the unusual gets around fast; an American woman asking
about things no tourist had business knowing would certainly
qualify.

We rejoined the main road on the other side of Philipsburg
and Kenny began telling me an involved story about a
Dutchman and a Frenchman dividing the island by walking
in opposite directions around its perimeter until they came
face-to-face again. Its punch line was that the French got the
lion's share because the Dutchman was fat and stopped on
the way for gin. Kenny, who had told me he lived on the
French side, laughed uproariously and slapped the steering
wheel. The story probably wasn't true, he said, but it was a
good one on the Dutch, wasn't it?

I laughed politely and agreed it was a good one—and
wished I'd chosen a less talkative driver. I appreciated his

efforts at making me feel welcome, but the combination of his chatter and the hot muggy air was now making me edgy.

Finally we crested a hill and a sign appeared saying we were entering St. Martin. After the congestion around the airport and Philipsburg, Marigot seemed tranquil, with a tropical French feel that reminded me of New Orleans in the sleepy off-season. The buildings were graceful pastel structures, many fronted by sidewalk cafés; small shade-dappled parks abounded. I supposed Kenny was giving me the full tourist treatment, because he drove down to the quay at the crescent-shaped harbor where freighters and a Cunard Lines cruise ship lay at anchor. The drizzle had stopped, and slivers of sunlight pierced the clouds; vendors at an open-air market along the waterfront were pulling tarps off their displays of T-shirts and other souvenirs. On the streets people in cruise clothes strolled, dazzled by the arrays of merchandise in the windows of the duty-free shops. Finally Kenny brought the cab to a stop at a two-storied white stucco building with ornate wrought-iron balconies draped in cascades of vermilion flowers.

Cam Connors's number was one of those painted on the building's wall below an arrow pointing to a narrow cobble-stoned passageway. I paid Kenny, taking the card he offered and promising to call him should I want a tour of the interior, and slung the strap of my travel bag over my shoulder. The passageway led to a courtyard with palmetto trees growing in its center; more blossom-draped balconies overlooked it. I climbed a staircase, located a door, and followed an interior hallway around two bends before I came to Connors's apartment.

The man who answered my knock was tall and well built, probably in his early forties, with a deep saltwater tan, sun-bleached hair, and brilliant eyes that regarded me with frank curiosity. "You're Sharon," he said. "Ripinsky gave me your ETA, and I've been waiting for you. Come in. How were your flights?"

"Long." I let him take my bag and stepped into a spacious room furnished spartanly in rattan. The parquet floors were bare, the whitewashed walls unadorned, and two ceiling fans turned lazily.

"Did Ripinsky tell you why I'm here?" I asked.

Connors set the bag down, motioned at a chair, and shook his head. "He just asked me to give you whatever you need and advised me not to cross you because you've got a temper and are stubborn as hell."

"I can always count on him to present me in my best light." I sank onto the chair, weariness creeping up on me.

"Actually he said some flattering things." Connors sat opposite me. "Sounded smitten, to tell the truth."

I smiled. "You've known him a long time?"

"We go back to the seventies when we both flew for K-Air in Bangkok."

"Ah, so you also worked for Dan Kessell."

"Yeah, my bad luck. Ripinsky said you're on a job for Kessell's firm. How is the old bastard?"

I shrugged. "I've only met him once; he keeps a very low profile."

"Smart of him, considering his past." Connors's gaze lost its edge and muddied a bit. I'd seen that same expression in Hy's eyes when he talked about those days in Thailand.

I said, "The partner I've been dealing with is Gage Renshaw. You know him?"

"Sure, we're old drinking buddies."

"Then you probably understand him better than I. I can't get a handle on him."

"Nobody can." Connors paused, reflective. "I think what it boils down to with Gage is compartments. He's made up of hundreds of little boxes, all strictly segregated. This person or this experience goes in here, that concept or that emotion goes in there. It's a good way to avoid personal conflict, but it doesn't make for much consistency."

"Interesting take on him. I'll have to remember that." I turned the conversation back to my host. "So you flew in Southeast Asia during the seventies and then . . . ?"

"Well, Ripinsky's probably told you how ugly it was over there. After a while, if you had any conscience at all, you got sick of the profiteering and the trafficking, and heartily sick of death. I was on a roller coaster that was about to jump the tracks when Ripinsky decided to bail out."

"That was around nineteen eighty?"

He nodded. "I remember it very clearly: we were in a bar in Hong Kong. This Chinese asshole was singing countryand-western and smirking at all us Americans who they were ripping off with their cover charge and watered drinks. Ripinsky took one look at him and said, 'Man, I've got to get out of this life and back to the high desert where I can feel clean again. If you've got any sense, you'll get out, too; otherwise you've got no future.'

"Now, the high desert's one thing, but me, I was raised in Gary, Indiana. Talk about dirty! I told him, 'No way. I'm making a fortune over here, and there isn't any place I want to go back to.' He said, 'You don't want to end up like Dan Kessell. Or dead.' And for the next couple of weeks he kept after me about it. When he finally wore me down, I spun a mental globe. It stopped and I said, 'Hey, I'm going to the Caribbean.'"

"And obviously it worked out."

"Took a while. First I headed down to Trinidad, flew for another charter service. I didn't much like it there, so I worked my way up through the Windwards—St. Lucia, Martinique. They were okay places, but I didn't feel enough of a connection to settle down. Then one day I hitched a ride on a freighter and when it sailed into Marigot Bay, I knew I was home. I've been here ten years. Used the money I stashed away while I was in Bangkok to buy a seaplane and started ferrying tourists around; later I branched out into intcrisland freight. Now I've got a fleet of seven planes and twenty-one employees."

"Not bad, for only ten years."

"Not bad, for a guy who by all rights shouldn't've seen his thirtieth birthday." The muddy look returned, but he quickly snapped back to the present. "No more about me now. You're down here on business. I'll get us a couple of beers, you tell me about it."

Connors left the room and I leaned my head against the back of the chair, watching the ceiling fans make their lazy orbit. They didn't do much good; I was damp with sweat. When Cam came back with a pair of ice-cold Beck's, I rolled the bottle against my forehead before sipping. Then I explained what I was after as best I could without going into unnecessary detail. "What I need now is more information about Jumbie Cay and Klaus Schechtmann," I finished.

Connors frowned and set his empty bottle on the floor; steepled his fingers and thought for a minute. "Well, something's wrong on that island, that's for sure. The natives talk about it in whispers. Of course, they've always been superstitious about the place—its name, you know."

"What does it mean?"

"A jumbie's an evil spirit. Can be either a person or an animal. It's said to walk at night."

"Why would anyone give an island a name like that?"

"Well, it isn't the most hospitable place."

"The people?"

"No, the land. Rocky shores, barren hills, bad water. About the only thing that can scratch out much of a living on it is a goat."

"Have you ever been there?"

He shook his head.

"The people who left the San Francisco area by ship—how would they get there, and how long would it take?"

"Tough question." He got up to fetch more beers. When he came back he said, "A lot depends on how fast they want to get there. They could stay on the ship they rendezvoused with, sail down the Pacific Coast and through the Panama Canal. But if this Schechtmann has made the trip often, he'd probably choose a quicker way. They might put into a small Mexican port where the officials're easily bribed, travel overland, and fly out of Mexico City. Or they might arrange to be picked up at the ship by helicopter or seaplane, then catch a commercial or charter flight at any number of airports. You say Schechtmann's rich; if money's no object, there're plenty of combinations he could use."

"Okay—assuming the fastest way, how long would it take them to reach Jumbie Cay?"

He calculated. "They're probably there now."

No time to waste, then. "How can I get to the island?"

"You're really determined to go there?"

"I wouldn't be here if I wasn't. Why?"

"Well, the kid *is* with her father. And there're things . . . that you probably shouldn't be getting involved in."

"Such as?"

He shook his head, looked away. "I've got a bad feeling about this, that's all."

"Cam, I need your help."

". . . Yeah, all right." He thought for a moment. "There's a fellow I know, gambler by the name of Zeff Lash, who might've been over there."

"Where can I find him?"

"He lives in the Quarter over near Philipsburg—you probably bypassed through there on your way from the airport."

"If you'll give me his address and point me at someplace where I can rent a car—"

"Whoa! Ripinsky asked me to give you what you need. I'm going with you."

"That's not necessary. I don't want to take up any more of your time—"

"I've got nothing doing tonight, and you don't want to go to the Quarter alone."

"I'll be okay."

"You speak French or Dutch?"

"No."

"You carrying a piece?"

I'd left the .38 at home; there was no way that someone with only a California carry permit could bring a weapon over international boundaries. "No," I admitted.

"Well, tourists've had some problems in that area recently. Besides, I doubt Lash'll talk with you alone. Me, he owes a favor."

The remark was reminiscent of Hy; sometimes I pictured him and his old buddies as points on a global diagram of interlocking obligations that resembled an airline's route map. "Okay," I said, "can we go now?"

"Not till at least eleven tonight. Zeff Lash is what you'd call a late riser."

I chafed a little at the delay, but my impatience was quickly overridden by weariness. "Then if you'll recommend a hotel—"

"I've got a guest room."

"Cam, you don't have to put me up, too."

"I want to."

"You must owe Hy big time."

His expression grew uncomfortable. "Well, I told you about that night in Hong Kong."

"Then I accept your hospitality. And I thank you."

"Why don't you get some rest now? Around nine we'll go to dinner at my friend Ben's restaurant. He makes a great curried conch that'll set us up fine for tackling Zeff Lash."

The potholed streets of the Quarter throbbed with a rhythmic beat emanating from a hundred different sources. The night was inky dark, warm, and velvety soft; the air caressed my bare skin and carried the scent of unidentifiable blossoms. Unfortunately, the bugs were out in force, and even the organic repellent Cam had made me rub on my face, arms, and legs didn't discourage them. I swatted furiously as we walked past a closed lottery shack toward a cluster of pale cinder-block houses.

Voices surged through the darkness—quick lilting talk, high-pitched laughter, angry shouts. Dogs barked, a child wailed, a woman sobbed. A cat screeched, and another answered. In spite of the lateness of the hour, the Quarter seethed with life—hidden, intense, vaguely dangerous. My body responded to it, adrenaline building and flowing.

Connors guided me to a pink house whose door and windows were shuttered; slanting shafts of light striped the packed dirt below them. He knocked, and abruptly the voices inside grew still. Footsteps came up to the door and a man with Medusa-like dreadlocks looked out. Cam spoke lengthily to him in French, and he stared at me, frowning deeper and deeper.

"Jus'so?" he asked when Connors finished.

"Jus'so."

"But, mon, I holdin' aces."

His words brought a bittersweet taste to my mouth as I remembered Hy folding at the RKI data-search section poker game last night. I swallowed, tucked the memory away for now.

Cam spoke in French again. The man—Zeff Lash, I assumed—looked irritated, then chastened. He shrugged and turned away, shutting the door on us.

"No?" I asked.

"Yes. He's cashing in, will meet us at Eudoxie's. That's a bar around the corner."

Eudoxie's was one small room crammed with white plastic furniture of the kind that appears worldwide at hardware and garden-supply stores on the day spring takes its first tentative breath. There was a pair of slot machines against one wall next to a pass-through window where you placed your drink orders. A middle-aged couple talking quietly at a corner table were the only customers.

While Cam went to order, I sat down, instantly recognizing the chair's contours from previous encounters with its American relatives. He returned from the window with three glasses, set one on the table, and handed me another. "What's this?" I asked, regarding the colorless liquid warily.

"Gin."

"I thought rum was the drink of choice in the Caribbean."

"But you're also in the Netherlands Antilles."

"I see." I remembered the cab driver's story about the Frenchman and the Dutchman. The gin was warm and raw; quickly I set the glass down.

Cam smiled at my grimace, his eyes moving toward the door. Zeff Lash had just come in; he nodded to us, his bony face creasing in a wide grin as he spotted his waiting drink. He picked it up, knocked it back, and handed the glass to Cam. Cam went to the window for a refill.

Lash sat down and looked me over. "You a dick, huh?"

"What?"

"Dick, like on TV."

"Oh, right."

"Connors say you want to ask me about Jumbie Cay. Little girl got snatched, they take her there."

"Yes. She's only nine years old. Her mother was killed when they took her."

He scowled fiercely. "I got girls of my own. Somebody messes with them . . ."

Connors came back with Lash's drink and sat on the other side of him. He asked, "So, mon, can you help the lady?"

Lash ran his tongue over his lips. "I don' know. The folks out there, they not just kicksin'—they mean business."

"Remember what I told you earlier." There was a warning note in Connors's voice.

"Yeah, mon, okay." Lash turned back to me. "Start at the beginning, huh? For a long time Jumbie Cay belong to the British, but it really be owned by the Altagracia family. Don' suppose you know them."

I shook my head.

"Don' matter. Zebediah, he be the only one left out there now. Regina, his oldest girl, live over here in Princes Quarter, keep goats on a little farm. She hate the old man, won't have nothin' to do with him, and the rest, they all in the States, think they havin' the good life, but what d'they know? Anyways, maybe twenty-five years ago old Zeb got a wild hair up his butt about the Brits. I don' remember what they done to him, but he wasn't takin' any more of it. So he rip a page out of your country's history book and declare independence. And you know what? The Brits don' even care. That island got no fresh water, not even weeds grow right. What the Brits want with it anyhow?

"Okay, months go by. Then Zeb get a letter from the Prime Minister at St. Kitts-Nevis—that be the seat of government for those islands. It say, 'We understand you unhappy with your status as a British dependency.' He answer back, 'You damn right. I want my independence.' And the Brits say, 'Okay, good luck.' So there was Zeb with no fight on his hands. I don' know what made him madder—belongin' to the Brits or bein' let go so easy." Lash laughed, smacking the table with his hand. He finished his drink, looked expectantly at Cam.

Cam went for yet another refill.

"Okay," Lash went on, "nothing much happen after that. Zeb bring up his kids, they go off, his wife die. The island kind of fall apart 'cause now the Brits ain't around to keep up the roads and such. Zeb, he always be a gambler, but eight, ten years ago he get into betting sports on this toll-free number. You know about that kind of book?"

"Yes."

"Well, Zeb, he get himself in big, and jus'so, he owe a lot

of money. But he think they can't touch him on his island. Then this fella from the States show up, tell him to settle or else, and Zeb can't."

"Was the fellow Speed—Klaus Schechtmann?"

"Yeah, that the one. Anyways, Zeb work a deal with him. He sell him Jumbie Cay, and Schechtmann let him keep his house and some land."

"What did Schechtmann want with the island?" I was reasonably sure my information was correct, but I wanted Lash to confirm it.

He smiled slyly as he extended his hand for the full glass Connors brought him. "It a damned good place to run a sports book from."

"You know for sure that's what he's doing?"

"Yeah."

"Have you been to Jumbie Cay since Schechtmann bought it?"

"Sure. Zeb and me're friends, go back a long ways. Sometimes I visit him."

"Have you ever seen Schechtmann?"

"Uh-uh. He got a compound out on Goat Point. Never leave it."

"What about a man named Dawud Hamid? Have you heard of him?"

Lash glanced at Connors. "Hamid. That the Arab. I hear about him, but I never see him."

"Okay, Mr. Lash, how can I get onto Jumbie Cay without attracting the attention of the people at the compound?"

Again he glanced at Cam. "Bad idea."

I suspected he was right, but I merely repeated the question.

He asked, "You just goin' to the island, or you want into the compound?"

"The compound."

"Bad, *bad* idea."

"I'll worry about that."

"Sharon," Cam said, "you ought to listen to Zeff."

"Maybe I ought, but there's a little girl on that island who needs my help."

"You said she was with her father."

"I also said that's the wrong place for her."

"How can you be sure?"

Good question, but I couldn't explain to him the violent stirrings of the gut-level instinct I'd always relied on. "I *am* sure—that's all I can tell you."

Connors compressed his lips. After a moment he said, "Ripinsky warned me you were stubborn."

"Too damn stubborn for her own good, maybe," Lash muttered.

I turned toward him. "Why?"

"That compound, it got guards, army of them. They using assault weapons, AK-forty-sevens. Then there's the Dobermans. You ever tangle with a Doberman?"

He was trying to scare me. It worked, but I wasn't going to back down. "Mr. Lash, for the last time—how can I get onto Jumbie Cay?"

He spoke swiftly in French to Connors.

"What?" I snapped, fed up with their cryptic conversations.

Connors shrugged, eyes troubled. "He's concerned for you, Sharon. So am I."

"I'm through with arguing, Cam. If the two of you can't help me—"

He sighed and nodded to Lash. "You better help her."

Lash studied me for a moment. "Okay—you a good swimmer?"

"Yes." It was the one form of exercise I really enjoyed, and recently I'd been swimming laps at the health club Adah had talked me into joining.

"Then you get somebody to fly you there in a seaplane. Drop you off at night off Marlin Landing. There be a restaurant, Nel's Place. Belong to Nel Simpson, friend of mine. You swim towards the orange lights on his dock."

"And he'll get me into the compound?"

Lash's lips tightened.

"Look," I said, "the little girl's mother was an American, and she was born on American soil; that makes her a U.S. citizen. I don't want to bring our State Department in on this because of some complicated circumstances surrounding it, but if I have to, I will. That might cause trouble for your friend Zeb."

Two two men exchanged glances that contained both reluctance and, on Connors's part, a warning. After a moment Lash said, "Okay, I tell Nel. Maybe he find a way to get you in there."

"And if not?"

Lash set his glass down and spread his hands. "Then, lady, you on your own. I tell you this much: you go near that compound without a damn good plan, for sure you gonna die."

Sixteen

Black star-filled sky, blacker water. Orange lights in the distance. I'm all alone. Should be afraid, but I'm not.

Waves gentle, water warm. Soft tropic breeze against my face. My limbs are leaden. Should swim for shore, but I can't.

I start to sink, but feel no panic. I want to lose myself in this warm darkness. The water closes over my head. Safe at last.

But what's that?

Something floating on the surface above me, great wings spread. A giant bat.

I glide closer, look up. Not a bat, a woman. The wings are a robe billowing on the swell. And her eyes . . . They're empty holes. I can see through them, down into her soul. But there's only darkness there.

Oh God, Mavis, your blank forever eyes—

I jerked upright, clutching at my throat, my heart pounding. My breath came in short, harsh gasps and sweat filmed my body. It was hideously hot. I itched from a hundred insect bites. Something had even stung the knuckle of my little finger; it felt as if a match were being held to it. Glaring light slanted through the half-closed louvers on the window next to the bed. I looked around at the simple furnishings, my travel bag, my discarded clothing.

After a minute my panic ebbed. I propped up the pillows, leaned back, reached for my watch where it lay on the nightstand. One thirty-three; I'd awakened from a nightmare in the middle of the day.

Anxiety, of course, over the prospect of striking off in unfamiliar waters toward a strange place in the dark of night. Dark of *tonight*, because I'd persuaded Cam to fly me to Jumbie Cay as soon as possible. At first he'd refused, then tried to talk me out of it for hours after we left Zeff Lash. When he finally gave in, he said he wanted to go along. I wouldn't allow it; his debt was to Hy, not to me.

The dream images returned: all alone in the dark sea . . .

For the first time my resolve weakened. I permitted myself to wonder if I'd be doing Habiba a favor by bringing her home to her despotic grandmother. After all, as Cam had repeatedly pointed out, Dawud Hamid *was* her father; he had a right to her. But then my uneasy feeling about Hamid returned, and I thought of Speed Schechtmann and what might go on inside his closely guarded compound. I suspected Malika Hamid was ignorant of how Schechtmann was accustomed to living, had only sent Mavis and Habiba with him to get them out of harm's way at the consulate. She fully intended for them to return to her control when the bomb threat was finally laid to rest. But now that Mavis was dead and Dawud had possession of his daughter, I doubted he'd willingly relinquish her. Whatever control his mother once exercised over him had been severely weakened, if not destroyed, when Habiba stepped ashore at Jumbie Cay.

My resolve firmed again. Malika Hamid might be tyrannical, but she loved Habiba and she wasn't a criminal. Better the little girl live with her than her father and his corrupt associates.

As Connors and I had argued into the small hours of the morning, he'd asked me why I cared so much about a child I'd only seen twice. I simply told him that she was an exceptionally appealing little girl who deserved a chance in life, but of course that wasn't the half of it. From the moment I'd seen her solemn eyes regarding me over the lip of the huge urn at the consulate I'd connected with her. From the moment

she'd owned up to her loneliness I'd been solidly in her corner.
I, too, had been a lonely child.

You wouldn't have suspected it, had you seen the McCone
household during my growing-up years. Five kids—two older
brothers, me in the middle, two younger sisters. Aunts and
uncles and cousins stopping in by day or night. Dogs and cats
underfoot; hamsters and gerbils escaping their cages; a pair
of turkeys named Gregory Peck and—my bawdy father's
contribution—Gregory Pecker scratching away in their pen.
A gaggle of friends belonging to each of us crowding the
rambling house that was constantly in the throes of an ongoing
renovation project that eventually would span two decades.
How, you might ask, could anyone be lonely in a place that
resembled a beehive on a June day?

It wasn't as difficult as it might seem. I was the middle
child, and middle children are often overlooked. I wasn't a
rowdy male ever on the brink of juvenile delinquency like
John and Joey, nor was I a rebellious female ever on the brink
of teenage pregnancy like Charlene and Patsy. Instead I was
the one who made no waves, was on the honor roll, made
the cheerleading squad and the prom queen's court. Oh, there
was one disgraceful episode when I was caught in a compro-
mising position with the captain of the swim team—now
family legend, Mick claimed. But if so, it was only legendary
because it involved the white sheep of the flock. Otherwise
I played it safe, as John once bitterly told me.

Always playing it safe makes for loneliness.

There was a coldness at the core of our household, too, in
spite of a lot of ritualistic hugging and kissing. Pa was a chief
in the navy, often out to sea; when he retired, his sojourns in
his garage workshop lengthened to the extent that he frequently slept there on a cot. Ma was busy juggling the demands
of raising five kids on a very limited budget; she had no time
for our questions or problems, and usually she put them off
until they were either unimportant or critical. I suppose the
emotional vacuum was what made John drink and get into
brawls and Joey go off on petty-thieving rampages. I suppose
it was what made Charlene decide to get pregnant while still
in her senior year of high school and Patsy run away from
home at fifteen.

I know for sure it was what made me a loner—a dreamer who spent hours by herself in the tree house in our backyard canyon. Eventually the web of schemes I spun there would bind me more firmly within my isolation. I went off to college at Berkeley, where I knew no one. I financed my education by taking lonely graveyard-shift security jobs. Then I moved from Berkeley to San Francisco as soon as I graduated. If I hadn't run into my old housemate, Hank Zahn, in front of City Hall one day, all my college ties would have remained severed. Even when I went to work for very little money at All Souls, I refused their offer of a rent-free room, preferring my tiny, overpriced studio apartment. I formed romantic relationships, but never let down my guard enough to allow true intimacy.

But then I met Hy, who was shaped by a similar emotional vacuum. Together we'd made a life that worked for us.

Those years before Hy hadn't been unhappy ones, but they'd taught me some bitter lessons; and the sum of those lessons made me afraid for Habiba. If she remained on Jumbie Cay, she might never be in real physical jeopardy, but she might be emotionally scarred by events no child need experience. Most certainly she would become more tightly bound within the web of isolation she'd already begun spinning. But unlike me, she would never have the chance to break free. Her world would forever be a wild and lonely one.

That was why I'd swim through those unfamiliar waters toward a strange place tonight. That was why I'd do my damnedest to take her home.

The previous evening Zeff Lash had mentioned that the old man who sold Jumbie Cay to Schechtmann had an estranged daughter living on this island. After I showered and dressed I checked the phone book, but there was no listing for a Regina Altagracia. Of course, that didn't have to be her name now—she might have married—and I wasn't sure where Princes Quarter was, anyway. Cam had gone out on an early charter and wouldn't be back till after six, so I couldn't ask him. As I paged through the directory to the section for rental-car companies, though, I remembered the card Kenny had handed me yesterday when I paid my cab fare.

I called the number on the card and found the driver at
home. Sure, he knew where Princes Quarter was, and he also
knew Regina Altagracia's goat farm. "Snazzy family around
here once," he added. "No more."

I asked him what he'd charge to take me there.

"Thirty bucks, U.S.?" He sounded so tentative that I was
certain he'd doubled his usual rate.

"Fine." After all, it was RKI's money. "Pick me up where
you left me yesterday, please. In an hour."

I set the receiver in its cradle and calculated the time difference between here and San Francisco. It was ten-seventeen
in the morning there. Cam had told me the best way to make
an international call was through an independent long-distance
carrier that accepted Visa; I punched in the number he'd
written down and gave the operator the numbers for my card
and for Adah Joslyn.

Joslyn's phone rang eleven times before I hung up. No
answering machine again. Had she been home at all since I
last tried to call her? Time to have someone look into the
situation.

I redialed the long-distance carrier, this time giving Greg
Marcus's extension at the Hall of Justice. The call went
through quickly, and Greg's voice came on the line as clear
as if I were phoning from across town.

Not so on his end. He said, "Where're you calling from?
You sound like you're in a tunnel."

"I'm in the Caribbean." To forestall questions, I added,
"Long-distance minutes here are as precious as diamonds.
Did you find out anything about the people I asked you to
run checks on?"

"Nothing except the gambling indictment on Schechtmann.
Nothing on his wife, Ronquillo, or Newton, but plenty on
Chloe Love. She's dead, was murdered in her apartment in
Oakland's Lake Merritt district on January twenty-sixth, nineteen ninety. That much I got from my lady, who knew her
from when they were both students at the Culinary Academy.
Yesterday I called an OPD guy who worked a couple of
homicides in cooperation with me a few years back; he
accessed their records on the case. Nasty business: she was

raped and strangled. Dawud Hamid was questioned about the murder—very briefly."

My skin prickled and I gripped the receiver more tightly. "Briefly, because an attorney appeared and put a stop to the questioning on grounds of diplomatic immunity?"

"You got it. He was in and out of headquarters within two hours."

And early the next month he'd dropped out of sight. According to Mavis, the police hadn't been called because it was too soon after some event she then refused to discuss. She thought her mother-in-law had hired private detectives, but I now suspected that was a fiction designed to keep Mavis from finding out that Malika had sent Dawud abroad to live. But why to Klaus Schechtmann, whose influence had already weakened the once-strong hold she had on her son? Why not back to Azad?

I could think of one reason: the born-again Sheik Zayid bin Muhammad al-Hamid had reinstituted the death penalty for murder and rape. The sheik had been rough on family members before and, as I understood it, Muslim law had worldwide jurisdiction. Malika didn't want to risk her son being tried for his crimes in an Azadi court—and possibly being stoned to death.

"Greg," I asked, "why did they question Hamid?"

"He'd been bothering Love. Not exactly stalking her, but close enough that she went to her attorney two days before she died to get a restraining order against him. The attorney told her nothing could be done because of his diplomatic status."

"Did they ever solve the murder?"

"It's an open file, and it always will be."

"Because Hamid actually was the perp."

"Right. There was enough physical evidence that he'd been in the apartment to bring charges, plus an eyewitness who saw him leaving the building at the right time. The D.A. was considering charging him anyway, maybe making a landmark case of it, but then Hamid disappeared." Even from thousands of miles away I could feel Greg's anger; it infected me, made me more determined to get Habiba off that island.

"Greg, one more thing—I'm worried about Adah Joslyn.

She left me a message on Monday saying she had a lead on the bomber and I should call her, but she hasn't been answering her phone and her machine's off. Can you check on her?"

"Sure. Do you want me to call you back?"

"No, I'd better call you."

"Wait—what're you doing in the Caribbean? Does it have to do with—"

"Thanks, Greg."

One more detail to take care of. I called RKI and was patched through to Renshaw at the consulate. "I can only talk for a minute," I said. "Did you get hold of Habiba's passport?"

"Yes. The kid has dual citizenship—U.S. and Azadi. Schechtmann took the Azadi passport, didn't want the American."

Better for me that way; an Azadi child traveling with an unrelated American might attract attention. "How'd you persuade Hamid to hand it over?"

"I didn't. Kahlil Lateef snagged it from the consulate safe."

"Good for him. Now—I need it tomorrow morning. Any problem with that?"

"I'll send it by courier, one of our people. Where?"

"The airport, by nine. If I don't show, he should hang around till I do."

"You'll recognize him by our blazer. Anything else?"

There was a soft rap at the door. Kenny, early. "Not now, but I'll be in touch." I told Kenny to wait a minute, then called the airline and made reservations for Habiba and me on tomorrow morning's flight to Miami.

Princes Quarter lay inland: a lushly green valley studded with cholla cactus, where trees and brambles that Kenny called thorn forest grew in profusion. Small rock formations protruded among the vegetation, and free-ranging goats scrambled over or perched atop them, regarding the taxi solemnly as we drove by. Rain-filled clouds lowered over the surrounding hills, threatening to sweep down their slopes and dump their burdens on us.

Kenny was curiously subdued this afternoon; perhaps he'd realized I was not a normal tourist. He commented once or twice on the scenery, called a goat that wouldn't move out of the road a "fuckwit," but otherwise we rode in silence.

After thirty-some minutes he reduced speed, pointing to two piles of stones that marked a dirt track. As he steered between them he said, "This Miz Altagracia's place."

"She's not married?"

"No mon in his right senses go near that dame. She jus' sit out here with her goats, dry up like a dead crab on the beach."

"Why?"

He looked puzzled, then shrugged. Clearly he wasn't one to question root causes. People did what they did, and that was that.

We drove through more thorn forest and then a house came into view: whitewashed shingles, with a peaked red iron roof and wooden louvers on the doors and windows. A second building stood next to it, joined by a latticed walkway overgrown by hanging vines; its windows were covered by storm shutters for hurricane season. Brown, black, and white goats noshed on what little greenery remained in front of the house; they scattered, bleating, when Kenny tooted the horn. As he brought the Toyota to a stop, the louvers on the front door opened slightly. I felt, but couldn't see, someone looking out.

Kenny asked, "How long you be?"

"I'm not sure. Can you wait?"

He shrugged. "I already miss the three o'clock plane from San Juan, so yeah, I guess."

"If I'm more than fifteen minutes, I'll pay ten dollars extra."

That satisfied him. He switched on the radio, leaned back, and tilted his Dodgers cap over his eyes. As I walked toward the house rhythmic, percussion-dominated music followed me.

Before I could knock, the door opened on well-oiled hinges. A tall, heavyset woman with tight gray curls above a high square forehead regarded me, eyes squinting myopically. "Yes?"

"Ms. Altagracia?"

She nodded.

I told her my name, showed identification. "I'd like to talk with you about your father."

"That old fool? What's he gone and done now?" Her speech had none of the local flavor; if anything, she sounded as if she were from New Jersey.

"Well, you know he's sold Jumbie Cay."

She blinked. "I did *not*!"

"He has, and he may be in serious trouble."

"You can depend on that—he's in serious trouble with me. That island is all that's left of my family's heritage. How *could* he sell it!"

"It was a forced sale. May I come in?"

"Of course. I've forgotten my manners." She opened the door all the way and let me into a room full of diffuse light. Its floors were covered by grass-cloth mats, its walls by color photographs of what looked to be local landscapes. The furnishings were simple rattan like Cam Connors's.

Regina Altagracia motioned for me to be seated and lowered herself into a recliner chair, moving carefully as though she suffered from back trouble or arthritis. She placed a hand on the yoke of her flowered shift dress and said, "What you just told me tears at my heart. Jumbie Cay—gone."

"You sound as though you love the island."

"Yes, I do." She nodded at the photographs on the walls. "I took those. Now they're all I have left."

"But you moved away from there."

"No, Ms. McCone, I moved away from my father."

"Why?"

She sighed. "Many reasons, but you don't want to hear them. Please tell me what happened. And where my father is now."

"He's still on the island; he was allowed to keep his home and some land. Are you aware that he has a gambling problem?"

"Yes. That's one of the reasons I can't live with him. I'm Seventh-day Adventist, converted when I was at college in New Jersey."

"I thought I recognized a Jersey accent."

She smiled, momentarily diverted from the sale of Jumbie Cay. "It always surprises people. I attended high school in Newark and Fairleigh Dickinson University in Teaneck. My brothers and sister, too."

"Why there?"

"My father's brother married a woman from Newark. They were unable to have children, so they encouraged us to come live with them and attend school. After graduating I stayed on and worked for an insurance company; my brothers and sister are still in the States."

"Why did you come home?"

Her smile became pained. "My mother died, and my father was getting out of hand. We all felt someone should look after him, and the task fell to me. I was not married, my sister was. We women, you know, usually end up the caretakers."

"But you didn't remain with your father."

"I couldn't; he made my life intolerable. He drinks, he smokes, he gambles. There is always a card game going on on his veranda. I'm a religious woman, but living in that situation taxed my faith. When I began to hate my own father, I knew it was time to leave. Besides," she added, her smile brittle now, "he didn't really want or need me."

I knew that feeling of offering and being dismissed. The previous Christmas I'd been concerned about Pa and his friend Nancy spending the holiday in our old house, with its trapped memories. Since none of my other siblings was offering, I called Pa and invited them to visit, much as I would have preferred spending the day with Hy and close friends. Pa's response had been abrupt and to the point: "Why would we want to do that? We're off to Reno on the twenty-third."

He didn't even thank me for the invitation, and it hadn't improved our relationship when I responded with sarcasm: "You're welcome, Pa."

"It hurts, doesn't it?" I said to Regina Altagracia.

She shrugged, quickly covering her feelings. "In a way it was a relief. I had saved my money in the States, and I knew there was a strong Adventist community here. I bought this farm, joined in, found a life. We're a very close community— closed, I realize now, since I didn't even hear about Daddy . . . my father selling Jumbie Cay. Who bought it, and why was he forced to sell?"

"The purchaser is a man called Klaus Schechtmann."

"Who is he?"

"A racketeer who ran a very lucrative phone-in sports book

in San Francisco. He was indicted by the grand jury and left the country. Now he's running the same kind of operation from a compound on Goat Point."

She closed her eyes, shook her head from side to side.

"Apparently your father was heavily in debt to Schechtmann. He took the island in lieu of payment."

"The old fool."

"I'm afraid the story only gets worse. Schechtmann is harboring an Azadi citizen named Dawud Hamid, who raped and murdered a woman in California. He was never charged because he had diplomatic immunity. Two days ago Schechtmann removed Hamid's wife and child from the Azadi Consulate in San Francisco; the wife either died accidentally or was murdered, and Schechtmann fled the scene with the little girl. By now he's brought her to Jumbie Cay, and I'm here to get her back."

Regina Altagracia's fingers had tightened on the arms of her chair. "Is my father involved in this?"

"I honestly can't say, although I doubt it. More likely he's as much a victim of Schechtmann and Hamid as the little girl."

"It's difficult to imagine him as a victim. How do you plan to get the child back?"

"A seaplane is dropping me off near the island tonight. I'll swim ashore. I have a contact there, a man called Nel Simpson, who'll help me and bring us back here in his boat."

"I know of Simpson. How did you come across him?"

"Through a friend of your father named Zeff Lash—"

"No! Do not trust that man!"

"Why not?"

"Did he say he was a friend of my father?"

"Yes."

"He is *not*. My father had him thrown off the island while I was still living there, for cheating at cards. Lash promised he'd get even with him."

But Lash had told me he visited often with Zebediah Altagracia, and demonstrated knowledge of Jumbie Cay since the time Schechtmann took possession. If he hadn't gone there to see the old man, then who? Nel Simpson? Or . . . ?

An uneasy feeling made me ask, "Ms. Altagracia, do you

know of a man named Cam Connors who operates an air-charter service out of Princess Juliana?"

"Connors, Connors ... Of course! He's a friend of Zeff Lash, and also a gambler. I met him on Jumbie Cay a number of times—in addition to coming to play cards, he also flew in supplies. It seems to me I heard something about him recently. What?"

I was silent as she thought, her teeth worrying at her lower lip.

"Cam Connors ... yes. He's heavily in debt to illegal gambling interests, and in danger of losing his charter service."

So Cam—who had claimed he'd never visited Jumbie Cay—used to play cards there. And now he was in over his head in gambling debts. Even if Schechtmann were not one of his creditors, those who collect such debts often have cooperative arrangements. Doing Schechtmann a favor would not hurt Connors. Doing him a disfavor would be sure to bring the vultures swooping down on his business.

Connors was setting me up.

Now I recalled things—little things, but significant all the same: the exchanges in French between Connors and Lash, the guarded looks. Lash's attempt to scare me off, my all-night argument with Cam. His later insistence on accompanying me to the island and, when I said no, his refusal to provide me with a gun to take along. He hated guns, he'd told me, didn't own any and wouldn't arm anyone under any circumstances.

At the time I'd accepted what he said as truth because of my own reservations about firearms, but now I revised my opinion. Hy had told me that Dan Kessell's pilots always went armed—too much danger of cargo or planes being hijacked otherwise. Here in the Caribbean, where drug trafficking and political instability were rampant, Connors would be a fool not to follow the same practice. Habits born of living dangerously don't die; Hy was the world's most cautious person where firearms were concerned, but I doubted the day would come when he didn't sleep with his .44 within reach. Connors would do the same.

Cam may once have been Hy's buddy, but the friendship was forged many years ago in different times. People change, and often we forget that they don't necessarily change for the better. If Hy had a dangerous flaw, it was believing in the continuing good intentions of those he had cared about.

He should have been more cautious where Connors was concerned.

I should have been more cautious.

My fists were clenched, and my fingernails dug into my palms. I bit my lower lip so hard I tasted blood.

Regina Altagracia frowned. "Are you all right?"

What would Connors do? Force me out of his plane over the open sea? Probably not; I'd put up a struggle, and he wouldn't want to risk the aircraft or his life. He might land at some location other than Jumbie Cay and drown me. Tourists drowned all the time; my death probably wouldn't trigger a serious investigation.

Still, Cam didn't strike me as the sort of man who would kill with impunity; certainly he'd tried every way possible to talk me out of making the trip to Jumbie Cay. For all he knew, I'd called Hy and told him our plans. We'd been seen together both at his friend Ben's restaurant and Eudoxie's last night; we'd be seen together at his charter service tonight. No, rather than kill me, Cam would let matters take their natural course. He'd drop me at Marlin Landing as promised.

And then? Easy. Nel Simpson would deliver me into the hands of Schechtmann and his people, and I'd end up in an unmarked grave on Jumbie Cay.

The images of what might happen before they killed me swarmed before my eyes like insects.

Through them I saw Regina Altagracia watching me. Awkwardly she got up from the chair and came over, put her hand on the back of my head and forced it forward. "Breathe shallowly," she said. "You're about to hyperventilate."

"I have to think—" The swarm became small black dots. Jesus, this hadn't happened to me in years! I thought I'd gotten over it—

Next thing I knew my knees were pressing against my temples. A hand restrained me from raising my head.

"It's all right," Regina Altagracia's voice said. "Relax and keep breathing shallowly."

"I'm so embarrassed," I said to the grass-cloth mat on the floor.

"You've had a shock. It happens."

I relaxed and breathed.

After a moment she took her hand away and I sat up. "Thanks," I said.

She leaned down, tilted my face toward hers, and studied me with coolly assessing eyes. Then she nodded and smiled grimly. "I will help you," she said.

I couldn't imagine how.

Her smile broadened, became wicked—and dangerous.

She said, "You probably see me as a good church lady. On the upper fringe of middle age, dowdy and overweight, with an undistinguished past and a future that is a gentle slide toward death."

I shook my head, confused as to where this was taking us.

"I am most of those things," she went on, "and something else entirely. And I will tell you this: anyone who tries to—pardon me—fuck with my island, my father, a helpless little girl, or a good person such as yourself . . . Well, anyone who tries that is in for one hell of a fight."

Seventeen

Regina told me to go outside and pay off Kenny. She didn't know the driver and didn't trust anyone unfamiliar to her and her associates—whoever they might be. "Here," she said as I started toward the door, "give him some of these. He'll clear out in a hurry."

I looked at the pamphlets she thrust into my hand. Seventh-day Adventist literature. When I came back I was smiling; Kenny had fended off the pamphlets as if they were capable of transmitting an infectious disease.

Regina smiled knowingly. "It hurts me that so many people are unwilling to see the light, but on the other hand, their horror of the Lord's word can be useful. Now, come with me."

She took me through the latticed walkway to the shuttered building at the side of the house. Its door was secured by a padlock and chain. She keyed the lock, unwound the chain, and entered ahead of me. The interior was totally black; I waited.

An oil lamp came on, its beam weak at first, then stronger. I stepped through the door and saw a large room that had once been a barn. It was spotlessly clean and the stalls were partitioned off with bedsheets; in one I glimpsed a neatly made cot. At the far end of the room was a cooking and eating area; at the other stood a grouping of shabby mismatched chairs. A toy box with a teddy bear perched atop it and a bookcase crammed with paperbacks sat beneath one of the shuttered windows.

"What . . . ?" I asked.

Regina switched on a ceiling fan against the trapped heat, lowered herself slowly into a chair, and motioned for me to sit, too. "I will tell you a story," she said. "When I first moved to this peaceful valley I began attending services at the little stone church two miles down the road. For a while I made no friends; I was out of practice. Then one day in the supermarket I ran into a woman who had sat next to me during the previous week's services. I was carrying a political history of the area; she commented on it and after some conversation during which we discovered we shared the same views on a number of issues, she suggested I might be interested in joining a study group at the church.

"Well, I told her I already knew my Bible backwards and forwards. She said the group wasn't a bible-study class; instead they discussed political situations in the Caribbean and South and Central America. That interested me, so I attended and got caught up in it. Every Thursday evening we had spirited arguments about the oppression and change sweeping our corner of the world.

"After six months the same woman called on me and asked me to join the group's inner circle. It seems the sessions I attended were a proving ground, their way of checking out the strength of my beliefs and commitment. The inner circle did more than talk; they assisted people in the troubled areas."

"How?"

"You have of course heard of your country's Underground Railroad?"

"Yes."

"Well, this building is one of the way stations on ours."

"You actually help them escape the trouble spots?"

She shook her head. "We're not equipped to do that. To tell you the truth, most of us are too old and fat for that sort of action. But we raise money for loans, we provide them shelter, we refer them to other associates in other places. We give them moral and spiritual support. The word is out that people in need have friends on this island."

"This is a remarkable coincidence," I said. "The man I'm involved with does similar work; right now he's helping a political dissident escape from Haiti." I told her Hy's name and the organization in Miami that had contacted him.

Regina didn't look surprised in the least. "I don't know of your friend, but I do know the group he's working for. And this is no coincidence."

"Oh?"

"As I said before, I'm a good church lady. I believe in divine guidance." My skepticism must have shown on my face because she asked, "What faith are you?"

"I was raised Catholic. Now I'm . . . nothing."

"Don't look so alarmed; I'm not about to begin proselytizing. But I very much doubt you're 'nothing.'"

"No?"

"If you were, you wouldn't be here to save the little girl. You believe. You just don't put a name to it."

". . . Maybe."

"No maybe about it. Now, when are you flying to Jumbie Cay?"

"Around ten tonight." I explained my reasoning about what Connors planned to do.

"I think you're quite correct," she said, "so we must insure that you're adequately protected. You see that toy box over there? Open it."

I went over, removed the teddy bear, and lifted the box's lid. Inside was a jumble of more stuffed animals. I frowned at Regina.

She tossed me a small key. "Take them out and use this to release the panel beneath them."

I scooped out the playthings and tossed them on the floor, then unlocked and removed the panel. It concealed an impressive cache of handguns.

"Before you leave here," Regina said, "we will see that you're equipped with the proper weapon in a waterproof, concealed package. But let's concern ourselves with that later. At the moment we have work to do."

* * *

Regina dropped me off in Marigot at quarter after five. In my head I had a list of facts and instructions. Taped to the small of my back and braced by the belt of my loose trousers was a waterproof package containing my money, I.D., and other essentials, a lightweight Glock nine-millimeter pistol and a final necessary item. My yellow shirt billowed out, concealing the extra bulk. Regina clasped my hands and wished me Godspeed, reminded me to contact her at her unlisted phone number should I need help when I returned with Habiba.

That she said "when," rather than "if," bolstered my courage.

Connors wouldn't get back from his charter for more than an hour. I turned down a side street, found a small sidewalk café, and ordered coffee. As I sipped it I reviewed my plans. A few more details had to be taken care of; I'd find a pay phone before going back to the apartment.

Even though I was a good actor, it wouldn't be easy to fake the rapport I'd previously shared with Connors. I was sure I could pull it off, though, and any slips I might make he'd chalk up to nervousness about tonight's excursion. I wouldn't have to fake that.

The plan was solid; Regina and I had gone over and over it—each adding bits and pieces from her own area of expertise, improving on it as we went. Details were crucially important, and I had them down pat. One would lead to another with smooth precision.

As I reviewed them I realized that my nervousness was fading. I felt in control, and somewhat high. Hell, any minute now I'd be starting to enjoy this!

Was this the way the Diplo-bomber felt as he homed in on one of his targets? Yes, I thought so. The powerful rush might not be the motive for the bombings, but it had to be a satisfying by-product. And the more he toyed with the authorities, the more he walked on the thin edge of danger, the greater the rush would be.

I was beginning to understand him in a way that reading a dry psychological profile couldn't duplicate. If I could get farther inside his mentality, until I was almost in sync with it, I might be able to figure out what he wanted as his ultimate payoff. There had to be one; he'd been escalating his activities, changing his patterns, revealing more of himself. He'd demand that payoff soon. And if, when he did—

Whoa, McCone! Take things one step at a time. The program for tonight is to get Habiba off that island.

I finished my coffee. There was a pay phone on the corner; I left money on the table and walked down there.

Early afternoon in California. Greg Marcus was out of the office. Still no machine and no answer at Joslyn's. Renshaw wasn't at Green Street, but the operator patched me through to the consulate.

"Goddamn time you called back!" he exclaimed. "What's going on?"

"I'm about to snatch Habiba and bring her home." I believed it now; it would happen. "What's going on there?"

"Nothing. No ransom demand, and Hamid's going about business as usual."

"Jesus, Gage, Mavis is dead and Habiba's down here. How can she remain calm? She knows what her son is—"

"What her son is?"

Bad slip; I couldn't go into it now. "Well," I said lamely, "he hasn't been the best of fathers. Have you heard from Ripinsky?"

Hesitation. "Yes. He got his party out and sent him on to Panama, where he's been granted asylum."

"Where's Hy now?"

"Santo Domingo. There were . . . complications."

"Complications? Gage—what?"

"He's sick, that's all. That damned bug he picked up in Managua. But he's seen a doctor and gotten some medication for it. Don't worry."

How could I not worry? "Do you have a contact number for him?"

He read it off to me. "Give me a number where I can reach you."

"Isn't any. And listen, Gage, if Hy calls in, will you tell him not to contact Cam Connors under any circumstances?"

"Connors. What's he got to do—"

"I've got to go, Gage."

"Well, stay in touch." He hesitated, then surprised me. "And, Sharon—take care of yourself."

Mellowing in his middle years, I thought as I hung up. Or maybe he's moved me to another one of those little mental compartments Cam was talking about. Labeled what, I wonder?

I gripped the receiver, looking at the scrap of paper on which I'd scrawled the Santo Domingo number for Hy. I could feel the pull; a simple call to the long-distance carrier and I'd hear his voice. Reassure myself that he'd be all right.

But I *couldn't* do that.

I'd never been able to lie to him, never even been able to hide anything from him. If I called, he'd have the whole story of Connors's betrayal from me in minutes. It would enrage him and, in spite of his illness, he might fly here in time to disrupt my plans. Besides, talking with him might bring me down, make me lonesome. I couldn't indulge in bad feelings now. I had to focus only on tonight and Habiba.

I'd let the promise of hearing Hy's voice be the radar signal that would guide me back here with the little girl.

One last detail to take care of, but it was the most important of all. I called a number on the nearby island of Anguilla and passed along some information that greatly interested my party. Then I braced myself and went back to Rue de la Liberté to face Connors.

Connors insisted we go to dinner at a restaurant on the quay where the ferries left for Anguilla—a grim variant on feeding the prisoner her last meal. The sunset was hidden from view by the point that formed the west end of the bay, but its glow turned the underbellies of the clouds piled on the horizon to flame, their tops drifting away like smoke. I took a cue from the sight and—in hope of shoring up what I feared was a badly sagging rapport—began to chatter about color photography. The more I talked, the more morose Connors became, slouching in his chair and staring moodily at the darkening water.

An attack of conscience over what he planned for me, I supposed. Well, good. Let him have a foretaste of how miserable he would feel before this night was over.

Our goat kebabs were being grilled on an oil drum on the rickety veranda. When they came I pushed them around on the plate; the adrenaline high cut my appetite as surely as a line of cocaine. Connors didn't notice and ate voraciously; he'd wrestled with his conscience and won.

Back at the apartment I checked my travel bag. Nothing there that I cared about, and a good thing, since the bag would have to be abandoned. I zipped it up and took it to the living room. "Okay to store this here?" I asked.

Connors nodded and stowed it in a closet. "All set?"

"Guess so."

"Those clothes don't look too great for swimming."

"I'm wearing my suit underneath."

"Then let's get this show on the road."

1,000 Feet Above The Caribbean Sea

May 24, 10:43 P.M.

The L4 Buccaneer skimmed above the glittering moon-shot water on a due-south course. Darkness enveloped us, and the roar of the engine made conversation impossible.

I was sitting in back, rather than up front with Connors. At first I'd climbed in beside him, fiddled with adjusting the seat, then announced I'd be more comfortable if I could stretch out preparatory to my long swim. He accepted the reason without question.

I began my preparations, moving slowly so nothing would alert him. It's all in the timing, I told myself. Don't rush.

Don't rush, and don't think ahead. Concentrate on each step, and then the one after it.

When I was ready I leaned forward. Tapped Connors on the shoulder and asked through the headset, "How much longer till we get to Marlin Landing?"

"Ten minutes, give or take."

I'd timed it perfectly. "Okay," I said, "we're changing course."

". . . What?"

I brought up the pistol that I'd carefully removed from the waterproof pack and jammed it against the base of his skull. "It's loaded, and I'm prepared to use it. Do exactly as I say."

Alarm tightened his features. "Are you insane? What the hell's the matter with you?"

"I'm a whole lot more sane than you and Zeff Lash were when you concocted your plan to get rid of me. You must've thought it would cancel out a hell of a big gambling debt if you did Klaus Schechtmann and Dawud Hamid a favor."

Abruptly he averted his eyes. That and his silence were all the confirmation I needed.

My anger rekindled. Easy now, I cautioned myself.

I said, "Your new course is due northwest. Rendezvous Bay. Got that?"

". . . Yeah."

"Good. Set it and don't deviate. I'll know if you do. I guess Hy didn't mention it, but I'm a pilot myself."

Connors muttered something I couldn't catch. Garden-variety expletive, no doubt. He began correcting course, and in a few moments the seaplane's wing dipped and we made our turn.

Connors remained silent for a while, but eventually his curiosity overcame him. "Why Anguilla?"

"I'm not sure you really want to know."

Eighteen

When I last saw him Cam Connors was trying to convince the Anguillan authorities that he didn't know how the packet of cocaine had gotten under the front passenger seat of his seaplane. The American tourist who had alerted them by phone that her charter pilot planned to smuggle the drugs in at Rendezvous Bay that evening was released into the hands of the Reverend Michael Gadieux, pastor of a nearby Seventh-day Adventist church.

Gadieux, a tall dour man, was silent as we drove away from the police station. I gathered he disapproved of Regina's method for getting Connors out of my life and into a place where he couldn't contact anyone on Jumbie Cay, but it seemed to me that Cam wasn't being punished nearly enough for conspiring to turn me over to Schechtmann and his people. In the end he probably wouldn't be charged with anything. There was no real proof that the drugs were his; only my smeared fingerprints were on the bag that Regina had confiscated from a Central American refugee earlier that year; and since I was leaving the island, there would be no witness against him.

Gadieux drove along a paved two-lane highway toward the west end of the island—on the left-hand side, as Anguilla was a British dependency. We passed through small settlements that were largely dark at this hour; I could tell little about my surroundings and quite frankly didn't care. This island was only a stepping-stone to Jumbie Cay.

Finally we turned onto a dirt secondary road; the car's headlights showed it cut straight through scrub vegetation toward the sea. At its end I saw a few lights, and as we drew closer I heard music—not the hard-driving beat I'd become accustomed to, but jazz with a faint calypso rhythm. Gadieux stopped the car at a low white frame house where a number of vehicles were parked.

"He's expecting you," he said. After a momentary hesitation he added, "Good luck."

I thanked him and got out, crossed sandy ground to the house. At its side was a latticed area; I stepped in, saw it led to a ramshackle deck overlooking the water. Below, the waves broke gently on a rocky beach; the wind blew warm and steady, dampening my skin with salty spray. Light spilled across the deck from windows and leaked around the door to my left.

When I knocked the music stopped abruptly. A male voice said, "Okay, we'll break till tomorrow night. I got business to take care of."

Voices murmured, chairs scraped, objects thumped. The door opened and a bony-faced man with very dark skin, a piratical blue headband, and a gold hoop earring looked out. Behind him two other men and a woman were stowing instruments in cases.

"Ms. McCone?"

"Yes. Mr. Fisher?"

"Lloyd."

"Sharon."

That established, he let me inside. The musicians brushed past me with their cases, nodding in greeting. Lloyd said, "A sideline. We play gigs at the tourist hangouts on weekends."

"And during the week?"

"I take more tourists out on sight-seeing charters. Visitors from your country are Anguilla's economic base. It's not the sleepy little island I remember from childhood."

"You're a native?" He didn't sound like one.

"Originally, but my family moved to Florida when I was

around eight. A few years ago when the developers finished ruining Fort Myers, I decided to move back—just in time to watch the developers ruin Anguilla."

"It's that bad?"

"On its way. But let's get down to business. You want to go to old Zebediah Altagracia's place."

"Yes. His daughter said you're familiar with it."

"I am. The old man's doctor lives here on Anguilla; I take him over there to make periodic house calls."

"Altagracia's ill?"

"No. The house calls are an excuse to play cards."

I looked at my watch. It was already after one. "How long will it take to get there?"

"Not very. I've got a high-powered speedboat."

"I'll need a couple of hours of darkness to operate in."

"You'll have them, but we better get started."

Lloyd cut the speedboat's power a good ways from shore. All I could make out were orange lights that blinked irregularly—tree branches moving across them in the sea breeze, I guessed. He said, "I could go in closer, but that might alert the wrong people. Can you swim it?"

I measured the distance with my eyes. "Yes."

"Okay. You strike out for those lights; they're on Zeb's terrace. When you get closer you'll make out a concrete pier anchored to the rocks. The current's strong through there, so swim hard or you'll get sucked past the pier to the south. When you grab onto it, be careful; it's crumbly and jagged in places. Up top there's a gap about halfway down where it's fallen apart and been bridged with some planks and a board; watch that, too. At the end of the pier you'll find a path through a palmetto grove; it ends at the terrace. Zeb'll be waiting for you on the veranda."

While he spoke I shed my sandals, stripped to the bathing suit I wore under my shirt and trousers, and carefully removed the tape that held the waterproof pack in place. It was considerably lighter than before, as I'd ditched the gun in the seaplane for the Anguillan authorities to discover. Now I stowed the pack in a pocket by the seat. I wouldn't need money, docu-

ments, or credit cards on Jumbie Cay—and if I didn't return
to the boat, I'd never need them again.

Lloyd added, "I'll be waiting where you told me. Can the
kid swim?"

"I don't know. If not, I can help her." I hesitated, gazing
at the shifting pattern of lights on shore. "Look," I said, "if
. . . something happens and we're not back by daybreak, don't
jeopardize yourself. Go home, call the San Francisco number
I gave you, and use the emergency code. They'll put you in
touch with a man named Gage Renshaw. Tell him what's
happened. He'll . . . do something about it and arrange for
you to be paid the rest of your money."

Lloyd nodded, looking grim. His hoop earring glinted in
the low light from the instrument panel.

I stood up, sat on the boat's side, swung my legs over.

"Remember to watch that current," Lloyd said.

*Black star-shot sky, blacker water. Orange lights in the
distance. I'm all alone. Should be afraid, but I'm not.*

*Waves gentle, water warm. Soft tropic breeze against my
face.*

*But my limbs don't feel leaden. I don't start to sink. I don't
want to lose myself in this dark water.*

*There's no batlike shape floating on the surface. No
drowned woman with blank forever eyes. Just me. Me and
my determination to get to Habiba.*

*I'm swimming strong and steady for shore. Easily winning
my battle with the current. And I'm not even winded.*

By the time the battle was over I *was* winded. I pulled
myself up onto the pier and lay on its rough concrete, gasping
and spitting seawater. Then something stung the back of my
neck and buzzing assailed my ear. A second sting on my
forearm, and I leaped up, swatting furiously. The concrete
was uneven and crumbling; it lacerated my bare soles as I
ran along. The board that bridged the gap rumbled and pitched
under my weight. I teetered, in danger of plunging back into
the water, regained my balance and rushed ahead toward a
sandy path bordered by conch shells.

Palmetto and sea grape grew densely there, and mangrove

roots encroached. Dry fronds rustled overhead and taller trees creaked and sighed. I felt my way through the darkness, alternately pushing branches aside and slapping at the persistent insects. The path went straight for a ways, then hooked back toward the sea. I'd begun to wonder if I'd taken a wrong turn when I swept through a thick stand of palmetto onto a tiled terrace. The lights I'd been homing in on were imitation torches mounted on poles along a low wall that bowed out above the water.

The terrace contained nothing but a dead coconut palm in a central planting area; there were deep cracks in the tiles. Cracks, too, in the walls of the single-story pink stucco house on its far side. The house's veranda faced me, three wide steps leading up to it. Its sagging roof was supported by columns to which stout vines clung, their peach and purple blossoms draping down onto the railings and emitting a scent so sweet it cloyed.

I remained where I was, flat brown leaves scudding around my feet. I could see no lights in the house, could hear nothing above the crash of the surf beyond the terrace wall. Then I spotted a red ember glowing on the veranda; it moved, grew brighter, described an arc, and went out. Almost immediately whoever was there lighted another cigarette.

"You are very prompt, Miss McCone." The Britishaccented voice was a man's, made gravelly by age.

I moved toward the veranda and mounted the steps. "Mr. Altagracia?"

"Who else would I be? Don't ask unnecessary questions."

I located him in the gloom some six feet away, reclining on an ancient aluminum chaise longue under a louvered window that opened into the house itself. He was long-boned and gaunt, clad only in a pair of madras shorts. His head was completely bald, but a thick white beard hung halfway down his chest, vivid against his dark skin. He regarded me testily through gold-rimmed glasses.

"Don't just stand there."

I approached him, acutely aware of the skimpiness of my bathing suit. A mosquito nailed me solidly on my thigh. I swatted, missing it. Another got me on my bare midriff. I swatted again.

"Oh, for God's sake!" Mr. Altagracia reached for a can of insect repellent that sat among a welter of objects on a rusty metal TV tray and extended it to me. "Use this. Then put on that shirt hanging on the chair over there. I'm not so old that I can't be distracted by the sight of so much female flesh."

I sprayed on the repellent, then donned the shirt. It came to mid-thigh, and I had to roll up the sleeves four turns.

"The shoes under the chair are for you, too. Abandoned by my daughter when she fled this den of iniquity."

They were rubber thongs, close to my size. I slipped my feet into them and turned around.

Mr. Altagracia looked me over and nodded. "It isn't Paris couture, but it will do. Bring that chair over here and sit down."

Regina had warned me her father was a curmudgeon, but she hadn't mentioned his fondness for giving orders. Well, from years of experience with my military father, I knew how to deal with the likes of him. I picked up the light aluminum chair and set it on the other side of the TV tray. Sat and looked attentive.

"I know you're not deaf, but have you by chance become mute?"

"No, sir, I'm just economical with words—even if I do ask unnecessary questions."

He frowned and his lips pushed out belligerently. "You think I'm a cantankerous old man."

"Does it matter?"

"It does not."

"Good. Let's get down to business."

He hesitated, eyeing me thoughtfully. "I like a young woman with spirit."

"And I like a cantankerous old man who agreed to help me sight unseen."

"We will work well together, then. I assume everything has so far gone according to plan?"

"Yes. The pilot's in custody on Anguilla, and Lloyd Fisher's moving into position off Goat Point. You told your daughter that the little girl has arrived. Were you able to find out how she is?"

"Lucinda Mumms, woman who lives down the road, cleans

for them out at the compound. I pay her to keep me informed about what goes on there. She says the child is very unhappy; she doesn't cry, but Lucinda can tell she's very upset."

Habiba wouldn't cry—any more than I at her age.

"Did Lucinda find out if they know I'm coming?"

"They do, but they're not worried because they believe Nel Simpson will deliver you to them. The child's father thinks you were sent by his mother. He is very angry and determined to retain custody of her."

"So the approach you suggested on the phone with Regina will probably work."

"It will work."

"If we can get into the compound to see Habiba."

Zebediah Altagracia stared haughtily down his long nose at me. "We will be welcomed with open arms."

"Are you sure?"

"Don't question me, young woman! Of course I am sure. In many ways this is still my island; the people who have lived and worked here all their lives did not change their loyalties, and Klaus Schechtmann knows that. Why do you think he encouraged me to remain after the sale? Mr. Schechtmann was afraid to be left to the mercy of what he considers a subspecies, and a savage one at that. I am here to keep the peace. As a result, Mr. Schechtmann grants me certain privileges."

"Such as?"

Mr. Altagracia smiled demonically and reached for a phone that sat in a drift of newspaper on the TV tray. "Such as the privilege of calling him in the middle of the night."

While he dialed a wind suddenly came up, setting the trees to bending and swaying. Rain began to splatter down on the tiles of the terrace and the roof of the veranda. Almost immediately the air became cool and fresh, bringing with it the scents of ozone and the sea. In the distance lightning flashed.

"Schechtmann," Mr. Altagracia said into the receiver. "Wake him." He covered the mouthpiece. "His staff recognize my voice. It's shameful how I terrify them."

After a moment his head cocked. Again he smiled wickedly. "Klaus, Klaus—such language. If you think I do not know what *schweinhund* means, you are seriously mistaken. And I was about to do you a favor. . . .

"No, it cannot wait until morning. I have a visitor, a Miss McCone. From what she has told me, I gather you are expecting her. . . . Ah, now I have your interest. By seaplane? No, by boat. . . . At around four-thirty this afternoon, on the beach near your compound. Somehow she found her way to me, and we have been talking. . . . That's right. She is a determined young woman, but I believe I have persuaded her to be sensible. Here is what we propose: you will allow us to come there and see the child. If Miss McCone feels she is in good health and happy to be there, she will go home and report to her client that it is in the child's best interests to remain with her father. . . . Very good, Klaus, but it must be within the hour. . . .

"Klaus, if my bible-thumping daughter were here, she would take a bullwhip to you for using such a word in reference to her sainted father. . . . I *know* the child is asleep, but wake her. Children are extremely flexible—a character trait about which you know nothing. . . . Yes, I assure you that Miss McCone will depart as soon as she is satisfied that all is well. . . . No, by helicopter from here. A pilot friend of hers is coming. . . . Very good, Klaus. We'll be there directly."

Mr. Altagracia replaced the receiver and smiled serenely at me. "That man," he said, "is entirely too trusting of this old 'pig dog.'"

The rain had stopped by the time we drove away from the Altagracia house in Zebediah's old Jeep, but lightning still illuminated gravid clouds on the horizon. Halfway down the puddled driveway the old man slammed on the brakes, forcing me toward the dashboard.

"Do you see that cannon over there?" he asked.

I looked where he pointed. Through an overgrown tangle of trees and shrubs I spotted it, floodlighted and aimed at a forty-five-degree angle toward the sea.

"That cannon," he said, "was used by your countrymen in their Revolutionary War against the British. I bought it and had it shipped here at great expense shortly before I began my own revolt against the Empire. Unfortunately, I was not required to fire a single shot. I keep it in working order, however, and fire it every November seventeenth to commemorate Jumbie Cay's independence." Once more he smiled wickedly, his teeth gleaming against his dark skin. "It will give me great satisfaction to fire the shots that will free Jumbie Cay from its present-day oppressors. In fact, I am looking forward to it."

"I can understand that." Regina's assessment of her father had been way off base; he was anything but an old fool. Quite mad, perhaps, but definitely nobody's fool.

The road we took skirted a salt pond that shone silver in the lightning's flash. The wind blew puffs of foam from it and chased them across the pavement. I clutched at the dash as we banged in and out of potholes, trying to make out something of the terrain.

Inland the island appeared hilly and barren, strewn with rocky outcroppings and sparsely covered with scraggly vegetation. We passed an occasional cinder-block house, but most of them looked to be falling into ruins. A tiny settlement containing a gas station, market, and tavern displayed a faded sign that proclaimed it Altagraciaville, Capital City of the Republic of Jumbie Cay. My companion didn't comment on it, and I followed his lead.

The night had turned steamy and insect-ridden once more. The repellent I'd sprayed on had long before ceased to work, and the bugs' stingers penetrated the cloth of my borrowed shirt. Mr. Altagracia didn't seem bothered by them; I supposed if you lived here all your life you developed an immunity.

When we thumped into a particularly deep pothole and I made an involuntary exclamation, the old man said, "After I evicted the British from my island, I took over the responsibility of maintaining the roads. When I sold it to Mr. Schechtmann, I informed him that the responsibility had transferred to him. You see how seriously he takes it."

"I *feel* how seriously he takes it."

"We're quite close to the compound now. You will recognize the site from the pictures my daughter showed you, of course."

The framed photographs on Regina's walls had proved invaluable to me. "I think so. It's on a rise and the beach below is crescent-shaped, with a stone jetty at either end. Beyond the western jetty is another beach with rocks that contain tide pools. It's above the tide line now, but at four-thirty this afternoon it was under water."

"Good."

"What about access to the beach from the compound?"

"You needn't concern yourself with that."

"But Habiba—"

"Yes, I understand. The buildings ... Wait, we're there; you'll see."

My stomach knotted. I pushed my hands downward against my thighs as if by doing so I could restrain my rising tension. Soon I'd come face-to-face with Klaus Schechtmann and Dawud Hamid. Soon I'd see the little girl.

Mentally I telegraphed a plea to her: *Remember. Please remember.*

We rounded a sharp curve and then I glimpsed luminescent breakers offshore. Buildings came into view: white, stark, and wedge-shaped, with the larger edges thrusting aggressively toward the sea. Their sides and backs were monolithic, with small doors and no windows. The largest building perched at the top of the rise, and a series of smaller ones descended steplike toward beach level.

Zebediah Altagracia said, "The main building contains the betting operation, as well as communal living and dining areas. The smaller ones are sleeping cottages. They are built on a grade, and a path in front of them leads to the beach. From there it is a short walk to the western jetty."

I nodded, studying the layout.

A stucco wall some ten feet high enclosed the compound; a guardhouse sat beside an automobile gate. Mr. Altagracia slowed the Jeep and blinked his lights; the guard opened the gate quickly, but the Jeep's bumper still grazed it as the old man imperiously drove through.

"Fools," he muttered. "Who would want to break in here, anyway? The people who work for them are only too glad to get *out*."

The driveway was lined with tall coconut palms; in spite of their size they appeared to be recent transplants, and the rest of the landscaping also looked raw and new.

"Another foolish idea," Mr. Altagracia said, motioning at the palms. "Klaus had those trees brought in full grown, plunked into holes, and never gave a thought to the soil conditions. They already look sick, and they'll be dead by Christmas."

"Schechtmann had this compound built?"

"He imported an expensive architect from the States, one who didn't understand the Caribbean. Look at those buildings: airless eyesores, warts on the face of this island. Now his landscape architect is about to commit similar atrocities—to say nothing of killing a multitude of perfectly good plants."

As we drew close to the main building, I had to agree with him. Its wedge shape, at least when viewed from this vantage, looked crude and ungainly. When we got out of the Jeep and crossed to the small door I felt vaguely menaced, as if I were about to enter a cold tomb from which there was no exit.

Mr. Altagracia ignored the bell and banged impatiently on the door with the flat of his hand. When it didn't open right away he banged again. Footsteps approached and a man's voice said something in angry German.

The old man nodded to me and said loudly, "Yes, my bible-thumping daughter would surely take a bullwhip to him for such language."

I recognized the short, compact man who glared out at us as Klaus Schechtmann. Not so much from his physical appearance—the few details I had were sketchy. But there was a stinginess and smugness to his mouth that fit with what I knew of him, as well as a sly, greedy cast to his pale blue eyes. He wore a black silk bathrobe that was supposed to convey he considered our visit so unimportant he hadn't bothered to dress. He had groomed his gray-blond hair and beard, though.

Schechtmann continued to glare at Mr. Altagracia for a moment, then moved his eyes to me. Their expression altered subtly. Automatic response to all women, I thought, because the look was sexually speculative; he probably wasn't even aware he was doing it. I met his gaze with a cold one of my own. His little mouth tightened and he turned back to Mr. Altagracia.

"This is the McCone woman?"

"Miss McCone to you, Klaus. You must mind your manners." The old man took a firm grasp on my elbow and pushed past Schechtmann into an entryway with stark white walls that slanted upward at such an angle that I felt we were at the bottom of a funnel. "Where is the child?" he demanded.

"All in good time, Zeb." Schechtmann shut the door and motioned for us to follow him. "First her father wishes to see Miss McCone."

He led us down a small hallway and through an arch into a large room with a window wall that showed the lightning flashes on the sea. Its furnishings were oddly shaped, fashioned of black- and green-veined marble, with brass trimmings and black leather cushions. They must have been costly, but they looked uncomfortable as hell. A man in a burgundy robe that was the twin of Schechtmann's sat in one of the chairs, his dark head bent over a snifter of amber liquid that he was contemplatively swirling.

He must have heard us come in, but he held his pose a few more beats before he looked up. Dawud Hamid hadn't changed much since the pictures concealed in Habiba's window seat were taken; his face had a few more lines, his hair had flecks of gray, but his mouth was still sensual, his eyes still brooding and intense. And he was still vain and self-involved; the way he held his head and the flick of his wrist as he tossed off his drink told me that.

He set the snifter on a table beside him. Leaned back in the chair, crossed his legs, and stared arrogantly at me. "My mother," he said, "she sent you?"

"I'm working under contract with the consulate's security firm. Naturally your mother is concerned about Habiba."

"How touching."

His tone made me want to shake him, but I said mildly, "It's true."

"Why? She arranged for Speed to bring Habiba here."

"Habiba and Mavis. She didn't intend for your wife to end up dead in San Francisco Bay."

Something flickered in his eyes. Not sorrow or regret or any of the normal emotions that even an estranged husband might feel, but the fear an entrapped animal displays. Then he blinked and extinguished it. "Mavis's death was an accident—and her own fault."

"Oh?"

Schechtmann said, "Mrs. Hamid was drunk. She staggered and hit her head as she went overboard."

"And you didn't try to save her."

He shrugged indifferently. "We were already well under way."

"Wrong. You were still in the marina. Mavis's foot was caught in one of the mooring lines in the *Freia*'s slip."

"Whatever. As I said, it was an accident."

"Did Habiba see this *accident*?"

No response.

I glanced at Hamid. His posture had altered slightly and he was watching his business partner.

I asked Schechtmann, "Weren't you concerned that you might be connected with Mavis's death? That the *Freia*'s crew might talk?"

"The crew are well paid."

"Still, others knew you'd taken Mavis and Habiba: Malika Hamid, the consular staff, Leila, Eric Sparling, Fig Newton. . . ."

Schechtmann sighed impatiently. Hamid was paying close attention now.

"Perhaps," I added, "you wanted Mavis's body found where it was. In the case of a suspicious death the authorities always think first of the spouse, especially an estranged one."

"What are you driving at, Miss McCone?"

"Well, if Mavis was murdered—and the possibility hasn't yet been ruled out—Mr. Hamid would be a natural suspect; if it wasn't for his diplomatic immunity he'd have been arrested for another murder in California."

Hamid's breath came out in a hiss.

I added, "In that case, he certainly wouldn't want to return to the States, might not even feel comfortable venturing off this island. Your hold on him would be strengthened, as it is by having his daughter here in the compound."

"This is sheer fantasy," Schechtmann said. "Why would I want a hold over my own business partner?"

I shrugged. "Maybe he knows too much about your organization, or your past. Maybe you're afraid you've placed too much trust in him, and you want it as insurance."

Schechtmann tried to look amused, but his eyes were cold and wary. I'd struck a nerve.

Mr. Altagracia's fingers tightened on my elbow. "Please excuse my young friend," he said. "She has an extravagant imagination, and her judgment is clouded at best. Some of the clouds may be dispelled by allowing her to see the child."

Schechtmann smiled ironically, nodded, and turned military-fashion. I half expected him to goose-step from the room.

"Prussian, isn't he?" Mr. Altagracia said.

Hamid had overcome his shock at my earlier pronouncement and now was looking thoughtful. He got up, took his snifter to a wet bar, and poured a couple of fingers of Remy Martin. As he swirled and tasted it, his motions were measured and somewhat theatrical. In his elegant robe he could have been an actor in a Noel Coward drama.

I wondered which of the many roles he'd played in his life was the real Dawud Hamid: indulged but closely leashed son; neglectful husband; loving but absent father; international sophisticate. And then there was obsessed admirer. And killer.

Hamid seemed to sense what I was thinking. He glanced at me, eyes hooded, then turned to stare at the window wall facing the sea. The lightning had stopped, and the wall was a black mirror. I watched his reflection. His eyes met mine in the glass, then slid away.

Sounds in the entryway now: clipped adult footsteps and the barefoot patter of a child. I turned expectantly.

Habiba entered, Klaus Schechtmann's hand firmly on her shoulder. She wore a yellow flowered nightgown, and her hair was tousled, her eyes sleepy. On her left wrist was a Garfield-the-cat watch, and on her thin forearms were bruises that looked like finger marks. When she saw me she stopped, her lips forming a little O.

Schechtmann nudged her forward. "Say hello to Miss McCone, Habiba."

Her mouth formed my first name, savoring it as she had on that not-so-distant evening in my MG, but no sound came out. I went to her, squatted down, and took hold of her hands. "How are you, Habiba?"

Her eyes flicked toward Schechtmann. "Fine."

"Are you happy here?"

". . . Yes."

Mr. Altagracia moved between Schechtmann and us.

"Are you glad to be here with Uncle Klaus and your dad?"

Her brow puckered. She glanced toward her father now. He hadn't acknowledged her presence, still stood with his back to us, but he was observing everything in the window glass. I moved slightly, turning Habiba so he could only see her profile.

"I know you've missed your dad," I said. "You told me, remember? You showed me the parrot bracelet he gave you, and then we went for a ride, and Mr. Renshaw escorted the lady back to her castle."

"I remember."

Schechtmann pushed around Mr. Altagracia. "Miss McCone, please stick to the reason you came here."

Habiba's bony shoulders flinched.

"So can I tell your Grams that you like it here?" I asked her.

". . . Yes, tell Grams I'm fine."

"I'm so glad."

She pulled her hands free of mine, threw her arms around my neck, and hugged me. Mr. Altagracia coughed loudly as she whispered, "Help me!"

"Of course. You miss her. But maybe she'll visit you soon."

Schechtmann was moving toward us. I broke Habiba's hold on my neck and pushed her back till she was looking directly into my eyes.

And I winked.

She started to smile. Bit her lip.

I said, "You don't know how worried we've all been—your Grams, Mr. Lateef, Mr. Renshaw, me. Do you know how I got here? I swam from a boat to the beach where the tide pools are, just past the jetty. Have you seen those tide pools?"

"My new nanny showed them to me this morning."

Thank God. Schechtmann was right behind her now, his hands reaching for her shoulders. "Well, I'm glad you saw them. I didn't. When I got here at four-thirty it was high tide and they were under water. I guess this morning at four-thirty they won't be."

She bit her lip again. "I guess." And then she yawned very realistically.

I let go of her hands. Stood and smiled down at her. "Well, now that I know you're okay, I'll go home and tell your Grams that you want to stay here. Shall I do that?"

"Yes, please."

"Tell me once again—are you really happy?"

"I'm really, *really* happy." She raised her wrist and glanced at the Garfield watch. "Uncle Klaus, I'm sleepy. Can I go back to bed now?"

As they left the room hand in hand, Habiba looked over her shoulder and winked at me.

Nineteen

Zebediah Altagracia brought the Jeep to a stop and shut off its lights. We were perhaps half a mile from the entrance to the compound on a sandy track that cut across open ground toward the sea.

"This is as far as I can go," he said in a low voice. "The road turns into a footpath a few meters from here. Follow it until you see a stand of mangroves, then go toward them. They're on the shore above the tide pools."

"I guess this is good-bye. I can't thank you enough for your help."

"I should thank you. Your problem gave my daughter occasion to break her years-long silence."

"She does care, you know. The reason she left was so she wouldn't end up hating you for the way you live."

"And I care, too, in my fashion. I was not a particularly good father, and probably never should have been one. Unfortunately, few of us are able to resist the temptation to find out what manner of offspring we will create." His smile was tinged with melancholy. "Oh well, perhaps after tonight Regina will realize I'm not such a heartless old reprobate."

"She already knows that." Halfway out of the Jeep I paused. "When they find out Habiba's gone, will Schechtmann and his people give you trouble?"

"Oh, I hope so."

"I'm serious."

"Young woman, don't worry about me! This old *schwein-hund* has learned many a new trick over the years."

I believed he had.

The tall mangroves leaned outward from the edge of the sheltered cove, their high-arching aerial roots knitting land and sea together in a chaotic tangle. I waited beneath them, watching the jetty and allowing the mosquitoes that bred there to feed on me. The trees' spindly trunks and overarching branches cast grotesque shadows as light began to show in the east; when they shifted in the wind their sighs sounded like a dying woman's last breath. It put a sharp edge on my tension, and I repeatedly glanced at my watch. Four twenty-seven, and the minute hand didn't seem to be moving.

Maybe the watch was broken. It was guaranteed to be waterproof, had stood me in good stead in the health club pool. But what if its recent hard service had been too much? What if I was late? Maybe Habiba had come and gone. Or come and been apprehended by Schechtmann's guards. Maybe the game I'd been playing with her in the living room at the compound had been too obvious—

Stop it, McCone! This is no time to panic.

Eastern sky getting dangerously light now. How much longer before sunrise? Long enough for Habiba to get here and for us to swim to the boat? What if—

Movement on the jetty. Habiba's dark head appeared. She pulled herself up, slipped on the loose stones, took a tumble down the other side. It must have hurt, but she made no sound. Just got up, brushed herself off, and kept coming.

Brave little thing, I thought as I kicked off the rubber thongs and stepped out of the mangroves' shelter.

Habiba saw me and began to run. We met halfway, and she threw her arms around my thighs. "You really came for me," she whispered.

I pulled her arms away, squatted down. "No time to talk, we've got to move fast. Can you swim?"

"Yes."

"Good." I stripped off the borrowed shirt and dropped it

on the sand. Let the tide take it. Let Schechtmann's guards find it. I didn't care.

Habiba stripped off her T-shirt and shorts. Underneath she wore a pink tank suit. "I knew we'd have to swim," she said. "When I told my dad I wanted to go home to Grams, he said there wasn't any way off the island except to swim, and if I tried that the sharks'd get me."

And Zebediah Altagracia thought he'd been a bad father!

"Don't worry about sharks," I said. "They're a lot farther out to sea than the boat that's waiting for us."

Habiba stiffened. "When Uncle Klaus took my mom and me on the boat back home—"

"I know, Habiba, but we can't talk about that now. We can't even think about it. All our energy has to go into swimming. You ready?"

"Yes."

"Then let's go." I took her hand and we waded into the water. The bottom was rocky, and I fought for balance. Twice Habiba stumbled; once she almost pulled me down with her. When the water was thigh high I ducked down and floated; she followed my lead.

I said, "I'm going to put you in a lifeguard's hold. Do you know what that is?"

"Uh-huh."

"I'll tow you. You help out by kicking. When we get on the other side of those rocks, we're going to drift for a few minutes till we see a light flash on the boat. Then we'll paddle toward it as fast as we can. I won't let go of you; we won't be separated at any time. Okay?"

"Okay."

I got hold of her around the shoulders. She was very light and swimming to the other side of the rocks was easy. Of course, if we had to move fast—

Follow your own advice. Put all your energy into the job at hand.

Beyond the rocks the current was stronger. I kicked hard to maintain position, reminded Habiba to do the same. The horizon was distinguishable now, but I couldn't make out the shape of the speedboat. I swept my eyes back and forth, watching for Lloyd Fisher's signal. Habiba was facing toward shore; I told her to keep an eye out for activity at the compound.

Minutes passed—more than I was comfortable with.

Maybe Lloyd had taken off and left us. Maybe Regina's information about him had been wrong and I shouldn't have trusted him.

In a scared little voice Habiba said, "Something's happening."

"What?"

"The lights just went on in my cottage."

Dammit! Where was Lloyd?

"Somebody's running out of there! I think it's my nanny." Shit!

"She's going up to the big house!"

I resisted the impulse to look around. Kept scanning the sea. Where was Lloyd? *Where?*

A light flashed—a good distance away, but not an impossible one.

"Don't panic, Habiba. We're on our way. We'll be at the boat before they start looking for you."

I began towing her for all I was worth.

"Here, dry yourself off. You don't want to catch a chill." Lloyd tossed a towel to me, wrapped Habiba in another.

"We've got to get out of here," I said. "They've already discovered Habiba's missing."

"By the time they figure out she's not on the island we'll be long gone." He pulled an oar from behind the seats and handed it to me. "Habiba, you're gonna have to crouch down on the floor in front of the seat there, so you won't get clipped on the head. Sharon and I are gonna paddle the boat out a little farther. That way when the engine starts it won't alert them."

She shivered and slipped down while Lloyd got the second oar. Then we set to paddling. I'd thought my arms ached before, but now every stroke grated. My head ached, too— a sharp throbbing in my sinus cavities. And my back—Jesus, was I turning into an old woman? I'd be forty in September. Forty wasn't old. Only the beginning of the prime of life, if you listened to Jane Fonda.

Of course, in the fifteen years prior to *her* fortieth birthday, Jane hadn't been stabbed, almost drowned, suffered numerous contusions and a couple of concussions, and once been shot in the ass. What did she know, anyway?

I paddled stoically, too proud to grunt and moan as I wanted to.

After what seemed like an interminable time but was probably only five minutes, Lloyd said to stop. I handed him my oar, nearly whacking him in the face with it, and he stowed both. "Put Habiba on your lap and belt youself in," he told me. "We're about to motate."

I pulled the little girl from where she crouched on the floor. She didn't speak, didn't seem able to help me, either. Anxiously I looked at her face. She was pale, and her eyes were blank and glazed.

"You okay, kid?"

She nodded unconvincingly.

"Just hang in there. The bad part's almost over."

The speedboat's engine boomed in the silence. I barely had time to secure the belt before we took off with a space-age thrust that pushed us deep into the seat's padding. We were motating, all right.

The bad part's almost over, I repeated to myself.

Some three hours later those words would make me a liar.

At shortly after nine the departures terminal at Princess Juliana was jammed. Long lines snaked toward the ticket counters and overflowed onto the sidewalk. One glum group of teenagers sat on their bags in the middle of the floor, making everyone detour around them. Many people looked rumpled and tired, as if they'd been up all night. In this crowd Habiba and I wouldn't stand out, in spite of our weariness and the cheap, ill-fitting T-shirt and shorts I'd bought for her from a sidewalk vendor after Lloyd Fisher dropped us on the Philipsburg quay.

Gage Renshaw had told me I'd recognize the courier bringing Habiba's passport by his RKI blazer. I spotted him quickly, leaning against the wall by the entrance to the duty-free shops, the too-heavy garment slung over his shoulder, sweat beading his forehead. Habiba and I threaded our way over there hand in hand, and I showed him my identification.

He examined it, nodded, and removed an envelope from the inside pocket of the blazer. As he handed it to me he said, "Looks like you've given me a vacation on the company."

"Staying down for a few days?" I checked the passport and placed it with my own in the straw bag I'd also bought from the vendor.

"I'm stuck here for however long it takes to settle it." He motioned around the terminal.

"I don't follow you."

"They went ahead and struck."

"What? Oh, *no!*" Vaguely I remembered reading in the San Francisco paper about a possible strike of American Airlines flight attendants, but that had been last week when I didn't know I'd be flying anywhere, so I hadn't paid much attention. "How'd you get here?"

"Continental. But the firm booked me an open return, since they didn't know when you'd show, and now all the seats're filled with people from the flights American canceled yesterday." He shrugged philosophically. "Guess I'll check into a hotel and find the nearest casino."

I turned and looked at the American counter. The line was still out the door, but I'd reserved first-class seats; there was a shorter line at that window. I started to speak to the courier and found he'd disappeared into the crowd.

Dammit! I could have used his help. Of course, he wasn't aware of the seriousness of our situation; RKI shared information with its employees on a need-to-know basis. I glanced down at Habiba. She was watching me, solemn and a little scared. I took her hand again. "Don't worry. We'll go talk to the ticket agent."

The agent wasn't optimistic. "The aircraft is here," he said in the soft cadence of the islands, "and we are trying to put together a crew. If we can do that, your flight will leave on time. If not, we will put you up at one of the nearby hotels— at our expense, of course."

I gripped the counter, fighting panic. By now Schechtmann and his people had figured out that I'd removed Habiba from Jumbie Cay; how long before they also figured out my probable course of action? How long before they searched the airport, canvassed the hotels?

"Ma'am? Are you all right?"

No point in taking it out on the agent; he looked as haggard as I felt. "I'm okay. When will you know if the flight's going?"

"Check with me in an hour." He glanced at our passports, issued tickets and boarding passes. I tried to take that as a positive sign.

Habiba grabbed my hand again and walked beside me, head bowed, as we went to a second window to pay our departure taxes. This was the point I'd been concerned about: would they examine her passport and see she'd never entered? But a person who is leaving legally from an airport is presumed to have arrived the same way; the woman in the booth took my money, stamped the passports, and returned them with receipts tucked inside.

Habiba was clutching at my trousers. I looked down and saw she was still staring at the floor. "Hey," I said, squatting in front of her, "are you feeling okay?"

She shrugged.

"You know what? We need to eat something. That'll make us both feel better."

She didn't look too convinced, but she nodded.

I took her hand again and steered her toward a stairway leading to the restaurant. It too was jammed, but we found a corner table and ordered cheeseburgers. The room was hot and muggy; ceiling fans gave little relief. All around us people talked in loud voices; some actually seemed to be enjoying the situation and others, who had probably been here all night, were on their way to becoming obnoxiously drunk. Through the windows overlooking the field I could see our plane—a 727 around which there was a suspicious lack of activity.

Habiba remained silent, but she ate her burger and fries with concentration, then asked for a chocolate sundae. I forced myself to eat and drank three cups of coffee, but I kept blanking out, my eyes focusing on the black-and-white floor tiles. The what-ifs echoing in my mind threatened to drown out the din around us. When Habiba finished the sundae, I tucked some bills under the edge of my plate and said, "Let's go see if they know anything more about when our flight's leaving."

She nodded and got up, slipping her hand into mine as we left the table.

Downstairs the terminal was even more crowded, and tempers were fraying. A man in a business suit began to berate the teenagers for blocking the center of the floor; a woman in a sequined T-shirt was screaming at a ticket agent. I started toward the first-class window, but Habiba hung back, tugging on my hand. I glanced at her, saw her eyes were filled with panic.

"What? Who do you see?"

"One of the guards from Uncle Klaus's. Over there by the shops talking to a man with a broom."

Surreptitiously I looked that way. A tall man in a khaki shirt and shorts was in conversation with a janitor. He held out his hand at Habiba's height, then moved it to mine. Describing us. The janitor frowned, then nodded and motioned at the stairs to the restaurant. The man in khaki handed him a tip and pushed through the crowd.

"We're out of here." I started toward the automatic doors. For a moment Habiba froze, holding me back, then she trotted along. Taxis lined the curb; I headed for the nearest one, but turned when I spotted a familiar face beneath a Dodgers cap.

"Kenny! Remember me?"

He squinted. ". . . You the lady I took to Miz Altagracia's." His expression wasn't particularly warm; I supposed that he feared that I was about to foist more religious tracts on him.

"Can you take us there now? Double the fare, since there're two of us?"

"You betcha, get in."

As Kenny closed the backseat door behind us, Habiba moaned. "There's Uncle Klaus in that taxi! He sees us!"

I looked where she pointed. It was Schechtmann, all right, staring at us from a green Datsun. Kenny got in and I leaned forward. "You see that green car that's backing out? He's going to follow us. Can you lose him?"

Kenny glanced at the Datsun and laughed. "Does a dog got fleas? That Slow Eddie Frazier. Hold on!"

He reversed the Toyota and kept backing, clear through the

driveway marked In Only. Made a sweeping turn in front of an oncoming limo. Jammed the car into first gear and gunned it through a narrow alley between a convenience store and a gas station, cackling maniacally all the while.

I looked at Habiba. Her eyes were livelier than I'd seen them, and her lips were parted.

Kenny sped between two rows of buildings. Made a screeching left into a side street. I peered through the rear window and saw no sign of the green taxi.

"Slow Eddie, he still tryin' to get outa the airport," Kenny assured me.

Next we were cruising at a stately speed up the driveway of a gaudy pink hotel. The palm trees sported Christmas wreaths in spite of it being May, and electrified reindeer sculptures cavorted on the lawn. Kenny saluted the doorman, who looked like one of Santa's elves, and we turned down a service road. When we emerged from the hotel grounds we were a block from the main highway.

"Hunky-dory, huh?" our driver asked.

"Uh-*huh*!" Habiba exclaimed—and actually smiled.

Twenty

Goats scattered and ran as Kenny wheeled the taxi into Regina Altagracia's yard. The front door of the small whitewashed house opened almost immediately, and the tall woman stepped out, shading her eyes with her hand. After having met her father, I could see her resemblance to him: they had the same long bones, straight nose, and strong jaw. The same steely will, too. She came over as Kenny stopped the car and peered in at us.

Kenny asked, "You want me to wait?"

Before I could say no, Regina told him, "Yes. I'll bring you some fresh-squeezed lemonade."

The driver gave her a look that said lemonade was not his drink of choice and why didn't she offer him a beer, then leaned back resignedly and reached for the radio's knob. Habiba and I got out and followed Regina inside.

"So this is the young lady you came all this way for," she said, leaning down and tipping Habiba's chin up so she could study her face. "I'm *very* glad to see you."

Habiba looked wary and remained silent.

I said, "I think Habiba's tired. We've had ... quite an adventure."

"I see. Would you like to lie down, young lady?"

"Yes, please."

"Then come with me. I'll put you in my bedroom, where we'll be able to hear you if you need anything." She took the little girl's hand and led her from the room. Habiba looked anxiously over her shoulder at me. I smiled reassuringly and sank into a chair.

It seemed a decade since I'd last been in this room—that much had happened in the past eighteen hours. Eighteen rough hours with no sleep, little food, and too much grueling activity. And now . . . I leaned forward, my face in my hands, unable to imagine what still lay before us.

Regina called, "I'll take your driver his lemonade, and then we'll talk."

"I don't think he needs to wait. We're likely to be here for a while."

"Yes, I heard about the strike. But you don't want him leaving here; he knows where you are and he can be bought."

". . . Right." Weariness was making me stupid.

Regina passed through the room with a big plastic tumbler, returned, and went into the kitchen again. When she came back she was carrying a bottle of brandy and a glass. I stared at it.

"Yes, we Seventh-day Adventists don't approve of liquor, but this is not for recreational purposes." She poured with the expertise of a seasoned bartender. "Medicine. Drink up."

She was her father's daughter—pragmatic as they come. I drank and felt an insidious warmth creep through my body.

Regina settled into her recliner, putting up its footrest. "My father called an hour ago and told me that you'd gotten safely off Jumbie Cay. Lloyd Fisher phoned him when he returned to Anguilla."

"Is your father all right?"

"Why wouldn't he be?"

"They discovered Habiba was gone while we were still in the water off Goat Point. I assumed Schechtmann would give him a hard time."

Regina smiled in the same wicked way as her father. "He tried, but Daddy drove him off. He loaded his cannon as soon as he got home, and when Schechtmann arrived, he threatened to open fire."

"My God."

She nodded, laughing softly. "When I lived with him, his craziness drove me wild. Now I can appreciate it."

I sensed a reconciliation brewing in the Altagracia family, but decided not to comment lest I derail it. Stubborn people like Zebediah and his daughter—and me—hated for others to realize that they were backing down from even the most unreasonable of positions.

Regina's smile faded. "Now tell me what's wrong. Something worse than a canceled flight has happened; the child is terrified, and you look unnerved, too."

I explained about Schechtmann and his people appearing at the airport. "There's no way we're going to be able to take a commercial flight out of here with them looking for us."

She pursed her lips. "What about a charter?"

"By now I'm sure the story of what happened to Cam Connors has gotten out among the air-charter operators. I doubt anyone will be terribly receptive to flying me anyplace."

"You're right. But there's Lloyd Fisher; he could—"

"Can't risk it. Schechtmann might have a helicopter or a seaplane at his disposal; they could drop on the speedboat."

"Mmm."

We fell silent. I finished the brandy, felt lethargy steal over me. I could sleep for a week. I could say the hell with it and just hole up in the building where Regina sheltered her refugees—

And how long would it take Klaus Schechtmann to make the connection between Zebediah's "bible-thumping daughter" and me? I couldn't do that to Regina—or to Habiba and myself.

I sat up straighter, shook my head when Regina motioned at the brandy bottle. I had to think; we had to make our move quickly.

"Sharon," she said suddenly, "what about that boyfriend of yours?"

"Hy? What about—" Of course! Hy was in Santo Domingo. I had a contact number for him there. Hy, who was so talented at getting people out of tight situations. I rummaged through the straw bag and came up with the paper on which I'd scrawled the number. Regina motioned to the phone, and I went over there and dialed.

Hy wasn't there.

He'd left for the airport two hours ago, the man who answered told me. I asked for the number, called it, and requested they page him.

And waited.

"Still paging."

Please be there.

"Still paging."

Please!

"I'm sorry, your party doesn't—Here you are, ma'am."

"Ripinsky?"

"McCone?"

"Thank God! Are you all right?"

"Why wouldn't I be?"

"Renshaw said you were sick."

"I was, but I got some pills for it, and so far they're working. Where are you?"

"On St. Maarten, and I need your help." Briefly I filled him in on what had happened since I left San Francisco. When I got to the part about Cam Connors, his rage was apparent in the single syllable he uttered. I went on, "As if that wasn't enough, then there was the difficulty of getting her off the island, and now I can't get us off *this* island. And sooner or later Schechtmann's bound to figure out where we are. Probably sooner."

"Damned inconvenient time for a strike, but I suppose some good came of it; you caught me here because *my* flight was canceled."

"So you can't get off *that* island." I laughed and heard a hysterical edge to my voice.

"Of course I can get off the island. Tell me this: is there a small airfield somewhere near you?"

I turned to Regina. "He wants to know if there's a small airfield nearby."

"Esperance, over at Grand Case. But your Mr. Schechtmann will have thought of that."

"Did you hear?" I asked Hy.

"Yes. Ask her about an airstrip—anything where I can land a small plane."

"An airstrip, Regina? Anything?"

She thought. "A man I know—not exactly a friend, but someone whom I trust—lives on a defunct sugar plantation, also near Grand Case. The former owner was a pilot and put in an airstrip; perhaps it's still usable."

Hy said, "Ask her to find out. If so, she should get its location in relationship to Esperance and some landmarks. I'll call you back in fifteen minutes or so, and in the meantime I'll look into aircraft rentals."

"Will do." I gave him Regina's number and turned the phone over to her.

She spoke with her acquaintance for a long time in French, jotting down notes on a scratch pad. When she finished she said, "The airstrip is in bad condition, but Marcel says a good pilot could land there. He's willing to assist us and has given me the landmarks. You'll have to fly out by daylight—too risky in the dark. Will that be a problem?"

"No, Hy's checking on rentals right now."

We sat back to wait for his call. It came fifteen minutes late, but he had good news. "I've got hold of a Cherokee One-eighty. It'll cost a king's ransom, but RKI's paying. Do we have an airstrip?"

"Yes." I took Regina's notes and described its condition.

"Piece of cake. Location?"

I gave him that, and the landmarks.

"I can be there in a couple of hours."

"Habiba and I will be waiting."

The sugar plantation had been established in the eighteenth century and allowed to fall to ruins in the nineteenth. Outbuildings were collapsed, palmetto had claimed the fields, and moss weighed down the branches of the trees. Only the dark stone house remained as a reminder of the days of cane and slavery. It too was in bad repair and covered with a tangle of vines; a ravaged and rusted Studebaker moldered in its garden.

Regina had insisted we have Kenny drive us there and cautioned me against paying him when we arrived. Instead she took the money and would turn it over to him only after we'd taken off and he'd delivered her home. The driver displayed little curiosity about our mission; probably he thought we were going to the plantation to bother its present occupant about joining the church. His only comment came as we entered the grounds; the plantation, he said, was "cheesy."

After we got out of the taxi Regina asked me to wait with Habiba in the shade of an overgrown arbor near the junked car. She went to the door of the house, knocked, and spoke for a time with someone inside. Then she returned to us, walking slowly in the oppressive midafternoon heat.

"Marcel has given me directions to the airstrip. He's a bit of a recluse, so he won't be accompanying us." She glanced at the taxi, then shook her head. "It's a good distance from the house. There's an access road, but we have time to walk it, and I don't want that driver seeing the plane or its identification number."

"You really don't trust him."

"As I said yesterday, I don't *know* him. Suspicion of strangers has become a habit of mine."

"Yet you trusted me when I came knocking on your door."

"I've also developed instincts about people. I recognize my own kind." She motioned toward the garden and we began to walk. Habiba, who hadn't said a word since she earlier accepted a glass of juice at Regina's, clutched the leg of my trousers. I squeezed her shoulder briefly, glad she didn't want to hold my hand; it was too damn hot for physical contact.

Beyond the overrun garden the trees grew thicker and the moss hung lower. Regina said, "Marcel has really let this place go."

"How long has he lived here?"

"Ten years."

"It looks like more than ten years' neglect to me."

"Things grow rapidly here in the tropics. The previous owner had the property well on its way to recovery; he planned to make it into a very exclusive resort."

"What happened?"

"He died."

Habiba's hand tugged spasmodically at my trouser leg. I looked down, saw her head was bowed again. The word "died," I knew, had triggered her response. Soon we were going to have to talk about her mother's death, before bottling up the experience caused permanent emotional scars.

Regina had noticed, too. "Sorry," she said softly.

We walked for nearly twenty minutes through the thick thorn forest and finally arrived at a cleared area through which a slender ribbon of runway stretched. I stared at the cracked and potholed tarmac in dismay. I couldn't have landed anything on that, wouldn't have attempted it. But Hy had landed all kinds of aircraft under all sorts of conditions. He could do it.

Regina was wiping sweat from her brow. I thought of her long walk back to the taxi. "Are you going to be okay?"

She smiled. "As my father's continued existence proves, tough old birds run in the Altagracia family."

"Still, I'm sorry for all I've put you through."

"I would rather be doing this than knocking on the doors of people who don't want to hear the Lord's word. I long ago decided that His message is better spread by action than by talk and literature."

Maybe if my life had been different she'd have made me a convert, but religious faith didn't work for me. Not that I was opposed to religion, expecially when there were people like Regina doing good works in its name.

We waited, sweltering under the trees that encroached upon the tarmac. Habiba let go of my trousers and sat down, her back against a palmetto bole. The birds had fled upon our arrival, and silence was heavy around us. I looked at my watch. How much longer?

The minutes dragged. There was a rustling in the thorn forest, and I whirled, peering around. It went on for a moment, then stopped. I glanced at Regina, who stood erect, fanning herself with her hand. Nothing to worry about, I decided. Regina knew this type of terrain, would have reacted to a suspicious noise. Still, I continued to look around, seeing nothing, until I heard a drone coming from the west.

A small plane appeared above the trees. Habiba jumped up and watched it, shading her eyes with her hands. Regina seemed to have been in a heat-induced trance; now she came out of it, smiling broadly.

The Cherokee was white and trim. It flew in a steady descent toward the strip of tarmac. Soon we'd be in the air, heading for a destination that would be one hop closer to home—and safety.

The landing gear was down and the flaps were partially extended. The plane neared the end of the runway. Made a pass over it and kept going.

Regina and Habiba looked anxiously at me.

"He's checking the condition of the tarmac," I told them.

The plane made its turn and started back. Habiba grabbed my hand and gave a little jump. The Cherokee descended steadily, its flaps fully extended now. It glided above the runway and touched down near its end. As it turned and taxied toward us, I peeled Habiba's fingers off mine and ran toward it.

The Cherokee came to a stop; its prop feathered and the power cut off. Its door opened and Hy looked out. "Anybody here want to hitch a ride to the Florida Keys with me?" he called.

PART THREE

THE JOURNEY

MAY 26–28

Twenty-one

Sunlight streaming down from a skylight, cooking me. More still, muggy air. More insect bites.

I've got to get out of here. Got to get to Habiba, to safety.

No, wait. I *am* safe, and so is she. We're not in the Caribbean anymore.

I sat up and looked around. A small white room, thrift-shop furnishings, double bed with the imprint of a head on the other pillow. Hy's head. But where . . . ?

Oh, right.

We were at the home of one of his network of old buddies, a man who hadn't been here when we arrived the previous night and whose name Hy hadn't told me. On one of the small Florida Keys, just large enough to accommodate a few buildings and the airstrip where we landed. Hy hadn't mentioned the island's name either, and his guarded manner told me that something was going on here, possibly something illegal. I didn't want to know what it was; I had enough to concern me.

I got up, went to the window, and parted the slats of the blinds. Shocking aquamarine water and a ramshackle dock. Two figures seated at its end, their bare feet dangling. Hy and Habiba. She was talking, and he listened intently, nodding now and then.

Should I disturb them? Probably not; if I did, she might relapse into that worrying silence. Besides, I had things to take care of.

First a shower. Then throw on my soiled, rumpled clothing. Then go in search of a phone.

The phone was in a kitchen that told me Hy's friend probably lived alone. A trash can was crammed with take-out food containers; beer bottles stood in the sink, linked by a trail of ants. I'm not the tidiest of housekeepers, but the smell in there would have launched me on a three-day binge of cleaning. I opened a window to let some of it out, then placed a credit-card call to Greg Marcus.

"It's about time you got back to me," he said. "You home?"

"No."

"Where, then?"

"Can't say."

"Why the secrecy?"

"If I told you, it wouldn't be a secret, now would it? Did you check on Adah Joslyn?"

"I did. Sharon, we have a . . . situation on our hands."

Bad news, when Greg used the word "situation" in that tone. "Tell me."

"Well, I didn't find anything out of the way at her apartment except for a huge cat that had torn a hole in a bag of Friskies and eaten the whole thing. Practically ripped my hand off when I put out some tuna."

Poor Charley!

"But," he went on, "someone claiming to be the Diplobomber has posted on the TechnoWeb that he's taken Joslyn hostage. He says he'll make his demands known soon."

Jesus. "How do you know it's really him? It could be some computer geek playing games. Did he present any proof he's got her?"

"No, but until we know otherwise, we've got to take him seriously. And if he doesn't have her, where is she?"

Guiltily I thought of Adah's guns, presently in the strongbox bolted to the floor of my linen closet. If what she'd said in her phone message to me was true, she'd gone up against the bomber unarmed—and it was my fault. "So what's being done about this?" I asked.

"Ed Parkhurst, head of the task force, is setting everything in place for getting her back once the bomber makes his demands; our chief is monitoring the situation. In case it's money he wants, they've made an arrangement with the Federal Reserve, and their people're working round the clock to identify him. Their court order for a list of the Web's subscribers was denied yesterday, but now it's a whole new ball game, and they've reapplied. We expect he'll ask for a ransom—"

"It's not money he wants."

"What, then?"

I'd begun to sense it, but it wasn't yet clear. "Greg, I've got to go." I broke the connection.

Adah, in the hands of the bomber. My God. What would he do to her? What was she feeling right now? She wouldn't break, not if I knew her. Wouldn't let him see her fear, no matter what. Poor Adah—full of bravado in the face of her career crashing and burning, skating on thin emotional ice to begin with. And now she'd fallen into the hands of a man who toyed with people's lives, who had killed indiscriminately, would kill again. . . .

What exactly had she said in the message on my machine? "I stumbled onto a lead on the bomber by coincidence, and it's too damn close to home for comfort. I'm heading out now to confirm it. Sure wish you hadn't appropriated my guns."

If Adah died because I'd done that, I would never, ever forgive myself.

Don't pick out your hair shirt yet, McCone. Do something. Dig at that motive you've begun to sense.

I picked up the receiver and placed a call to my office.

"Shar!" Mick's voice was an octave higher than normal. "Have you heard about Adah? Her mother called, and then her father. They've both gone round the bend, and it's not pretty on their side."

"I can imagine. If they call again, tell them we're working on a promising lead. It won't be a lie; I need you to dig up some more data for me. Get Charlotte Keim to help you. You have something to write with?"

"Yes, but where—"

"No time for questions. Get moving on this."

When they heard my footsteps on the dock, Habiba and Hy turned. "Thought you'd never wake up," he said, grabbing my ankle and squeezing it.

"I suppose the two of you have been up since sunrise."

"Damn near, huh, Habiba?"

She nodded and smiled shyly.

I sat down beside them, let my bare feet dangle, too.

Hy said, "It's too pretty here to sleep all morning. In a few minutes I'm taking Habiba for a spin in the outboard. Come along, if you like."

"We're not leaving right away, then?"

"I've booked us a flight out of Key West at five-forty."

"Commercial flight?"

"Uh-huh. American Eagle. The strike's been settled, and we'll connect with our San Francisco flight in Miami."

"Good. Where's your friend? Still not home?"

"He came in early this morning, and now he's ferrying the Cherokee back to Santo Domingo."

"Nice of him."

"He owes me."

"So did Cam Connors."

Hy's jaw grew tight. "Let's not ruin a beautiful morning by talking about him. So, do you want to come along with us?"

"I don't think so. I want to call Renshaw to tell him we're safe, and I'm waiting to hear from Mick."

He raised his eyebrows inquiringly.

I shook my head, motioning at Habiba; she was staring down into the water but appeared to be listening intently.

"Well, suit yourself. We'll be back in a couple of hours." He stood, held out his hand to the little girl. "Come on, sailor."

I watched them as they walked along the dock and angled across the sand to an old Chris-Craft that was beached under a stand of mangroves. Then I got up and went to the house.

I was back on the dock when they returned. Habiba was wearing a new floppy-brimmed straw hat that was more my size than hers; beneath it her face looked sunburned and weary. Hy didn't look much better. Habiba waved at me and trudged toward the house. He came along the dock carrying a shopping bag.

"Is she all right?" I asked as he sat down beside me.

"Just tired. I sent her in to take a nap."

"What about you?"

"I've had better days."

"Feverish?"

"Some." He patted my knee. "Don't worry, McCone. It's just taking the drugs a while to work."

And that in itself worried me, but all I said was, "You'd better see your own doctor when you get home. What's in the bag?"

"Fresh clothes for you and her. We stopped off at Marathon."

I opened the bag and pawed through its contents. The sizes of the jeans, Tees, light jackets, and athletic shoes were right. "Thanks. You did good."

"You're welcome. Habiba helped me choose; she was very picky about your stuff."

"Funny kid. I saw her talking with you this morning. Did she tell you about her mother?"

"Yeah. The kid's gone through hell the last few days."

"Did she see what happened to Mavis?"

"No. She was below deck in the main cabin, but she heard Schechtmann and her mother arguing above just before they got under way. There was a thump, then they were quiet, and after a bit Schechtmann came below and told her Mavis had changed her mind about making the trip. That panicked Habiba, and she wanted to go ashore, but Schechtmann said it was too late and locked her in the forward cabin. I think at that point she suspected what had happened but wouldn't let herself believe it."

"She knows now, though."

"Schechtmann told her when they got to Jumbie Cay. He said Mavis had an accident."

"Sounds like murder to me."

"Yeah, and Habiba's a potential witness. You can see why

old Klaus wanted to keep her on the island—and why he'll probably try to get her back. You talk with Renshaw?"

"Yes. I didn't have our flight number, so we're to call him with our ETA when we change planes in Miami. He'll send a car to SFO for us. I also talked with Greg Marcus." Briefly I explained the situation with Joslyn. "I'm still waiting on Mick. He's pulling together some data for me, and if it indicates what I think it will, I'll have a handle on the bomber's motive."

"Oh?"

"Yes, but I don't want to talk about it till I'm sure." I glanced at my watch. "It's taking him a long time."

"Why don't you call him?"

"No, we'll be in San Francisco later tonight. That'll be time enough."

At five o'clock that afternoon the heat at the Key West airport had given me a headache. To avoid dwelling on the pain, I concentrated on Habiba while Hy checked us in at the flight gate. When I'd awakened her from her nap she'd been curled in a fetal position on the bed in the room next to ours; now she looked as though she'd like to lie down on the floor and curl up again.

"Are you excited about seeing your Grams tomorrow?" I asked.

She shook her head. "She'll be mad at me. Everything that's happened is my fault."

"Habiba, none of it is your fault."

"Yes, it is."

"Why?"

"My dad said so. He said that if I wasn't born he and Mom would've been okay together, and then a thousand bad things wouldn't've happened."

A thousand bad things—including him killing Chloe Love and and Schechtmann killing Mavis. The son of a bitch had no right to blame anything on this psychologically abused child!

I squatted down and put my arms around her, feeling more bone than flesh. "You know," I said, "fathers aren't always right. Sometimes they have . . . things wrong with them that make them say things that just aren't true. Remember what your dad said about the sharks getting you if you tried to swim away from Jumbie Cay?"

". . . Yes."

"Did the sharks get us?"

"No."

"See?"

Hy came up behind us. "We'll board in about twenty minutes."

Habiba stiffened.

I said, "It's only Hy—"

"No, there's my dad."

I turned my head and looked around Hy. Dawud Hamid stood at the podium talking to the clerk. She frowned and shook her head. He leaned forward, banging on the counter with the flat of his hand as he spoke.

Asking if a child of Habiba's description had checked in. Thank God the airline wouldn't give out that sort of information!

But how the hell had he known we'd be flying out of Key West?

Hy had looked over his shoulder, too. Now he stepped between the podium and us. He held out his hand to Habiba, and she grabbed it. Clung to it with whitened knuckles as they turned and began walking away from the gate. I followed, staying close behind her and blocking her from Hamid's line of sight.

Halfway to the security checkpoint Hy ducked into a recessed hallway leading to a service door. I slipped in behind him.

"Is it Hamid?" he asked.

"Yes. Let's wait and see what he does."

Habiba stood between us, her panicky eyes moving back and forth between Hy's face and mine. "Please don't let him take me back!"

"No way," he said tightly.

I took the oversized straw hat from her head, pushed my hair up, and plopped the hat on top. Then I looked out toward the flight gate. Hamid was striding up the concourse, a scowl spoiling his handsome features.

I motioned for Hy and Habiba to get back. Stepped out after Hamid had passed and began walking the same way. He moved stiffly and angrily. Brushed against an old woman struggling with two carry-on bags and didn't bother to apologize. As he headed into the ticket lobby he seemed to calm down; his step became sure and fluid—the gait of a predator.

The small airport was sleepy at this early evening hour. The season was over here, the heat intense; the few people in the terminal moved in slow motion. I kept a good distance from Hamid and drifted toward a bank of phones.

He went to the American Eagle counter. Took out a credit card and brandished it self-importantly, motioning toward the concourse.

He planned to take our flight.

The clerk took the credit card. She ran it through, then issued a ticket and boarding pass. Hamid snatched them up and strode toward the phones; I slipped into one of the kiosks, watching him as he made a brief call. When he hung up he went directly to the gate where our flight was boarding.

Hy and Habiba were still in the hallway where I'd left them. He was squatting, his arms around her, her face pressed against his shirtfront. I touched her lightly on the head and said to him, "Let me have my ticket."

"What?"

"Hamid's taking the flight; so am I. You and Habiba grab a cab and check into the nearest hotel."

"McCone—" He hesitated momentarily, then held out the ticket envelope. "I'll page you in Miami."

The plane was a turboprop, some thirty seats, max. Too damn small for traveling incognito. I pulled the straw hat lower on my forehead as I approached the gate. Hamid had already crossed the tarmac and was ascending the steps. When I handed my boarding pass to the woman at the gate I pointed to him and said, "That good-looking dark-haired guy who's getting on—do you remember what seat he's in?"

The attendant grinned and winked. "You noticed him, too. Next to last row, and you're at the front. Try switching after they reach cruising altitude."

"Thanks." I hurried outside, one hand clamped on the hat.

As I crossed to the plane I hunched so I appeared a couple of inches shorter; once inside, I kept my head lowered. My seat was in the second row, and I slid in quickly. Curled up, my feet on the companion seat that Habiba would have occupied, and pulled the hat over my face.

The flight was forty-nine minutes and uneventful. I was first through the door and into the terminal, where I staked out a position in the nearest bank of pay phones. Hamid came through the gate and stopped, looking around impatiently. A man approached him and offered his hand. They conferred briefly, then began walking up the concourse. After a moment I followed.

They say socialites and criminals can immediately sense their own kind. Maybe that's also true of investigators. Everything about this nondescript gray-haired man in resort clothes told me he was a private detective.

The two followed a hallway to the concourse where the American flights departed, went into a cocktail lounge, and took a table next to the railing that separated it from the main traffic way. I kept on to the next gate where a plane was arriving and mingled with the people greeting it. Hamid seemed on edge and kept looking around for a waitress; finally one appeared and took their order.

I was trying to gauge how close I could get to them without being spotted when a familiar name came over the loudspeaker: ". . . Hy Ripinsky. Paging Hy Ripinsky . . ."

Clever man. I smiled and moved toward the courtesy phones, still keeping an eye on Hamid's table. "Where are you?" I asked when Hy came on the line.

"A Ramada near the airport." He gave me the number.

"I'll call you back."

The waitress was setting drinks on the table now. She offered popcorn, but Hamid waved her away. I moved to a pay phone where I had a better vantage of the bar and inserted my credit card. Punched out the number Hy had given me while watching the two men talk. Hamid gestured impatiently. The other man listened and replied calmly, the way I would to a client who was being unreasonable but whose business I didn't want to lose.

"So what's happening, McCone?"

"Hamid's meeting with someone who I'm ninety-nine percent certain is a private investigator. They walked over to the concourse where the San Francisco flight leaves, so I guess he plans to take it. How's Habiba?"

"Relapsed into speaking words of one syllable."

"Are you worried about her?"

"Not particularly. I'd do the same in her situation."

"And how're you?"

"Better, now."

Hamid's companion was talking, sculpting his words with his hands. He motioned toward the concourse where the American Eagle flight had landed, then in the direction of the field. Hamid shook his head and leaned forward, speaking intensely and tapping the table with his index finger.

"McCone?"

"It doesn't look as though the meeting's going too well. Hamid's upset."

The investigator waited until Hamid concluded his tirade, then made a conciliatory motion and started to speak. Hamid cut him off and spoke loudly—delivering an ultimatum, I thought. The other man shook his head. Hamid stood, and this time his words carried: "I don't have time to listen to your excuses. You're fired!" Then he strode out of the lounge and down the concourse toward the gate for the San Francisco flight.

"Looks like he's going to board the flight," I said to Hy, "but I want to make sure. I'll call back in a while."

The investigator still sat at the table, looking both rueful and faintly amused. I glanced along the concourse and saw Hamid push through the crowd around the podium, his anger loosely reined now, his expression making people move aside. He waved his boarding pass at the gate attendant and rushed down the jetway.

I left the phone booth and went to the cocktail lounge.

Hamid's investigator was ordering another beer. He didn't look overly concerned about being fired, and he didn't seem surprised when I sat down opposite him.

"Nice surveillance, Ms. McCone. My client didn't make you, and I wouldn't've either, if I didn't know you."

I frowned. "We've met?"

"A number of years ago at the National Society of Investigators convention in San Diego. You wouldn't remember me, but of course you made an impression because of the murder and the job you and your colleague from San Francisco—I forget his name—did of solving it."

"I see. If you made me, why didn't you tip Hamid?"

"He and his associates aren't interested in you, only the kid, and she's not in evidence. Besides, Hamid's a horse's ass and too violent for his own good; he'd've probably attacked you on the spot. That kind of trouble I don't need."

"You're right about that violence, Mr. . . . ?"

He produced a business card: Kent Maynard, Maynard Associates, Boca Raton.

"Mr. Maynard, am I correct in thinking Hamid fired you?"

He smiled and reached for the beer that the waitress set down. When he cocked an eyebrow questioningly at me, I shook my head and he motioned her away. "He can't fire me."

"Why? Because the person who actually retained you is Klaus Schechtmann?"

Maynard merely smiled and sipped his beer.

"Did Hamid tell you why he's going to San Francisco?"

"That isn't completely clear. He seems to be ricocheting around, hindering more than he's helping."

"So why didn't Schechtmann come along, keep him in line?"

"I think you know the answer to that."

So Maynard was aware of the warrant on Klaus. "Have you worked for Schechtmann before?"

"Collected some accounts receivable."

Read that gambling debts. Kent Maynard wasn't the mild-mannered man he appeared. "I suppose he presented this as a child-custody case."

He nodded.

"Then you'd be better off fired. It's not that simple. The child's mother was killed—"

He held up his hand like a traffic cop. "I don't want to know."

Typical attitude of the nineties-style investigator, and one that probably would have made me more successful had I embraced it. "No, I guess you don't. And since you've seen that I don't have the child, you really have no further interest in me, now do you?"

He smiled. "Oh, yes, Ms. McCone, I have a great deal of interest in you. I assume that you had the kid in tow when you spotted Hamid at Key West. You've stashed her someplace, probably with your pilot friend, and you intend to hook up with them again. And I intend to stick with you—very closely."

He knew about Hy.

"Right now," he went on, "my people are canvassing the Key West hotels and charter and rental services. We've got people on surveillance at general aviation here, as well as at Orlando, which is the only other airport they could take a commercial flight to."

"Why are you telling me this? I can contact him and warn him."

"I'm telling you so you'll be aware of how hopeless your situation is—and how thorough and well financed we are. By all means, go ahead and warn your friend. Won't make any difference in the long run. Why don't you save yourself a lot of trouble and turn the kid over to me?"

I ignored the question. "My pilot friend—how do you know about him?"

He shook his head and smiled again.

Didn't matter how he'd found out about Hy; he still didn't know his name, or he'd have recognized it when it came over the loudspeaker. He would have flaunted that knowledge now. It wasn't a large advantage, but an edge nonetheless.

I suspected how Schechtmann and Hamid had found out we'd flown to the Florida Keys: Kenny the cab driver had not been as uncurious about our visit to the old sugar plantation as I'd assumed. He'd followed us through the thorn forest, heard Hy ask if we wanted to go to the Keys, and later contacted Schechtmann through his fellow driver, Slow Eddie Frazier. In a tourist area with a poor standard of living the residents are alert to the slightest scent of profit, and they'll sell anything they stumble across.

I should have paid more attention to the rustlings I'd heard in the thorn forest. I'd take a lesson from that mistake and be doubly on guard now.

Maynard said, "Why don't you just tell me where the kid is? Give her up and go home. Nobody's interested in you or your friend."

The hell they weren't. Maynard had to be stupid if he actually believed that.

I studied his face: lines around the eyes that suggested long nights of vision-straining surveillances; lines around the mouth that suggested long years of disappointment. In spite of the embossed card and the talk of his people, I sensed Maynard's operation was a small one, and that Klaus Schechtmann was a major client whom he wouldn't want to disappoint.

Maynard's muddy brown eyes were studying me in a similar fashion.

A good private investigator has to be a good actor: we adopt false facial expressions; we tell lies with body language; we alter our personas with vocal tone. We're two-sided: lying while seeming truthful; dripping sincerity while drowning in duplicity. Maynard was doing all of that, and pretty well. But not well enough to fool *this* actor.

I said, "Well, we both know the business. You do what you have to."

He spoke a bit too eagerly. "You'll turn the kid over?"

"No." I pushed away from the table and stood. "Right now I'm going to those phones—right over there where you can see me. I'll make some calls. Long ones, so you might as well stay here and finish your beer. In fact, have another, on me." I dug a five-dollar bill out of my pocket and set it on the table.

Maynard looked at it and then at me. "What the—"

"You're free to try to keep as close a surveillance on me as possible, Mr. Maynard. But it'll have to be on my terms. If you come any closer to me than, say, the distance from this table to those phone booths, I'll call Security. Your Florida P.I.'s license doesn't give you the right to harass or intimidate women, you know."

I let that sink in, then added, "As you said before, that kind of trouble you don't need."

Twenty-two

My first call was to Greg. "Anything on Joslyn?"

"No. Sharon—"

"No further postings on the Web?"

"Nothing. Where—"

"I'll be in touch."

Kent Maynard was finishing his beer, narrowed eyes fixed on me. I saluted him. He scowled.

For a moment I debated calling Renshaw to ask if he could help us out of this situation, but then I decided against it. Renshaw's methods tended to be high risk, and I was damned if I would allow him to endanger Habiba. Besides, I had RKI's best man only a Touch-Tone dial away. Between us, Hy and I would manage.

Mick's recorded voice was all I reached at my office. I redialed, this time Charlotte Keim's extension at RKI. Keim answered, sounding too frisky for someone laboring in the data-search section. Mick's voice in the background explained why. Oh, well, at least Keim had promised to be gentle with him. . . .

Charlotte became even more animated when I identified myself. "Sharon, you were right. We're definitely onto him!"

"Go ahead." I pulled a pad that I'd appropriated at Hy's friend's house from my bag.

"No, I'll let Mick tell you. These're really his findings."

Keim knew how to reel my nephew in, all right. When he came on the line he sounded as puffed up with self-importance as a blowfish is with air. "We just finished," he said, "and we found incidents like you described for each country—some of them outside the ten-year time frame that you originally set. You ready for this?"

"I'm ready."

In less than fifteen minutes I had it all. "Good work, Mick!"

"Thanks. So what should I do? Turn it over to the task force?"

I hesitated; something was cautioning me against that. "What you do is sit on it."

"But your friend Adah—"

"Could be in more danger if the bomber realizes how close we're getting. Do you think Parkhurst would keep this information confidential? It's the first substantial break in the case; he'd call a press conference. You are to do nothing with the information. Understood?"

"Yes."

"Now, I've got another assignment for you. How good are you at surveillance?"

"I'm—" He seemed about to extol abilities that he'd seldom tested, then retrenched. "I'm okay."

"Can you pick up somebody at the airport tonight and keep tabs on him indefinitely?"

"Yes."

"Good. Subject's name is Dawud Hamid. He's on American's ten-nineteen flight from Miami." I gave him Hamid's description. "Take that ridiculously expensive cellular phone you bought last month along with you so I can get in touch. And Mick—"

"Don't worry—I'll be careful, I won't run up any more expenses than I absolutely have to, and I won't fuck up."

Kent Maynard was still watching me. I returned his gaze with a steady and measured one of my own. Then I moved down the concourse to an empty gate and spread the pages of notes I'd taken during my conversation with Mick on a table between two chains of molded plastic seats. Tucked my legs under me and swiveled sideways so I could examine them. In a moment Maynard came out of the bar and moved to another gate, keeping exactly the distance I'd prescribed. I ignored him and hunched over the pages on the table.

Brazil: assault w/ deadly weapon, Washington, 1982

The son of the Brazilian ambassador had allegedly stabbed a bouncer at a nightclub, leaving him permanently disabled. The suspect spent a few hours in custody, then was released because of his diplomatic immunity. The embassy could have waived privileged status, but refused.

Saudi Arabia: rape, D.C., '83

A fifteen-year-old girl was allegedly raped at a party by the son of a diplomat attached to the Royal Embassy. The father was persuaded to repatriate the young man to their native country, but he reappeared in the D.C. area several weeks later. The authorities told the girl's parents there was nothing they could do because he was immune from prosecution.

Pakistan: child molestation, D.C., '82

A military attaché to the Pakistani Embassy fondled an eleven-year-old girl at the post exchange at Fort McNair, Virginia. Both the military police and the Criminal Investigation Division told her mother that their hands were tied because he was a technical staff member at a diplomatic mission—a category granted full immunity from criminal prosecution.

Ghana: rape, New York City, '81

The alleged perpetrator was the son of a United Nations delegate. In spite of a positive identification by the victim, he spent only forty-five minutes in custody and left the police station laughing. Later he voluntarily repatriated to Ghana.

Yemen: vehicular homicide, NYC, '86

The son of North Yemen's ambassador to the United Nations was driving along Park Avenue at lethal speed; his victim, a pedestrian, was dead on arrival at Bellevue Hospital. No charges were filed.

Mexico: assault w/ deadly weapon, NYC, '85

The Mexican Ambassador to the United Nations broke another driver's window and threatened him with a semiautomatic pistol in a dispute over a parking space. No charges were brought, although a cash settlement was later tendered to the victim.

Panama: reckless driving, D.C., '74

A cultural attaché to the Panamanian Embassy ran a red light and broadsided another car, permanently paralyzing one of its occupants. He carried no liability insurance and offered no financial restitution to the victims. Again no charges were filed and the diplomat was later posted elsewhere.

Libya: murder, London, '84

A Libyan assassin fatally shot a London policewoman in front of the embassy, where a peaceful demonstration of Libyan exiles was taking place. The murderer was never apprehended and the murder weapon never found, presumably because he had it in his sealed diplomatic baggage when he fled the country.

Belgium: drug trafficking, La Guardia Airport, '85

The chancellor of the Belgian Embassy at New Delhi, India, delivered heroin smuggled into the U.S. in a diplomatic pouch to an undercover agent of the DEA. Diplomatic immunity carried no weight in this case, as the chancellor was not posted to a U.S. mission; he received six years in prison. The high-profile case revealed that drug smuggling in diplomatic pouches was not an uncommon practice.

No wonder, I thought, that the Diplo-bomber's attacks seemed to follow a completely random pattern. They occurred anywhere from five to eighteen years after the diplomats' crimes. They were not necessarily directed at the perpetrators or even at the same missions. But now that I'd discovered the common link among his victims, it was apparent that the bomber was enraged at diplomatic crime—and that the specific crime that had fueled his anger was Chloe Love's murder.

Interesting that his last attack before the attempt at the Azadi Consulate had been on a diplomatic mission of a country whose lawbreaker had been brought to justice. A message, perhaps, about his future intentions?

What had the bomber been to Chloe? Friend? Relative? Lover? What had he been doing in Washington, D.C., and New York City? Why the two-year period of inactivity preceding the San Francisco bombings? And why play this contrived game of cat and mouse with the Azadis, rather than locate Dawud Hamid and deal with him directly? Why take innocent lives, injure innocent people?

Because originally he wanted to make a statement, but now it had gone beyond that. He was enjoying this, getting off on it. It had produced the biggest high of his life, and he would do anything to maintain it.

I glanced along the concourse. Kent Maynard was sitting patiently at the empty gate. I was certain his eyes hadn't left me the entire time I'd studied my notes.

I looked down at the pages again, staring at my scribblings till they blurred. The felt-tip lines and whorls bled out to an asymmetrical Rorschach blot and, like a psychiatric patient who has lost all other hope, I searched it for a vision of the bomber's face.

Nothing materialized.

I sighed and looked up. Maynard nodded pleasantly.

As if I didn't have enough problems, now I was cursed with this nuisance!

I got up and walked along the concourse to the phones. Called the Ramada in Key West. Maynard took up a position at the closest empty podium.

"Everything okay there?" I asked Hy.

"Still very silent on our young friend's part, but nobody's come looking for us, if that's what you mean."

"My colleague here claims his firm has people scouring the hotels for you." I related my conversation with Maynard and his actions since then. "He doesn't know your name, but he probably has a description, so watch out."

"How'd they find out we were in the Keys?"

"A money-hungry cabdriver, I think. But that doesn't matter now. What am I going to do about Maynard?"

"Well, do you suppose he's got the manpower he claims?"

"I really can't guess at that."

"Can you lose him?"

"I doubt it. He knows the territory here; I don't."

"Okay, let me do some phoning. I'll get back to you."

"McCone? Is Maynard still watching you?"

"Uh-huh."

"Okay, we've got a plan. I've set things up with my buddy, the one whose house we stayed at; he's a real helpful guy. Trouble is, you're going to have to spend the night there in the airport."

"I've spent the night worse places. Besides"—I glanced at Maynard, smiling faintly—"misery loves company."

"And you'll do your best to make sure he's miserable. Okay, tomorrow morning there's a Vanguard Air flight to Fort Myers at seven. I've already made you a reservation on it and a connecting flight to Tampa."

"What good's that going to do? Maynard'll buy a ticket at the podium and go along."

"That's the idea. When you get to Fort Myers, here's what you do . . ."

Vanguard Air was a grandiose choice of name at best. The ancient twenty-four-seat turboprop was the kind of aircraft that reduces passengers unaccustomed to small planes to babbling, quivering lumps of terror. The pilot looked to be around twelve years old; through the open cockpit door I could see him reading the operations manual. After a few minutes he announced our takeoff would be delayed because nobody could figure out why the baggage compartment door wouldn't close.

None of it bothered me. When you've flown upside down over the Sierra Nevada, you've seen it all from every angle— literally—and you know that the moment you set foot inside a plane you've turned your life over to random chance or fate or a higher power, whichever you happen to believe in. Apparently Kent Maynard didn't share my stoicism; from the instant he belted himself into the seat across the aisle, his face was tinged an unbecoming shade of gray. Our rattling, stuttering takeoff bleached it to white.

Serves him right for being so relentless, I thought as I pulled Habiba's hat down and closed my eyes. As Hy and I had counted on, Maynard had purchased a ticket at the podium as soon as he saw me present mine to the gate attendant. When he entered the cabin he looked somewhat tentative: it wasn't large enough for him to keep the prescribed distance; would I summon the pilot, as I'd threatened to summon airport security? I eased his concern by motioning cordially at the opposite seat.

Now I kept my eyes closed, conscious of Maynard's gaze. When I finally opened them, he was looking puzzled. Probably it had dawned upon him that I'd made it altogether too easy for him to stick with me. Soon he'd realize that I'd lured him into a situation where he would be unable to contact any of his people for forty-five minutes. Forty-five minutes that Hy and Habiba needed to make their move.

Fort Myers was another standard-issue airport, quiet at this time of morning when few flights were arriving. I spotted the women's restroom, crossed to it, and followed a woman in a long flowered skirt, flimsy pink blouse, and absurd floppy hat inside. She took the hat off immediately, turned, and extended her hand. "Edie Rosen."

"Sharon McCone."

Edie Rosen was about my height and had shoulder-length black hair styled very much like mine. She kicked off her sandals and began stripping off the skirt and blouse. "We better hurry; your flight was late."

I traded my jacket, jeans, and Tee for them, then sat on the floor and began unlacing my athletic shoes. Edie jammed the floppy hat—also pink, with mauve roses—on my head. And started to laugh.

"What?" I asked.

She pointed toward the mirror. "It's definitely not you."

The image that confronted me was a cross between Blanche DuBois and my neighborhood bag lady. "My God," I said. "And I have to go out in *public* like this?"

Edie sat down next to me and began putting on my shoes. "Yeah, you do look kinda pathetic, but you'd fool your own mother, and that's what Lanny said you wanted."

"Lanny?"

"The guy whose house you stayed at in the Keys."

"Oh. He wasn't there and his name never came up."

"That's Lanny—real careful about his name, and too damned casual about his place." She stood up and dumped the contents of a plastic purse decorated with seashells on the counter, then handed it to me. I transferred my things to it and gave her my straw bag and airline ticket. She handed me another ticket envelope.

"Okay," she said, "stand up and walk for me."

I took a few turns around the restroom. Edie watched, then imitated me.

"Not bad, huh?" She smiled confidently, pulling the straw hat low on her brow. "I'm an actress, or at least I'm trying to be. Lanny promised that after this next flick we're making he'll get me some legitimate work."

Legitimate work. So porno film-making was what went on at Lanny's island. God, Hy had collected a motley assortment of buddies over the years!

Watch it, McCone, I cautioned myself. That motley buddy and his friend Edie are getting you out of a tight spot.

Edie handed me a shopping bag she'd been carrying. "Ther're some jeans and stuff in here. I didn't think you'd want to travel all the way cross-country in that getup." She checked her watch. "Time to go now. Lanny will've called and had your guy paged right after we came in here. If I know him, he's managed to keep him on the phone the whole time, and from the booths you can't see anything but the backs of people leaving the restrooms. You go first; your flight to Tampa's already boarding. My Orlando flight's about to board. With any luck at all, your guy'll follow me."

I clasped her hand. "Edie, thanks."

"It's nothing. I love to act." She winked. "I'll do almost anything to act."

I winked back and went out onto the concourse. As I moved toward the gate I slumped a little and altered my walk. The door to the field seemed miles away; I forced myself to keep my pace normal and not look back at the phones. When I finally held out my ticket to the attendant he said, "*Love* your hat."

I couldn't wait to get on the plane and rip the ridiculous thing off my head.

At the top of the steps I allowed myself to take a quick look back at the terminal. Through the window I saw Maynard buying a ticket at the podium for the Orlando flight.

Twenty-three

"Worked like a charm, McCone!"

Hy gathered me in his arms and swung me around; one of Edie's too-large sandals flew off my foot and fell to the tarmac. Hy's skin felt damp and overly warm. When he set me down he looked me over. "What the hell're you supposed to be?"

"If you think this is bad, you should've seen the hat I ditched on the plane." I reached with my toes for the sandal and slipped it on while studying him. His color was high and his dark eyes glowed with erratic fire. "You feverish again?"

He put a hand on my shoulder and walked me away from where Habiba was watching the line people refueling the twin-engine Beechcraft his friend Lanny had rented for us in Key West. "I'm not going to lie to you," he said. "The fever keeps spiking, then falling off again. I think they gave me the wrong kind of drugs in Santo Domingo."

"I think we should—"

"No time. You've been checked out in this type of aircraft. If I can't pilot, you can take over."

I looked at the Beechcraft. I'd logged some hours in one with a friend of Hy's, but still . . . Wouldn't we all be better off if he saw a doctor and we holed up for a while?

He sensed what I was thinking. "I mean it when I say we've got no time to waste. Lanny made some calls, asked around about Maynard. He runs a good agency and they're hooked in with Associated Investigators."

Associated was a nationwide network whose members provided one another services on a cooperative basis. "Damn. By now he knows about the switch, and it won't take him long to figure out which cities I could've flown to. He could have someone here pretty quick." I paused. "What's the range for this plane?"

"Around twelve hundred miles. That's approximately five hours at near max airspeed. I figure we'll take her to New Orleans, see if you and Habiba can't pick up a commercial flight there."

"I don't like that; it's exactly what Maynard would expect us to do."

"Well, we could try Houston or even Dallas-Fort Worth, but it'll slow us down."

I considered. By now Dawud Hamid was in San Francisco. His arrival there could set in motion events that would further endanger the Azadis—to say nothing of Joslyn. I needed to get to the Bay Area quickly, but I also needed to insure Habiba's safety. The little girl had to be my first priority.

"Let's go to Dallas," I said.

Dallas-Fort Worth International Airport, 2:21 P.M.

Hy went to the phone to inquire about flights to San Francisco, and I settled Habiba's sleeping form on the backseat of the Beechcraft before taking the shopping bag full of more practical clothing to the restroom in the general aviation terminal. The little girl stirred and threw out her arm; her fist was clenched tight. I held it for a moment, uncurling her fingers, then gently laid it on her chest.

It was hot here in Texas, but without the oppressive tropical humidity I'd endured the past five days. For a moment I stood on the tarmac, looking across the flat landscape at the distant towers of the metropolis. Then I asked the lineman to keep an eye out and not let anyone near the plane, and walked toward the terminal.

Hy leaned on a counter, receiver to his ear, his back toward me. At a machine I bought a cup of what I call cardboard coffee and carried it to the restroom. The jeans and purple Tee that Edie had provided me fit on the loose side; the long gaudy skirt and flimsy blouse went in the trash can. I washed my face, then went looking for Hy.

He stood next to the Beechcraft, chatting with the lineman while he refueled it. His color was still too high, but he looked better than he had that morning. When I came up, he shook his head to my offer of a sip of coffee, said "Thanks, buddy," to the lineman, and steered me toward the plane.

I said, "No flights, huh?"

"Oh sure, plenty of flights. No seats, though. We forgot one detail—it's Memorial Day weekend."

"Damn!" I'd totally lost track of the date—the day, even. "You also tried flights to Oakland and San Jose?"

"And L.A., San Diego, and Sacramento, as well as anything departing for Houston, San Antone, Austin, Wichita Falls, and Amarillo. *Nada.* You could go standby, but that's not a good idea, in case Maynard's got associates looking for you along the obvious routes."

I slumped against the plane, tired and discouraged. "So what now?"

"We push on to Phoenix. Maybe we'll get lucky there."

Sky Harbor Airport, Phoenix, Arizona, 7:48 P.M.

Habiba was awake but still silent when we arrived in Phoenix. I took her to the bathroom while Hy went to ask about commercial flights. My attempt to wash some of the accumulated grime from her face left her muddy-complected and passively miserable, so I gave up on it and bought her a Coke and some Doritos for consolation. She consumed them hungrily, but without pleasure.

Hy came over to where we sat and shook his head.

"Terrific," I muttered.

Habiba looked up anxiously, trying to read our expressions.

"Look, Ripinsky, why don't you take Habiba outside and show her the planes in the tie-downs? I think I saw a Citabria there. In the meantime, I'm going to make a phone call."

He held out his hand. "Come on, copilot."

Surprisingly, she responded, "You called me sailor before."

"That was in Florida. When there, we sail; when in Arizona, we fly."

She took his hand and they left the terminal.

I went to a pay phone and placed a call to Mick's cellular unit. When he'd bought it I'd thought it a waste of money; now it was a lifeline. He answered on the first ring. Simultaneously we asked, "Where are you?"

"Phoenix," I told him.

"Russian Hill," he said. "Hamid's holed up in a building on Francisco near Leavenworth. Condo belongs to—"

"Alejandro Ronquillo. Hamid went straight there from the airport?"

"After a couple of phone calls, yeah. Came out once, bought a bottle at a corner store, and hasn't shown since."

I considered, then thought of Ronquillo's housekeeper and dug in the hideous shell-encrusted bag for my notebook. "Take this down, please: Blanca Diaz. She works for Ronquillo. Here's the number there." I read it off to him. "Call her and tell her you're my assistant and Ricky Savage's son—"

"What's Dad got to do with this?"

"She's a fan, the one you asked him to send the autograph and tape to, remember? Ask her what's happening with Hamid; I'm sure she'll be willing to tell you whatever she knows."

"Will do. Anything else?"

"Not now. I'll be in touch." Hy was approaching, minus Habiba. I hung up and went to meet him. "Where is she?"

"In the plane. She closed up on me again, said she was tired."

"Poor kid. She's really been put through it these last few days. Ripinsky, what should we do?"

"Take the Beechcraft all the way to the Bay Area."

"Flying time?"

"Probably four hours or more."

"That seems long."

He hesitated, his expression guarded. "I didn't want to

mention it before, but the starboard engine's been acting up. Nothing we can't live with, but we'll want to baby it some. And I'm feverish again; I need you to pilot. Feel up to it?"

I glanced out the window at the gathering desert shadows, then shrugged. "I feel up to anything that'll get us home soon."

6,500 feet above the Mojave Desert, 11:48 P.M.

"Ripinsky?"

No response. He slouched in the seat beside me, eyes closed.

"Ripinsky!" I put my hand on his knee and shook it.

"Unh?" He jerked his head up, blinking.

"I'm losing power in the starboard engine. And listen to that."

He cocked his head to the side.

"You hear it?" I asked. "It sounds like a car that's leaking exhaust."

"Yeah, I hear it." He leaned over, checked the fuel-pressure gauge. "Well, there's no blockage or pump failure."

"I know. What is it, then?"

"Maybe a leaking cylinder head gasket. Where're we?"

"About fifty miles southeast of Barstow."

"Shit. Let me take over, study on this."

I relinquished the controls gladly. When I glanced into the backseat I saw Habiba curled into a little ball under a blanket. Her face was covered and she lay very still; I couldn't tell if she was asleep or awake and listening.

Hy said, "Yeah, got to be a leaking gasket, or maybe just a stuck valve."

"Can we make Barstow?"

"I don't want to chance it. I know a little airstrip not far from here. Not much of one, but the guy who runs it is a mechanic, lives at the field, and stocks parts. We'll put down there."

I looked out at the black and seemingly limitless expanse of the Mojave. How the hell was he going to *find* the airstrip in that untamed land?

"Relax, McCone," he said. "I've found smaller strips in far worse places."

How had he known what I was thinking? How did he always know?

Mirage Wells Airport, 12:10 A.M.

The tiny airstrip was eerily deserted, a hot gritty wind blowing from the Granite Mountains to the north. As Hy ran toward the Quonset hut by the side of the field, I stood next to the Beechcraft, breathing air that had a faint chemical tang and trying to locate the source of a ghostly whine and clacking that came from beyond the glowing landing lights.

Large shapes hulked over there. I moved toward them, saw tidy rows of jetliners, some two dozen, with heavy protective material secured with tape over their windows and engine housings. As I went closer I made out faded insignia on their tail sections: Pan Am, Midway, Eastern.

Ghost planes of dead airlines?

The clacking was louder now. I slipped under the belly of a 747 and looked up at its wings. The protective material had blown off its engines and their turbine blades rotated in the wind; its once-sleek body was sand-scoured and pitted. How long had it sat grounded here in this strange imitation of flight?

Soft footsteps behind me. Hy.

"Why're these here?" I asked, surprised to hear a faint tremor in my voice.

"Storage. The Mojave's an airplane graveyard. Climate prevents corrosion, and space at little airports is cheap."

"What'll happen to them?"

He shrugged. "They might be returned to service if the airline industry ever picks up. More likely they'll be sold for scrap."

I looked at the derelict craft; scrap was all they were good for now. The wind from the barren Granites shifted and set the turbines to spinning faster. In spite of its heat I felt chilled.

"You talk to the mechanic?" I asked Hy.

"Place is locked up tight. He's probably gone off for the Memorial Day weekend."

My spirits dipped further. How much more of this grinding disappointment could we take before we wore down? "Can you call somebody else?"

"I wouldn't know who, and besides, the receiver's been ripped off the pay phone. If I had the right tools and parts I could fix the engine myself, but as it is . . ."

"You know," I said, "maybe it's time to call on RKI. Get on the radio to Barstow, ask them to phone Renshaw and have him send the company jet."

He considered, then shook his head. "Bad idea."

"Why?"

"I know Gage. He may operate on the edge of the law, but one thing he's not going to leave himself open to is a charge of accessory to kidnaping. He'd insist on turning Habiba over to her grandmother as soon as we got to the Bay Area."

"Well, what's wrong with that?"

"Think, McCone. The Azadis are still a target. Dawud's in San Francisco. For all you know, he's contacted his mother and convinced her Habiba should go back to Jumbie Cay with him. We hand the kid over, we just might be at square one again. It's your case, your call, but—"

"No, you're right." I looked speculatively at the Quonset hut.

Hy's eyes followed my line of sight. We began walking toward it.

"These huts," I said, jiggling the door latch, "are not put together too sturdily. You suppose he's got an alarm system on it?"

"Out here?" Hy laughed.

"I wish I had my lock picks."

"You want one of my credit cards?"

"The Visa method of entry isn't as easy as they make it look on TV." I gave up on the door, walked along the length of the building to its rear, where there was a small window. When I tested it, it slid up without protest.

I looked over my shoulder and grinned. "The forgetfulness of the human animal is a wondrous thing. You want to climb in, or shall I?"

"I don't think I'm up to it. You go, and let me in at the front."

"Feeling bad again?"

"Like shit."

"Are you going to be able to work on the engine?"

He shook his head. "I'm gonna supervise. You, McCone, are about to get your first course in aircraft mechanics."

3:48 A.M.

I closed the access panel to the engine and wiped my oily hands on a rag. Hy made a circle with his thumb and forefinger and grinned weakly at me, his face drawn and flushed in the light from the heavy-duty torch he held.

He said, "Bet you didn't think you'd replace a cylinder head gasket before this trip was over."

"I guess it shows you can do anything, if you have to." I started gathering up the tools. "I'll put these back and leave some money on the desk in there. Then we can get going."

"Uh-uh. My fever's raging; I can't pilot her. And you don't want to be mountain flying in the dark; you haven't logged enough hours for that. It'll be getting light by five, five-thirty, time enough to start out."

"Why don't you try to get some rest, then? Take the couch in the Quonset."

"I think I will, if I can totter in there."

"It's that bad?"

"That bad."

"Lean on me." I walked with him to the hut, got him settled on the couch, and went back for the tools, torchlight, and extension cord. By the time I replaced them, he was out.

I went over to the old wooden desk that nestled in the curve of the far wall and set some twenties on top of the papers and parts manuals strewn there. Then I sat down in the creaky swivel chair and reached for the phone. It was an ancient black rotary dial model, and it took a long time to get an operator on the line. When my credit-card call went through to Mick's cellular unit, it rang and rang with no answer.

I felt a flutter of alarm, but the lack of an answer didn't have to mean anything. Mick probably fell asleep on stakeout.

So why didn't the phone wake him?

Maybe he was away from the unit.

No, he'd have taken it with him.

Well, I couldn't do a damn thing about the situation now, and worrying wasn't going to help matters. I pushed away from the desk and went over to Hy, felt his forehead. It was excessively warm and he didn't stir when I touched him. More unconscious than asleep—and that was something else to fret about.

Finally I left the Quonset and checked on Habiba. She was sleeping deeply on the backseat of the Beechcraft, once again curled into a fetal position. For a while I sat up front listening to her soft breathing. Then I climbed down to the tarmac and sat there.

The wind from the Granites was still strong but cooler now; the sky had begun to lighten toward the east. I'd wait an hour, then call Flight Service's 800 number for a weather briefing. Half an hour later I'd awaken Hy and we'd be on our way.

For now, though, I was content to sit here and listen to the plaint of the ghost planes.

6,500 Feet Above The Tehachapi Mountains

May 28, 6:27 A.M.

The vast arid waste of the Mojave was behind us now, but the deathlike loneliness of the tiny airfield and the shroud of white smog drifting from the chemical plants at Trona had left nightmare traces in my mind. Below sprawled the Tehachapis, their wrinkled, jagged peaks thrusting aggressively. They seemed to telegraph a warning: we can claim you.

I pulled my gaze from them before my imagination could cloud my judgment, looked instead at the last ridgeline separating us from the Central Valley and an easy flight home. Piece of cake, as Hy would say. Only Hy wasn't saying anything just now—hadn't for some time.

Anxiously I glanced into the Beechcraft's rear seat, where he'd crawled after I'd awakened him with difficulty at Mirage Wells. He was slumped against the side—unconscious again, and maybe better off, since the chills had passed and the fever raged again. The little girl sat rigid beside him, silent as she'd been the whole grueling journey. Her dark hair was matted, her face begrimed; her eyes had a bottomless quality that said she'd seen too much in too few years. I wished Hy were able to hug and reassure her, but for the moment my smile and the words "Not long now" would have to do.

She didn't respond.

Well, who could blame her? After we were on the ground, I'd hug and reassure her. And get badly needed medical help for Hy.

I checked the instruments, looked back at the ridgeline. The morning sun was turning its striated brown rock to gold. Some of my tension was draining away, but the grit of the desert was still on my skin, overlaying the clamminess of the tropics. I made myself feel it so I wouldn't become careless.

So much could go wrong yet. Could go wrong at any moment, as events of the past days had proved—

The impact felt like slamming into a concrete wall.

My stomach lurched and I felt a surge of panic. I scanned the instruments as the plane shuddered. The VSI showed we were descending fast: fifteen hundred feet per minute, sixteen hundred . . . When I looked up the ridgeline tilted crazily, then leaped to the top of the windscreen. All I could see was a fractured stone cliff face.

Downdraft—bad one.

Extreme clear air turbulence here, and why the hell hadn't Flight Service warned me? Not that I'd've had any choice but to brave it. . . .

I glanced into the rear seat again. Hy was still unconscious; no help from that quarter. The child's eyes were wide, her face drained of color. Afraid I'd betray my panic if I spoke, I tried instead for a reassuring smile, but it didn't come off.

Okay, I thought, you know what to do. You've watched Hy deal with downdrafts a hundred times or more. Stay calm and change course. Get away from that ridge, turn toward lower ground.

I turned. Another draft slammed us. For a minute the Beechcraft shuddered so violently that I imagined its wings being torn off.

Two thousand feet per minute now and still falling!

Sweat coated my forehead and palms. I gripped the controls, struggling for focus.

"Mountain flying course," I said. "Mountain flying—what did they teach me?"

My mind refused to function.

Oh God, not this! We've come too far, through too much. Twenty-three hundred.

This can't be happening! I can't die this way.

Twenty-five hundred.

Jagged brown peaks below. Sunny gold cliff ahead. The last things I'll ever see.

Sunlight, you idiot! Mountains facing into the sun create updrafts. Get closer to them, not farther away.

Find an updraft, and you can use this machine as a glider. Find one, and you'll clear that ridge.

I began to test the controls, banking toward the cliff.

For God's sake, McCone, find an updraft!

Twenty-four

As the starboard wing dipped lower and the fractured stone cliff loomed closer, I shut down the part of me that felt until all that remained was a cold focus. I was in command once more, hands gentle and precise on the controls.

I completed my turn, banked again. The VSI still indicated we were losing altitude. I felt a fresh flutter of panic, forced it down and maintained my concentration.

If I was going to die, I was going to die fighting.

A slight bump. Then it felt as if the Beechcraft was sucked into an inverted whirlpool.

Updraft! Strong one.

I glanced at the VSI. Three hundred feet of indicated climb already!

A joyous bubble rose in my chest; tears stung my eyes. For an instant I gave in to emotion, gripping the controls. Then I took a deep calming breath and held the plane in a tight, steadily climbing spiral.

One thousand foot gain now. One thousand five hundred. True altitude forty-five hundred.

I'd need at least sixty-five hundred feet to safely clear that ridgeline.

I banked away from the edges of the updraft, deep into its core.

Five thousand. Fifty-five hundred. Six thousand.

We cleared the ridge at over seven thousand feet. I maintained a steep and rapid ascent, rolled out at eighty-five hundred, and set a northwesterly course toward Bakersfield.

Only then did I allow myself a small yelp of victory.

It was echoed through my headset. Habiba's hand touched my shoulder. She was leaning forward, lips parted, dark eyes intense.

"We made it," she said.

"You bet we did!" My voice shook with the tears I was holding in check, and I gripped her fingers tightly.

She added, "Hy slept through everything."

I turned my head. He looked terrible: gray now, his eyes sunken, his mouth flaccid. Oh, Jesus . . . "Habiba, do you know how to take a person's pulse?"

"Yes."

"Check his, please."

While she took his limp hand and fumbled with his wrist, I scanned the terrain below. A few rounded hills, then the flat expanse of the great Central Valley. How far to Bakersfield? By my calculations, no more than forty miles.

Habiba said, "His pulse feels awful weak, Sharon."

"Is his forehead hot?"

"Burning up, but it's like he's cold, the way he's shivering."

The fever-chill cycles were shortening. "Listen," I said, "we're going to land at Bakersfield, get him to a hospital." No reason not to; nobody would be looking for us there. By now, I doubted anybody was looking for us at all.

She asked, "What should I do?"

"I think that blanket is under the seat. See if you can find it and wrap it around him." It wouldn't help against his chills, but it would keep the little girl occupied.

We were well into the valley now, approaching the farm towns of Arvin and Weed Patch. Flat fields striped by crop rows stretched for miles; armies of electrical towers marched from east to west, held in formation by their power lines. I reached toward the radio to call in to Bakersfield air traffic control, but my eyes stopped at the starboard engine's oil-pressure gauge.

The needle was dropping into the red.

For a moment I stared in disbelief. Then I laughed—a hollow, on-the-edge sound. So much for my ability as an aircraft mechanic!

Jesus Christ, what now?

I checked the engine for smoke. None visible. But then I smelled burning oil.

Okay, okay, it's bad, I admitted. You keep running the engine, it could freeze from lack of oil. And then all sorts of disastrous things can happen—flying pistons, smashed fire walls . . .

Don't imagine. Think what to do. Remember that multi-engine course back in March.

Maintain altitude. Feather the propeller.

I feathered. The prop stopped immediately.

Good. Now, secure the power plant. Mixture to idle cutoff. Fuel selector off. Boost pump off. Ignition off. Close cowl flaps.

Nonessential electrical equipment? None on, that's good.

Coddle the port engine; it's all you can depend on now. Fuel mix rich, power back to the minimum to maintain airspeed.

And now what?

Notify air traffic control.

"Sharon? I can't find the blanket."

"That's okay. We'll be on the ground soon."

"But Hy—"

"He'll be okay without the damn blanket!"

Habiba sucked in her breath and became very still.

"I'm sorry I snapped," I said. "Is your seat belt fastened?"

". . . No."

"Fasten it, please. We're . . ." I paused, unable to think what to tell her. Oh, hell, why hand her a lie? After what she'd been through since we swam away from Jumbie Cay, she deserved to be told the truth the same as an adult.

"We've got an engine out," I went on. "No reason to worry, the other's still good, and we're very close to the airport. It might make for a rough landing, though. I need you to see that your belt and Hy's are fastened tight. And I need you to be very quiet so I can concentrate."

Silence.

"Will you do that for me, Habiba?"

"Yes." There was no tremor in her voice, no threat of tears. The kid had guts, for sure.

"Thanks. I'll have us on the ground in no time."

I reached toward the radio, flicked on the mike, and began my transmission. "Bakersfield Tower, this is Beechcraft four-eight-three-three-Echo. I'm VFR three-zero miles southwest with my starboard engine out and a seriously ill passenger. Request assistance."

Static.

"Bakersfield Tower, acknowledge."

"Roger, three-three-Echo. Are you declaring an emergency?"

"Affirmative, Bakersfield."

"Three-three-Echo, are you able to maintain altitude?"

"Affirmative."

"Three-three-Echo, plan straight in to runway three-zero right. You'll be number one. Do you request an ambulance for your passenger?"

"Affirmative, Bakersfield. And I'll need assistance on this landing; it's a first under these conditions."

"That's what we're here for, three-three-Echo. Three-zero right is ten thousand feet, so you've got plenty of runway."

I acknowledged and heaved a sigh of relief.

7:01 A.M.

Phrases from the emergency flight manuals I'd studied over the past year filtered through my mind as I approached Bakersfield.

When making an engine-out landing, keep your pattern close to the runway, and lower landing gear at the normal point in the pattern.

"Three-three-Echo, are you able to lower your gear?"

Dammit, I didn't know which engine the landing-gear extension system operated off of. If it was the starboard . . .

"Sorry, Bakersfield, I had to take over for the pilot, and I'm not familiar with the system."

"What is your full aircraft designation, three-three-Echo?"

"Beechcraft Delta-five-five Baron."

"Stand by." Half a minute elapsed. "You're in luck, three-three-Echo. Gear operates off the port engine."

"Thanks, Bakersfield." I waited till I was two miles out, then lowered the gear and cranked in fifteen degrees of flap.

Maintain blueline airspeed and delay final flap extension until you are established on final approach.

The runway stretched ahead of me. I kept my approach fast and high.

"You're doing fine, three-three-Echo. Suggest thirty degrees of flap."

If you have trimmed the rudder to counteract yaw from the out engine, the rudder pressures will change once the flaps are down.

I had, and they did.

Over the tarmac now. Totally focused. Nothing in the world but this aircraft, the voice from the control tower, and me.

Once the flaps are fully extended, there is no possibility of a go-around. You are committed to land.

I pulled back on the power.

Close to the normal touchdown point now.

"Doing just fine, three-three-Echo."

Past the touchdown zone and still floating!

". . . doing fine . . ."

End of the runway coming up, and beyond it there're trees!

. . . you are committed to land . . .

In the trees? In the fucking *trees*?

". . . easy now, three-three-Echo, easy . . ."

A sudden spine-jarring thump. The Beechcraft yawed violently, but I controlled it, braking gingerly. And then we rolled to a stop—as if this were the perfect finish to a perfectly routine hop.

Except the end of the runway was only yards away.

"You did good, three-three-Echo, and your ambulance is on the field. Taxi to crosswind runway and hold."

I taxied to the runway and brought the plane to a stop. Shut down all systems, leaned my head against the controls, and burst into tears.

"Ambulance is on its way to you, three-three-Echo."

I sucked in a sob.

"Acknowledge, three-three-Echo."

I choked out the words, "Roger, and a *big* thanks, Bakersfield."

Habiba's hand touched the back of my head. "Sharon, don't cry. Hy's awake!"

I raised my head and swiveled around, mopping tears from my cheeks as I stared at my lover. He looked even worse than before: sweat sheened his gray pallor, and his eyes were bloodshot and dull. His droopy mustache twitched as he tried for a smile, and when he spoke his voice rasped painfully.

"McCone," he said, "that was the lousiest landing you've ever made, and I loved every second of it."

PART FOUR

NORTHERN CALIFORNIA

MAY 28–30

Twenty-five

We spent a couple of hours at Bakersfield Memorial Hospital getting Hy admitted and conferring with the attending physician. The bug he'd caught in Nicaragua was rare but—now that it had been properly diagnosed—treatable with sulfa drugs and would require a few days' stay. After I finished with the doctor I went to Hy's room; when I told him Habiba and I would be leaving for San Francisco, his droopy mustache sagged lower.

"Jesus, McCone, I never thought you'd abandon me in *Bakersfield*!"

"You're in perfectly good hands and, besides, what's wrong with this town?"

"Well, when I was a little kid in Fresno, my daddy used to say that on a clear summer night you could sit on your front porch and listen to Bakersfield suck." He paused. "Of course, that's what the porch-sitters in Bakersfield were saying about Fresno."

"Then you'll just have to let go of your old prejudices and rivalries, because the people here have been really good to us. I'll keep in touch by phone and be down to get you as soon as you're released."

"In the Citabria?"

I hesitated.

"Planes're like horses, McCone. You've got to climb right back on."

"All right! I'll pick you up in the Citabria." Quickly I kissed him and got out of there before he could extract any further promises from me.

I collected Habiba from the nurses' station, got a cab back to the airport, and dealt with the necessary formalities—including notifying the aircraft rental agency of the whereabouts and condition of the Beechcraft. Then, at the suggestion of the air traffic controller who had talked me down, we rented a limo from a firm called Bring 'em on Home, whose drivers wore western attire rather than uniforms—Bakersfield being the country-and-western capital of California. Habiba and I slept all the way to the Park 'n' Fly near SFO where—eons ago—I'd left my MG.

Anne-Marie Altman and Hank Zahn lived in a two-flat building on Twenty-sixth Street in the Noe Valley district. It was the safest haven I could think of for Habiba.

I hadn't bothered to call ahead; my former boss and his wife were my best friends and advance notice wasn't necessary. Anne-Marie came to the door of the lower flat wearing her usual at-home attire of a knee-length Tee and leggings; her normally pert blond hair stood up in little points and she had on no makeup. She didn't seem particularly surprised to see me, but she did glance at Habiba with ill-concealed displeasure.

Anne-Marie, an attorney for a coalition of environmentalist organizations, claimed to hate children more than strip miners or clear-cutters, but I knew better. Babies didn't interest her—to tell the truth, I don't find them all that interesting myself—but she'd often betrayed a liking for children who were on the cusp of becoming fully realized individuals. In no time, I was sure, Habiba would ingratiate herself and join the select ranks of young people whom my friend respected and was even fond of.

"So who is this?" she demanded.

"Habiba Hamid," the little girl said, extending her hand.

Way to go, I thought. The kid had a good sense for what worked with people.

Anne-Marie shook with her, somewhat nonplused. "And to what do I owe the honor?"

I said, "It's a long story. You have any coffee?"

She waved us inside and led us to the kitchen at the back of the flat. The coffeemaker was on, so I poured cups for both of us, listening as my friend stiffly asked Habiba, "Would you like some milk? Or juice?"

"Coke?"

"Diet?"

"Yes, please."

Anne-Marie fetched it, and we sat down at her butcher-block table. "So what's the long story?" she asked.

"I don't have time to go into it. Habiba can fill you in later."

"Later?" There was a touch of alarm in her voice.

"Yes. I need you to put her up for a while." Before she could protest, I asked, "Is Hank around?"

"He went upstairs to shower a couple of hours ago, but I think he got sidetracked because I've been hearing Thelonious Monk—a new sound-enhanced compact disc he bought on Friday. You want me to get him on the intercom?"

"Yes, ask him to come down here, if you would."

Anne-Marie and Hank are one of those married couples who found out early on that they can't live together. She's what he calls a cleanliness Nazi; he's what she calls a slob. Separate flats in the same house and frequent conjugal visits have proved their ideal solution.

She went to the intercom that joined the flats and spoke in hushed tones. Half a minute later Hank came through the door from the interior staircase. He wore a terry bathrobe that gave evidence to an impressive number of spills and clutched a big coffee mug that said Superlawyer. Behind his thick horn-rimmed glasses his eyes were sleepy; he'd probably been napping to Thelonious.

As he sat down I introduced him to Habiba, adding, "She needs an attorney."

Hank studied her with mock severity. "What's she done?

I don't defend litterbugs or people who fail to return their library books."

Habiba giggled.

I said, "She may be seeking a divorce from her father. Perhaps her grandmother as well." Briefly I explained the situation, omitting only the part about her father being a murderer. I'd fill him in on that outside the little girl's hearing.

Hank listened thoughtfully, running his hand over his curly gray-brown hair. "Is this what you want, Habiba?" he asked.

"Yes. My dad scares me, and Grams will insist I go back to Jumbie Cay with him."

"What if we could arrange it so you could remain with her?"

"That'd be okay."

"And you want me to represent your interests?"

"Yes, please."

"In that case, you'd better give me a retainer."

She frowned and looked at me.

"I'll loan it to you." I picked up the tacky shell-encrusted bag from where I'd shoved it out of sight under the table.

Anne-Marie asked, "Where the hell did you get *that*?"

"It's a small part of the long story."

"Habiba will definitely have to tell all." She unbent and smiled at her. Habiba grinned slyly in response.

I asked Hank, "How much?"

He calculated. "Seventeen bucks'll do it."

"Why such an odd number?"

"It's the cost of a complete meal for three from El Pollo Supremo. Anne-Marie tells me Habiba's visiting for a while, and that's what I think we should have for her first dinner chez Altman-Zahn."

"Fair enough." I counted out seventeen dollars and handed the bills to Habiba. She in turn gave them to Hank and they shook on the transaction. I added another ten to the pile.

"What's that for?" he asked.

"A bottle of wine, on me. By way of thanks for helping out."

"I don't know, Shar." Hank folded the money and stuffed it in his bathrobe pocket. "You're getting too high-toned for us. Ten bucks might even buy a bottle with a cork."

* * *

Ten minutes later I was driving along Mission Street toward Bernal Heights and trying to raise people on the car phone. No answer at Mick's cellular unit; none at his home, my home, or the office. Greg Marcus was off duty and away for the weekend. I even tried Joslyn, on the slim chance that the posting on the Web had been a hoax and my friend would be in her kitchen feeding Charley his Sunday dinner.

No answer anywhere.

The intersection at Mission and Army was blocked by an accident. One of the big articulated Muni buses sprawled across the south-bound lanes, a van was pinned against a power pole, and police officers, SFFD rescue crews, and paramedics scurried around. I looked for an escape route and spotted an alley several yards ahead. To reach it, though, I'd have to drive over the curb and across the sidewalk, exposing my nearly new tires to possible damage.

"Screw it," I said and snapped on the radio. It was after three; maybe there'd be something on the news—

". . . a sheet of flames, and firefighters are battling to control it. The bomb squad is on the scene, as well as personnel from the Diplo-bomber Task Force, and the mood here on Jackson Street in Pacific Heights is one of—"

"Oh, my God!"

To hell with the nearly new tires. I eased the MG forward, bumped up onto the curb and across the sidewalk. Gunned it down the narrow alley all the way onto Valencia Street and headed across town to the Azadi Consulate.

I couldn't get anywhere near Jackson Street, so I finally detoured around Lafayette Square and double-parked beside RKI's mobile unit. It was locked and deserted. I scribbled a note and stuck it under the car's windshield wiper: "Consular security vehicle. Please do not tow." Then I ran along Laguna to where it crossed Jackson.

People jammed the intersection and sidewalks there, trying to see past the barricades. A reporter with a Minicam stood filming on top of a Channel Five van. A still photographer had shinnied up a plane tree in the fenced front garden of a white Victorian; a second man, probably the house's owner, was shaking his fist and yelling for him to get down. A pall of smoke lay on the air, tinged with evil-smelling chemical fumes. For an instant I flashed on the explosion at Bootlegger's Cove, then I put the memory behind me and pushed through the crowd to the barricade. I showed my I.D. to the uniformed officer there, explaining that I worked for RKI. He shouted, "What?" and leaned closer. I repeated my explanation, but he wasn't impressed. He shook his head and turned his back.

I was about to go look for a roundabout way onto the scene when I spotted Craig Morland. The FBI agent was trying to mingle with the crowd, but his dark suit and red tie stood out among the others' weekend attire. I shouted his name and he turned and came over to the barricade.

Morland showed his I.D. to the officer and motioned for me to join him. "So when did this happen?" I asked.

"Three o'clock. I'll tell you, there must've been enough black powder in the bomb to take out a mountain." He put a hand on my elbow, shoved some bystanders aside, and began guiding me along the street.

I said, "When did you get here?"

"Approximately seventeen after. Since then the fire's spread to the outbuildings and houses on either side of the consulate. Their annex behind, too."

"Jesus. Fatalities?"

"Of course, but it's too soon to know how many, or who."

"Survivors?"

He shrugged.

As we moved closer to the fire the air grew thick with smoke and drifting particles of soot. In spite of it being a coolish day, I felt heat on my skin. The voices of the crowd and the shouts of the firefighters were muted by the roar and crackle of the flames.

Now I could see the consulate and its outbuildings—more accurately, I could see their blackened skeletons. The houses to either side had caught fire; streams of water poured onto them from hoses, hissing and vaporizing. The firefighters were moving to the sides, struggling to keep the blaze from spreading down the block.

In spite of the heat, a chill struck deep to my bones. Once

again the memory of the conflagration at Bootlegger's Cove intruded; once again I pushed it away.

Morland put an arm out and shoved aside an elderly couple who were blocking our path. The woman turned, outraged, but the FBI man kept going without an apology. Mild-mannered, by-the-book Craig had the same violence within as most of us, and he wasn't keeping it in check all that well. I disengaged my elbow from his grasp and followed along cautiously, in case he should erupt into more extreme behavior.

The street ran with water; I slogged through it, feeling it squish in and out of my too-large sandals. Several yards away, behind one of the SFFD four-by-fours, I spotted a knot of civilians: Gage Renshaw, three RKI security staff, Kahlil Lateef, and—surprisingly—Mick. Their faces were streaked with soot; Renshaw's trousers were soaked to mid-calf and splashed with what looked to be fire-retardant chemicals.

I said to Morland, "I'll be over there. Thanks for getting me past the barricade."

He nodded and headed toward a bomb squad car that was pulled up on the sidewalk.

I went over to the group by the fire department vehicle and touched Renshaw's arm. "So what happened here?"

He turned, taking me in with an expression of surprise that quickly transformed to fury. "Where the hell've you been?"

"Traveling home with Habiba."

"Where is she?"

"In a safe place." Thank God we hadn't contacted Renshaw and had the company jet fly us home from the Mojave! If that scenario had played as Hy predicted, the little girl would have been inside the consulate when the bomb went off.

"Where?" Renshaw demanded. "What safe place?"

I ignored the question and turned to Mick. "I've been trying to call you. Why didn't you answer your phone?"

"Damned thing died. That's what I get for buying a cheap model."

He looked exhausted and discouraged, and my heart went out to him. Silently I vowed to buy him the best cellular unit available and never again to belittle his addiction to technology. "Let's talk," I said, and led him away from the others.

Renshaw glared and moved to stop us, then shrugged angrily. Mick and I went to the front of the four-by-four and sat on its bumper. "What happened with Hamid?" I asked. "Start from the beginning."

He closed his eyes and took a deep breath, as though to clear his head. "Okay, I contacted Blanca Diaz like you told me to. She was glad to help, kept me posted on Hamid's activities. He arrived at the condo very upset. Blanca was staying over; she does that when Ronquillo and Schechtmann are into heavy entertaining, and Friday night it was dinner for thirty. After the guests left, Leila, Sandy, and Hamid stayed up all night drinking and doing coke. Blanca was in and out of the room clearing the party things, and she heard plenty.

"Seems Hamid called his mother from the airport. She wouldn't let him come to the consulate, and she said that her head of security had told her Habiba was in good hands. She also said that under no circumstances would she let the kid return to the Caribbean with him, and that Dawud had better go back before, as she put it, something dreadful happened. I guess we know what the dreadful thing was." Mick motioned at the blazing buildings.

"Go on."

"Okay, eventually Hamid got out of control, ranting about his mother stealing his kid and insisting he wouldn't leave the city without her. Finally Ronquillo gave him something to bring him down, and everybody went to bed. Hamid was up early though, yelling at Blanca at ten in the morning because there wasn't any single-malt Scotch left. He went out for a bottle, and they all stayed in on Saturday, doing more drinking and drugs.

"I stayed put in my car across the street. Nothing happened. The fucking phone gave out sometime, and I didn't discover it till around ten, when I tried to call Maggie to ask her to bring me more sandwiches and coffee. I was starving, and I still had some Cokes, so I drank them to fill up and then I kept having to take a leak. One time an old lady walking her dog caught me in the bushes and threatened to call the cops. After that I stayed in the car and pissed into an empty can."

Welcome to the real world of the private investigator, I thought. "Okay, what happened today?"

"Hamid left the condo around two-thirty in a Yellow Cab; I got its number. He came here. It didn't look like the security guards were on the side door; he went right in, and he hadn't come out when the bomb went off. Shar, I've never seen anything like it. . . ."

No security people on the side door? Renshaw never would have permitted such a lapse. But Malika Hamid could have ordered them away, or diverted them in a manner that wouldn't have prompted them to notify their supervisor. Habiba had told me that her grandmother always sent everyone except for her old nanny away from the consulate when Dawud came to call.

Her insistence on preserving the fiction that her son disappeared years ago had gotten both of them killed.

I asked Mick, "Did anybody follow Hamid?"

"Besides me? Nobody that I could make."

"Any deliveries after he got there?"

"No."

Then the bomb had been in place beforehand. The bomber had known the security guards would be taken off; he'd known Dawud would be there. I thought about Joslyn's phone message: ". . . too close to home for comfort."

Too close to the Azadis' home for comfort?

Mick and I went back around the four-by-four. Renshaw wasn't there anymore, but Kahlil Lateef sat on the curb, tears making tracks in the soot on his rough-featured face. I sat down next to him.

"Such ruin," he said. "Such ruin."

"Where were you when the bomb exploded, Mr. Lateef?"

"I was taking my daily walk. I walk to the Marina Green and back—early on the weekdays, later on Saturdays and Sundays."

"Mrs. Hamid—do you know what she had planned for today?"

He shook his head.

"Did anyone survive besides you?"

"I do not know."

I looked thoughtfully at Lateef's bent head, recalling his frank dislike of Malika Hamid, his fondness for Mavis. When

I glanced up, I saw Renshaw and a tall man with iron-gray hair whom I recognized as Ed Parkhurst, head of the task force, walking my way. "Excuse me," I said to Lateef and went to join them.

Renshaw scowled and motioned for me to back off. I kept going. "Mr. Parkhurst," I said, "Sharon McCone. I'm a consultant to Mr. Renshaw."

Parkhurst ignored my extended hand. "You're the investigator Adah Joslyn was leaking confidential information to. We found out about that after we placed her on leave."

I didn't acknowledge the implied accusation. "Any word on her situation?"

"That's also confidential."

"I hardly think so, since he's boasted on the TechnoWeb about taking her hostage. Why do you suppose he hasn't made his demands?"

Parkhurst sighed. "As you see, he's been otherwise occupied."

I turned to Renshaw. "Any idea how Malika Hamid got your people to leave the side door unguarded?"

"Sharon, enough!"

"Have you told him yet?"

"What?"

"About the—"

Renshaw grabbed my arm, excused himself to Parkhurst, and hustled me off to the other side of the four-by-four. "Goddamn it, Sharon, when're you going to stop trying to dictate how I conduct my business? I'll tell Parkhurst about the messages when I feel it's appropriate."

"And when is that?"

"After I consult with my client."

"Consult with Malika Hamid?" I motioned at the smoking skeleton of the consulate. "Not likely, unless you're into channeling."

"We don't know that Mrs. Hamid is dead. But even if she is, I'm still bound to act in Azad's best interests. I'll discuss what to do with Ambassador Jalil—"

"Oh, stuff it, Gage! It's a little late to worry about protecting Azad's image. People have died. Some of *your* people have died. It's time to get everything out in the open. We need to sit down with Parkhurst and tell him everything; I need to tell both of you what I've found out."

Renshaw's eyes narrowed and his nostrils flared. He leaned toward me on the balls of his feet, poking his index finger against my shoulder as he spoke. "I've had about all I can take from you, Sharon. You're to deliver the Hamid girl to me by six o'clock, latest."

I stepped away from his prodding finger and matched his glare. "You're not getting your hands on her."

"You'll do as I say if you want to avoid trouble."

"Trouble?"

"In three little syllables—kidnaping."

"Well, Gage, in four little syllables—accessory."

"I never authorized—"

"Yes, you did."

"There are no witnesses, nothing in writing."

"But, as you pointed out, RKI paid for my ticket and expenses. Habiba's return ticket, plus a couple of aircraft rentals. You sent her passport down by courier. I reported to you all along; my phone bill will show the credit-card charges." He opened his mouth to speak, but I played my ace in the hole. "Besides, your partner Ripinsky was with Habiba and me all the way back."

He was silent.

"Gage," I went on, "there's a lot you don't know. Let me tell you what I've—"

"No, Sharon. End of discussion. Go ahead and refuse to turn the kid over to me, if it satisfies some twisted need you have for power. But I doubt you'll be able to refuse a request from Ambassador Jalil—particularly when our State Department lends it some muscle." He turned and stalked away.

I watched him go, rage spilling over. "Twisted need for power, my ass," I muttered. So much for sharing what I knew with RKI or the task force. The hell with them.

"What?" a voice behind me asked.

I turned. Craig Morland. "Nothing!" I snapped.

Morland took a step backwards.

"Sorry," I said. "If you're looking for Parkhurst, I don't know where he went."

"Doesn't matter. I'm through here for now."

I looked around for Mick, but couldn't spot him. Didn't matter; he'd turn up at the office sooner or later. Morland was still standing next to me, looking as though he wanted to say something but was afraid I'd bite his head off again. I'd better treat him decently; he was now my only contact on the task force.

"Craig," I said, "you look like you could use a drink. Buy you one?"

Twenty-six

        An hour later Morland and I were sitting in a
booth at the back of a dark Mexican restaurant on Lombard
Street's motel row. Usually I can't eat when I'm upset and
depressed, but the day's events—combined with the depriva-
tions of my recent journey—had quite the opposite effect on
me. I'd already put away huevos rancheros with beans and
rice, two Dos Equiis, and an indecent quantity of chips and
salsa. Craig had nibbled at a few chips, drunk two margaritas,
and was working on a third.

"Used to come here a lot when I was attached to the San
Francisco field office back in the eighties," he said in a sepul-
chral voice.

I braced for yet another installment of his life story. In
spite of my repeated attempts to question him about the case,
Morland had deftly steered the conversation to his career
history. Without actually revealing much of himself, he'd told
me about his work on the New York City bomb squad; about
attending Columbia University Law School; about his first
and only job as an attorney, in the Brooklyn public defender's
office; about joining the Bureau.

Now he seemed to run out of steam. He looked around the
restaurant morosely, as if it didn't measure up to his memories.
"What the hell," he muttered.

Upset about the bombing, I thought. And about Adah; he withdraws every time I mention her name, cares more for her than he lets on—or than she realizes.

Once again I tried to bring the conversation back to the investigation, this time taking a roundabout route. "How long did you work out of San Francisco?"

"Two and a half years. Then I was transferred back to D.C. For a couple of years I was on an interagency exchange with Scotland Yard. I'd just gotten back to the States when I was tapped for the task force." He paused. "I wish to hell this waiting was over. Why doesn't he make his move?"

"Maybe the bombing was his move. Maybe he's gotten what he wants now."

"Don't count on it."

"Azad is the only country he's hit more than once, and in more than one location."

"But those other attempts weren't successful."

"His attempt on the Panamanians back in ninety-two wasn't successful, and he didn't repeat it."

Morland shook his head. "I don't think the Azadis are central to the case."

"Why not?"

"There's nothing to indicate it." His eyes narrowed as he regarded me over the salt-encrusted rim of his glass. "Unless you have information we don't."

For a moment I considered telling Morland everything; I sensed I could trust him. But he'd have to turn the information over to Parkhurst, who would love to see me charged with obstructing a federal investigation. I couldn't risk it.

Damn Gage Renshaw and his client confidentiality!

I said to Craig, "I just have a feeling about the Azadis, that's all. I asked Parkhurst if there was anything new about Adah's situation, but he wouldn't tell me. Has the bomber posted anything further?"

His eyes clouded and he sipped his drink before replying. "There's been nothing."

"You know about the message she left on my machine?"

He nodded. "Marcus on the SFPD passed along the gist of it."

"If she was right . . . a man like that—he'd kill anyone who could identify him."

"We're acting on the assumption that he's holding her alive as an insurance policy. We get too close, she's his ticket out of here."

I wanted to believe that as much as he did.

My doubts must have shown on my face, because Morland launched into a monologue on the psychological profile of the bomber, much of it aimed at easing his own anxiety. After a few minutes I cut him short by signaling for the check. His earlier recital of his personal history had given rise to an idea, and I wanted to get back to the office and explore it.

I'd expected All Souls to be holiday-weekend quiet, but instead I heard angry voices coming from the law library as soon as I walked through the door. Ted and—I thought—Mike Tobias, one of the flock of new partners and associates who had come to the firm within the past couple of years. I fled up the stairs, the words "intolerable inefficiency" and "insufferable workaholic" following me.

There had been entirely too much bickering around the co-op of late—serious arguments, as well. During the dozen or so years Ted had presided over the front office I'd seldom heard his voice raised in anger. Now, it seemed, something or someone set him off at least once a day. The co-op had turned into a place that most people were eager to quit at close of business; those who remained stayed closeted in their offices or living quarters.

Upstairs I tossed the horrible shell-encrusted purse on my sofa and dug out a canvas tote from the bottom drawer of one of the file cabinets. My possessions went in the tote and the purse went in the wastebasket. Damned if I was going to carry around that reminder of the hideous journey. Next I sat down at my desk and called Hy's room at Bakersfield Memorial.

"Much better," he replied in response to my question. "They've still got an I.V. going, and they won't let me have solid food, but what the hell—I'm alive. How're you doing? Is Habiba okay?"

"Fine, both of us. She's with Anne-Marie and Hank. But, Ripinsky, he blew up the Azadi Consulate."

"Hank? Oh, Christ, what am I saying? When?"

"Three this afternoon. Both Hamids were there, and presumably killed. The only survivor that I know of is Kahlil Lateef, the trade attaché."

He was silent, and I knew he was thinking Habiba could have been there. "The guy's got to be stopped, McCone."

"Yes. I have an idea that may help identify him, or at least narrow the range of suspects. Let me run this by you." I detailed what I'd thought of at the restaurant with Craig Morland.

Hy said, "What surprises me is that nobody's thought of this before. Or maybe they did, but checked out the wrong group of people."

"I'm going to get hold of Mick and start him working on it right away."

"Why not use Charlotte Keim, too?"

"I'd just as soon steer clear of RKI."

"Why?"

"Renshaw and I are having a disagreement. I insisted he take all his information to the task force. He was willing to do it—with or without Malika Hamid's consent—when the bombs were sent to the Azadi Embassy and U.N. delegation. Now he's backpedaling—protecting the client's interests, he claims, but he's really protecting himself. He wouldn't listen to the new information I have; all he wanted was for me to turn Habiba over to him."

"Sounds like it's cover-Gage's-ass time. What did you tell him about Habiba?"

"I refused to hand her over. He accused me of being on a power trip."

"So?"

"Ripinsky, I'm *not*. I just want to keep the kid safe."

"I know that, but don't you think it's possible you may also enjoy calling the shots where Gage is concerned?"

"Well . . ."

"Exactly. You can fault him in any number of ways, but not for pointing that out."

"But he said I have a *twisted need* for power!"

Hy laughed. "The cad! You want me to duke it out with him?"

"Ripinsky!"

"Okay." Serious now. "You know, I like calling the shots, too, and I own a good chunk of that company. Nothing to stop me from phoning Gage from my bed of pain and setting him straight."

The offer was tempting, but I had to fight my own battles with Renshaw. Besides, this was a time when I should be distancing myself from RKI. "Thanks, but Mick and I can handle things as far as the data search goes. And you're in that bed of pain to recover from this malady, so please concentrate on that."

My nephew had come to the connecting doorway between our offices, freshly groomed and probably well fed. I said good-bye to Hy and set the receiver in its cradle, then swiveled toward Mick. "You look ready to go to work."

"Shar, get in here!"

"What?" I started at the urgency in Mick's voice.

"Now!"

I pushed up from my worn oriental rug, where I'd been poring over the spread-out files on the people involved in the case. Mick sat at the computer, its screen glowing in the darkness of his tiny office. We'd been working together for several hours, narrowing our list to a small number of suspects.

He pointed to the screen as I came in. "I took a break and checked the boards on the Web. Look at this. He's signed it differently, but I'll bet it's him."

I leaned over his shoulder and read the line he indicated.

I AM NOT FINISHED. I WILL POST MY DEMANDS SOON.

The message was signed "Tied Hands."

"Of course!" I said. "Tied hands—the first signature on the bombs was a metal device that looked like praying hands tied at the wrists. It fits the motive perfectly. Dawud Hamid couldn't legally be punished because the authorities' hands were tied by his diplomatic immunity. As were the hands of the authorities in all the other cases."

"Fine, but why isn't he finished? He blew Hamid to hell this afternoon."

"*Did* he?"

Mick turned from the screen, and his pale eyes fixed on mine. In that instant I realized how alike we were, and felt a connection click into place between us that would hold firm for the rest of our lives.

I asked, "You still have the number of that cab that picked up Hamid on Russian Hill?"

But he was already digging a notebook from his shirt pocket and reaching for the phone. He punched in a number and gave the person who answered a name—Inspector A. Joslyn—and an SFPD shield number—also Adah's. Asked his questions and sat back, tapping his pencil impatiently.

"Have you gotten information that way before?" I whispered.

"A time or two."

"Adah'll have your ass for that."

"Not if we save *hers*." He scribbled in his notebook, thanked the dispatcher, and broke the connection.

"Hamid's alive," I said.

"Right. He asked the cab driver to wait around the block in front of the consulate's annex on Pacific. Showed up less than twenty minutes later."

"And went where?"

Mick held the notebook out. "The trip log shows an address on Manzanita Lane in Brisbane. Mean anything to you?"

It certainly did.

Twenty-seven

    At eleven-ten the fog hung thick and motionless in the eucalyptus along Manzanita Lane, reminding me of the night I'd returned there after pulling Mavis Hamid's body from the Bay.

I drove past the plank bridge that led to Langley Newton's bungalow, kept on to where the potholed pavement ended in a tangle of scrub vegetation, and U-turned. A stand of cypress blocked my view of the bridge now; I tucked the MG behind it and cut the lights. Then I reached for the car phone and called Mick.

"Anything?" I asked.

"I checked with all the cab dispatchers on that part of the Peninsula. *Nada*. If Hamid left Newton's place, it was by private car."

"You talk with Blanca?"

"Reached her at the condo; more entertaining tonight. She overheard the three of them arguing this morning. Ronquillo picked up on some sexual tensions—woman-man things, Blanca calls them—between his lady and Hamid, and told him he had to leave. Hamid's run short of cash, and Visa has started kicking back his card because he's over his limit, so Leila called Langley Newton and asked him if Dawud could stay with him after he visited his mother."

"Why couldn't he persuade her to let him stay at the consulate?"

"Newton asked that, too; apparently he didn't really want a visitor. Leila told him Malika had granted an audience of no more than twenty minutes, on the condition that Dawud take the first flight back to the Caribbean. But he's determined to stay around till he can collect his daughter."

"So it's safe to assume he's still here at Newton's."

"Yeah, but . . ."

"I know; I'd better make sure." I looked glumly out the window at the thick, uninviting fog. "You making any headway on our list of suspects?"

"Some. Blanca was able to answer a few of the questions I couldn't find in any database, so I should have something for you within the hour."

"Then I'll call you back after I take a look around here."

I set the receiver back in its cradle and took the .38 that I'd picked up at home from my tote bag. Slipped out of the car, locked it, and stood listening for a moment. Mutters came from a TV in one of the downhill dwellings; a dog barked monotonously on the ridge. I stuck the gun into the waistband of my jeans, pulled my jacket collar up against the chill, and slid down the incline to where the little creek trickled over moss-slick stones. As I moved along the creek bed I braced my hands against the slope. When I sighted the plank bridge I scrabbled to higher ground and struck out through the grove.

Soon I sighted two rectangles of light: the front window of the bungalow and a smaller one toward the rear. I stopped at the edge of the trees and scrutinized them; both were like projection screens on which the film had yet to run. I waited for several minutes, smelling the distant sea under the more insistent cat-spray scent of the eucalyptus.

The black Citroen was pulled up in front of the bungalow, and beyond it the junk on the porch was a shadowy mare's-nest where anything or anyone might lurk. The dark hulks of the pickups didn't look much more inviting, but they presented good vantage points for watching the windows. I glanced around, then sprinted toward the closest one and crouched in its shadow, studying the front window some more.

Newton had told me he seldom used that room except when he had company.

After about ten minutes an elongated shadow rippled from left to right across the pulled-down shade. It seemed to grow smaller, then lengthened again and rippled back the way it had come. The tang of woodsmoke drifted through the air.

I looked up at the bungalow's roof. There was a metal chimney above the spot where I recalled a woodstove standing, and it now emitted a plume of smoke. Someone had stirred the fire. Who? And what about that light in back?

The other pickup was closer to the rear window. I ran to its shelter.

The shade back there was also taut, and the window was covered by a security grille. I watched, resting my eyes frequently when the shadows cast by the bars began to play tricks on me. Five minutes. Ten. Fourteen—

Someone moved inside the room, had probably just come in. An indistinct shape passed the window. Passed once more, and a third time. Then another figure appeared—larger and to the left. The first shape pivoted, and I imagined an exchange of words. In less than a minute the light in the room went out.

I glanced at the front of the bungalow. The parlor window still glowed. Bent over, I dashed toward the other pickup. Reached it in time to see the same tall shape pass the front window.

One person going to bed, one sitting up late. Two people in residence, anyway.

Quickly I retraced my path to the MG.

"Anything?" I asked Mick again.

"Yeah, but I don't think you're gonna like it. This analysis isn't working for us."

"Go ahead."

"Okay, I used the variables you gave me: presence in San Francisco during nineteen eighty-nine; presence in D.C. from ninety through ninety-one; presence in New York City from ninety-one through ninety-two; and absence from the country from ninety-three to late ninety-four. Based on that I came up with only two names of men connected with the case."

"Who?"

"One's Langley Newton."

Newton, the bomber? Not too damn likely, given that he was currently playing host to the bomber's primary target.

"No, I don't like that," I told Mick, "but give me the details, anyway."

"Okay, he worked at Das Glücksspiel from the mideighties till it was sold in fall of eighty-nine. Remained in the city through the holidays, then took a job with a firm that manages food services on military installations. Was in the D.C. area till ninety-one, New Jersey from ninety-one through -two. Then he left that company and went to work for a franchise that was setting up outlets in Europe. Was overseas where he couldn't've mailed a bomb during ninety-three and the early part of ninety-four. It all fits."

"Except for the fact that Dawud Hamid is alive and well in his back room. Who's the other possible?"

"Kahlil Lateef, sole survivor of today's bombing."

I liked that better, though not a lot. It did fit with my suspicion that the bombing might have been an inside job, though. Lateef would have known Dawud was coming to the consulate; he could easily have planted the bomb before he took his daily stroll to the Marina Green. But had he known Chloe Love? Very likely; Das Glücksspiel had been a diplomatic hangout.

"Okay—the details?"

"Assistant trade attaché at the San Francisco consulate, eighty-seven to November of eighty-nine. Personal aide to Ambassador Jalil, eighty-nine to June of ninety-one. Trade attaché, United Nations delegation, ninety-one through -two. Returned to Azad due to family tragedy, ninety-three through October ninety-four, when he was reposted here."

So Lateef had been in San Francisco when Love was murdered and Hamid disappeared. Somehow he'd given me a different impression. I reviewed my luncheon conversation with the trade attaché; he'd been vague on the date of Dawud's disappearance and said nothing about him being a suspect in the Love case. That was odd, for such a malicious gossip as Lateef. Unless he had a bad memory, or feared the consul general's wrath too much to open that can of worms. Or unless he had something to hide. . . .

"Shar?"

"Nothing more on the Web?"

"I haven't checked in a while."

"Do, then. I'll hold."

Both the suspects fit the physical profile of the bomber, such as it was. Both had been in the right places at the right time. Lateef had had access to the consulate this afternoon. And yet . . .

Did either of them have it in him to coolly walk up to the door of the consulate and hand a bomb to a nine-year-old girl? Was either a sociopath who would taunt and toy with the authorities? Was either a thrill-seeker who got off on power?

Who could tell? The bomber was a good actor; he'd proven as much time and again.

"Shar? Nothing new on the boards."

"Well, keep monitoring them. I'm going to pay a call on Newton."

Langley Newton's eyes narrowed when he saw me standing in the circle of light from the overhead bulb on his porch. He wore the same threadbare bathrobe as the last time I visited, and a pair of half-glasses perched on the end of his nose. "Ms. McCone," he said, removing the glasses, "what is it? Has something else happened?"

"That depends on what you mean by 'else.' The Azadi Consulate was blown up this afternoon, and all but one person are presumed dead."

"I know; I saw it on the TV news." He glanced over his shoulder, then stepped out in his stockinged feet onto the porch and pulled the door shut behind him. "I'm sorry I can't invite you in. I've a guest, someone who's a light sleeper. I don't want our voices to carry."

"Ah, you have a friend visiting."

After a slight hesitation he nodded, his low-slung halo of silver hair looking tarnished in the light from the bulb.

"Or is he a friend of a friend?" I asked.

". . . I'm sorry?"

"Perhaps your visitor is a friend of Leila Schechtmann?"

Newton frowned, probably wondering if Leila had told me Hamid was there. He took a step to the side and leaned against the old wringer washing machine that sat next to the door, folding his arms across his chest.

"Mr. Newton," I said, "how long does Dawud Hamid plan to stay with you?"

"Hamid?"

"Come on, I know Leila sent him to you earlier today. I know he's sleeping in your back room. For how long?"

". . . I don't know."

"Guess."

"Well, a day or two anyway."

"So he can try to get hold of his daughter."

Newton nodded slightly and shifted his weight, his gaze sliding away from mine. "Why are you interested in Hamid?"

"Someone I know is looking for him. I want to put them in touch before Hamid leaves the country."

He scanned the darkness around us, as if he thought the person might be lurking in the trees. "You're lying to me."

"About what?"

"Nobody you know is looking for Hamid. The only person besides you who's interested in him is the Diplo-bomber."

I hesitated, framing my reply, warning myself to proceed cautiously. "What do you know about the bomber?"

"Only what I've seen on the news and what Hamid's told me. I know about the woman Dawud killed, and about the bomber torturing the Azadis with messages every time he struck."

"Does Hamid know who he is?"

He shook his head.

"And he admitted to the murder?"

"Yes."

"Yet you're letting him stay here, even though he killed your friend?"

"My . . . ?"

He didn't know. "The woman Dawud raped and strangled was Chloe Love."

"Chloe . . . Chloe's dead?"

"Yes, in January of eighty-nine. Hamid was the prime suspect, but he walked because of diplomatic immunity. Since he told you he killed a woman, that pretty much erases any last doubts about his guilt."

But Newton wasn't listening; he seemed to have withdrawn, as though the news of Love's murder had been too much for him to absorb.

"Are you all right?" I asked.

He moved his hand in a blind gesture, his eyes focused somewhere behind me.

I said gently, "Why don't you call the police, Mr. Newton? Turn Hamid over to them?"

"Why? You said they couldn't do anything to him when it happened."

"Times have changed. A case might be made otherwise. They're starting to crack down on diplomatic crime; the D.A. brought charges against the Irish consul general last year when he injured all those people in that drunk-driving accident. And this is a far more serious crime."

Again he made the blind gesture. "A lawyer of the caliber Dawud can afford would surely get him off. Why should I start something that never can be finished?"

It was the response I'd been hoping for. I wanted Hamid to stay safe and unsuspecting at Newton's bungalow; he was my only bargaining chip with the bomber. With Kahlil Lateef, apparently.

"Mr. Newton, can you keep Hamid here?"

He shrugged. "Not if he doesn't want to stay. He's younger and stronger than I."

"What if you tell him that someone who has a lead on his daughter will contact him in the morning? Would that make him stay put?"

"Probably, if I don't give away . . . what you just told me. And that may be difficult."

"Please try. The bomber's aware that Hamid wasn't in the consulate this afternoon. He's been posting on the Techno-Web—do you know what that is?"

"Yes."

"Well, he's been posting that he'll make his demands known soon. One of those is sure to be Hamid, in exchange for the policewoman he's holding."

Newton glanced nervously at his front door. "You'd give him over in exchange? Just like that?"

"In a heartbeat. The policewoman's a friend of mine."

"But it's like . . . cold-blooded murder."

"No, Mr. Newton, it's more like justice."

He seemed to think about that, and after a moment he nodded. "All right, I'll keep Hamid here by the method you suggested—or barring that, any other I can come up with."

"Thank you."

He turned, then paused with his hand on the doorknob. "Do you have any idea who the bomber is?"

"I think so: Kahlil Lateef, trade attaché at the consulate. He's a consummate actor, has hidden his true emotions extremely well."

"I should take a lesson from him," Newton said. "After what you've told me tonight, I'm going to have to keep my own feelings on a very tight rein."

Twenty-eight

I retreated to the eucalyptus grove and watched Newton's bungalow. There was no sign of activity in the back room where Hamid was staying, and after a while the light in the parlor went out. I stayed put for about fifteen minutes, but the house remained dark and no one came outside. Finally I cut through the grove to the MG and checked in with Mick. Nothing further had been posted on the TechnoWeb.

"It's weird, Shar," he said. "I'm sitting all alone in front of this screen in the middle of the night, and I can feel hundreds of thousands of other people doing the same thing out there. We're all waiting to see what he does next."

"You really think that many people are following what's happening?"

"Oh, sure—and not just law enforcement and the press. The boards're buzzing. Nighttime's when they get heavy use, anyway; people are lonesome and it helps them feel connected."

I thought of our cross-country flight and the long, dark leg between Phoenix and Mirage Wells. The mutterings across the nighttime radio waves had helped me feel connected while Hy and Habiba slept.

"Well, keep monitoring the boards," I told Mick, "but I need you to do something in addition to that: locate Kahlil

Lateef. The operator at RKI can probably tell you where he is, if you don't let on that you're asking for me."

Mick said he'd think of some way to get the information, and I settled down for a long surveillance. Stakeouts were just a notch below paperwork on the list of things I didn't like about my work, but I couldn't lose track of Hamid and I needed Mick at the computer, so the tedious task fell to me. God, how I wished I could afford to hire another operative! Rae had been making noises lately about leaving All Souls; she'd be perfect. But how to manage it? The reward money the feds had posted for the bomber? If I could claim even a portion of that—

Don't get ahead of yourself, McCone.

Time dragged. The fog began to drift, fooling me more than once into thinking I saw a person slipping through it. It grew cold in the car, and I discovered that the blanket I usually kept in the trunk had mysteriously disappeared. I desperately wanted a cup of coffee, but had to content myself with some stale chocolate I found in the glove box. Over the past couple of years my passion for chocolate had waned; the Hershey Bar looked and tasted as if it had been melting and solidifying in there for at least that long. I threw half of it out the window and continued to watch the edges of the grove and the plank bridge. No one came or went by either route, and by one-fifteen I was half crazed with boredom.

The phone buzzed, a welcome diversion. "Yes, Mick."

"Shar, brace yourself! The bomber's posted again. He wants to communicate with *you*, personally!"

"What! How?"

"He's switching from the boards to the Web's live discourse. And he wants you on-line at quarter to three. The task force called here; they're setting up for you at their headquarters. Parkhurst wants to see you right away."

"Jesus." I glanced at the plank bridge. "This surveillance— we can't let Hamid go anyplace, and I don't know if Newton can hold him if he gets it into his mind to leave. I'll need you to take over down here."

"I'm already on my way; I'm talking to you on a cellular unit I borrowed from a friend this afternoon." He recited its number, and I scribbled it down. "You better leave now. It won't hurt if the place is uncovered for a few minutes. Now listen: the press is already onto what's happening, and they're massing outside the Federal Building annex. You're to go to the back of the building, down the alley that opens off Larkin Street. Park by the red dumpster. Craig Morland'll be waiting to take you upstairs."

"Okay." Heart racing, I reached for the ignition. "Oh, Mick, did you locate Lateef?"

"Nobody knows where he is. I spoke directly with Gage Renshaw, pretending to be a worried relative. Lateef walked away from Jackson Street this afternoon and nobody's heard from him since."

Nobody except the authorities, the press, and half a million hackers.

When I got to task force headquarters I met with Ed Parkhurst in his office and briefed him on the bomber's probable identity. Although I hadn't intended to, at the last minute I kept RKI out of it, citing instead an "anonymous source" at the consulate. It wasn't that I was trying to protect Renshaw, or even the firm in which Hy held a substantial interest. What it boiled down to was a clear-cut matter of ethics: I'd signed a contract with them guaranteeing confidentiality. Once I'd given my word, I wouldn't retract it.

Besides, my fit of moral purity made me feel several steps farther removed from the thin line that separated them from me.

Parkhurst called in two of his people and assigned them to tracing Lateef. "If he is our man, he'll be stuck at his computer for a while," he said. "You get a quick fix on the son of a bitch, and we might take him unaware."

The pair didn't look any too optimistic as they filed out, and I couldn't say as I blamed them. They'd been handed a near impossible task.

Parkhurst remained at his desk, rubbing his stubbly chin and regarding me with thinly veiled dislike. "I thought of keeping you out of this, Ms. McCone," he finally said. "I don't like involving outsiders, especially ones who don't play by my rules. The bomber isn't going to be able to see you;

any member of this task force could deal with him—and much more effectively."

I bit back a sarcastic remark about the task force's effectiveness up to this point and asked, "So why *did* you bring me in on it?"

"Two reasons. One, he was adamant that he would communicate only with you. There's a reason for that and until we know what it is we can't risk noncompliance. Two, he may ask a question that only you can answer, as a means of identifying you. And now, if this Lateef is really our man, we have a third reason: he's personally acquainted with you and thus equipped to pick up on some nuance of phrasing that might tip him if we used a ringer."

"How do you know it's actually him you're dealing with, rather than someone who's fooling around?"

"All along he's revealed details that we've never made public—but that doesn't concern you. Now, a few pointers on how to play this: Don't let on that you think you know who he is. Don't antagonize him. Don't ask questions unless absolutely necessary for clarification. Feed into his game, agree to all of his demands, no matter how outrageous. Get instructions, and we'll take it from there."

"Won't he be afraid you're trying to trace him by keeping him on-line?"

"Communication by computer can't be traced like a phone call, if that's what you're thinking. Posting on the boards creates a paper trail; he left one, of course, but once we got our court order we found he'd been using a password belonging to a woman in Tennessee who'd never heard of the Diplo-bomber and hadn't logged on to the service in six months. Since then he's been using other borrowed passwords. Now that he's moved to live discourse, he's selected the perfect method of communicating undetected; it doesn't create any trail at all." Parkhurst looked at his watch. "Let's get on with it, shall we?"

He led me to the office Adah had occupied only ten days before: a small high-ceilinged room rendered claustrophobic by the two women and seven men assembled there. They all looked tired and on edge; the air was thick with cigarette smoke, and Styrofoam cups littered every surface except the desk. Craig Morland sat there, a Macintosh PowerBook in front of him. When Parkhurst and I came in, he motioned for me to take the chair next to him.

The flashing numerals at the top of the Mac's screen said 2:40 A.M.

As I sat down, Morland was scrolling through a menu: eco-freaks; lesbian forum; writer's heaven; post divorce; over thirty; badass males; feminist backlash; stressed out; looking 4 love—the list seemed endless.

"What're those?" I asked.

"Conversation rooms." Morland moved the cursor to an item near the bottom of the window.

DIPLO-BOMBER.

"That's ours?"

"No. It's just a public room; there're eighteen people in there babbling about the case. I lurked, checked out what they're saying. None of their theories is as improbable as what's really happening."

"Explain this 'room' business, would you."

"I take it you're not familiar with the boards or live talk?"

"My computer's strictly for business purposes, and I only use it when my assistant's unavailable."

"Then I'm glad I waited for you before setting this up."

The words WELCOME TO LIVE DISCOURSE appeared on the screen. Below them were listed two options: PUBLIC ROOMS and PRIVATE ROOMS.

"Imagine a large house," Morland said. "A mansion, actually. It contains hundreds of rooms, each devoted to a different topic of conversation. Right now we're only in the foyer."

The other agents had been milling around and talking, but as he spoke they grew silent and crowded behind us.

"Most of the rooms in the house," Morland went on, "are public. Any subscriber to the service can select and enter one, and either converse or lurk—just listen. Anyone can also set up a private room dedicated to any topic he wants, simply by selecting that option." The cursor moved to it. "You name the room with a password of your own choosing, but the name doesn't appear on the menu. The only people who know it exists are those you give the password to. I'm now going to set one up, using the name the bomber specified when he last posted on the boards."

"Wait a minute—if he posted it, don't all the people using the service know what it is? What's to stop them—"

"Our guy's too clever a bastard by far." Morland smiled grimly. "He told us to use the last two words of his last note to the Azadis. We've never made that public." He began to type.

REMEMBER C.L.

I glanced at the top of the screen. 2:42 A.M.

"That's all there is to it," Morland added. "We're now in the room and waiting for him to arrive."

In my mind's eye I visualized a shadowy room and Craig standing beside me, his features barely distinguishable in the gloom. There was a door, open just enough to let in a thin stripe of light. Any moment now I'd hear footsteps—

I pulled myself back from the scene, gripped the desk with cold fingers. Was that what they meant when they talked about getting lost in cyberspace?

Morland hadn't noticed my absence. He said, "This particular service is a very fast one; it's about as close to actual conversation as you can get on-line. When our guy logs on and enters the room, he'll type and send his first message. You'll hear a chime, and his words'll appear on the screen. You'll then tell me how to reply, and I'll enter it word for word. If you don't know what to say, consult with Special Agent Parkhurst. Take your time; delays are normal."

2:43.

In a low voice I said, "I just briefed Parkhurst on what I've been able to find out. I'm reasonably sure that the bomber is Kahlil Lateef, the Azadi trade attaché."

Morland looked sharply at me, then shook his head. "You *did* know something we didn't. What's Lateef's motive?"

"It's complicated and, frankly, I'm too nervous to go into it. What if I screw this up?"

"You'll be fine. Just bring him along easy, let him enjoy his game."

"And it *is* a game to him."

He nodded. "I've got a theory about players like this guy. Something happens to them—a shock, a loss, or just an irresistible impulse to go against the acceptable norm. So they start to alter their behavior a little at a time, moving farther and farther away from society's standards until they're finally free of all the emotions the rest of us feel: guilt, pity, remorse, empathy, even love. Eventually only one emotion remains: the fear of being caught out. You've lived with fear, I assume. So have I. We both know what happens after a while."

I thought back to the tremendous rush I'd felt while sitting in the sidewalk café in Marigot, before I'd pulled my trick on Cam Connors and gotten Habiba off Jumbie Cay. Intoxicating stuff—effective if used wisely, dangerous if it got out of hand. "Fear can become how you get your kicks."

"Yeah. And tonight our guy is getting the biggest kick of all."

I studied the staid-looking FBI man, surprised to find a kindred soul lived within his conservative facade. Adah could do far worse; Craig, like Hy, understood and accepted the darkness that inhabited us all.

2:44.

The room was very quiet now. The flick of a cigarette lighter made me start; a cough set my heart to pounding. Tension connected all of us like an intricate web of electrical current. I thought I imagined the hair on my arms bristling, looked down and saw that it was.

Still 2:44.

Come on.

2:44.

Come *on*!

2:44 ... 2:44 ... 2:45.

The Mac's chime was incongruously whimsical for such a prosaic piece of equipment. Words appeared on the screen.

GREETINGS, MS. MCCONE. YOU THINK YOU KNOW WHO I AM, DON'T YOU?

I stared at the message, as if somehow I could bring his face into focus.

"What do you want to say?" Morland prompted.

". . . Say 'You have me baffled. Why do you want to talk with me?'"

Morland typed and pressed the send key. The reply came quickly.

AS TO YOUR STATEMENT, YOU ARE LYING. AS TO
YOUR QUESTION, I THOUGHT YOU WOULD ENJOY
MATCHING WITS. DO YOU KNOW WHERE DAWUD
HAMID IS?

Right to the crux of the matter. "As of an hour ago, yes. I
spoke with the man he's staying with."

AN HOUR AGO ISN'T GOOD ENOUGH. WHERE IS
HE NOW?

I snapped my fingers, motioning for the phone. "Give me
a minute and I'll find out."

Morland pushed the phone toward me before he entered
my words. I punched in the number Mick had given me for
his borrowed cellular unit. When he answered, he sounded
agitated.

"Thank God you called, Shar! Has he—"

"I need Hamid, Mick. Is he still at the bungalow?"

"No. Newton's car was gone and the place was empty when
I got here. But listen—I checked the office machine. Blanca
Diaz called; Hamid's at her house."

"What!"

"I guess Newton drove him to Ronquillo's condo; he got
there around two, drunk and raving about the bombing. Ronquillo wouldn't let him stay, so Leila asked Blanca to take
him home to her place in the Mission. I'm on my way there
now."

"Okay, Mick, call Blanca and tell her not to let him out of
her sight and not to turn him over to anybody but me. Get
there as fast as you can, so you can help her in case he tries
to take off."

"Will do."

I broke the connection and said to Morland, "Tell him,
'I've located Hamid.' "

JUST LIKE THAT? MY, MY. THEN YOU MAY BE ABLE
TO HELP ME—AND YOUR FRIEND INSPECTOR
JOSLYN.

"How?"

DON'T BE SO TERSE, MS. MCCONE. TRY TO ENJOY
THIS. I AM.

"I'm very concerned for Adah Joslyn."

YOUR FRIEND IS FINE, ALTHOUGH SHE COULD DO

WITH A MORE PLEASANT DISPOSITION. I AM WILL-
ING TO EXCHANGE HER FOR DAWUD HAMID.

I glanced at Parkhurst. He nodded.

"It's a done deal," I said. Quickly Morland entered and
sent the words.

I LIKE A DECISIVE WOMAN. BUT WILL THE FEDS
ALLOW YOU TO MAKE THE EXCHANGE?

"You have my word on it."

I TRUST YOU, BUT I DO NOT TRUST THEM.

"They will make good on this."

I DON'T SUPPOSE IT MATTERS.

Now what could that mean?

HOW SOON CAN YOU GET HOLD OF MR. HAMID?

"Within the hour."

THEN I WILL RETURN TO THE ROOM AT FOUR
O'CLOCK.

"I'll be here."

Morland said, "He's logging off now."

Parkhurst put his hand on my shoulder. "Well done, Ms.
McCone." He sounded as though it pained him to acknowledge it. "Now where's Hamid?"

Blanca's address was in my notebook. "I'll take you there."

"You'll give me the location and we'll—"

"No way." I wanted to be there when they hauled Hamid
downtown.

Morland interceded quickly. "Sir, what's the charge for
picking him up to be?"

"Material witness in a federal investigation. And you get
that ambassador who arrived from D.C. a few hours ago—
what's his name?"

"Jalil."

"Get Jalil over here. Tell him . . . ask him to exert pressure
on Hamid to play it our way."

"Yessir."

"And you, Ms. McCone—"

"Mr. Parkhurst," I said, following Morland's tactful lead,
"you're going to need me. As I was about to say before,
there's no way the woman who's sheltering Hamid will turn
him over to anyone other than me."

Parkhurst eyed me mistrustfully. "Why?"

"Because I'm Ricky Savage's sister-in-law."

His eyes narrowed, and for a moment I thought he might deliver an ultimatum. Then he raised them to the ceiling and rolled them dramatically. "If I don't go along with you, it's going to be more hassle than it's worth. Come along, if you must." Sourly he added, "Whoever the hell Ricky Savage is."

By the time we got back to task force headquarters with our sullen, booze-saturated material witness, Ambassador Jalil had arrived. I could see a family resemblance to Malika Hamid in the portly diplomat's facial features, but little of her intelligence in his small eyes. Jalil proved to be crafty, though: when Dawud refused to cooperate, citing his immunity, the ambassador exerted strong and swift influence to change his mind. He could, Jalil said, waive Dawud's immunity, as was the prerogative of the senior diplomat, but that would be too lenient. Instead he thought he'd repatriate him to Azad, where a tribunal of Muslim judges would try him for the rape and murder of Chloe Love. Slyly he reminded Dawud that the penalty for those crimes in their native country was death by stoning.

Hamid decided he'd stand a better chance against the Diplo-bomber.

At ten to four, as Morland and I were about to resume our positions in front of the Mac, one of the ATF agents rushed in and handed Parkhurst a message slip. He scanned it, then announced, "Listen up, people. An anonymous tip was phoned in to the SFPD an hour ago. Caller said the bomber was operating out of an apartment on Fillmore between Bay and North Point. He's not there anymore, but they got their warrant from the judge who's standing by, and they're going in to collect evidence."

The reactions ranged from whistles and foot-stamping to grumbles about the police horning in on the task force's investigation.

"Fillmore between Bay and North Point," I said to Morland. "That's right around the corner from Adah's building. I'll bet she came across what Lateef was doing by coincidence, like her message to me said. Went investigating, and he grabbed her. He's superconfident—thought nothing of telling me he took daily walks to the Marina Green."

Morland grimaced. "You mean daily walks to his private bomb factory."

WHAT A COOPERATIVE WOMAN YOU ARE. OR ARE YOU LYING TO ME AGAIN?

Lateef had logged on at exactly four o'clock.

"No, I'm not lying. We have Hamid in custody."

WHERE DID YOU FIND HIM?

What does it matter? "At the home of a woman named Blanca Diaz, in the Mission district."

I AM SATISFIED. NOW HERE ARE YOUR INSTRUCTIONS. FOLLOW THEM TO THE LETTER. UNDERSTOOD?

"Yes, understood."

TAKE HAMID IN YOUR LITTLE RED CAR TO THE MARINA GREEN AT TWENTY MINUTES AFTER FIVE. THERE IS A PARKING LOT AT THE EAST END NEAR THE PAR COURSE. IT IS CLOSED TO THE PUBLIC UNTIL SIX. DO YOU KNOW IT?

"The one by the Gashouse Cove boat slips?"

YES. DRIVE INTO THE LOT, TURN, AND PARK AT THE GATE FACING MARINA BOULEVARD. TELL THE TASK FORCE TO HAVE A HELICOPTER AND AN UNARMED PILOT WAITING ON THE GREEN JUST BEYOND THE PAR COURSE.

I glanced up at Parkhurst. He nodded.

"It will be there."

LEAVE HAMID IN THE CAR AND GO TO THE FIRST PHONE BOOTH BY THE BOAT SLIPS. I WILL CALL YOU AT EXACTLY FIVE-THIRTY.

"I've got it."

There was a stir behind me, a rustling of paper. I ignored it.

THE POLICE ARE TO CORDON OFF THE AREA. THERE ARE TO BE NO CONCEALED SHARPSHOOTERS AND NO HEROICS ON ANYONE'S PART. I WILL BE WATCHING THE AREA AND WILL KNOW IF A TRAP IS SET. IS THAT CLEAR?

"Yes, it's clear." Parkhurst had handed a message slip to Morland. He passed it to me before typing my reply.

The slip gave the address of the apartment on Fillmore and noted, "Bomb-making materials in kitchen. Press-on lettering and stationery stock on desk. No other evidence except a photo of an unknown woman in a chef's hat and apron with an Arab who bears a strong resemblance to Richard Nixon."

Chloe Love and Kahlil Lateef.

"Sharon?" Morland nudged me with his elbow. I looked at the screen.

THE MARINA GREEN AT FIVE-THIRTY, THEN. DO NOT FORGET: I WILL BE WATCHING YOU.

Twenty-nine

The Marina Green extends several long blocks east from the St. Francis Yacht Club to the Gashouse Cove boat slips next to Fort Mason. In between stretch a level lawn and bayside esplanade. On the clear, sun-shot days that are fairly standard in a district that has always reminded me of a Mediterranean village, the grass is dotted with picnickers, lovers, kite-flyers, and sun-worshippers. Joggers, walkers, dog-walkers, and bench-sitters crowd the esplanade. Tourists photograph the elegant yawls and cabin cruisers or poke around the small clapboard building that sits midway on the seawall and is used by the navy as a sonar tracking station. The views, from the Golden Gate to Alcatraz, are postcard-perfect. It is a place of joy and peace.

But not so at five-twenty in the morning after a harrowing, foggy night. Not so when a sociopath riding an enormous power rush is dictating the terms of your behavior—and watching you.

The nighttime sky was beginning to gray, backlighting the spires of Russian Hill. The fog had retreated to the Gate and lay like a dirty smear between the reddish towers of the bridge. Scattered lights twinkled on the Marin hills and the beacon on Alcatraz flashed. The wind blew cold and steady off the Bay.

On the lawn some hundred yards from my car an SFPD helicopter idled—red lights winking, an unarmed officer at its controls. Marina Boulevard was cordoned off for two blocks between Webster and Steiner Streets. The everpresent press and curious residents drawn by the activity massed against the barricades. Here, on my side, the Green lay dark and deserted.

I got out of the MG and peered into the shadows. He was somewhere in them, not far away.

The task force had followed Lateef's instructions to the letter, except for the team of sharpshooters smuggled into an apartment building facing the Green and now stationed on its roof. They would do nothing to jeopardize Joslyn, and there would be no heroics—least of all on my part. I was playing it straight all the way.

I turned from the MG and started toward the phone booth by the boat slips. The hooded sweatshirt I'd borrowed from one of the women on the task force to conceal the body wire I wore was much too big; I rolled up its sleeves some as I walked. I'd objected to the wire at first, afraid Lateef would somehow realize I was relaying his instructions to the task force, but now I was glad I'd given in. It made me feel less alone out here.

I still didn't understand Lateef's insistence on dealing only with me. Was it because I was Adah's friend and would do everything I could to make this operation go smoothly? Or was there some other factor working here—something I'd yet to figure out?

Another thing that puzzled me: how had he known he was actually dealing with me? He hadn't asked any question that only I could answer, but he'd demonstrated himself too clever to proceed this far on blind faith. Something in our initial exchange had reassured him, but I was damned if I knew what.

Five twenty-four now. I reached the phone booth on the walk next to the slips. "In position," I said into the wire. Behind me mooring lines creaked as the craft rode on a light swell; a buoy bonged monotonously in the channel. Again I peered into the shadows, searching for a sign of him and knowing I would see none. Finally I gave it up, listened to the drifting murmur of voices from the barricades, watched the trickle of traffic on the distant bridge.

Five twenty-six now. God, I was sick of dancing attendance on him!

In my peripheral vision I caught a motion inside the MG, where Hamid was shackled and handcuffed to the seat-belt support. Unnecessary precautions, since he—while still sullen—was cooperating fully, but Parkhurst wouldn't let him out of task force custody otherwise. I'd tried to get Hamid to talk on the way here, but all he'd told me was to go fuck myself. Brazening it out, I thought, and he hadn't even asked me what I'd done with his daughter. Neither, for that matter, had Ambassador Jalil; from the way he'd turned the subject aside when I'd broached it, I gathered he considered Habiba an inconvenient detail that was best ignored.

Poor kid. The Azadis wouldn't want the motherless offspring of a drunken American and a murderer. And now that she'd ceased to be the prize in a bitter mother-son tug-of-war, she no longer interested her father.

Five twenty-seven.

My body tingled from an excess of adrenaline. My head ached and my eyes stung from lack of sleep. My hair hung limp to my shoulders. I hadn't washed or brushed my teeth since late yesterday afternoon at All Souls. I felt and probably looked like hell.

Five twenty-eight. Time now.

Deliberately I began to shut down my thoughts and emotions. I tuned out everything, even physical discomfort, and strove for the kind of focus I achieved in the cockpit. I let myself open to one, and only one, stimulus: fear. Accepted it, allowed it to boost me to a new level of awareness.

Getting high. As high as he must be right now.

Five twenty-nine.

I stared fixedly at the phone. Its burnished surface reflected the graying sky behind me. "Ready," I said into the wire. And placed my hand on the receiver.

The phone rang.

"Hello."

"Is everything in place, Ms. McCone?" The voice was high pitched and unreal, without a trace of an accent. He was using a distorting device.

"Yes, everything's as you requested."

"They are tracing this call, of course, but it will be too brief for that. You have on a body wire."

Damn! I knew he'd have anticipated that.

"Disconnect it, please. I am watching."

He must be very close by, using a cellular phone. He could even be mingling among the press beyond one of the barricades. I hesitated, hating to lose my link to the task force. Then I recalled Parkhurst's last words to me: "Give him whatever he wants."

"All right, I'll disconnect the wire." I set down the receiver, unzipped the sweatshirt, ripped the wire free. Held part of it up so he could see—wherever he was.

On your own now, I thought. It's just you and him.

I picked up the receiver. "You saw?"

"Yes. Now look in the phone book hanging below the shelf."

I stepped back, raised the book to the shelf, and opened it. Half the pages had been ripped out, and a mini-cassette recorder was attached by duct tape to the inside of the cover.

"You have it?" the voice asked.

"Yes."

"Play the tape. When you finish, erase it and take it with you."

"Where?"

He hung up.

I replaced the receiver and switched on the recorder. The same strange voice said, "We will resume our conversation now. After you have listened to this tape and erased it, you will return to your car. At twenty minutes to six there will be a diversion. While the authorities' attention is elsewhere, you and Hamid will leave."

A long pause.

"Come on!" I said.

"Look to your right. What do you see?"

A marina.

"Think of what you see. Then think of a drowned bird floating in the water. A drowned *bird*."

What does that—oh.

In my dreams Mavis Hamid's floating form had looked like a bat, but a more appropriate symbol would have been a bird—because that was what her name meant.

Mavis. And Salt Point Marina.

"By now I believe you will have grasped it, Ms. McCone. I regret being so cryptic, but surely you can appreciate my need for extreme precaution."

Another pause, as if he was gathering his thoughts.

"You have forty minutes to arrive there with Hamid. Make sure no one from the task force or the SFPD follows you. I'll have fixed the gate so it will remain open; come in and bring Hamid aboard the yawl. I'm sure you remember her name."

The *Freia*.

"Now erase the tape and go back to your car."

The helicopter, the police cordons: all a sham to confuse the authorities. The phone call and recorded message: his method of getting Hamid and me alone.

And Adah? *Was* she alive, or was that another of his lies? *Give him whatever he wants.*

I rewound the tape and pressed the erase button.

As I slipped behind the wheel of the MG Hamid said, "So what did the lunatic demand this time?" His voice was steady but underscored by fear.

My watch said five thirty-eight.

"I asked—"

"I heard you. There's been a change of plans. In about two minutes we're going to take a ride. I'll need you to watch and make sure nobody—fed or cop—follows us."

"Oh, no! I will not go anywhere without—"

I motioned at his handcuffs. "You don't have much choice in the matter, now do you?"

Hamid looked away and slouched lower in the seat.

I kept my eyes on the second hand as it inched around. What sort of diversion—

A muffled thump, like a potato sounds when it blows up in the oven.

Hamid jerked. I looked around him in time to see the lid fly off a dumpster halfway between the helicopter and the St. Francis Yacht Club. Flames shot into the air and debris rained down on the esplanade.

"What the hell?" Hamid said.

Another thump, and a second dumpster exploded.

An SFPD car started up and careened around the barricade at Webster Street. A press van followed. Spectators surged through the tape and over the sawhorses as the uniforms struggled to control them.

On the Green, flames shot high from heaps of burning rubble. The roof of the small clapboard naval tracking station caught fire. An SFFD hook and ladder that had been stationed on Webster pulled out, lights flashing.

I started the MG.

The fire truck turned onto the boulevard, cutting a swath through the people racing along the pavement. I shot out of the parking lot in its wake. In the rearview mirror I saw a task force car attempting to follow. The foot traffic blocked it as I took a hard left and crashed past the barricade onto Fillmore.

"You watch out the rear window," I told Hamid.

His face was pale. Wordlessly he nodded and looked back.

Not much traffic here on the side street. Intersection clear at Beach, clear at North Point.

Fillmore between North Point and Bay! What's that address where the bastard was making his bombs? There it is, that peculiar-looking Bavarian-style building with the For Sale sign.

Nobody coming, slide across Bay Street.

"Anybody behind us?"

"No."

"Keep watching."

What's the best way out of town? Lombard to Gough and over the hill to the freeway? Yes.

Peculiar-looking Bavarian-style building with a For Sale sign. The one across the back fence from Adah's. That must be how . . .

I turned left on the tail end of the yellow light at Lombard, jumbled words and phrases that I'd heard over the past ten days bubbling up from my subconscious in no logical order.

Mr. Duck . . . sure makes a lot of trash . . . he is having trouble selling it . . . I'm heading out now to confirm it . . . waddles in and waddles out . . . probably the most kind and decent person I've ever known . . . it's too damn close to home for comfort . . . one of those funny European cars . . . stumbled onto a lead . . . by coincidence . . . left him an apartment building . . . she went to bat for me . . . someday I'm going to pick through it, too . . . you'd give him over, just like that?

"Mr. Duck," I said softly.

No wonder the bomber hadn't questioned my identity when we'd talked on the computer; I'd told him something only the two of us knew.

I ran the red and turned right on Gough.

"Hamid," I said, "where were you before you showed up at Leila's last night?"

"In a bar. I stopped for a quick beer, and the special report about the bombing came on. I just kept drinking."

"No, before that."

"The consulate. I thought Habiba might be there. If she was I planned to play that game you used to get her away from me at Jumbie Cay. Too bad I didn't remember it until afterwards; I wouldn't be in this mess now. Anyway, I had a cab waiting around the block, but Habiba wasn't there. And my mother wouldn't loan me any money; she wouldn't even give me a glass of water."

"Then what did you do?"

"Went down the Peninsula to a friend of Leila's. She arranged for me to stay with him, but when I got there he wasn't home. The place was so damned depressing that I decided to go back to the city. I was sure Leila would make me a loan if I could get to her when Sandy wasn't around. I left her friend a note and walked down the hill to Brisbane. And that's when I stopped for a beer and found out how close I'd come to being killed."

How close *he'd* come to being killed. No grief for his mother or the others who'd died in the explosion.

We crested the hill onto Gough. Into the homestretch to the freeway now, traffic light, and still no one following.

I asked, "So you never saw Leila's friend?"

"No."

And he hadn't been in that back room at Newton's bungalow last night.

Adah had.

Thirty

There were a number of cars in the parking lot at Salt Point Marina, but quite a few of the boats were gone. Holiday weekend, I thought, carefree start of summer—for some people.

I pulled into a space at the far side of the pavement, turned off the MG, and checked my watch. Ten of the allotted forty minutes remained.

"We'll be going into the marina soon," I said to Hamid. "He wants us on board Eric Sparling's sailboat."

"Do you have a plan?"

"We'll take our cues from him. I think I know him well enough that I may be able to push some of the right buttons."

"Kahlil doesn't *have* buttons."

"He's also not the bomber."

Hamid stared at me. "I thought they were sure he was. What about that picture of him and Chloe that Parkhurst said they found in that apartment?"

"Planted by the bomber, who also tipped the cops. He knew I suspected Lateef; I told him so."

"Then who—"

"No time to explain. We'd better get going."

He rubbed at his wrist where the handcuff had chafed.

"This is all so unnecessary. Let me go, and I'll pay you handsomely."

"I thought you were broke."

"I have access to a great deal of money. I hold the keys to Speed's entire operation; I can tap into his bank accounts."

Which was why Schechtmann had contrived to get a hold over him. The two were shackled to one another as securely as Hamid was to the seat-belt anchor.

I said, "Money wouldn't buy my friend's life back."

He made a dismissive sound. "One life. What is that, when you can become very rich?"

"Adah would be one more ghost to visit me in my nightmares. I can't afford that, even if I cared about money. Which I don't."

"Then you're a fool."

"And you're entitled to your opinion. Now listen carefully: as I was saying, we'll take our cues from him. You watch and listen. Don't talk. He'll probably taunt or threaten you. Don't react. Let him think you're resigned, that he's going to get what he wants. As he warned me, no heroics."

Hamid shrugged and looked away.

"Is that clear?"

He grunted.

I got out of the MG and studied the marina. The *Freia*, a yawl of at least forty feet, was in the slip where Mavis's body had floated, but several of those to either side of her were untenanted. It was quiet there; I could hear only the hum of light traffic on 101 and the cries of seabirds out for their breakfasts. A thick mist hung over the cove, although a quicksilver line had appeared between the cloud cover and the tops of the East Bay hills. I walked around the car and opened the passenger's door.

"This is supreme stupidity on your part," Hamid said.

"Shut up." I took the cuff keys from my jeans pocket, unlocked the ring that held him to the seat-belt anchor and clicked it around my left wrist. Then I squatted and freed his ankles. "Come on."

He got out, making a great show of overcoming his stiffness.

Joined at the wrist, we walked toward the gate. It looked locked but opened when I touched it. Jimmied latch, and no manager available to fix it on the holiday. I pushed through it and led Hamid along the pier to the *Freia*.

She was a sleek yawl, hardware and teak damp and shiny from the mist. No one was above decks and when I glanced at the cabin portholes I saw they were tightly covered. No crew in evidence; he planned to take her out alone.

"Go ahead," I said to Hamid. He stepped awkwardly from the dock to the afterdeck. I followed. The companionway steps were to our left; I motioned him toward them. Dim light shone below. Hamid stopped, resisting.

Briefly I yearned for my .38, which I'd left with Craig Morland. Its weight would have been comforting now. But I was still playing it straight. Would continue to play it straight as long as possible.

I nudged Hamid and we started down the steps.

The main cabin was teak paneled and reasonably spacious; the only light came from a bare bulb on the bulkhead near the bottom of the steps, and shadows gathered in its far reaches. To our left Adah hunched on the settee behind the dinette table, her ankles shackled to one of its supports, her hands tied behind her. She was gaunt-faced and disheveled, but not broken. There was fire in her eyes; it flared higher when she saw me.

I didn't feel so alone anymore.

I gave Hamid a final nudge. As we came all the way into the cabin he stiffened. I looked to our right toward the galley.

Langley Newton stepped forward in his ducklike gait, holding a snub-nosed pistol. Mr. Duck, who deposited telltale trash in the dumpster behind the building where he had his bomb factory. A factory much closer to his primary target than the bungalow above Brisbane.

Newton was a changed man. Gone was the mild-mannered recluse of San Bruno Mountain. His eyes glittered and his color was high; he stood tall, a contemptuous smile curving his thin lips.

"Good morning, Mr. Hamid," he said. "I'm sorry I missed you when you stopped by yesterday. No, that's a lie; having you fall so conveniently into my hands would have ruined the whole game."

Hamid's mouth twitched, but he didn't speak.

"You're alone?" Newton asked me.

"Yes."

"You erased the tape?"

I nodded.

"Set the recorder on the table."

Slowly I took it from the sweatshirt's pocket and set it down.

"Now unlock the handcuffs."

I removed the cuff from my wrist, leaving it dangling from Hamid's. Placed the keys next to the recorder.

Newton motioned for Hamid to come farther inside, near the closed door to the forward cabin. I remained where I was, halfway between him and the steps. He regarded Hamid thoughtfully as he passed him. "My, we look subdued, Mr. Hamid. Afraid, even. But then, men who prey on helpless women usually are cowards."

Hamid flinched.

Joslyn's eyes were focused intensely on me. Now they moved to her right. I glanced that way but couldn't make out what she was trying to indicate.

Newton said to me, "You don't seem surprised to see me."

"I figured it out a while ago."

"I thought you would. So tell me, how did the show on the Marina Green come off?"

"As you planned it. This scheme must've been in the works for a long time."

"Actually I improvised it bit by bit from the time I found Hamid's note under my door and realized he'd escaped death at the consulate. I added the final pieces after you came to my house and told me you'd exchange him for Inspector Joslyn. I did have some concern about you locating Hamid in time, but I hoped you'd trace him through Leila. Once you had, it was quite a scramble to get everything in place."

"And now that you have him—what?"

"My statement to the world will be made."

"Your statement?"

He looked scornfully at me. "Surely you've figured that out by now. My statement is on the evils of diplomatic immunity. I will reveal the reason for the bombings by making an example of this scum." He jabbed the gun toward Hamid.

"How?"

Newton didn't reply. His eyes sparked brighter; he drew himself taller. If he hadn't been so dangerous, I'd have found his oratorical pose comical.

"A few hours' improvisation," he said, "and I made an entire city and the federal authorities bend to my will. I kept hundreds of thousands of people on-line, breathless for my next word. By tomorrow I'll have captured the attention of the entire world. All that, with only a few hours' planning."

His statement to the world was now secondary, I realized. So was exacting his revenge on Hamid. Chloe Love and the manner in which she had died was only a dim memory. What mattered to Newton was power. He'd gotten it, and he was glorying in it. The years of hidden criminal activity had nurtured a controlled psychosis; the intoxicating payoff had tipped him right over the edge.

Joslyn said, "McCone asked you a question—how, Newton?"

His gaze shifted to her, which allowed me to look again at where she'd been directing her eyes. Now I saw it: a Very pistol for shooting distress flares, in a hinged glass case mounted on the bulkhead next to the companionway. Standard equipment on a large yawl like this. I couldn't tell if the pistol was loaded, but there was a box of flares next to it. . . .

Newton said, "Death at sea."

"Where?"

"There's no need for you to know. We will sail, the four of us. I will drop you and Ms. McCone at a location where you will be unable to contact the authorities until Mr. Hamid and I are well under way."

"Under way to *where*?" Joslyn pressed.

". . . That's my business." Newton's eyes still glittered with triumph, but now I saw uncertainty creep in, as if in his haste to stage a big show he hadn't thought far enough beyond it.

Hamid seemed to sense it, too. He said, "This is Eric Sparling's yawl. He'll have the Coast Guard after us when he realizes it's gone."

"Have you always been stupid, or is this a recent occurrence? Do you think I would take her without Sparling's permission? I do odd jobs for him; a recent one was to drive him and his wife to the airport to catch their flight for France, where they are spending a month's vacation. He offered me the use of the yawl, gave me the keys."

"But he didn't mean for you to use it without the crew. You can't possibly sail her alone."

Hamid, damn him, was pushing too hard. Before Newton could reply, I asked, "What about your statement to the world? When will you make that?"

"Once we're under way I'll reveal the reason for the bombings—and Mr. Hamid's punishment."

"How?"

"My laptop." He nodded toward the forward cabin.

"Won't you need a phone connection to do that?"

Newton suddenly looked stricken. He *hadn't* thought it through. He shook his head as if to deny the lapse in planning.

Hamid took advantage of his preoccupation and stepped toward him.

Newton jerked the gun up, jabbed it at him. His hand was far from steady. Hamid froze, then backed off.

Newton glanced at the handcuff dangling from Hamid's wrist, then seemed to think better about moving any closer. "If you make another move toward me," he told him, "I'll shoot you dead. You," he added to me, "get back there and cuff him to—"

But I'd found the right button to push. "You won't kill him," I said quickly. "Not with a gun, not face-to-face."

"No? I killed three people prior to yesterday. Who knows what the final body count at the consulate will be?"

"There's a difference. You weren't there when they died. You didn't see your victims go up in flames. Smell their flesh burn, hear—"

"Stop that!" The gun's muzzle wobbled toward me.

"You won't shoot me, either," I said gently—and with more conviction than I felt. "It would hurt too much—the way you hurt for Chloe. That's what started all this, her pain—"

"She's right," Hamid interrupted. "You're a fucking coward."

"Shut up!" I snapped at him.

He ignored me, seeming to take strength from my words

to Newton. A rising tide of anger and hatred had submerged his fear; I could see sudden fiery resolve in his eyes.

"You think you're a man, Fig? You're nothing. All this nonsense over a cheap cockteaser who got exactly what she asked for! You're nothing but a robot. You talk through a computer. You kill by remote control."

"Hamid! *Shut up!*"

"I wouldn't be surprised if you fuck long-distance, too— if you can get it up at all." He took another step forward.

"Hamid, goddamn it—"

But there was nothing I could say or do to stop him now. His rage had made him recklessly self-assured. I watched his muscles tense, knew he was going to rush Newton the instant before he acted. All I could do was set myself to react.

Hamid lunged, pawing at the gun. He missed it, and before he crashed into Newton, the muzzle flashed and the bullet tore somewhere into Hamid's upper body.

I was moving by then, deafened by the boom reverberating through the cabin. Not forward; Newton still had control of the gun, and there was too little room to try to disarm him. Backward, two quick steps, so I could reach out and smash the lightbulb by the companionway. Just as Newton staggered clear of Hamid's toppling body, the cabin plunged into darkness.

I fumbled along the bulkhead for the case containing the Very pistol, blood flowing from a gash in my hand. Behind me, sounds filled the gray-black: the heaving, bubbling gasps of a dying man; frantic grunts from Newton; Adah's accelerated breathing. I found the case, yanked on the knob. It wouldn't open. Oh, God, not locked! I tugged harder—and this time the door squeaked open.

The pistol, where was—

There! I grabbed it. Felt for the box of flares, took it, too, and then scrambled up the steps to the afterdeck. I had to take the chance Newton would come up there after me. If I was forced to fire the pistol, I didn't dare do it in the close confines of the cabin because of the risk to Adah.

On my knees I slid across the mist-slick teak, digging inside the box. One cartridge. One chance. I jerked it out as I reached the port rail and crouched there, panting, fumbling now to break the pistol open so I could load it.

Sounds boiled up from below. If he stayed down there with Adah, tried to use her as a hostage . . .

I jammed the flare into the pistol. Held it ready.

Newton's head appeared in the companionway. Then the rest of him, alone, as he quickly climbed up. His breath was ragged, his eyes wild. The gun still trembled in his hand.

"Newton! Put the weapon down!"

For an instant he froze. Then he swiveled both his head and the gun toward the sound of my voice, trying to locate me in the thick mist.

"I mean it, Newton! Put the gun down! Don't make me shoot—"

He saw me before my last word was out. He was too far gone to listen.

He fired.

Once, twice—wild shots, but the second came close.

I heaved the flare box at the gun. It bounced off his arm. The next shot came closer.

How many did he have left? I didn't know, couldn't take any more chances. No choice, dammit, he'd left me no choice—

I braced myself and pulled the Very's trigger.

The flare hit him square in the chest, drove him backward to the starboard railing. Ignited clothing and flesh. In an instant he turned into a human torch.

You didn't see your victims go up in flames. Smell their flesh burn—

Sickened, I watched as his back struck the railing, just above the hips. It jackknifed him up and over. He didn't make a sound—not a sound. When he splashed into the water I heard the hiss and saw the steam rise. The flames died, but the stench lingered in the cold morning air.

I threw the pistol down and doubled over.

Thirty-one

I was on my back deck trying to keep my mind off Langley Newton by fashioning a new tail out of some old silk scarves for W. C. Fields when Joslyn arrived on Tuesday afternoon. Her eyes were deeply shadowed, her face strained, and there was a tentativeness to her normally jaunty step. It would be a while, I thought, before she recovered from her ordeal.

"Cat got him, huh?" She motioned at the silk parrot.

"Right."

"Which one?"

"So far neither is copping to it."

"Those repairs aren't gonna last five minutes around the beasts."

"I know. I'm taking him up to Bootlegger's Cove, where neither of them can ever lay filthy claw on him again."

Adah dropped a key on the table next to me.

"What's that?"

"Your spare. When you didn't answer the door, I used it. I'm giving it back now."

"Don't," I told her. "You never know when you might need it."

Our eyes met and after a moment she nodded and pocketed it. "Thanks." Then she set a paper sack on the table and pulled out a bottle of wine. "For you. Deer Hill ninety-three Chardonnay. I had to visit six wine shops before I found it."

I noticed that the bottle was chilled. "Why don't you go inside and get the corkscrew and a couple of glasses?"

"Thought you were saving it for your fortieth."

"What's a birthday, compared to us both surviving the other morning?"

She grimaced. "Amen to that."

When she came back I took the corkscrew from her and used up some time opening the bottle. Joslyn was here to deliver news; I suspected it was negative and didn't really want to hear. "How're you feeling?"

"Like shit, but I'll mend." She took the glass I offered and tasted. "Good stuff." Then she toed off her athletic shoes and headed for the lounge chair. "I tell you, McCone, I am *never* going to go through anybody's trash again, no matter how fascinating it might be. There's nothing like getting waylaid by a maniac and spending Memorial Day weekend trussed up in a moldy little room in his moldier little bungalow. Not to mention having Barbara and Rupert on my back for upsetting them."

Her mention of Langley Newton made me sick all over again.

Adah peered keenly at my face. "Just glad I was below deck and didn't see it. It's gonna take you a lot of time to get over that. Some ways, you never will."

"I know. Did he . . . say anything to you?"

"You mean about the woman? Not really. He was a very withdrawn guy, McCone. He just didn't connect with other people, especially at the end—even though he had every means of connecting at his disposal. Computer, cellular phones, fax, tape recorder, you name it. I did pick up on one thing, though: he never had a relationship with her."

"Oh?" It didn't surprise me.

"Nope. You know what the task force found at his bungalow? An album of pictures, probably taken by him at some party at Das Glücksspiel. Love was in every one, posing with staff and customers. It's where the one of her and Lateef that he planted in the apartment came from. There wasn't a single picture of them together, though; too shy to ask, I guess."

"And yet she touched him in a way nobody else ever had, just by being nice and going to bat with the D.A. for him. That's why all this happened." I tried to imagine how it must be to live in an emotional void, distanced from one's fellow creatures. It wasn't difficult, since I'd had some experience along those lines myself. But to imagine having the one person who made the void bearable violently torn away . . .

I thought of Hy, of almost losing him—not once but twice now. Maybe I could understand Newton's grief and rage, as I'd earlier understood his addiction to fear and power.

I pushed the thought away. Understanding him more deeply would only make it harder to live with the memory of killing him.

"McCone?" Joslyn said. "Aren't you going to ask me about the reward?"

"I was waiting for you to bring it up. They're not going to give it to me, are they?"

"Well, Parkhurst didn't want you to get anything. He says the bomber came to you, rather than you tracking him down. And that you didn't even get his identity right. He blames you for Kahlil Lateef threatening to file suit against the SFPD for false arrest; he was having breakfast in the dining room at the Stanford Court, where he was staying yesterday morning when they nabbed him. Parkhurst also claims it was a task force member—me—who first made the Diplo-bomber, conveniently forgetting he'd suspended me, of course. *And* he's pissed about you blowing Newton away and letting Hamid get killed. Actually that's only the short list of his reasons for denying you. I won't bore you with the rest."

"Jesus!" I dropped W.C. on the deck, jumped up, and began to pace. "What the hell did he expect me to do under the circumstances? You're alive, aren't you? There won't be any more bombings. What else does he want? He damned well knows Hamid provoked Newton, and wasn't worth the powder to blow him to hell anyway. You found Newton by *accident*, for Christ's sake! Talk about a situation that illustrates why we have the word 'coincidence' in the language! And it's not my fault that Lateef's litigious—"

"You're getting part of the money."

"I'm ..." I stopped pacing and stared at Adah. "How much?"

"A quarter."

". . . A quarter of a *million dollars*?"

"Uh-huh. Craig and I leaned on Parkhurst, and a number of the others on the task force backed us up. You know what he said when we settled? 'It should keep that dreadful woman off my back until I can pack up and leave town.'"

"Asshole." But I said it without much rancor. My mind and emotions had slipped into low gear. A quarter of a million dollars. So much money. What the hell would I ever do with it?

"I want you to have part of it," I told Adah.

She shook her head. "Can't accept, much as I'd like to. If I did, the tarnish would really be on the old shield."

"They're reinstating you?"

"To Homicide, providing I see a shrink for a while." She scowled.

God help the poor shrink, I thought.

"Craig convinced me that I should at least give it a shot," she added.

"Craig, huh?"

Adah looked down into her wineglass. "He's not so bad, McCone, once you get to know him. And he's sure let me lean on him in the past twenty-four hours." Quickly she changed the subject. "So, what're you going to do with the dough? Take a trip around the world? Buy yourself a fancy car and duds? Upgrade your sorry lifestyle?"

I hadn't a clue. Fortunately, I was saved from contemplating it by the doorbell. "Excuse me a minute."

Anne-Marie, Hank, and Habiba stood on my front steps. The little girl's hand was tucked into Hank's and she stared down, her head bent, much as she had throughout our long journey from the Caribbean. Well, small wonder: First she'd lost her mother. Then she'd lost her father, her grandmother, and her home all in the space of forty-eight hours.

"Hope you don't mind us stopping by," Hank said. "We've just come from a conference with Ambassador Jalil."

"Of course I don't mind. And I'm very glad to see you, Habiba." When she didn't respond, I squatted and tipped her chin up. Her eyes looked dully at me, but she took her hand from Hank's and thrust it into mine.

"Let's go out to the deck," I told all three of them. "Adah's here too."

I ushered them back there and, with Habiba clutching at the leg of my jeans, fetched wineglasses for the adults and a Coke for her. When I sat back down she crawled into my lap and I cradled her protectively. "So," I said, "tell me what happened with Jalil."

Anne-Marie glanced at the little girl, smile lines crinkling around her eyes. "Kahlil Lateef was also there; he's been named to succeed Mrs. Hamid as consul general. Both he and Jalil feel that since Habiba's been raised in America and attended American schools, going to live with relatives in Azad would prove very difficult for her. And they also feel that remaining in familiar surroundings will help her to get over her loss."

Hank added, "Lateef's going to be operating out of a hotel for some time, and while he wants to play a major role in Habiba's life, he admits he doesn't know a thing about child rearing. As a result, Jalil's consented to grant Anne-Marie and me temporary custody of her. Mavis had no family, and he's her next of kin, so it should pose no problem."

The little girl was sitting with her back against my chest; all I could see was the top of her bowed head. "Are you happy with that arrangement, Habiba?"

She mumbled something I couldn't hear.

"I'm sorry, I didn't catch that."

"That child-rearing stuff? They don't know anything about it, either. But that's okay. My"—her voice faltered briefly—"my nanny Aisha and my Grams already taught me table manners and things like that. Besides, I like Anne-Marie and Hank, and Uncle Kahlil promised I can see him whenever I want to. And . . ." She tipped her head back, presenting me with an upside-down view of her pale face. "And if I stay in San Francisco, I can see you and Hy, too. If you want to."

"Of course I want to, and so does Hy."

Habiba regarded me solemnly for a moment, gave a brisk nod, and went back to staring down at her lap.

Joslyn asked, "So which one of you is she going to live with?"

"Oh, Hank," Anne-Marie said quickly. "I'm too much of a . . . cleanliness Nazi, but he won't mind the . . . disorder a child can create."

"What she means is she hates kids." Allie had just jumped onto the deck's rail; Habiba pushed off my lap, went over, and began petting her.

We all exchanged concerned looks.

Habiba looked over her shoulder and flashed us a weak grin. "Joke. This morning she told me that I'm a lot more interesting than most adults she knows, and next week she's taking me to the Academy of Sciences." She went back to petting the cat.

Anne-Marie watched her thoughtfully—and affectionately. She saw me observing her, shrugged, and quickly changed the subject. "So how're you two doing?"

"Fair," Adah said. "McCone has some good news, though: she's a quarter of a million dollars richer."

"The reward?" Hank asked.

"Uh-huh."

"What're you going to do with all that money?"

"Oh, I don't know. Buy Mick a new cellular phone, I guess; he's heartbroken over the demise of the old one." I paused. They all looked expectantly at me. "And there's a woman in the Caribbean who helped me a lot; her organization could use a donation."

"That's it?" Joslyn asked.

"Hey, let me get used to the idea of the money before I start spending it."

Hank glanced meaningfully at Anne-Marie. She nodded. He said, "I'd better bring this up now, because I hope it'll affect your plans. I'm leaving All Souls."

"What!" Hank had founded the co-op. He was its senior partner. No, more than that—he was the soul in All Souls. "Without you, it'll wither up and die."

"No, it'll just become something else. We've agreed to dissolve the existing partnership; the partners who choose to remain will reincorporate under a different name. I'm betting they sell the building and move downtown before the year is out."

A wave of sadness swept over me. Every time I'd considered moving my offices elsewhere it had comforted me to think that my old friends and associates would still be there for me in the big Victorian in Bernal Heights.

"Don't look that way, Shar," Hank said. "The co-op you're mourning doesn't exist anymore."

"I know, but . . . What're you planning to do?"

He smiled at Anne-Marie and took her hand. "How does Altman and Zahn, Attorneys-at-law, sound?"

"You're leaving the Coalition for Environmental Preservation?" I asked her.

She nodded. "I'll still act as counsel to them. And guess what else? Ted's coming along as our office manager."

Suddenly my sadness vanished. I knew what they were about to propose.

Joslyn said, "Well, all three of you are going to be in the market for office rentals. Anybody have an idea where you'll relocate?"

My friends looked hopefully at me.

I said, "I don't know about the neighborhood, but I'm certain of one thing: I want to be next door to a brand-new husband-and-wife law firm."

6,500 Feet Above The Central Valley

May 31, 11:21 A.M.

       It was a high beautiful world up there and not the least bit lonesome, because a fully recovered Ripinsky rode in the rear seat of the Citabria.

Through the headset he said, "You told Clearance Delivery we were VFR for Little River."

"You bet I did. We're going straight to Bootlegger's Cove and not stirring for a good long time. You need to convalesce, and I want to sleep for a week."

"Sounds good to me." He was silent for a moment. "How're you dealing with what happened?"

I shrugged, my attention on the controls.

Again he was silent. A few minutes later he said, "Maybe you should consider it your personal Ban Kach."

My breath caught. He had only once discussed the incident that for nearly two decades had lived in the darkest corner of his psyche. I'd thought it forever off-limits.

He added, "You knew you were setting Hamid up to die, just like I did those Cambodians. When Dan Kessell changed my return flight plan from Chiang Mai to that abandoned village near the border, it was clear what would happen. I told myself it didn't matter because I was being well paid and they were corrupt, murdering druglords. And when one of them came at me begging for help in that clearing where the other corrupt, murdering druglords were slaughtering them, I didn't think twice about putting a bullet through his head so the guys with the Uzis would think I was on their side. It was only afterwards that it mattered."

In the intimate confines of the plane, with his voice coming close through the headset, the retelling took on special meaning. I nodded, turning it over, seeing the parallels.

He added, "Just let it go, McCone."

Below us farmland gave way to the foothills of the Coast Range as I set course for the South Bay and a quick jog up the continental shelf. I found my thoughts drifting to early June at Bootlegger's Cove—a time of foggy beach walks and woodsmokey lovemaking in front of the fireplace.

On the other side of San Jose Hy suddenly asked, "Say, did Renshaw make good on your ten-times-or-nothing wager?"

"Well, he paid my fee in full, plus a bonus for keeping RKI out of a mess—again. But he welshed on our bet."

"You want me to send out the leg-breakers?"

"Nah, I'm forgiving it. The reward's overwhelming enough; I seriously don't think I'm equipped to handle too much money."

"Don't underestimate yourself."

"Oh, hey—I just remembered something. Take a look at the clipping from last night's *Examiner* that's tucked in the side pocket of my bag. I think you'll find it interesting."

As he read I could follow along because of the surprised and appreciative sounds coming through the headset. I'd practically memorized the wire-service story that had appeared on a back page devoted to peculiar incidents. Datelined Marigot, the headline read FREAK ACCIDENT CLAIMS GERMAN CITIZEN.

> Klaus Schechtmann, a German national residing on Jumbie Cay in the Leeward Islands, was killed late Sunday afternoon when a cannon belonging to a neighbor accidentally misfired.
>
> Schechtmann, 43, owner of the sovereign island, was visiting Zebediah Altagracia, 76, when Altagracia's Revolutionary War relic discharged while he was cleaning it. Schechtmann was killed instantly.

Altagracia, a local celebrity since he successfully declared the island independent from the United Kingdom in 1971, said he was preparing the cannon for Monday's celebration of the United States' Memorial Day.

"We celebrate damn near every patriotic holiday known to mankind here," Mr. Altagracia told the press, "especially those of people who have been subjugated. I plan to dedicate today to the memory of Klaus Schechtmann. He was a fine man who cared deeply about this island and its inhabitants. I speak for all of us when I say he will be sorely missed."

An investigation by Interpol is pending, but sources close to the agency say there is little likelihood that charges will be filed.

Hy whistled softly. "All I can say is *vive la révolution*."

The end